Rosalie Ham is the author of three previous books, including the sensational no.1 bestseller *The Dressmaker*, now an award-winning film starring Kate Winslet, Liam Hemsworth, Judy Davis and Hugo Weaving. Rosalie was born and raised in Jerilderie, New South Wales and lives in Melbourne, Australia. She holds a Master of Arts in Creative Writing and teaches literature.

Also by Rosalie Ham

The Dressmaker
Summer at Mount Hope
There Should Be More Dancing

THE YEAR of the FARMER

Rosalie Ham

PICADOR
Pan Macmillan Australia

First published 2018 in Picador by Pan Macmillan Australia Pty Ltd.
This Picador edition published 2019 by Pan Macmillan Australia Pty Ltd.,
1 Market Street, Sydney, New South Wales, Australia, 2000

A catalogue record for this
book is available from the
National Library of Australia

Typeset in 11.9/16 pt Adobe Garamond Pro by Post Pre-press Group
Printed by IVE

Cover images: Rowena Naylor/Stocksy, FoxyImage/Shutterstock, vectorkat/
Shutterstock, Justin Hannaford/Alamy stock photo.

The paper in this book is FSC® certified.
FSC® promotes environmentally responsible,
socially beneficial and economically viable
management of the world's forests.

For the Hams, farmers all

Here is a rural fellow
That will not be denied your Highness' presence.
He brings you figs.

William Shakespeare, *Antony and Cleopatra*, Act 5, Scene 2

PROLOGUE

Except for the busy nocturnal creatures and a light wind rocking the bushy gums, all movement in the camp had ceased. Evening had settled into night and the people were asleep. One dog sat up, stretched, and crept to sniff around the smouldering fire. Others raised their heads and joined him, tails up. They milled together in the lifting smoke, ears and tails moon-tipped. One moved off and the others followed, slinking behind. At the river, they paused and lifted their snouts to the dark air, then turned and moved westwards, a handful of mongrel pets pattering along the edge of the water. As they ran behind the caravan park, a Labrador joined the pack, a fluid line of hunt-coloured ghosts moving with purpose. The dogs rounded the pump station and ran under the bridge, continuing along the riverbank behind the shops. No lights shone in the houses on the flood plain opposite, and traces of rabbit and fox slipped across the river to them, but the pack were drawn towards a bigger chase, lust warming as they ran, blood on their minds. They travelled along the exercise track and over the levee and vanished way beyond the swimming hole, past the hospital and the new service station, outrunning the westbound flow of the sluggish river to the sleeping sheep captured in their paddock and yards, innocent to the coming game.

1.
WATER AND SHEEP

The dust staining the thin sheet of clouds peeping from the horizon told Mitch the sheep were coming. He stopped the ute, tied the steering wheel to the rear-vision mirror to keep the vehicle on course, and wedged a square of timber against the accelerator. He paused again to check the clouds sneaking up, then put the ute in gear and climbed onto the tray, the truck grinding along at a walkable nine k's and the sun hot through his shirt. The hungry, thirsty mob hurried towards him so he jumped onto the feeder trailer and pulled the outlet lever. The middle of the seed in the bin fell away, and wheat trailed on the dry dirt. Soon the thread of skinny, unhandsome sheep were falling into line, like a zipper closing, either side of the thread of golden feed. He pointed. 'Those clouds will slide over here and water will fall from the sky.'

Tinka, Mitch's mostly black dog, understood many words but there were none she recognised in the sounds he was making, so she turned her ear back to the gathering mob of dull sheep.

'I see you don't believe me, Tinka, but I'm reliably informed that weather works in seven-year cycles and I choose to believe it.' He climbed across and stood on the roof of his ute. 'This is my year, *our* year. Rain will fall and life will change.'

Tinka moved to the very far corner of the ute and examined the contents of a passing breeze. The ute kept moving, the rams kept eating and Mitchell Bishop sat down, his feet dangling over the headboard. He reached for his phone and held it up to the meagre clouds, hoping a signal was passing, a lean, broad-shouldered young man in his prime, expectation in his heart despite the drought and his just mildly successful marriage. No marriage was perfect and, in the way of things, his would tick on until change presented itself. There were no messages on his phone, but Mitch's main concern was survival. Specifically, water. While his ravaged sheep nibbled with their tender lips and noses in the dirt and their own hard dry shit, he looked again to the promising horizon. Rain would be good to grow a bit of feed, though it would have been better months ago at sowing time. His crop was poor, sparse and starved, but that crop had come to represent survival. An adequate harvest could see him break even, just, though no income he'd get from his poor sheep or any sort of crop would dent his debts. He checked his phone once more then put it in his pocket. As he climbed back to the feed trailer his dog swivelled one ear to him.

He shut off the seed outlet and drove to the yards to fill the bins for the next day's feed then drove back to his flocks in the fire truck to fill the water troughs. He let the farm dogs off for a run while he refilled the fire truck tanks, then tied the dogs up and fed them, and drove home. Pulling up next to his wife's car, he looked at the old house. Within its chilly walls his father would be watching *The Morning Show* and Mandy scrolling through Mitch's emails. He wished he had more sheep to go to. He opened the door and Tink jumped down off the tray and they paused to watch a vehicle out on the road

4

roaring through the morning stillness. It was Cyril Horrick heading towards Riverglen and Glenys Dingle, most likely. They would sit together in Glenys's shiny, dustless office and discuss the forthcoming meeting. Any discussion with the Water Authority meant announcements, and announcements meant changes to water supply allocations.

o0o

In town, Jasey White dropped two slices of bread in the toaster, flicked the kettle on and went to the back verandah. She unlocked the wood box, took out her .22 rifle and paused to inspect the churning grey sky and inhale the dusty eucalyptus air. Then she loaded the rifle and moved to the back step, where she stood in a sun shaft which cast her white hair golden. She trained the scope on the reeds along the low river. The riparian areas no longer shuffled and whirred with busy ecology; the long, dry years had made the river gums still and brittle and the birds had migrated to a richer place. Dieback had crippled their canopies and where once great tree limbs had stretched out over a wide, strong flow, there was nothing, just exposed roots clinging to bare sloping clay, hardened where the tide had receded. Sometimes the crash of a branch being shed echoed all the way to the main street. In the small flow of turbid water, one fowl and her three chicks were paddling towards the reeds. Along a low, fat branch of a thirsty gum, wild ducks were lined up, their little boxy heads snapping from side to side and their thin, flat feet lifting. The hen in the water turned abruptly and paddled away, her chicks following as fast as their small webbed feet allowed. Jasey moved her scope to the reeds. She found the black-rimmed red ears of Mr Fox, watching like a sphinx. Then he rose and Jasey held the crosshairs on his shoulder as he slunk across the clay bank towards the thick, slow stream. Mr Fox put one foot in the water, took it out, but was drawn in towards the chicks. He swam delicately, his nose high, a gentle wake rippling out from his fluffy tail. Jasey held, exhaled and squeezed the trigger but the bullet punctured the water high of Mr Fox's shoulders and he flinched. The hen squawked and turned, wings flapping and water splashing, her beak spearing at the retreating fox. Her chicks swam in confused circles and the ducks on the branch flapped away. In the kitchen, the kettle clicked off and Jasey's toast popped up.

'You are toying with a woman who has the patience of a gate post, Mr Fox.' She unloaded the gun and put it into the wood box with the bullets, locked it and hid the key under the mat.

She ate breakfast, dressed and waited on the front step, her name tag large on her left breast. The clouds had turned soft and flat and crept away across the blue sky. Galahs and magpies flew past towards morning business, and the rye grass fluttered stiffly with a passing zephyr.

Two houses westwards, the Jovetic family had heard the gunshot but resumed their morning routines. Lana Jovetic's father turned his small sticky eyes to her. 'Home today you will come to help your mother the potatoes to plant.'

'I will,' she said, and watched him struggle towards the back steps and his garden. These days the old man moved slowly and stiffly up and down his rows of vegetables, swearing at the damage the fat rabbits had done in the night. Papa was beyond physically hurting them now; he hated his diminished status in the family, though, and remained a tyrannical presence.

Mati said, 'Vile you can enjoy, go. Do.'

Lana kissed her mother and left. As she crossed the yard she lit a cigarette and looked at the grey-streaked sky. At her precious 1990 Holden Commodore, she brushed the dew and soft white spheres of dandelion seeds from the windscreen.

At exactly ten minutes to eight, Jasey and the rest of the river dwellers heard Lana's car rumble to life.

She drove slowly down her gravel drive, turned east and, about twenty metres later, turned into Jasey's gate, bouncing over her stock grate and rolling up the potted driveway, thin boree fronds brushing her car. She pressed play and the first bars of the song filled the car as Jasey opened the door. They sang, '*You didn't love me like you said you would but I loved you as much as I could, though you made me cry . . .*'

It took three minutes and fifty-eight for their favourite song to play through but it took them about two minutes to get from Jasey's to work, so they drove past the house where their friend Neralie had once lived, and crossed the bridge and turned and drove on through the town past Jasey's IGA. They smiled at the men hanging the SOLD sign from the pub balcony, drove on past the op shop, then the hairdressers – Beau Monde – the deserted butcher's shop and empty frock shop and the people waiting outside the newsagency. They waved to Kevin, standing by a tractor outside his garage. The car turned at the swimming hole, where Larry Purfeat exercised his thin, languid greyhounds and the morning walkers trudged – some elderly folk with their Zimmer frames, the Rural Women's Club and the smart set, with their blonde ponytails swinging. The blue car drove around and around the barbecue area until the last note of the rousing crescendo – '*I stopped loving you though I knew I could because you didn't love me as much as you should, so now it's your turn to cry*' – faded. Then the faster walkers in their tight activewear crossed the road to Maria's cafe for a skinny decaf latte. Lana parked in her spot beneath the kurrajong outside the abandoned butcher's shop. Opposite, customers still waited outside the newsagency. Jasey said, 'Something should be done about that,' and Lana replied, 'You've been saying that every morning for five years.'

They headed to the IGA, where Paul was sorting letters into the mailboxes in the window. Jasey picked up some money waiting near her cash register. 'Debbie's been in for milk and cereal?'

Paul continued sorting the mail. 'Yep.'

Jasey counted the money. 'She take Rice Bubbles too?'

Paul paused to read a postcard. 'Yep.'

'She owes me five cents. That card from Zac?'

'It's raining in Noosa.' He poked the card into Zac's parents' mailbox, wondering at the cruelty of Mother Nature for giving Zac rain on his holiday, but none on his farm.

Lana was paying for a packet of cigarettes, a carton of chocolate milk and some lamingtons when Nurse Leonie Bergen approached silently in her nursing shoes. Her shopping trolley held fizzy drinks, sweet biscuits and cakes for the Activities afternoon tea. 'You know,' she said, 'some old people don't bother with the newsagents, they just turn up to Activities at the hospital and listen to the allied health girl read out the headlines.'

The four people in the IGA turned to the newsagency, where the queue remained.

Nurse Leonie said, 'Now's the time,' and they all shifted their gaze to the SOLD sign hanging from the pub balcony.

Jasey nudged Lana. 'She's right. Do something before she finds out who bought the pub.'

Lana nodded. 'She's been asking.'

On the fifty-metre walk to her office, Lana stopped to light a cigarette and speak to the queue outside Mandy's newsagency. 'I'm starting an evening class for youse to come to, on learning how to read newspapers on a computer.'

The people in the queue looked doubtful.

'Without even getting out of bed, you'll be able to read the papers on your iPad or computer.'

They shifted. A few eyebrows rose.

'What night?'

'Monday.'

They hesitated.

'Before *Australian Story*,' Lana added, and they looked like they might just warm to the idea. She walked the rest of the way to the shire offices, where she carefully stubbed her half-smoked cigarette out in the powdery mortar between the worn bricks and popped the remaining half back into the packet.

oOo

Isobel Prestwich's first thought of the day was always of her Merinos, her pretty green-eyed girls with neat, clean arses and rich, uncontaminated wool. She left her high, wrought-iron bed and her snoring husband, his sun-fried nose hidden between the Italian cotton-sateen Chine sheets, their lace flowers meandering along the edges, and dressed. On the broad verandah Isobel raised her arms, inhaling, then stretched. Rain was in the air. Above, soft fat clouds floated. She looked to the river – perhaps the cranes and moorhens had returned? But there was just blue-green algae and cumbungi weeds reaching from one dry expanse of riverbank to the other across a slow, fetid flow of fermenting excrements and dead fish.

9

Midway through her hamstring stretches some kooka-burras laughed, and fifteen speedy minutes on the treadmill later, Isobel set off on a brisk walk through the grey country morning, magpies singing to her. At the shed, she wrenched open the doors and a cushion of warm vapours – sheep shit, urine-soaked straw and pungent lanoline – engulfed her. Her calm, friendly Merino ewes shuffled together, their large eyes expectant.

When she'd announced her business plans to Digby over dinner, her husband had gestured to the great outdoors. 'We've already got a business – all those cattle and sheep out there.'

'Really? I thought they were for keeping the grass down,' she deadpanned. 'You specialise in meat, Digby; I'll specialise in wool.'

'Darling, all that extra work, I don't think –'

'I said *I'm* going to start a business. If I need your help or advice, I'll ask.'

He raised his eyebrows and drank some fine red wine.

'I will breed with Bishops Corner's best – Mitch's finest fleeces and the better stud ewes and rams. I'll send fleeces to be scoured and washed and they'll come back in skeins.'

'You won't make any money out of knitting jumpers.'

'Weaving,' she said. 'My mother, if you remember, was a very fine spinner and weaver, and the ladies from the Rural Women's Club's craft group will make pashminas and what-ever other fine wool garments they please and we'll sell them in Verity's shop.'

Verity, Digby's cousin, ran a fashion boutique in Melbourne.

Digby shook his head. 'Really, Isobel, you can't –'

'I haven't finished speaking so don't start patronising me just yet. Sheep are pleasant. They're not threatening, they're unassuming but social, reasonably small and neat; ewes are generally very good mothers, they're vegetarian –'

'Herbivore.'

'And, as you know, they produce lovely meat and wonderful fibre and we have two children, a boy and a girl. Rory will inherit Girri Girri, and I want Philippa to have my sheep and Bishops Corner because Mitchell won't have children.'

'How do you know?'

'Girls know these things.'

'Nonsense.'

'She had an infection. We all knew that before she married Mitch. And we all know why.'

'Bishops Corner's got no water frontage. Wool-growing requires water.'

'Mitch is a sheep man, he'll keep his channels for stock. He's bound to trade some of his water allocation for an upgrade and there's Esther's water. She'll fall off her perch sooner rather than later.'

'Isobel!'

'Well, it's the way it is. But we need to be in first if Philippa is to have ample water.'

Half a minute passed while they chewed their steak and sipped wine and thought resentfully of Glenys Dingle and Cyril Horrick and the Water Authority.

'You'll need your own sheep shed, extra yards,' Digby said. 'It all costs money. Why sheep? Why not chooks or puppies?'

'Same reason you don't breed chooks and puppies.'

And here she was, five years later, almost a triumph. Isobel remained slightly disappointed her beautiful Merinos were slow to succeed at wool shows; nonetheless, she was well on her way to achieving fine micron fleeces and smooth-skinned sheep.

And the Rural Women's Club garments – Digby called them 'glorified hankies' – were to feature in Verity's Melbourne boutique. So Isobel did not want her legacy to end when she did. She needed Bishops Corner for Philippa – and she also needed its water entitlements. Water was money. But to get everything she wanted, she had to manoeuvre Mandy, cautiously.

'Hello, girls,' she said, and climbed into the sheep pen. She cornered one ewe and ran her hands over her back. 'Cold weather, you've got dry wool.' She filled their water trough and fed her girls lucerne hay and oats for breakfast, and headed back to the house, where her husband stood at the kitchen sink with a cup of coffee in his hand.

He pointed through the window. 'Clouds.'

'Not much in them.'

'How are your girls?'

'Wool's a bit dry.'

'Graze them on pasture for a couple of days.'

'What if it rains? The shearers won't come.'

Digby drained his coffee and put his cup in the sink. 'Anyway, there are dogs about. I see online that one grazier's lost ten thousand dollars' worth of sheep in the night.' He headed off to get dressed and Isobel said she would phone Bennett Mockett, the stock agent, 'ask him what he's doing about the dogs'.

oOo

Glenys Dingle wandered back through apartment number six in the brand-new Riverglen Lake Resort Apartments, constructed on what was once prime farming land, and sat at the kitchen bench. The agent, a fragrant young man wearing thin-soled shoes, told her the apartment was 'A magnificent investment property, an ideal place to live for people like you, Mrs Dingle, with a modern twenty-first-century attitude'. Then his phone rang and he answered, saying, 'Yes, they're selling fast because they're a magnificent investment, ideal for people with a modern twenty-first-century attitude.'

Glenys looked pointedly at her wrist, then remembered she had abandoned her watch in favour of her smartphone. 'You programmed that phone to ring,' she said, picking up her handbag. The agent abruptly ended the call, apologised and resumed his pitch. Then Glenys's phone rang. She declined the call and the agent waited while she sent a text message.

He hadn't programmed the call. There was little interest in the apartments and he was taking every opportunity to sell, that was all. She was high up in the Water Authority, granted, but she had no right to turn up late and ask too many questions about internet accessibility, intrusive mobile phone towers, wind farms, future property developments and zonings.

oOo

A badly parked Volkswagen Jetta and a late-model Ford Territory took up all four parking spaces outside the apartments, so Cyril parked his company car in the bus zone. Except for the short, dry scrub twitching in the wind, the new estate was lifeless. Nonetheless, he switched his hazard lights on. The earthy smell of farmland and the sound of bleating sheep came to him. His phone pinged and he read the message from Glenys Dingle: *Wait*. He sighed, checked his wrist, then remembered he used his phone to check the time these days. The new Riverglen Lake Resort Apartments were a cumbersome, stepped apartment block with concrete balconies and reflective-glassed floor-to-ceiling windows. Frondless pine saplings promised shade if one day their roots found moisture. The lake itself was empty save for three supermarket trolleys. A billboard showed it full, two kiddies sans life vests waving from a small boat skimming the small, white-capped waves: ENJOY RIVERGLEN LAKE RESORT APARTMENTS FOR YOUR HOLIDAYS.

'Yes, do,' Cyril said, 'but bring a footy because there won't be any boating.'

The door opened, filling the car with a cold, dusty turbulence, and Glenys Dingle was beside him. She leaned over and turned the rear-vision mirror to herself. Her fingers sparkled with glittery gemstones – aquamarines, Cyril assumed – and she ran them through her ruffled hair then faced him, leaving the mirror skewed. He'd never been this close to her but remembered she had a decent arse for an old boiler. Her face was spongy but taut, like his wife's. It was the hardcore Spakfilla they used, good stuff. He used Pam's on his calluses after he'd trimmed them with the potato peeler. Some women didn't care that they weren't attractive to men, but not Glenys. She was like the glittering fairy godmother on the cover of a book he'd bought for the grandkids last Christmas. He smiled at Ms Dingle and gave her a wink.

'Right, Mr Horrick,' she said, 'the southern region is experiencing a pretty terrible drought.'

'Most of eastern Australia's had the same drought so –'

'I'm perfectly aware of that. I am, after all, the head of the Water Authority and I have not been in a lead-lined safe at the bottom of the Atlantic for the past five years, though I imagine you'd prefer I was.'

The fondness Cyril felt for fairy godmothers started to fade.

'You're also hosting a strident and somewhat demanding irrigators task force from your regional office.' She flipped through manila folders in her business handbag.

For the life of him he could not remember any official task force, just a few dozen farmers anxiously discussing their future at the pub. 'They're not exactly a force.'

'I will not be bullied. Meet with them and explain properly our intentions to save water.' She offered him an envelope, though she wouldn't let go of it. 'You are to read this hard copy and then shred it. Do you understand?'

He said slowly, gravely, 'I un-der-stand,' but he failed to convey self-deprecation.

'You've been trying to be effective in your job for many years, have you not?'

'Well, I haven't been in a safe at the bottom of the Atlant–'

'So at this point in your career you're probably considering retirement.'

'Not yet, but –'

'Then you'll be thinking about your superannuation situation.'

Cyril did indeed have a plan in place to boost his super-annuation. He'd borrowed to purchase many solar-powered water pumps and meters, and planned to flog them to farmers as part of their infrastructure upgrade. His wife's shed was stacked high with them.

Glenys let go of the envelope. 'And you won't want to jeopardise your severance pay in any way, either.'

'Well –'

'Here's what you're going to do, Mr Horrick. A new colleague, Mr Stacey Masterson, will arrive soon to assist you. Task force or no task force, you will get your farmers to install

15

new irrigation systems to save water then you will cut water allocations so that I can please the minister and the Federal Government and the green factions and every other club, organisation and committee that's arguing over water.'

'When Mr Masterson arrives he can perhaps tell me how much water my region will actually get this coming season and then I'll finally know how much water we can retrieve for the factions and ministers –'

'For the next irrigation season, farmers will be awarded *some* percentage of their full allocation.'

'You must have some idea how much?'

She glared at him. 'They'll get enough. You will be informed in good time.'

'Good to know.' He wondered if Glenys had a handgun in her cream-coloured business handbag, and imagined a pub full of disappointed locals once the announcement went up on the site. *How's a bloke expected to grow crops and pay drought debt and live with only a bucketful of water?*

Glenys checked her hair again in the mirror. 'There is one last round of water buybacks. You will retrieve one hundred gigalitres from irrigators and you will take two hundred gigalitres of water from on-farm improvements. That means there will be three hundred more gigalitres in the system.'

'Yes, I added that up myself, but we only agreed to one hundred gigs from buybacks and fifty from on-farm –'

'You should listen. I will not repeat myself again. You will buy back one hundred gigalitres and you will retrieve two hundred gigalitres from on-farm improvements. I believe you have the on-farm improvements well in hand, that water savings are being achieved through a company called C. & P. Water Pty Ltd.?'

16

He didn't speak because he thought she would just cut him off and he was wondering exactly what she knew about C. & P. Water – Cyril and Pamela Horrick Water. Did she know he had a garage full of pumps and meters?

'The farmers are expecting to relinquish only one hundred and fifty gigalitres in total,' he said weakly. He had a vision of the river, fat and flowing, and rows of irrigation channels with an inch of water in them, thin farmers and skeletal stock draped across the banks, riots due to lack of bread, world famine . . .

'We need to save water, Mr Horrick, for everyone. Rivers are the soul of life for a great many creatures and people, like business investors and those who just need a holiday.'

Cyril looked at the Riverglen Resort and its empty lake. But the drought was not yet over; farmers needed time to recover and the only way to recover was to grow crops. Recovery required full water allocations, not cutbacks. The manila folder in his hands suddenly felt heavy. 'You'll announce these changes at the meeting?'

'As a representative of the Water Authority, you and C. & P. Water will deal with customers in your region.'

He needed to keep his job long enough to unload the pumps and meters in Pam's garage and he needed the severance pay in his super for Pam and the puppies. 'Not a problem,' he said feebly.

'For the sake of expediency you will also make your records and dealings accessible at all times. We will be in touch regularly.'

Glenys opened the car door. 'I'll see the lake full before Christmas, then.' She slammed the door, leaving him sitting in his company car, holding a manila envelope, his balls retracting in his underpants.

o0o

The Morning Show told Cal and Mitch the news as they ate breakfast; then the back door slammed and they watched Mandy walk to her car, leaving the yard gate open. Tink wandered down to the back step and settled on the mat. The weather girl said, 'And now for the weather,' and the two men stopped chewing. The map showed a low at the bottom of Australia and a few wispy white threads moving westwards across the Riverina, and no clouds of any significance anywhere else on the continent. The men resumed eating. In the paddock, the donkeys stood with the ewes and their new lambs, their rears to the crisp wind. They watched Mandy's small white wagon roar past and swung their heads to see if another vehicle was coming with breakfast.

As Mandy turned onto the road her phone rang. It was the landlord. 'Shit.' She put the phone on speaker, still grinding along in third. 'Good morning,' she said brightly.

'You got three people waiting on the footpath outside the newsagents. I've told them you're on your way.'

'Thanks,' she said, grinding up to fourth gear.

'People expect their newspapers at six o'clock in the morning or, at the very least, seven. I'm sick of people complaining to me.'

'I'm sorry,' she whined, 'but it's hard for me to get away until old Callum's right for the day, had his breakfast. You can open up for me if you like?'

'I just own the premises.'

'Exactly.' It was her business – not that it made any money after rent and expenses. 'Anyway,' she added, 'it's not as if they can go anywhere else to get a newspaper.'

'That's the point.' He hung up.

Mandy threw the phone on the seat beside her. 'Miserable old prick.'

She changed up to fourth gear then immediately encountered Esther Shugg's dumb, hungry sheep grazing the hard grass along the roadside. She should have just ploughed on through, but Esther was parked by the road up ahead, and dead sheep just got everyone all worked up, so she rolled down to five kilometres an hour, the engine chugging, then let it stall. The smell of sheep permeated the car and all around the plains were brown and grey. The air was perishingly dry and it was only eight in the bloody morning. And always, the stalking ravens on electricity wires and prehistoric eagles hanging overhead. Nothing was as it was supposed to be. Nothing exciting ever happened. The stupid drought came and everyone went broke or left town; those who remained succumbed to the drought and it just continued on and on and her life was with bloody old Callum and a dead-end job day after day and dull people who only ever talked about the weather. It was like one big boring club, except she wasn't part of the club, never had been, really . . . *I should have left.* In fact, she'd been about to move to the city when Mitch's mother died. Then Neralie McIntosh decided to leave and two golden opportunities to enter the central social structure were hers for the taking. First she took Neralie's job: Mandy Roper became the manager of a small business smack in the middle of town. And then she lost weight and got fit and took Neralie's old boyfriend, Mitchell Bishop, most eligible bachelor in town. She got both fair and square, but it turned out that she was chained to a dull, profitless job in boring isolation and a marriage that didn't give her what she wanted.

The flock dribbled to a standstill in front of her car and shat themselves, so she held her hand on the horn and screamed and the sheep scuttled to Esther's dry, weed-choked irrigation channel.

As she passed she waved at Esther as she would a bothersome fly and pressed the accelerator to the floor.

The main street moved into view through Mandy's insect-splattered windscreen – dopey Denise's op shop, then Beau Monde, Kelli's fancy hairdressing shop, and frigging Jasey White's IGA. And there was Jasey's best friend's car, parked in its usual spot under the kurrajong. Those two, Jasey and Lana, thought the entire town loved them, but they weren't members of the Rural Women's Club either. It was bloody Isobel Prestwich, Mandy's very own sister-in-law, who'd rejected her application to the club, she was certain. Mandy was born and raised in this town, volunteered at the footy club, the race club, the bowling club, the tennis club, but was never asked to a girls' weekend or a hen's party or baby shower. Once, years ago, she'd complained to Kelli, and Kelli said, 'Well, don't bloody argue with everyone.'

But she didn't argue, she just said what she thought.

Then Kelli said, 'When anyone else says what they think, you get shitty.'

Suddenly, Mandy saw the SOLD sign. She braked, stopped dead in the middle of the main street. There it was, hanging from the pub balcony. It was true! Rumour was the pub had sold, though no one knew who had bought it. The building showed no sign of activity, but maybe they'd put on music and nice food and people would start having fun again; maybe she'd join a pool competition, or even darts.

The usuals were queued outside her newsagency, Larry Purfeat with his shiny, thin dogs and old Morton Campininni and his obese Chihuahua, and a handful of fat, thin and medium locals stepping from one foot to the other in the cold. They watched her drive past and swing down into the

20

lane behind the shop. Through the plate-glass window they saw her bring the papers in at the back door; Mandy took her time unpacking the daily papers and setting them up on the counter, but her customers were attuned to her ways. Finally, she opened up. 'Held up by sheep on the road,' she said, issuing papers and change and asking if they wanted lotto tickets and if they knew who'd bought the pub, but her sullen customers spoke only of the clouds on the horizon, the possibility of rain, and the floods in Queensland. Lately, no one seemed to know the heart of matters, the interesting bits, like the details of the last will and testament or the bank statement that triggered the farmer's suicide in the first place, or the *exact reason* why so-and-so had left her husband – was it because of the drought or was one of them having an affair, and if so, who with? No one, it seemed, was interested in details anymore.

She moved to her stoop and watched, but nothing moved around the pub. Then a truck appeared at the end of the street and slowed. It stopped and, from the crowded cab, a weighty plastic bag flew at the real estate and solicitor's office opposite. The laden vehicle drove off, all that remained of someone's farming life piled on the trailer behind. Runny contents from the burst bag oozed down Joe Islip's shop window and onto the footpath. When Joe came out onto the street with a bucket of soapy water, Mandy strolled over. Joe was a bankruptcy expert, a man who knew how to persuade property from a jaded, exhausted farmer, so she asked him if he knew anything about one certain farmer, a customer of hers.

He scooped cow shit onto a spread newspaper. 'Why do you want to know?'

'He hasn't been in for weeks. And he hasn't paid his bill.'

Joe rolled up the paper and dropped it in the bin on the path. 'He hasn't paid for anything for a long time.'

'Right.' She pressed on. 'You don't know who bought the pub?'

'Couldn't tell you.' Joe Islip knew full well who'd bought the pub, he just couldn't say, that was all. Some legal thing, she supposed.

She left him to sweep the shitty water into the gutter and ambled down to the IGA with an armful of papers. Paul the postie was at his counter sorting parcels but Jasey was nowhere to be seen. Jasey often fled to the storeroom when she saw Mandy coming with the newspapers for Paul's mail run.

Mandy explained that a farmer had just thrown a bag of shit at Joe Islip's real estate and solicitor's office.

'Poor bastard. The farmer, I mean, not Joe.' He rolled newspapers up and put elastic bands around them.

'There'll be another one, I bet,' she said. 'Who bought the pub?'

Paul shrugged. 'What have we got for lotto this week?'

'A million.'

'Million dollars won't dent a farmer's four-million-dollar mortgage.'

'Jesus, what I could do with a million dollars.' She sighed. 'There has to be someone in the town who knows who bought the pub.'

He took the newspapers out to his mail van and Mandy wandered back to her shop, stuck her *Back in 5* note to the door and sneaked down the back lane with some useless newspapers and a couple of cardboard boxes. She leaned into the dumpster behind the pub to see what the bin revealed. A voice behind her said, 'What can you see?'

'Jesus, Denise, don't sneak up on me!' Mandy dropped her rubbish into the dumpster.

Denise was an older woman with thick yellow hair swept back over her grey regrowth and the charisma of a grouper. 'Not sneaking.'

'Stickybeaking?'

'You're the one who's got her head stuck in someone else's bin. What have you found, anyway?'

'Nothing. Plastic wrappings, boxes and papers, wood and plaster, old taps, pipes . . .'

'Renovating.' Denise chucked a pile of old shoes into the dumpster and walked back to her shop.

Mandy tugged the padlock on the corrugated-iron gates but it held firm, so she peered through the gap. There were just a few tradies' utes parked at the back door. She hurried back to her shop, got in her car and drove to the new twenty-four-hour servo, where she instructed Andrew to put extra butter on her sticky bun and to make her cappuccino very hot.

'The usual, then?'

'The pub sold.'

'So I see.' Andrew heated the milk.

'Your dad still selling firewood to the pub?'

He shrugged. 'They bought gas heaters for the beer garden.'

'Who did?'

He shrugged again. Mandy drove straight to the pub. The front door was locked so she went to the side and pushed through the gate into the beer garden, which doubled as a playground. The barman, Levon McIntosh, was tidying up. Mandy sat on the swing, which meant Levon had to walk around her to pick up the cigarette butts from under the seesaw. The barman was a man whose life was made complete by fantasy fiction. He was balding yet had long hair, his beard was a wizard's beard and a golden circle hung from a one lobe. He gathered empty stubbies from under the slippery dip and said that someone from Sydney had bought the pub, 'But I couldn't tell you exactly who'.

'Were there a lot of people looking to buy the place?'

'A few.'

'Will you keep your job?' The day he left school Levon joined his father to work at the pub.

'No one's told me I can't.'

'You're the manager – I thought they'd tell you everything.'

'Maybe they don't know everything.' He walked away with the empties and a plastic bag full of cigarette butts.

She got up and headed for her shop, leaving the beer garden gate open for kiddies to wander in and play on the monkey bars and fall and break their necks.

oOo

When Esther Shugg saw Gottlob Bergen's ute pull over by the side of the road she was inclined to put her old Dodge in gear and drive off. But he'd only catch her next time, and it wasn't neighbourly, so she waited while he rolled to a stop. The farmers nodded to each other across the asphalt.

'Dogs about,' Gottlob said. 'Other side of town, I'm told.'

Beside him, Gottlob's brother Vorbach nodded, and for a moment the three of them sat in their cabs while Esther's woolly sheep nibbled the verges and their thoughts all turned to wild dogs tearing at the hind legs of exhausted, terrified sheep as the town lights twinkled in the distance.

Gottlob hung his arm through his open window and aimed his thumb at her block. 'Those bloody weeds, Esther.'

She looked through her windscreen at the morning sun. 'Silage, you mean.'

'You seen Mitch's crop? It's contaminated to buggery.'

Esther checked her rear-vision mirror, adjusted her hat.

'Weeds come with the cheap feed you buy, and there's rain coming. Come summer –'

'I understand the life cycle of a plant,' she said.

'A bit of hot wind, we'll have weeds thick as wool as far as Sydney and that'll be enough fuel to burn the entire continent.'

'That's one scenario.'

'If my goats eat noxious weeds they'll be dead in twelve hours. There's a drought, they'll eat anything.'

'Goats are vermin too.'

Vorbach, who'd been sitting quietly beside his brother, said, 'We eat the goats. Chevron! It's better than beef, but your weeds breed rats, foxes, rabbits, and they bring raptors to eat the lambs.'

His brother asked, 'What are you doing with your allocation – watering your weeds again, selling, or rolling it over until next year?'

'I heard you're selling up,' Esther countered. 'Selling our land to foreigners.'

'What's wrong with foreigners?' Vorbach yelled, but Gottlob said they didn't know what they were doing; maybe they would keep the farm, just sell the water.

'To the Jeongs or the Water Authority?'

'To whoever pays the best price. But are you or are you not going to spray those bloody weeds?'

Esther pinched the brim of her hat, put her truck in gear and turned her eyes to her sheep. 'I'll see what I can do.'

Gottlob called, 'You want a hand? Happy to give you a

hand,' but her truck roared off, the hammock on the back lagging in the slipstream.

Beside him, Vorbach said, 'It would have been more gratifying to talk to the weeds themselves,' and scrolled through the contacts on his phone for Bennett Mockett, stock agent. He said, '*Verdammtes Ungeziefer, schieß alles,*' and his brother said, '*Ja*, time for a cull.'

oOo

Mandy Bishop drove home through the same dull landscape to the same old house and the same old man sitting in his usual chair. She went immediately to the phone-charging spot in the kitchen where she scrolled through Mitch's texts and emails. There was nothing of interest. She found her husband at the computer. 'What are you looking for?'

'A new irrigation system,' he said. 'I'm told I need an above-ground lateral sprinkler. Fantastic things, very efficient.'

'Terrific,' she said, almost sincerely, and went to the living room and Cal, sitting there like a ponce in his jacket and tam-o'-shanter as if he were in Scotland. She had every mind to buy a laptop, but the internet service wouldn't cope.

'I guess I'll cook dinner,' she said.

Later, the men in the house heard her call, 'Ready!' and sat at the table in front of the meal she had prepared for them, waiting for her to initiate conversation, if there was to be any. Failing to find a napkin, Cal removed a clean hanky from his breast pocket and spread it across his lap. Mandy settled at the head of the table, reached across and patted Mitch as if he were a good puppy. 'How's everyone's day been?'

'Good,' they said in unison, and Mitch mentioned roaming dogs and Cal started on about the forthcoming water meeting so Mandy cut him off. 'The pub's been sold.' They didn't comment.

'They're renovating. Surely there'll be an opening night party, free beer and bar snacks.'

Cal said he hoped the cook was better than the last one.

'It might change our lives, liven things up a bit. Anyone know anything about it?'

Mitch shook his head and Cal said, 'Can't tell you anything about it.'

She watched TV but Cal clung to the remote so finally Mandy hopped into bed with her dictionary and her mobile phone. 'Hearthrob.10+' thrashed her with five words, so she closed the game and put her phone aside. She was in her bed, but it wasn't hers. The furniture wasn't her furniture, it was theirs, and it was old, dark and heavy, like her life, a small-town life, and they were too broke to go anywhere or do anything. She wriggled under the covers and nestled into the soft pillow.

When he came to bed, Mitch lay with his back to her and in the dimness she touched where his black hair rested on his brown neck. He didn't respond, so she closed her eyes and rocked in her bed so that the bedclothes tucked into the small of her back and held her like a long, soft hand.

2.

DISAPPOINTMENT

In the night he heard the donkeys in the paddock hawing and a pack of feral dogs, low and hunting, panted through Mitch's sleep. He thought about getting up to check his ewes and their new lambs, then decided it was the fox that lived in the thickets of lignum over at Esther's. The dogs were the other side of town. But when the sun rose, Mitch leaped from his bed and went straight to the window. Tinka waited peacefully at the yard gate and high thin clouds softened the first rays. 'Jeepers,' he said, for they might just be emissaries for rain clouds. His wife groaned and pulled the covers over her head, and a momentary sensation, a faint emotional residue of someone happier, more positive, came and went. But the residue returned as he dressed and so he conjured Neralie McIntosh and carried her to the ute. Tink jumped onto the tray and smiled and turned a circle and they drove to the ewes and their new lambs. Mark and Cleopatra, his guard donkeys, waited together at the gate, their furry ears drooping against their long grey heads. In the paddock beyond them he saw one single dead lamb, its bewildered mother standing beside it. Bitter, cloudless nights and the lack of real feed made new mothers and their lambs weak, no match for a strong, fit fox. He slapped Cleo's dusty flank – 'Well done' – and patted Mark: 'I know you tried.' He aimed his gun at the ravens picking at the small pale corpse but the canny birds lifted and flapped sluggishly away, their bellies full. He dropped a wad of lucerne hay and the donkeys took a frail mouthful each and chewed. Mark's ears rose almost to full mast and he thought he saw his rude old jenny Cleo smile. The ewes and their lambs moved towards the hay and Mitch pointed to the dull sky. 'Remember rain? We get a bit of rain, breakfast will improve.'

He emptied a line of seed, checked the sheep had water, refilled the seed bin and went home. Tink settled at the house gate, rested her chin on her paws, her eyes following Mitch across the yard. The gate slammed behind him and the dull shadows of the grapevine moved up his back as he walked through the green tunnel to the door. He eased his boots off. The spring whined as the screen door opened and he vanished into the dark oblong. The dog closed her eyes, her ears still forward. At some point he would appear again and she would leap up onto the machine and they would go somewhere together and there would be a job for her.

There were two ways to get to the laundry in the Bishops Corner homestead: you could turn left inside the sleep-out door and follow the enclosed verandah around, or you could take a shortcut through the bathroom. Mitch discerned no sign of movement in the kitchen or beyond so assumed Mandy was sleeping, and decided to take the shortcut to wash his face and hands in the laundry. His mind returned to the happy prospect of rain. By the time he realised she was in the bathroom, it was too late. His wife was leaning into the mirror, a pair of tweezers in one hand, and she was naked. Her arms hid her breasts but he caught a glimpse of some residual tummy folds and her bottom. He hadn't seen it for a couple of years and didn't remember it being like that. She turned, eyes wide, mouth open, and grabbed the shower curtain over the bath, kicking the door so that it slapped shut in his face. He winced, focused on the door just millimetres from his nose. 'Sorry!' Something shocking had just occurred. It wasn't so much what he'd seen, but the fact that he *had* seen . . . and it conjured a feeling, new but familiar, and suddenly thick and present. It had been there since he married Mandy, though he wasn't sure what the feeling actually was.

He went back outside and, while he pissed on the lemon tree, gazed at the bald brown paddocks. Memories assembled like pictures along a wall: Mandy Roper at the bar in a tight dress, smiling, seductive; then Mandy waiting in his ute, topless; Mandy dragging him, half-pissed and lonely, into the little white wagon and shagging him outside the pub. There were flashes of lusty, whirlwind liaisons and then Mandy's eyes, brimming: 'I'm pregnant.'

And somehow, there was a secret trip away and the registry office and when they went to the family with the news, Mandy announced, 'I've never been as happy as I am at this moment and I never will be again.' Mitch's sister Isobel said, 'No, you won't,' and the happiness left Mandy's face. Then there was the miscarriage and a few sad weeks, and life resumed and moved through a hundred mostly unhappy scenes of some sort of marriage. He seemed to be the protagonist in the story and so remained in every scene of sleeping, waking, eating and working, but all the other cast members knew more about the meaning of the story. He was without them now at this unanticipated and brutal turning point; Mitch had just seen his marriage, acknowledged it. It wasn't what it appeared to be.

And now for the denouement. He had an inkling of what his sister meant about momentary happiness.

Feeling breathless and light-headed, he leaned on the strong, kindly lemon tree and looked at his dog sitting beside him, her small brown eyes gazing back into his.

'Holy shit, Tink.'

Eventually, he plodded up the path under the arbour and vanished through the dark oblong again and Tink put her head on her paws.

Mitch washed up in the laundry, plugged his phone in to charge and stood in the doorway between the living room and the kitchen. *The Morning Show* was on the TV and his father's bald head leaned uncomfortably from the edge of his reclining rocker. 'You right, Pop?'

'Righto,' he said sleepily, his head moving upright along the side of the chair.

Mitch poured half a cup of rolled oats into a bowl with a cup of water and put it in the microwave, made tea and four pieces of toast – two with Vegemite and two with honey. When the microwave pinged he removed the bowl and dribbled milk and sugar all over the gruel, grabbed Cal's analgesics and placed them on his father's stable table with a cup of sweet milky tea. Then he saw Mandy's deflated bum again and the hateful defiance in her face. Why wasn't she at work? It was well past seven-thirty. All those customers outside her shop! He changed the picture in his head to something good . . . Shane Warne, his slow run-up, the roll of his right arm, the ball travelling straight down the cricket pitch, spinning, the lovely drift to leg, Gatting moving towards the ball, his bat to the fore and it bouncing outside his leg stump. The ball passes, spinning to the outside edge of Gatting's bat, it clips the top of his off-stump, the bails flip through the air and Gatting stares at the ground where the ball has bounced. The crowd in the Bong erupts. The world erupts. 1993. Ball of the Century. Mitch felt better.

Callum Bishop – happy in his recliner rocker, neat as a pin in his clean blue shirt and woollen jacket – tucked a napkin into his collar, put the painkillers in his porridge, scooped them up and ate without taking his eyes from the TV. Milk spilled from his spoon, splashing into the gutter around the edge of the stable table then eking down into the deep crevice between the seat cushion and the leather rest.

The Morning Show told them news about tollways in cities and car accidents on highways, hurricanes in other countries and stranded whales in Tasmania. Then the attractive girl with pillow lips and stiff hair said, 'And now for the weather,' and the two men stopped, their tea halfway to their mouths. The low was still at the bottom of Australia and there were still no rain clouds anywhere on the continent. The men resumed breakfast, then Mandy was in the kitchen. They stopped chewing. Mitch turned his head from side to side to ease the tightness. Cupboard doors shut fiercely and water ran for too long. The microwave opened, slammed and then was quiet while she scrolled through Mitch's text messages. The microwave pinged, cutlery and crockery collided and when the back door shut, the two men watched out the window, cups in hand, as she emerged from the end of the corridor of the sparse arbour into the dry air. She passed the shrivelled garden and the brittle orchard, her thumb moving across the keypad on her mobile phone, her small, triangular handbag bouncing against her disappointing bum.

She reversed without looking. Tink jumped up onto the back of the ute and the farm dogs danced away from the wheels and her little white station wagon diminished into a low, brown dust cloud. The men resumed their breakfast. Mitch couldn't remember if he had actually seen Mandy's bum before he married her, but he knew he hadn't seen her stark naked and sitting at the kitchen table like Neralie had on the rare occasions she lost at Strip Scrabble. And he understood with sinking certainty as he sat there in his recliner rocker, next to his father in a matching rocker, that his life wasn't going to pan out the way it should have. And, come to think of it, he probably already knew that. 'And so does she.'

'What?'

He looked at Cal, his old face screwed up in frustrated anticipation. 'I said, do you want more tea?'

'I've still got this one.' He raised the mug, unsteady in his hand.

Marriage was meant to make things solid. When you gained a partner the pressures eased because you kicked on *together*. Every Sunday the presenters on *Landline* introduced couples in clean work shirts standing side by side at the silo, shed or tractor: '*My wife and I* run three hundred hectares of wheat . . . The adoption of new digital technology has helped farmer Mitchell Bishop achieve greater efficiencies in his cropping . . . *Together, he and his wife . . .*'

He thought about Neralie again, her brown legs rising from the creek water as she practised handstands after a hot day burr-cutting. But it had been five years and she wasn't here so it was best he stop thinking about her once and for all. The immediate problem was Mandy. He ran the footage of Warnie's Ball of the Century again but found himself wondering if Neralie had actually said she was never coming back, and then his thoughts went back to strip poker and Neralie's breasts, and he rubbed his elbow where Mandy's breast had connected with his arm at his mother's wake . . . at his mother's *wake*, for Chrissake. He'd recoiled from that soft pressure on his arm and saw Mandy Roper holding a tray of sandwiches, smiling up at him. He said, 'No thanks.'

'I should have just married Neralie,' he said.

His father said, 'Speak up!'

'How's your brekky?'

Callum scooped up the last of his porridge. 'It doesn't taste the same . . .'

'I know.' Not since Mandy turned off the AGA because it was too hot in summer and how was she supposed to cook on it if it had no dials? The new electric stove was meant to improve her cooking. It hadn't. And the life Callum had built and Mitch had inherited began to wilt as the drought ripened and Callum's whining about Mandy's rejection of the AGA joined her whining about how boring life was and it all became part of the music of the house. He got up and checked his phone. No messages.

'Shit,' he said, and dread settled in Mitch's heart as he poured his porridge into the dogs' scrap bucket.

Mandy Bishop drove in third gear because she was texting with her thumb as she steered. 'Blot', she wrote and gained three points on her word game. She flipped to the game of Lolly Crash but her thoughts went to the bathroom door opening and Mitch standing there looking her up and down. 'What an arsehole.' Her life as Mrs Mitchell Bishop of Bishops Corner was floating along smoothly up until that morning. She was the thinnest she'd ever been; Mitch even rolled over in his sleep and snuggled right up to her a few nights ago. There'd been no text messages from Neralie McIntosh for ages, none that she could find, anyway. And this morning, Mitch ruined it.

oOo

At lunchtime, Lana smoked half a cigarette from her packet as she walked to the library. When she stopped to screw the butt into the grass with her shoe she glanced across to the news-agency just in time to see Mandy pull back between the Lotto sign and the flag advertising prepaid rechargeable phone cards. As ever, Mrs Goldsack sat at her walnut desk staring in the general direction of the door. The long-time librarian suffered sugar diabetes and her eyesight was very poor. Above her, Queen Elizabeth, aged but vivid in satin and fat gems, watched from her gilt frame. The two women shared the same hair – a sophisticated shade of mauve featuring a curled tunnel at the temples – and both were a regal presence amid the crowded shelves and toppling stacks of dusty books. The door squeaked open and Mrs Goldsack leaned towards the sound. 'Good morning, Mrs Goldsack. Your sugar level, how's it today?'

'Ah, it's Lana. My sugar levels are level, thank you.' She held out one hand to receive a book. '*No Name* is under Collins on the shelf to the left.'

Lana said, guiltily, that she hadn't finished *The Woman in White* yet.

Mrs Goldsack folded her hands in her lap. 'You've had it three months. Big Brother will send you a message.'

Lana said she'd received the email and had already extended the loan online. Mrs Goldsack sniffed. Lana explained that she hoped to use the back room of an evening. 'I'll be running a class using the new computers that the council bought, okay?'

At the word 'computers', Mrs Goldsack shrank from the door that led to the back room, but she reached into the pocket of her knitted cardigan and drew out a bundle of keys. She dropped them on the table. 'What are you going to do with them?'

'I'll teach people how to send emails, join Buy Swap and Sell and read the newspapers online.'

Mrs Goldsack clutched her Silver Jubilee brooch and raised her chin. 'I think you'll find your students will be disappointed. Computers are not what they say they are.'

'You heard there are dogs roaming, didn't you?'

'Oh, no!'

'Well, see, I heard that on the email from Bennett Mockett and now everybody knows.'

'Anyone can tell you that. All you have to do is walk down the main street.'

'Monday nights,' Lana said. 'Before *Australian Story*.'

Lana didn't speak when she walked into Mandy's news-agency. She just selected a sheet of school project cardboard, a packet of colourful pens and a box of drawing pins. Mandy scanned the items wordlessly. It wasn't until she got to the door that Lana called, 'Thanks.'

Mandy watched her go straight to the IGA and when she walked back to her office a short time later, Mandy stuck her *Back in 5* note to the door and headed for the supermarket. The sign was between the notice about the water meeting in three weeks' time and the Buy Swap and Sell items.

Basic computer skills class starting soon.

Learn to read the paper online, buy lotto tickets, check results, make appointments with the visiting health service and more.

Library: Mondays, 6 pm

Lana

36

She dumped a packet of two-minute noodles, some dehydrated cheese sauce and some frozen vegetables on the counter. 'It'll never work,' Mandy declared. 'People around here won't even be able to find the on button.'

'You probably struggled the first time too.'

'Yeah, but I overcame it, that's the difference.' Mandy turned to Paul at his post office counter. 'How do you feel about it, Pauly? Less people coming into the shop, everyone sending emails and greeting cards online and not buying anything from you?'

Paul jerked a thumb at the parcels piled behind him. 'Online shopping.'

Triumphant, Jasey scanned the Bishop family's dinner. 'You got your own bag or you want one for twenty cents?'

'Don't need a bag.' Mandy gathered her groceries. 'Why, in this small town, do you bother to wear a name tag every day?'

'Because, Mandy Roper, *I've* got nothing to be ashamed of.'

'Everyone's got something to be ashamed of.' Mandy didn't bother to close the door after her, and when Jasey stomped over to shut it, Paul said to his fierce landlady, 'Might be an idea to install an automatic door.'

oOo

Mandy stepped through the door of Beau Monde, saying, '*Some* people in town still call me Mandy Roper. They need to get used to the fact that I'm Mandy Bishop.'

Kelli put aside the magazine she was browsing and looked at Mandy. This week Kelli's fringe was striped red and green. 'What can I do for you, Mrs Bishop?'

'I want my nails done.'

37

'The Japanese is popular.'

'Can you do the Japanese?'

'I can do whatever's in the bloody stamp book.'

Mandy reached for Kelli's appointment book, wrote *Mandy BISHOP* at a convenient time and went next door to see Denise. The shop smelled of stale people and cured shoes. Mandy asked her if she'd heard who bought the pub. Denise shook her grouper face.

'No one seems to know . . . and that's very unusual, wouldn't you agree?'

Denise shrugged. 'Paperwork probably isn't finalised. Did Kelli show you her nail-art book?'

'Yes.'

Denise said, 'I'm getting Japanese. What are you getting?'

'Haven't decided. Black's fashionable.'

'Why don't you get something fun?'

Mandy looked out at the dying trees lining the straight black road that brought new things to the town and took people other places. 'There's no fun here.'

'See those clouds on the horizon? That means rain.'

'That won't change anything.' At the door, Mandy said, 'Nothing ever changes.'

'Well, you just never know,' Denise cried, and went to close the door because Mandy always left it open.

Mandy walked straight back into Kelli's shop and studied the nail stamp book. 'Everyone's getting the Japanese.'

Later, she found there was still no sign of movement at the pub but there had to be something going on behind those closed doors. She spent the afternoon out on the street washing her front window. Denise popped in to see Kelli then wandered across to the IGA and came out again, having purchased nothing. They always knew something, those women. Then, when Paul left the IGA in his little postal truck, she abandoned her half-clean front windows and followed him home. In his small bachelor kitchen, Mandy trapped him against the stove, one hand on the fridge and the other on the bench. 'How much rent is Jasey charging you?'

'A reasonable amount.'

'I'll halve it. The landlord just wants his rent, he doesn't care who pays it.'

'Half, you're offering?'

'Half. And you can put your counter along the side so you still get a view out onto the street.' Mandy didn't want him to obstruct her view entirely, but the space she was offering was substantial.

He rubbed his chin.

She wanted a holiday, she wanted to save money so she could take Mitch to a beach or a mountain, eat nice dinners and watch films. And Paul would look after the shop. 'You'd have a quarter of the shop and of course there'll be free newspapers and magazines.'

He shifted his weight from one foot to the other. He was a tall man, heavy set, and she was quite short. She took a step closer. 'A nice *big* counter and everyone knows big is best.' She put her hand on his chest. 'Come on, Pauly, do it for me,' and Paul was swept back to that wet and slippery night on the bank of the swimming hole with Mandy Roper. Maybe she'd let him do that to her again?

'I suppose it makes sense, since I've got to deliver newspapers every day on my mail run.'

'Yes! Oh, Paul, I hadn't thought of that! That's such a good point!'

He looked into the distance. 'Give me a twenty-four-hour cooling-off period.'

He watched her go, studying what he could see of her bottom beneath her long shirt. He smoothed his substantial moustache. There had to be somewhere out the back of the shop where they could do it.

She gave him an hour to cool off before she rang him and said she'd moved the old cupboard and was waiting for him, then she told anyone who came into the shop that Lana's computer classes were pointless, 'because the internet reception's not up to it, anyway'.

oOo

Mandy's affable husband would not meet her eye, but Mandy had decided to erase the bathroom incident from her life. Uncomfortable things ignored went away, eventually. She checked his phone and email accounts and focused on dinner. She drained the vegetables and noodles from the boiling water, poured cheese sauce over them, sprinkled parmesan on top and shoved them under the grill. When the cheese had melted, she yelled, 'Ready!' Over dinner she introduced the topic of Lana's computer classes. 'She's deluded, your old friend Lana. It'll never work. And she's stealing customers, from Paul . . . and me, not that you'd care.'

Callum lifted a fork full of steaming noodles and said people would care if she opened up earlier, that she would keep her customers, and Mandy responded, 'I knew perfectly well you'd say those exact words, Cal. But why should I open up at six am? Where do all my customers have to rush off to that early? And why should I spend from six-fifteen in the morning until five pm waiting for nothing and no one? What's so important in a newspaper that all those boring old farts need to know before six-thirty in the morning, anyway?'

Callum put his cutlery neatly on the plate and Mitch said they weren't 'boring old farts'.

'And that's the difference between you and me, Mitch. You think they're nice, even entertaining?' she said, licking sauce from her finger. 'I don't. Anyway,' she continued, 'all they have to do is turn on the telly to get the news.'

'You've defeated your point.'

'What?'

'You're arguing that Lana took your customers but you're saying they may as well stay home and watch the news on telly.'

For just a moment she was taken aback. It was unlike Mitch to argue. 'There's only one point to this whole situation, Mitch, and that is: I do not care.'

Callum pushed his plate away and Mitch felt the bathroom door slamming in his face. He would have said thanks for dinner, but today he said to himself, *I don't care*. It was the residual bruise he was nursing, a niggling thought that he might not have been as astute as he thought he was, and he could not make that feeling go away.

Cal settled in for the news then fell asleep and Mandy ran a deep bath because she knew it annoyed them. *All that water . . . in a drought.* She poured in bath salts and soaked until she felt pampered and cosy. She ignored the mirror while drying her homely pink body, but finally, checking the door was snibbed, she craned to see what Mitch had seen when he burst in on her. 'You're thinner than Denise or Kelli, anyway,' she told herself. Besides, it wasn't as if Mitch could rush out and find someone new, someone perfect. She wrapped her pampered self in her nightie, snakeskin dressing-gown and fluffy bunny slippers, and expunged the morning bathroom incident from her memory, again.

Mitch checked the mail, again, in case there was a bill from the telco. The invoice was due; he needed to get to it before Mandy did, and it was sad that he did. Then he found that Mandy had wiped his careful history of irrigation systems, government subsidies, efficiency savings and commodities markets. He started his online research again but was soon distracted, wondering where it had all gone wrong. What had happened?

3.

WATER FROM THE SKY

Something was wrong. The air was different. It was thicker, sounds were duller, the morning light subdued, and there was that lovely smell . . . Petrichor. Wet dirt. Mitch flung back the covers and pulled the blind aside. In bed, his wife said something about too much light, so he said it was part of his job to know what the day would be.

'Why? So you can change it?'

'It's a grey sky.' He smiled, reaching for his clothes. 'No sun.'

'Government must have bought it back,' she said, and he almost laughed. She used to be interested in government buybacks, water and even his sheep. She could be funny, too, and she was warm, or was it just sex? But he'd told her all his dreams and all his secrets too. In the beginning – the very beginning – she was sociable. But as soon as they were married she refused to go anywhere with Lana, Jasey or Kevin. Now he rarely saw them. And had he ever actually proposed? Or was it a decision somehow arrived at in his small, lusty bed? He remembered the lurch of fear when she arrived at the breakfast table that first morning. His father said nothing. Absolutely nothing. Mitch put it down to shock, decided things would change when she cooked nice dinners, scrubbed the place up a bit and the kids came along. But there weren't any kids. The first night back from Melbourne they stepped into the beery post-harvest, pre-Christmas celebration at the pub, and the place erupted. There was much backslapping and toasting and laughing . . . but were they laughing *at* him? Kev put his pale freckled arm around Mitch's shoulders and said, 'Mate, sometimes relationships aren't what they seem.'

'Kev, you of all people are surely not trying to give me advice about relationships.'

And Isobel . . . speeding over the stock ramp in her big square vehicle and striding past him. 'You're an idiot.' She walked straight into the house then stormed back out with their mother's jewellery box in her hand and her engagement ring on her finger.

'What's it got to do with you?' But he knew even as his words melted lamely into the void that it had everything to do with her. Everyone had everything to do with it. Decisions like marriage and inheritance and reputation and worthiness were a family concern, a community discussion.

Denise had patted his back, saying, 'I think this secret marriage is just the thing for poor old Mandy.' He thought she meant that Mandy, like everyone, deserved the chance for happiness. But was that what she meant? Because, somehow, Mandy had never achieved happiness. Neither of them had.

His ruminations ended with the sound of first one, then two, then three raindrops on iron, and then a solid splattering that grew to a torrent on the roof. He dragged on his jeans, and ran in his socks, eager to see what the farm held for him on this day. 'Rain, Cal!'

Callum was at the living room window. 'Too late for rain,' he said. 'It'll just ruin that crop of yours.'

'Not much of a crop anyway.' But as they ate their porridge the late winter rain clouds floated away across the sky, turning it from grey to blue again. The main point was: water fell from the sky, and it would grow a bit of green feed for his sheep. And then the weather report promised more rain in the next twenty-four hours, so he checked the Bureau of Meteorology and it told him the same thing. 'So if it rains on my crop now, well and good.'

Cal called, 'What?'

He lifted the tin his father kept his hearing aids in, looked him in the eye and rattled it. 'I said, I'LL BE BACK ABOUT NOON.'

Cal retrieved the remote control from under the stable table and turned the TV up.

oOo

The donkeys watched him ride away, sighed and sniffed the bare ground at their hoofs. Above, the wedge-tailed eagles hung in the thermal, two huge silhouettes, their loose wingtips black against the cumulus. As he followed the track along the channel towards his crop, he scanned the gaunt paddocks for dead or dying sheep. There were no puddles in the channel bed, just dry, rain-punctured dust, and though more rain meant he wouldn't have to cart water to thirsty mobs all over the farm, there was also the niggling thought that a storm, or rain, could damage those acres of thin but promising wheat heads.

Under the great blue hat of the sky, the shallow horizon at his shoulder, Mitch waded into the sparse crop and broke a stalk. He rolled the head in his palm and ground out some seed. He chewed it and said to Tink, 'Too soft yet, but I should get enough for next season's seed, and maybe some stock feed if it's not shot and sprung after the rain.'

45

They set off across the bare paddocks to fill the bin for the animals. At the storage silos, Mitch positioned the auger beneath the silo hatch, making sure it was well positioned to suck up the grain. When he pushed the ignition button and the little engine sputtered to life, he went back to the silo and opened the hatch and grain was sucked up and fell like water into the feeder bin. The donkeys wandered down from the far end of the paddock and stood watching him. Cleopatra hung her long head over the fence. Mitch chucked a few scoops of nutrients into the mix for his boys, his wethers and handsome rams. When the feeder bin was full, he pulled the lever to close the silo hatch and cut the auger engine. Tinka jumped up onto the back of the ute. Mitch told the donkeys he'd be back to feed them next, then they drove away.

The donkeys raised their noses and caught the floating trace of golden oats. The ewes and their lambs arrived to see what their guardians were doing. They stood against the fence staring at the feed silo. It was Cleopatra who pushed on the wire gate that separated her from all that grain, and it was also the jenny who nudged the end of the auger with her big strong nose – and, because Mitch had failed to secure the brakes, it rolled from under the silo, catching on the outlet lever and pulling it open. A great pile of wheat came gushing out, tipping the auger forward so that it dropped its nose and emptied another small pile of wheat from its mouth. Mark went to that pile, Cleopatra stayed at the biggest pile, and then the ewes gathered around, heads down, their lambs gambolling behind.

Way off in the paddock, Mitch looped the string around the rear-vision mirror and wedged the square of timber between the seat and the accelerator. He climbed onto the tray and then stepped across to the feeder trailer. He sent Tink to gather a few confused stragglers, and soon all the wethers were in place along the thread of grain, heads down, and Tink was looking up at him on the roof of the cab.

'I once thought I would have a son or a daughter who'd help me with things . . . but all I really need is a block of wood and you, Tink.'

The dog blinked and looked uncertain.

When they headed back for the fire truck, he saw the strange sight at the storage silo. The donkeys were hunkered in under the great metal cylinder, sheep loitering and a thatch of pink and grey galahs at their feet. The gate to the silo hung open. 'No!'

He braked and ran at them, yelling, 'No, no, no, no!' The galahs lifted, fluttered and settled again, and the ewes scattered, their lambs calling from behind. Mark and Cleopatra were together, kneeling under the silo hatch, steadily working away at the grain as it leaked free. He slapped at them, kicked their rumps and they stood, appalled. Tinka rounded, yapping, and Cleopatra kicked out, her muzzle reaching again for the pile of grain. Mark turned to Mitch, wheat grains lacing his soft wet nostrils and decorating his thick, lovely eyelashes. Mitch smacked their rumps, careful to avoid the sideways kicks, and eventually Cleopatra gave up and trotted away. She came to a juddering halt just beyond the open gate, suddenly conscious of her very full stomach. Mark stopped, raised his tail and farted, then his nose and ears lowered, and Cleo heehawed painfully.

'Serves you both right! You are asses, mules and hinnies.' Though it was his responsibility to prevent harm.

He caught Mark, tied him to the ute and dragged him slowly away. At first Cleo refused to follow and turned her rump to her vanishing brother, but the smaller he got the more often she turned her great fluffy head to him and, in the end, it couldn't be endured. She hurried to him as fast as her bloated, fermenting guts would allow.

Mitch spent the next hour walking them in circles behind the ute. Then he untied them and left them with the ewes and their lambs again. 'You may as well get used to the walking,' he said. 'You'll be walking miles every day for a long time and I want you to consider that I'm being punished for your gluttony too.'

The sky was empty above the dry, hard farm, the topsoil curled away in low eddies and the house across the paddocks looked bleak, with its dull trees and dead gardens. The donkeys stood before him, looking truly contrite, their noses close to the ground and ears drooping. 'I don't blame you, and I'm sorry I called you asses. It has been shitty lately, but there's been a splash of water from the sky, rain, and things can't get any shittier, surely.'

oOo

Neralie McIntosh lay in bed in her Sydney flat while the sounds of the waking city filled her small bedroom. The motorcycle parked beneath the flats banged to life and idled as it did every morning, the engine clacking back from the concrete walls. Then the loud black and chrome thing thwacked all the way down the Coogee Bay hill and its noise was consumed by the din of the faraway day, where it would meet with disaster, Neralie hoped. Outside, a smoker cleared his watery lungs and doors slammed up and down the concrete stairwell. The girl from the flat above shouted instructions about the cat's dinner from the bottom of the stairwell, and heels clacked on the concrete steps: '. . . and if you don't clean up your room by the time I get home you are not going out this weekend, ya hearmee, Nay-th'n?'

Neralie's boyfriend, Beau, shut the shower taps off. He did not understand the value of water. He stayed too long under a hard-running shower, let taps flow for no purpose. He wasn't the sort of boyfriend you could be truly human with. She could never consider taking a pee behind a tree when he was present. Mitch, however, had accepted it was suitable to excrete according to need. She quickly segued from Mitch to panoramas of scrubby plains and oh! round grey sheep. Never had she imagined she'd long to see sheep again. And to hear the high trill of pink-tipped galahs disappearing into messy gums (perfect for peeing behind) and then Mitchell Bishop crept back into her mind . . . but he was with another woman.

Beau came into the bedroom and she heard the elastic of his clean boxers smack against his lovely tanned hips and his arms slide into his shirtsleeves. It was quiet while he buttoned up, then his substantial lips touched her temple, leaving a tiny wet spot.

'You know,' she said, 'there are as many people in this bloody apartment block as there are in my whole home town, but when I wake up there, I don't hear any of them.'

He kissed her again and was gone. He was the only boyfriend she'd ever had who wore a suit to work. She wept for a minute then tried to weep a bit longer but she was too happy – today was the end of this life; tomorrow another would commence. Or recommence. In the five years Neralie had lived in Sydney, she'd made three real friends: her boss, Steve; Steve's wife, Wanda; and Beau. She'd been to art galleries and museums, nightclubs and parties, the beach, the opera, the ballet and she'd taken the train to the Blue Mountains and woken in a warm bed that looked at the misty mountains. And she'd been to Fiji and Hawaii and Las Vegas. But always, life felt like a temporary thing. Then one morning, a year prior, on a day like any other, she woke and said, 'Bugger this,' and phoned home.

Her brother answered. 'What's up?'

'I'm coming home.'

'What happened?'

'Nothing.'

'Why?'

'Because I've been living in a blaring shithole for four years.'

There was silence for two seconds. 'Make it five.'

'Levon!'

'Wait till it rains – there'll be something to come home to, and I've got a proposition for you.'

'Levon, I need to come home.'

'The pub's for sale,' he said, and she let him speak.

When he'd finished, Neralie understood that her grinding life in Sydney had a purpose after all, and that purpose muted her longing. Within the hour she'd enrolled in two business courses that would see her return home with a Diploma of Business Management and a licensed premises management degree. Then she went straight to her boss. 'I've got a proposition for you.'

Steve closed his laptop and phoned for his wife to join them. When Wanda arrived in the office, he said, 'What have you got?'

Half an hour later it was decided that Wanda and Steve would go for a long drive to the country and take a look at this Billabong Hotel.

'It was a bit of a blood house last time I saw it,' Neralie warned, 'but life support for a hundred square kilometres.'

Steve winked at her and Wanda rubbed her hands together. It was a business opportunity for them, and an opportunity for Neralie's father and brother to invest in the place where they'd spent their working lives. It was a wonderful opportunity for the town and, most importantly, a good reason to go home.

She told Beau over wonton soup and, to hide her happiness, bent down to steady the table with a folded paper napkin.

'I'll come too.'

'You can't come. There's no work for performance and productivity managers there.'

Her boyfriend replied through a mouthful of lemongrass chilli chicken, 'I'll do IT.'

'Low demand – and anyway, you won't last a month in a small town.'

'I come from a small town.'

'Thirty thousand people is not small. Five hundred is small.'

He looked around at the Friday-night diners in the restaurant: couples and families, groups of girls, blokes on their own. 'I don't think I'll ever find anyone like you. You're different.'

'Yeah.' She shrugged, and put the problem of sad Beau at the back of her mind, along with 'Mitch' and 'find good hairdresser'.

oOo

Midmorning, Jasey was bending down under her cash register, searching for coins, while three customers leaned on their produce-laden trolleys and gazed through the front window at the pub opposite. A man in overalls was renovating the sash windows and an air conditioner was being hoisted up to the roof.

Debbie sighed and looked over to Paul. 'Moving up to the newsagents, I hear?'

Paul stopped bundling mail.

Jasey straightened, red-faced from bending. 'That right, Pauly?'

He nodded, then picked at a roll of sticky tape with his thumbnail.

'And just exactly when will you be vacating my premises to move your post office business to the paper shop?'

Paul put the sticky tape down and smoothed his pale moustache. 'Mandy's offered me cheaper rent.'

'She would, knowing *as I do* that rent's important for a struggling business.'

Paul said weakly, 'There's a bit more space for me and my mailboxes in her shop.'

The people in the IGA tried to visualise where the extra space in the newsagency might be, but couldn't. Paul felt the burn of Jasey's blue eyes.

'I'm sorry, I never noticed you struggling for somewhere to put the dozen letters and two packages you get in here every day.' Jasey found a small bag of change. 'Anyway, where exactly in your old girlfriend's shop is this so-called space?'

'She was never my girlfriend.'

Debbie said, 'You all say that.'

'She's removed the books and calendars and stuff because people don't use them anymore; they use the internet.'

'We still make stuff from colouring paper and pencils,' Debbie said, and her two kids nodded.

Jasey started ripping at the zip lock on the coin bag. 'She just wants you to open up for her at six in the morning while she lies in bed.'

'I don't think so.' Paul's chin went up, but if it was true, he'd get to root Mandy, for sure.

Jasey looked across to the shelves behind Paul. She'd changed everything in her shop to accommodate his desk and his postboxes, and now he was leaving.

'She'll read all our postcards,' Debbie said, and her two kids looked disapprovingly at Paul the postie.

'Debbie, that's a slanderous thing to say.'

'True, but.'

Suddenly Jasey smiled. 'Okay, you organise to get the post-boxes removed from my front window and you pay to put it all back exactly how it was, right?'

'Course.'

She gave up trying to open the small plastic bag and tore at it with her teeth, poured the golden coins into the cash register then slammed it shut so hard that the rack of peppermints and Tic Tacs rattled. She grabbed Debbie's bananas and dropped them on the scales, jabbed at the keypad, ran the baked beans under the scanner and dumped them in on top of the bananas.

In the car Debbie said to her kids, 'First drop of rain, everyone goes mad. Best not to cross anyone.'

That evening, the landlord settled in front of the news, feeling pleased because Paul's presence would bring more people to Mandy's newsagency. He could finally put the rent up. Over dinner, Debbie informed her husband that Mandy and Jasey were at war and her husband said he wasn't surprised, everyone knew Mandy was always the unhappiest person in town. Denise and Kelli discussed the tension between Jasey and Mandy and Denise said, 'Mandy Roper's been like a knife slicing through polystyrene since she was born.'

Over a drink in the beer garden of the Billabong, Jasey

looked at Kevin, her large, red-haired, pale-skinned boyfriend. 'Bicycle Mandy is being a bitch.'

Kev said, 'It's going to get worse, you know that,' thinking about Neralie, and Mandy, the lank-haired, sullen girl who bullied from the swing at school. She used to twist around and around so the rope was tight then lean back and lift her feet, swirling, watching the sun whorl through the peppercorn canopy, her shoes chopping close to the kiddies waiting for a turn. Happily, Mandy's attendance at school was sporadic so there were days when other kids got a proper go on the swing. Kev recalled one bitter winter's day, little Mandy slumped on the swing scraping her shoes in the dirt. The puddles froze that year and the wind was icy, and Mandy Roper's dad had died suddenly. Lana held out her lunch bag. 'You can have my sandwich.' Mandy Roper told her to stick it up her bum.

Mandy Roper had been warming her fingers over the toaster when her dad walked through the kitchen. Her mother butted her cigarette out and said, 'Bye, love,' and her husband said, 'See ya.' Gloria Roper reached for her coffee and Mandy turned back to her toast and they heard the ute door slam. The sound of a dull shot thwacked through the freezing air. Gloria stood up, took the bread from the toaster, spread it with butter and Vegemite and shunted her daughter out the door and into her car. She drove her to the school bus stop with her breakfast in a plastic bag and left her standing on the side of the road in the sideways rain.

When Mandy's grandmother retrieved her, the old woman put the girl in her car and said, 'My son is dead. It's your mother's fault.'

oOo

Apart from the light rain, which was only enough to make visibility poor, Isobel's day had gone to plan. She'd left on time – 5.30 am – unloaded a wool bale at the mill, and over a cup of tea and a sliver of homemade lemon slice had confirmed financial matters, estimated processing times and appointed a date to return for the skeins to coincide with end-of-term school pick-up. She texted the craft ladies and was on the road again by eight-thirty, had reached the outskirts of Melbourne by ten and was double-parked outside Verity's Collins Street boutique by eleven. At one point, a parking inspector stood in front of her four-cylinder, six-speed Isuzu twin cab and typed information into his small machine. Isobel emerged from the shop in her pale jeans, sky-blue shirt, pearls and puffer vest. 'Good morning,' she said, smiling. 'I'm very sorry, I'll just be a minute more.' She picked up a stack of flat boxes and asked, 'Have you been in the country long?'

'No.' He was looking at the Pipparoy spun-wool garments Verity was draping around the stiff shoulders of angular mannequins.

'Where are you from?'

'Sudan.'

'Oh, the Nile. Were you a farmer?'

'Yes.'

'I'm a farmer. Did you grow rice and cotton?'

'No, millet and goats, and I had some sheep too.'

'Me too.' She put some boxes in his arms, picked up the remaining boxes and asked him if he irrigated with water from the Nile.

'Yes, but it is not like here.' He followed her into the shop.

Half an hour later, Isobel took a photo of Azim smiling in front of the pashminas and shawls in the Collins Street window.

She texted them off to the craft ladies, shook Azim's hand and gave him her card and told him again where to catch the train and then the bus and that she was looking forward to meeting his wife and children. 'There's plenty of room at Girri Girri for you all.'

She headed off to the college, without a parking ticket, to meet the children. Philippa and Rory were scolded over their debit-card and phone accounts, then Isobel spoke to the house mistress and left her children with homemade biscuits and pink lipstick on their cheeks. As she drove towards Aunt Opal's, she fought the urge to go straight home, pop down to her sheep, sort the mail and organise dinner but there was the matter of the future, specifically Philippa's future, and, of course, Bishops Corner. As she drove, she planned: first the Bendigo show, next year the Royal Melbourne then Royal Sydney . . . then China. She would go to China and they would love her fine – superfine – merino wool, 15.5 microns, at least. For that, she would need more fine Merino hoggets. Many more hoggets. For these reasons, Isobel diligently attended her duties as niece. Her aunt was both elderly and wealthy.

Isobel served smoked cod on a round white plate and dribbled the white sauce over it, adding a sprig of parsley. Her bosomy aunt drained her crystal tumbler of Scotch and soda, her other hand poised, mid-note in Mozart's Serenade Number 5 in D major, then she lifted her large mono-breast and shuffled to the table, spreading her napkin and lifting the corner of the cod with her fish knife, her lip curled. 'Kippers?'

'Fish is good for you.' Isobel draped her napkin across her lap.

'So are Brussels sprouts but I haven't eaten them for sixty years. I suppose we're not having chips?'

'No.'

'Will you collect me for Christmas this year?'

'Yes, unless you'd prefer to take the train.'

'I haven't taken a train since your mother and I travelled up from school.'

There was a pause while Margot Bishop came to mind, Aunt Opal handing a lace handkerchief to young Margot while she waited with their father at the church door on her wedding day. Isobel pictured her dear mother, withered and smiling from her hospital pillow, her flattened hair a fan on the back of her head.

'You might not have to bother – anything could happen to me in the next couple of months.'

Isobel didn't respond. Aunt Opal pushed a tiny amount of cod onto her fork. The fish didn't taste as bad as she'd anticipated.

Finally Isobel said, 'We've had rain. Mild, but still . . .'

'Well, that'll ruin everything.' Aunt Opal tucked into her fish.

'Possibly. I'm surprised Mitch's not suicidal – the drought wiped out about ten years of investment into the property. His crop's no good, his sheep are poor, he won't get all his water allocation, though it doesn't matter much because his machinery's worn and his overdraft is huge. And we're all terrified of what they'll tell us at the water meeting.'

'Who'd be a farmer?'

'My Merinos are beautiful. I've put Digby on a diet.'

'Your husband has a tendency towards portliness. What about my dear brother, Callum?'

'He's slower. And needs his eyebrows trimmed.'

'When I phoned last week *she* answered.' There was a beat, and Isobel thought perhaps her aunt would stop there. 'I didn't want to speak to *her*. I wanted to speak to my brother. Or at least my nephew. She's entirely inappropriate.'

'Mandy hasn't had *our* start in life.'

'We all get a start in life, it's what we do with it that counts. She uses her feminine wiles to get what she wants. Her mother was the same.'

'If she was a bloke it wouldn't matter.'

'She's Mitch's wife.'

'Precisely,' Isobel said, 'so we must bear with her.' Though she was certain Mitch couldn't possibly love Mandy.

'What about that other lass, the barman's girl?'

'Neralie moved to Sydney and did very well, according to Jasey.' Isobel started on her salad.

'I quite liked her,' Aunt Opal said.

'We all liked Neralie.'

'Your mother didn't like her.'

'She's not Mum's type.'

'Neither is Bicycle Mandy.'

'Aunt Opal –'

'Everyone, and I mean *everyone*, knows everything in a small town. You know that so there's no sense pretending otherwise.'

Isobel continued, 'It was a long time ago and we all make mistakes, especially when we're young.'

'Not the same one over and over. All those boys on the riverbank.' Aunt Opal chewed some lettuce as though it were laced with snail killer. 'You wouldn't accept her to the Rural Women's Club.'

'No one would second her! Not one single woman in that town would endorse her application! She has nothing to contribute, she just objects to everything.' Isobel drained her wine and poured another and there was a pause while they ate, glumly. 'What I can't cope with is that the entire town let it happen. I simply do not understand how she got Mitch to the registry office.'

'Who bought the pub?'

'Someone from Sydney.'

Aunt Opal's knife paused, mid-air. Isobel had never seen her aunt breach table manners before. 'You say Neralie McIntosh has done very well in Sydney?'

'I'm told.'

Opal pointed to her niece with her knife. 'I said it five years ago, didn't I? I said, "I'll give Mitch's marriage five years."' She sat back, her eyes narrowing, cutlery facing the ceiling.

Isobel looked glumly at the fish bones lined up neatly on the plate. 'A divorce would mean the end of Bishops Corner. Mandy will take as much as she can; we're in no position to pay her out *and* survive.'

'So it's true! Surely he's signed some sort of agreement, or taken insurance for divorce? Fidelity and surety insurance? And anyway, she won't go, she'll just join the countless others living perfectly adequate lives in loveless, sexless marriages because it suits everyone. Mitch will be miserable forever for the sake of the farm.'

Isobel put her knife and fork side by side. 'Someone needs to invest an awful lot of money to make that farm a viable business, but not so that it can be taken by someone who doesn't deserve it.'

'My money's invested.' There was no way the weed-infested dust bowl that was Bishops Corner was getting Opal's money, especially since half of it might go to Mandy.

'The bank will have invested your money in some overseas company,' Isobel said.

'What's for dessert?'

She pressed on. 'If I had the money I'd take on Bishops Corner. For my daughter.'

Aunt Opal looked to the kitchen bench for the sweets.

Isobel continued, 'Farming isn't actually as physically arduous as it once was. These days they have all sorts of modern technology to drive tractors and grow things, consultants and specialists for everything from soil testing to air quality control. Women contribute forty-nine percent to farming . . . there are more and more solo women farmers.'

'Did you bring anything for dessert?'

'Fruit salad.'

'You feed me kippers and fruit salad and tell me you want my money for your daughter so she can be tricked by the weather and ruined by the banks and trapped forever?'

'Do not underestimate Philippa. If she gets a good start she'll run a good business. She has very firm ideas on farming. Times have changed; women rule the world these days, Aunt Opal.'

'And the smart ones let their husbands think they run the world. What time are you heading back to rule over your husband's empire?'

'As soon as I wake up.'

4.

TWENTY PERCENT

The week rolled on, the rain stayed away, then things went bad again. The computer kept telling him he was 'not connected', his wife was scrolling through his phone messages and his father was bellowing for more sugar on his porridge, and when reception finally dropped in, an email from Bennett Mockett said that another farmer had lost a dozen sheep to dogs in the night. He deleted the email but it did not delete the image of entrails stretched across the wet, red ground so he moved on to the email from the Water Authority. This coming irrigation season, their total water allocation would roll out to just twenty percent. He swore at the computer, went to the kitchen and got the sugar and dumped two tablespoons on the analgesics in Cal's porridge. 'We're only getting twenty percent of our water this season.'

'Twenty? That all?'

'Better than nothing,' said his wife.

'They'll bloody charge me twice as much for each megalitre then ask me to pay forty grand to maintain my twelve kilometres of channel so I can get the mere twenty percent of the water that I'm entitled to.'

'Just hide a pump in the reeds at Esther's,' she said.

'You can't do that sort of thing.'

'You told me you'd like to.'

'I was just dreaming, it's illegal, not ethical.' But he probably did tell her that; everyone thought about doing it, but nobody ever would. No one would steal, especially from neighbours.

He left before his father started his lecture on how farmers grew all the food and fibre which was an enormous percent of all global exports and what about the $160 *billion* a year agriculture added to the GDP and how farmers cared for sixty-one percent of the landmass to feed ninety-three percent of Australia.

Tinka's head was out the side of the ute, catching the early morning smells. He stopped far away from the donkeys and crept towards them, rope in hand. They watched him, listening to his kind words, and when he was finally just an arm's length from them, they turned and walked away. 'You need to get well and get back to work, there's dogs about.' They started trotting. Mitch ran, driving them forward, swinging the lasso. Finding themselves against the wire, the donkeys turned to follow the fence line but stopped to catch their breath behind a sapling, their fat tummies either side of the thin trunk. 'I can see you,' he called. 'Coming, ready or not.' And they moved off again. Finally, when they were tired, Tink rounded in front of them, stalling them, and Mitch managed to lasso Mark. Cleopatra turned her rump to him but he knew her deadly hoofs, had seen the slain foxes, their folded torsos like old socks, their heads a mass of bone and flesh, so he jumped, but fell. Mark slipped away and Cleo followed, leaving Mitch sitting in the dirt with his head in his hands. Tink pressed her wet nose to his arm. 'You're right,' he said. 'We won't give up.' They went to the ute and pushed the donkeys, drove them around and around, making them run in circles until eventually Mark gave up, his breath like a steam train. Cleo trotted away to the ewes and their lambs and Mitch dumped a hand of hay at Mark's feet. 'It's for your own good, and soon you can eat wheat again. Maybe.'

They drove next to the yearlings, Mitch's favourite type of sheep – shy, but not terrified, young, clean and light. It was a long day, and it always took a day to coax them along and get them into the yards, but Tink nudged and prodded, coaxed and guided and then gleefully hurried them down the narrow race to Mitch, drafting according to the pretty coloured tags in their dun-coloured ears – ewes to the left, rams to the right, wethers in the middle and the Sundays (the less-than-perfect sheep readied for Sunday roasts) straight into the holding yards. Late afternoon, when the wethers were looking through the fence at the rams and the ewes were looking back at the wethers, the wind picked up and moved the clouds in, and Mitch sat on the roof of his ute to eat an orange and survey all around while the setting sun put on a show. His pale crop, made golden in the evening light, illuminated the barren plains and turned the clouds mauve. Rain still threatened, and what sort of crop would next season bring with just twenty percent of his water allocation? How could he grow enough to clear debt and secure income? Would he still be viable if rain ruined this year's crop? Why was the weather never straightforward, timely or generous? The black forms of the eagles drifted across the sky towards their eyrie, a huge messy bowl in an ancient pine, the last of the stand. Mitch ignored the fact that the eagles might be responsible for lamb losses over the years; he was grateful that they preyed on rabbits and foxes, possums and myna birds. They might even have chicks in their nest – chicks that would grow and kill every raven in the place. He took a photo of the birds against the purpling sky and held the phone up. 'Please, God of technology, let reception drop in.' Two bars showed up on his screen, so he sent the photo off and waited.

The image that came back to him was a view of roofs, electricity poles and treetops. The caption said, *More please*, so he sent back a photo of a desolate landscape featuring a fat orange sun, painting a giant pine golden. He inhaled and wrote, *Smells like dirt and sheep shit. When are you coming home?*

One day you will stop asking. Don't forget to delete.

Mitch deleted the messages and checked his mail just in case the phone bill had landed.

A few fat raindrops stung the bonnet of the ute and spattered across the dirt, and were carried on the chilly wind almost as soon as they burst. Cleo and Mark brayed indignantly to him from across the paddock, but no amount of braying would make Mitch feed them. Tink barked because it was tucker time and suddenly Mitch felt keenly the absence of Neralie. She would tire of Sydney, surely. Her trips around the planet would tell her where home was. Why hadn't he understood that five years ago? She would come home, one day, maybe with a husband and kids, but they would be friends and she would be in his life again. The sky dimmed as it does when the sun finally slips from sight and Tinka barked again. 'Alright,' he said.

As he drove home he saw that the north fence needed re-straining. 'You can tell how good a farmer is by the state of his fences, Tink.' He would fix it. First harvest cheque or wool cheque, he'd fix everything.

oOo

64

Near the plate-glass window where Paul's personal mailboxes once darkened the view, the carpenter installed a rotating wooden card rack while Jasey made a dash to the two-dollar shop at Riverglen. On her return she filled the rack with coloured notepads, stickers, small satin-covered horseshoes and tiny paper hearts filled with confetti, sequins and streamers, sparklers and novelty candles, greeting cards and matching envelopes. She stacked Paul's old counter with magazines, board games, playing cards, calendars, novelty caps and socks, shoelaces that glowed, needles, pins, iron-on denim patches, headbands for babies, statuettes for wedding cakes, safety pins, earrings made from buttons and Christmas decorations. Then she put a small sign at her cash register: POSTAGE STAMPS FOR SALE. She continued to inform all customers that they could actually read newspapers online – 'Much bloody cheaper and better for the planet' – while handing out enrolment forms for Lana's computer classes. Finally, Debbie said, 'You told me about the classes . . . yesterday *and* this morning.'

'Well, plan your week's meals and write a comprehensive list and you won't have to pop in three times a bloody day.'

5.

IT CAN'T GET ANY WORSE

Mitch left the sleeping house as the sun rose and a slight breeze presented. A breeze was sometimes a good thing for sheep work if it stole the dust in the yards, and it would most likely take the clouds away. Isobel arrived and slid out of her shiny four-wheel drive. Mitch's big sister was dressed for work, though she still managed to look elegant. 'Mitchy-itchy,' she said, and gave her little brother a kiss, leaving two thin lines of pink lipstick on his cheek.

The yearlings, noisy as one-year-olds are, saw them coming and bleated like a million rather than a couple of hundred, rounding each other in their pens. Mitch and Isobel herded the wethers into the shed and the drenching races and, amid the cacophony of baas and hoofs pucking on boards, they checked their drenching bladders and inoculation guns and moved through the crowd, shoving the gun into mouths, squirting a dose, then pushing the sheep behind until there were no more in front. Mitch herded them out into the paddocks, where they jumped and found their bearings and ran to join their mothers, but they couldn't – there was a fence between them – so they cried again instead.

Mitch came back with a mob of young rams and herded

them into the race. He washed, and joined his sister sitting on a wool bale with a cup of tea and a date scone. She handed him his morning tea and he wondered if Neralie would have joined them to drench sheep. Would she have arrived bearing fat sandwiches and pikelets and a gallon of hot sweet tea at shearing time? Possibly not. Neralie's idea of helping was to steal his finest wool to line Tinka's kennel, and she bellowed wretchedly over the death of an orphaned lamb. She was a good crier; she bawled sincerely and with gusto – as he remembered well.

'A penny for your thoughts,' Isobel said, and Mitch said, 'Sorry, miles away. How are you? What's happening?'

She shrugged. 'This water business . . .'

'It can't get any worse.'

Isobel smiled, stood up and said, 'Mitchell, there is one thing I know for certain: your life will change and, one day, you will be happy again. For a start, we've got all that land and all those beautiful sheep, and they all need drenching.'

He threw the dregs of his tea away and followed his sister.

oOo

Five years earlier, on a very hot day that Mitch would later realise had heralded the drought, Neralie dragged a hoe through the ryegrass and Scotch thistle searching for Bathurst burrs. On the other side of the ute, chugging slowly between them, Mitch chipped at a spiky green bush, a net of flies across his sweaty shirt. He threw the weed onto the ute as Neralie half-heartedly chucked a lone burr. It missed the round pile. falling to the ground again. 'Can we stop for lunch?'

Mitch checked the position of the sun. 'It's not even noon yet.'

'I'm going burr-blind.' She opened the ute door and pulled the plank from the accelerator, stalling the engine. Mitch leaned on his hoe. Around him, as far as the eye could see, the skyline shimmered where it met the brown paddocks and bleached stubble, and he knew fat seed heads were drying out and bursting seed pods with every second that ticked by. 'Just have a drink and we'll keep going,' he suggested, but she was already sitting against the wheel in the slim rectangle of shade, an orange in her hand and her hat on her thighs.

She looked back at him standing in the blazing sun, squinting from under the brim of his hat. 'You should wear sunglasses,' she said. 'Those things will grow on your eyes.'

'Pinguecula.' He let the hoe drop and sat down beside her. She dug into the orange, peeled away the skin and handed him half, the juice dripping. The breeze scrooped by; the Scotch thistles scratched together, thin and irritating; flies buzzed and in the distance ravens cawed and cockatoos screamed. A dust devil eddied past, bouncing tufts of skeleton grass. Somewhere, way off, a gunshot sounded.

'Jesus,' she said.

'I get the feeling you're not having fun.'

'Sensitive, aren't you?'

Mitch threw his arms wide. 'It's beautiful here. I love it.'

'Only because you've got no choice.'

'I do actually love it,' he said, shoving a wedge of orange into his mouth.

They each chose a different part of the horizon to focus on.

There it was. The truth out loud, a declaration to the land around them, the dirt they sat on, and it was also a declaration to Neralie. Mitchell Bishop was going to run the family property and, though they loved each other madly, Neralie just did not see her life matching the life he wanted. At that moment, it was like a screen had parted and what they each expected was now revealed to the other in 3D technicolour. Neralie bit her bottom lip and hoped that he wouldn't touch her. Then he put his hand on her bare knee and she started bawling, and he gave her his hanky.

'Star-crossed lovers,' he said, which made her howl, so they huddled together against the wheel of the ute in the middle of the dry paddock, seeds splitting and noxious weeds scattering for miles. Mitch needed a partner who would be happy to spend a Saturday afternoon in mid-January burr-cutting when everyone else was at the swimming hole or lying on their couch under a fan watching the cricket. At that moment, Neralie would have given her left hip to be sitting in the cool of the public bar at the Bong, an icy beer in front of her and a pile of two-dollar scratchies to plunder. But she loved Mitch, and if she had just a bit more courage she would get out of this town and find out if there was another life, a better one.

She blew her nose. 'I can't do this anymore.'

'You can drive, I'll cut burrs.'

'No. I mean *this*. I don't want to be your secret part-time girlfriend anymore.'

'You keep telling me.'

'Your mother hates me.'

'She doesn't hate you . . . and I would leave you alone but I can't help it. It's hard to find someone else when there's only one pub.'

'I know, but you need to let me go.'

'Well, stop leaping out from behind things and dragging me for a kneetrembler every time you see me.'

'Well, you stop climbing through my window.'

'Don't leave it open for me. I don't know what you want.'

'What do you want in life, Mitch?'

'Rain to arrive in a timely manner.'

'I want to go somewhere else and do different things. I'd even go to an art gallery if there was one.'

Mitch said he'd get a paper and wait for her in the coffee shop and she started to cry again. He sighed. 'Okay, I'll look at the statues, they're usually nude.'

'I'm moving to Sydney.'

'Move to Melbourne, it's closer.'

She wailed. He stood up, put out his hand to her. 'Come on, let's go for a swim and have one last root . . . again.'

The rest of the afternoon passed in creamy, ribald delirium that left them exhausted, elated and a little embarrassed at their abandon, and when he dropped her back at her car he said, 'Goodbye ex-secret part-time girlfriend,' his throat hurting with love and lust and grief, but still, he didn't quite believe it was over. It would never be over. She was absolutely gorgeous: petite but shaped like the number eight, sun-bleached blonde and lush-lipped. A startling girl standing on the landscape holding a hoe in her workmanlike hand with the dry clay plain behind her. Nature was a wonderful mother.

When he knew his mother was going to die he told her he loved Neralie, had always loved her. Margot tugged her blankets up to her chin. 'She's trashy.'

'She's not,' Mitch said. 'She wears the same clothes everyone else does, she just looks sort of . . .' Fuckable, he thought, but his mother said, 'Trashy. She's a barman's daughter. You need to marry someone who grew up on a property, someone who'll be a good partner running things.'

On that day, Neralie determined that she would leave Mitch. But deep in her aching heart lurked the truth that he had always been there and always would be. You can't erase the past and you can't deny something that is, but around her there was nothing, just paddocks, faintly ticking, crackling as they baked in the sun. Through the windscreen, the flat land of survival and natural catastrophes stretched to nothing. Ravens abused her from the fence and hawks hung in the hot, windy sky. She turned the ignition key and drove home. Her mother was in the orchard. Birds gathered in the trees and on the electricity wires, watching her splash around in her homemade irrigation system. She called, 'Hey, Nelly!'

But Neralie didn't want to sit on the verandah shooting at birds. She went straight to her room and locked her window.

Then her mother was there. 'Where's Mitch?'

'In his element,' she said, thinking of his burr-caked socks and his sweaty shirt with its hovering black flies.

'His mother's back up at the hospital. Had a seizure.'

Neralie turned to Elsie, who was fanning her hot, red face with her hat. 'Minister's on his way.'

He would drive somewhere and reception would drop in and his phone would ping and tell Mitch that his mother was dying. Neralie unlocked her bedroom window.

On that same day, while a whirly wind whipped in from the plains, bringing topsoil and wheat dust, Mandy Roper heard a dog bark. She stopped and leaned on her bike, and that's when she saw Mitchell Bishop. He was at Kev's bowser filling his ute. The sleeves were torn from his shirt and his jeans were worn, the oil on them velvety with dust, and he held one brown hand over his eyes. He took that hand and reached out to a black kelpie on the back of the ute, stroking its head soothingly. The dog smiled, circled and settled, and an unfamiliar yearning in Mandy's sore, fatty heart flickered to life. Mitch's mother was dying, everyone knew. As a kid, Mandy had seen her own mother and father die, and when she returned from boarding school she settled in with her grandmother to care for her, though her grandmother didn't really require a carer. But Mandy stayed and then, finally, her grandmother died, only weeks prior to Margot Bishop's sad demise. Mandy was left with a shack that was only fit to demolish, which she sold to pay for the funeral. Mandy and Mitch were soul mates, obviously.

The day after Margot Bishop was buried, Neralie tearfully gave the landlord a month's notice. 'I have to leave this town.'

The landlord, speechless for a moment, took off his fake Panama and put it back on again. Then his face turned cunning. 'I'll put a comfy chair behind the counter, and you can have maternity leave.'

'You've got it wrong. Girls only get pregnant if they want to *stay* here.'

oOo

The envelope on the kitchen table from the Water Authority had been torn open, the letter removed and shoved back in. It was addressed to Messrs Callum S. and Mitchell S. Bishop, 1105 Bishops Road. While the porridge cooked, he read:

Dear Mr Bishop,

Your State Water Authority, in conjunction with the Sustainable Environment Department . . .

Then he skipped to:

At particular issue is the health of the river and this crucial subject will be central to a discussion to be held by the Water Authority . . .

But it was the section addressed to irrigators that he was most alarmed by, though he'd been expecting it:

As part of the upgrade to the region the Water Authority will be instigating modifications to your irrigation water supply channel. In preparation for the forthcoming meeting between the Water Authority and irrigators in your region, we write to advise you of the implementation of Total Channel Control (TCC), that is, end-to-end automation for efficiency and water-saving. Measures that need to be taken include the installation of solar-powered gates, meters and radio networks that will gradually replace Dethridge wheels and this will in turn ensure a low-energy, low-carbon solution . . . there will be an opportunity to ask questions and voice concerns at the above-mentioned meeting . . .

He put the letter down. 'Modifications,' he said, and in the living room Cal said, 'What?'

'The channel,' he said, and Cal said he didn't want to change the channel, the news was about to come on.

The truth of the matter was that the pages on the table condemned his lifeblood. The twelve kilometres of channel that fed water to his farm were to be decommissioned, ploughed in, graded flat. Mitch was the only farmer on Bishops Road who used water from the channel, the only farmer, apart from Esther (who only watered weeds), who waited each season for that lifeblood to come babbling down the channel to feed his crops. And he was the only farmer left who maintained and used Dethridge wheels. The shiny black waterwheels once ubiquitous on channels through rural Australia were now obsolete; the lovely dark blades that steadily pushed clay-coloured water out to the thirsty bays were being replaced. Dethridge wheels were not efficient enough to meet the exacting needs of water conservation. Everywhere, farmers were busily ploughing in irrigation ditches and channels and replacing them with pipes and C. & P. Water automated pumps and application systems; everywhere irrigation bays glinted with solar-powered meters, small metal trees buzzing in the blazing sun. All very good to save water, if you could afford to. He'd made a half-hearted attempt to comply by lining his supply channel with plastic to stop seepage but his thirsty sheep found no purchase and were claimed by watery suffocation, just slid to the bottom of the black channel to become yabby food like the emus and koalas that came to drink at dusk. But change was vital for progress, everyone knew. At least there was the meeting, where he could *ask questions and voice concerns*.

'That could make it a long meeting,' Mitch said, and sifted through the remaining letters, because there was always another one. And there it was, the envelope with the bank logo in the corner. *Dear Mr Mitchell* . . .

'Christ. Please.' He rubbed his forehead.

Callum crept into the kitchen, looked at the fridge, then the stove, then Mitch.

'What now?'

'The bank is asking us to sell some of our water allocation.'

'We'll need it next season.'

'They want us to pay some of the overdraft and the mortgage and the hundred-and-fifty-thousand-dollar loan for the header. Interest costs us five thousand a year – seventy-five grand all up over fifteen years.'

74

'Sell the house to pay half the mortgage.' Cal opened the fridge, squinted inside, then closed it.

Mitch pulled some bread from the freezer. 'Baked beans on toast?'

'Good-o.' Cal crept back to his TV and his chair, his cane *thucking* gently on the worn floor.

'And we could do with a new harvester,' Mitch said, because each year the costs associated with maintaining it rose.

oOo

Jasey and Kevin came up from the sluggish, brackish river with their catch. Between them they had seven European carp, one undersized redfin and a gasping, insubstantial yellow belly. They, too, found a letter from the State Water Authority.

> *Your State Water Authority, in conjunction with the Sustainable Environment Department, understands that community engagement and support is crucial to gaining successful environmental outcomes. The active engagement of the community's energy, knowledge and intelligence is a vital ingredient in sustainability and ongoing education in communities. At particular issue is the health of the river and this crucial subject will be central to a discussion to be held by the Water Authority in the shire hall . . . there will be an opportunity to ask questions and voice concerns.*

Jasey dropped the letter on the kitchen table next to the fish and they looked towards the house opposite. Bennett and Megan Mockett's house boasted a spa bath and sauna, a plunge pool and evaporative air conditioning. In stark contrast were the surrounding homes where the riparians, the people of the flood plain, lived. Jasey's humble house was serviced by two yard taps, a laundry and a bathroom. Mrs Maloney's shack had a rainwater tank and no bathroom at all, and her cow drank from the river and ate its grassy verges. The McIntoshes' neat house and the Jovetics' spare cottage bled recycled water from their single bathrooms onto their rows of struggling fruit trees and lines of luscious green vegetables.

The station wagon parked in Bennett Mockett's driveway had a Water Authority logo on its door. This told anyone who drove past that Bennett Mockett, the local stock agent, was friendly with the enemy – the Water Authority. And Megan Mockett was Kevin's very own sister.

'I understand that she's your sister, Kev, but that car in her drive belongs to Cyril Horrick and that means they're up to no good.'

'Possibly.' He picked up the letter from the Water Authority. 'We'll go ask Megan.'

'Good one, Kevvy – make her choose between her husband and her brother.'

'Isn't blood thicker than water?'

'At this point, water is blood.'

They gutted and cooked the redfin and sat on the back verandah to eat it with lettuce, tomato, onion and vinegar in brown bread, all the while watching for the fox in the brittle reeds by the creek. Jasey was draining the last of her wine when the carp leaped and splashed and the fox shot from the reeds. Kev put down his can of beer as the fox trotted past, metres away, smiling at them on his way to the plains. The gun remained against the wall.

'Yeah,' Jasey said. 'Enjoy your day. You're going from "is" to "was" real soon, Mr Fox.'

Kev picked up the letter again. 'That redfin tasted like rotten mud.'

'And cow shit.'

They walked down the drive and across the road and up the gentle slope to their local stock and station agent's double-storeyed concrete house. Cyril's Water Authority car was still there, but only Bennett came to the front door. He opened the metal, laser-cut, gum leaf–designed front door of his eco-friendly, low-impact, high-performance, carbon-neutral bunker, holding a yabby stick. He smiled, pointed the skewer at their boots and said, 'Coming in?'

In unison they said, 'No, thanks.'

Kevin thrust the bucket of carp at Bennet.

'Don't eat 'em, mate, but thanks anyway. Maybe the Jovetics can do something with them?'

Jasey held up the letter from the Water Authority and tried to see beyond him into the house. 'We've come to be actively engaged and to offer some of the community's energy, knowledge and intelligence for sustainability, and we're also here to ask questions and voice concerns.'

'Do that at the meeting, but I want you to know I'm on your side.' Bennett bit a curled white yabby tail from his skewer. 'These yabbies are from the swimming hole, harvested them myself. Sure you won't come in and have one?'

Kevin put the bucket of fish on his sister's whiter-than-white carpet next to Bennett's white ankle socks. 'Since you're on our side, you can fix a few things for us. We don't call you Two-shits Mockett for nothing.'

Bennett stood there in his you've-only-done-one-shit-but-I've-done-two house with his gourmet snack and bigger-than-most front door, shaking his head. 'That name's not fair; I don't play one-upmanship.'

'That bloody creek is so low and slow it's an environmental hazard to everything except carp and leeches and you reckon you're environmentally conscientious?'

'I *am* conscientious! Have you seen the size of my compost heap? The size of my water tanks? This house is insulated with six inches – not four or three but *six* inches – of wool *plus* a reflective barrier nailed to the beams. I'm all for recycling and eco-living and most especially sustainability of the river and the bottomland we live on. I'm a riparian, I live across the street from the riverbank houses –'

'We can see Cyril's car, it's got the Water Authority logo on it,' said Jasey. 'No one's blind, we can also see this big cement fortress up here *above* the flood plain.'

'You're always the first to say the flood plains should be maintained.'

'We can live with the odd flood if it means the river stays healthy, and I speak for the ferals, the McIntoshes, the Jovetics and Mrs Maloney and her cow and the kiddies who drink her milk.' The riparians looked to rainfall in the high country and gauged when a flood was coming, but would the Water Authority tell them when water would be released from catchments? Would the riparians have time to load kids and chooks and cows and heirlooms and flee?

'But,' Kev added, 'if the barons have purchased all the water and run it off for resale to all the poor suckers desperate to buy it, we don't have to worry about floods, eh?'

Bennett said there was no such thing as a water baron, but Jasey stepped back to look at his brand-new, very big and very expensive house. 'So you just live in some other baron's house, eh? You're taking water from the irrigators, right, they're only getting twenty percent of what they've bought, but how much of the remaining eighty percent will go back to the river for "sustainability"? Where will it be stored so the irrigators can go and scoop out a bucketful when they need it? Where and how will you release water back into the river system? Will it stay in the catchments and how much of it can we have? Just pop inside and ask Cyril for us, will ya?'

'Restored river flow is good for the ecology.' Bennett smiled, but Jasey had yet more questions.

'We, the riparians, and your other clients, the farmers, want you to ask old Glenys Gravedigger Dingle how we are meant to do two shits instead of one without anything to shit. How much of the area's production will vanish because of water buybacks? How will I run my store when most of my customers have no money? When can we all expect to die from fatigue and starvation, and how much money will all you water traders make out of our water?'

Bennett repeated that there were no water barons, but Kevin said, 'I'll still have to pay increased water rates so that the riparians can go fishing and swimming without getting cholera, and the irrigators will be happy with their whizz-bang water toys, but none of them will be able to pay me the money they owe me for the repairs I've done because they won't have any money left.'

Bennett's taut-faced, hard-lipped wife Megan came to the front door. 'Kevin! Jasey! Come see my new couch.'

'Can't, sis,' Kevin said.

Jasey explained that they were there in their capacity as the enemy.

'Oh,' Megan said, nodding in an understanding way. Megan, unlike her brother and his girlfriend Jasey, moved with the smart set. The women of the smart set, waterskiers all, were slim, marvellous cooks and belonged to the Rural Women's Club. Their husbands played golf and cycled all over the back roads in colourful synthetic suits on unnecessarily expensive pushbikes.

'So, old friend,' said Bennett, 'I'm actually not your enemy –'

'We're concerned that you might just be paying lip service to the idea of conservation while actually working with Gravedigger and your friend Cyril.' Kev tried to see beyond Bennett into the house where Cyril hid.

'It's not true, but have it your way if that's what pleases you.'

Kevin and Jasey turned to go.

'Come back and see my new couch sometime, Jase,' Megan called.

'Love to.'

The Mocketts watched their neighbours walk down the drive, Kevin one step behind his girlfriend.

Bennett shook his head. 'We're just trying to help them.'

'Depends how you look at it, Benny.'

They returned to their guests by the barbecue on the roof terrace.

oOo

When his phone sang the opening bars of 'Blue Suede Shoes', Paul was coming to terms with the fact that he had less room at the newsagency than he'd had at Jasey's IGA. He looked at his phone screen. It was Mandy. 'I'm running a bit late, Pauly, you'd better let anyone in who's waiting, they get a bit shitty. Thanks. Sorry.' She hung up.

He went to his phone's settings and selected 'Blister in the

Sun' for Mandy's personalised phone alert. Then he opened the front door and beckoned to the waiting customers, saying, 'Help yourselves,' and went back to the mail.

When Mandy eventually arrived, she found a pile of coins on the bench and her stack of newspapers raided and sloping across the floor.

'Thanks, Paul,' she said. 'Real good work.'

Larry Purfeat left his greyhounds stretched across the door and bought a magazine titled *Internet for Beginners*. As she handed him his change she said casually, 'We open up earlier these days.'

'Oh yeah? How early?'

'Seven-thirty.'

'Still too late.'

Then Morton Campininni came in, carrying his football-shaped Chihuahua, and she told him she'd be opening up early. He waved his newspaper at her. 'I'm going to start with the online newspapers soon as I figure it out.' So she short-changed him five cents.

A stroll by revealed nothing of interest at the pub, though there were fresh tracks at the back gate, so she wandered back to her shop to find Debbie there with her two kids. She and Paul stopped chatting when Mandy opened the door. She paid for a colouring book and pencils and asked if Mandy did gift-wrapping and Mandy asked if she knew anything about the pub owners. 'Nah,' she said, 'but I saw a van out the front the other day. "Hospitality Industry Specialist", it said.'

'I can read,' Mandy snapped. 'What we need to know is who bought the pub and when it opens for business.'

But no one could tell Mandy anything more. It was beginning to irk her.

Then a tradie, a short man covered in grey cement dust and flecks of old plaster, came in to buy a magazine on lead-lighting. When questioned, all he said was 'I don't care who owns the joint – I'm just doing me job quick as I can so I can fuck off out of this shithole.'

Paul was sitting behind his computer, absorbed in a game of solitaire, and there was no movement on the street, so Mandy researched holiday flats in Noosa Heads then moved her search to public house licensees. She'd decided to pop down to the pub to see if anything had happened when a late-model Ford Falcon with a lean, red-and-green racing bike crouched in its roof rack swung in to the kerb. The postie and the newsagent watched the car door open, showing them the Water Authority logo, and a young man get out. The cyclist was clean-cut and of medium height. He was focused on the smartphone in one hand while, on the other, two fingers searched for coins in his pocket. His blue shirt was untucked at the back and his thighs were thick and pressed against his white jeans, which were ruched from hours of sitting behind a steering wheel. He didn't bother shutting the car door, so he wasn't a city boy. Mandy squared her shoulders, yanked her top down at the front and leaned on the counter to maximise her depleted cleavage. 'Hi.'

He walked towards the newspaper stand, his boots heavy on the timber flooring, didn't even notice Paul at his counter. 'Got *The Australian*?'

'Have to be early for that one,' she said, because she only ever ordered just enough to go around. 'Nice bike.'

'Not fast enough,' he said, and she laughed a little too forcefully.

'Believe it or not, I did triathlons,' Mandy said.

'State champion?'

'How'd you know?'

Every school had at least one state champion of something. 'Takes one to know one, I guess.' He looked at her. The newsagent had her tits on show and her grin was smug – she was definitely sending messages, but her outfit, though designed to seduce, made her come across a bit used, more like a salvage job. There would be better in this small town, but he'd have to establish who was married to whom first. Couldn't risk offending a potential client before he'd even started trading water. 'What about the *Financial Times*?'

'Sure,' she said cheerfully. She tapped the computer keyboard. 'I'll make sure I get plenty.'

'Keep me an *Australian* tomorrow, will ya?'

'You're staying around, then?'

He dropped some coins onto the counter. 'What's the internet reception like in these parts?'

She rolled her eyes. 'Not good, but there's a hot spot on the corner opposite Kev's service station, and I know for a fact that the pub balcony's reliable . . . and the mantelpiece at my house is good.'

But he was reading the front page of the regional paper. 'I'll get you to keep *The Land* and the *Weekly Times*.'

'Every day,' she said, then remembered they were weekly papers. 'Or every week,' she added, 'depending on, you know . . .' But he was walking away, opening the paper as he went, so she called, 'What's your name, so I can reserve the paper for you?'

'Stacey.'

She held the coins he'd left on the counter. They were warm from his pocket. 'I look forward to seeing you tomorrow, Stacey.'

He started his car and reversed out, not bothering to check for traffic. Paul went back to his game of cards and Mandy grabbed a local paper to see what had captivated Stacey so much. A photo of Glenys Dingle, commissioner of the Water Authority, headed a fragment declaring: *Local task force agrees to release 300 gigalitres of water entitlements to the latest round of government buybacks, and on-farm efficiency improvements . . .*

Mandy liked taking bad news home to Mitch and Callum but, even better, she would see this Mr Stacey every morning. She phoned Kelli, two doors down. 'I want my toenails done the same as my fingernail art.' Then she erased her previous searches – coastal resorts and pub sales – and began a new search. The Water Authority website told her only that Stacey Masterson was a recent employee and that he was born in a large coastal city. Irrigation was his stated speciality. Research told Mandy that the government was committed to water-saving through improving the current irrigation system, over a hundred years old, by lasering, installing reuse systems, automation of bay outlets, farm channel decommissioning and much more, but the most captivating thing she discovered was the cost of water, per megalitre. A quick calculation told her that her husband, or rather his water, was worth over a million dollars. Mitch was rich! But they would be worth much more money if Mitch could use all of his allocation, not just the twenty percent, to grow lots of food. And they'd be worth even more if they installed a new irrigation system. Suddenly Mandy understood how water conservation and irrigation affected *her*. Rows of linear move sprinklers straddling Bishops Corner, like so many West Gate Bridges, equated to paddocks and paddocks of thick green crops. She'd be rich!

Reading on, Mandy was dismayed to learn that the conservation program required water savings. *This will require the irrigators to obtain approvals from their financier*... Mitch would have to sell water to implement the new system.

Shit. Water was the most valuable asset they had. They would be poor, deeper in debt.

She would have to be the breadwinner.

She would spend the rest of her life right here in the newsagency. With no holidays.

But she was entitled to some of his farm, maybe even half, and half of its water allocation, and the more water it had, the more money it was worth. Maybe she should leave – take her half of the farm and move to Bali. Do it now, before Mitch forfeited water. Or wait and sue for divorce when the property and its water were worth more? No. That would take years, and he might never pay off any debt. The dream she'd lived for those few short minutes was ruined and she was still at her counter in her shitty shop in shitsville.

The front door and the world outside drew her. She looked towards Bennett Mockett's office, now Stacey's office too.

oOo

Kelli was also watching the new boy drive the twenty-five metres from the newsagency to Jasey's IGA. She noted the bike on the roof but it was his hair that captivated her. It wasn't necessary for a man to use product way out here.

The women in the IGA noticed the new car and its flash bike – the type to join the smart set.

Stacey got out of the car and strode into the shop, picking up a shopping basket as he passed the cash register. 'How are youse?' he asked, without looking at the watching women.

Via the convex security mirrors they studied him searching for and finding bananas, bread, butter, Vegemite, coffee, sugar, a packet of biscuits and a roll of toilet paper. While Jasey scanned and packed his groceries, the others stared. Someone memorised the name on the credit card he was holding and they all checked out his shirt, trousers and boots, and if his ears were clean.

'I sell postage stamps here too, if you like,' Jasey said.

'Good onya.'

He strode out to his car, chucked his shopping onto the back seat and made his way across to Bennett Mockett's deserted stock and station agent's office, also home to Cyril Horrick and his Water Authority renewal project. He opened the door with a key, went in, came out less than ten seconds later, and crossed the street to his car. He chucked a U-ey, parked outside the Billabong Hotel and vanished through the beer garden gate, carrying his groceries and an overnight bag. The women were still watching when he came out, unstrapped his bike and disappeared into the beer garden again, carrying the flash red and green contraption in one hand. Upstairs, a window over the balcony opened and they saw him briefly. 'He's in room nine,' Jasey said.

The women went home to google him and do a Facebook search, and Jasey went to the back office, picked up the phone, dialled the shire offices and said to Lana, 'Want to go for a country one night this week, just us?'

oOo

Stacey had studied the Water Authority maps, specifically the outdated supply channels that ran from the river to service farms. He would show them just how good he was at this

86

water-saving game. Glenys Dingle herself had hand-picked him for this important posting, a position whose responsibilities would garner a promotion and a fat pay rise. He would do Glenys Gravedigger Dingle proud. And he would buy himself a new Ford 290 HP 3.5-litre V6 and possibly a new bike, a Giant Defy Advanced for a cool two grand.

He spread the map over his bed and put a red sticker on the eastern supply channel and the one farm it still fed, Bishops Corner. Then he turned his attention to the river. The river missed Bishops Corner entirely, and there was no way the property could feed from it. That was a couple of million dollars' worth of upgrade, right there. And then there was Miss E. Shugg, owner of the very last property on Bishops Road. Miss Shugg's was the first property the river encountered on its slow meander westwards from the mountain, the river forming the eastern boundary of her property. Stacey ran his finger around the sharp bend where the river headed north after Miss E. Shugg's property, missing Bishops Corner entirely. Then it turned again and fed water to the Bergens, and to the Jeongs' many plots and, finally, before it was lost completely to the west, the river embraced the town in its helix.

Stacey folded his map and descended the pub stairs three at a time, rushing past the renovations and out the door, where he jumped in his nice new company car and, wheels skidding, took off into the sunset, every eye along the main street watching.

oOo

Mrs Horrick arrived at the newsagency and purchased a copy card from Mandy, who made a point of not complimenting her on her new fingernails – sky blue with tiny handguns. Mrs Horrick inserted the USB, programmed the printer and stood back with her fingers in the back pockets of her skinny jeans. Mandy called, 'Need a hand?' and Mrs Horrick said, 'No, thank you,' so she turned her attention to her web search again.

Mrs Horrick wordlessly printed many pages of something, then purchased a packet of plastic A4 sleeves, said, 'See you at the water meeting,' and marched up to the Water Authority office, two busy tan puppies flopping along at her Cuban heels. Mandy went to the computer, took the master copies forgotten in the paper exit tray and studied them, smiling.

INTERNATIONAL ACCREDITATION CERTIFICATE

Mr/Ms . . . . is hereby *instructed and accredited in*

Submersible and Surface Solar Irrigation Pump and Meter Installation

by Southern Water Supply and the State Water Authority.

Mrs Horrick had printed off twenty certificates. The water meter installer – once deemed accredited – had only to write his or her name on the certificates. She had saved herself two dollars by printing the instructions for the installation of solar-powered meters and pumps on the back of the certificates.

Also in the exit tray was a C. & P. Water Pty Ltd invoice made out to the Water Authority for $500 for 'administrative services and consultation'.

oOo

The sound, like a falling log, told them that Papa had toppled again. Lana and Mati stood at the top of the back steps looking down at him, lying stiffly in the damp dirt, a smooth-skinned man with a body like bluestone. It was the cloudburst – water on dry, greasy steps – that caused the old man's fall. He extended his hand but Lana decided he'd fallen on purpose, that he knew it was Monday, the first day of her computer classes, and had decided to ruin it for her. When they didn't come down to help him, he let his arm fall to his breast and looked wounded and pained. She thought of the home he had not seen for decades, the terrible civil war he'd fled, the siblings he'd left behind, all dead now, and because she wanted her mother's night to be as peaceful as it could be, she came down the steps and nudged him across to the bannister. Papa reached for the sturdy post and she helped him pull himself onto his feet. Then the old bugger raised his fist and swung, but these days Lana had plenty of time to duck. When he swung a second time she gently shoved him and watched him topple to the dust again. 'You can't hurt us anymore, Papa.'

'*Jebena kučka*.'

Mati came and they pulled him up again, brushed him off and helped him to the table, where he ate dinner sullenly.

As she got ready to go out, Mati came to her, 'Find nice boy, have baby. You haf to go.'

But Lana didn't have to leave to do any of that. Leaving meant you just did the same thing somewhere else. She fluffed up her dark hair, sprayed another mist of eau de parfum and walked through it to kiss her mother. As she brushed the seeds and leaves from her Commodore, she lit a cigarette and drove away, music thrumming through the car doors.

The computer lesson got off to a good start. Mrs Goldsack found her way to a chair at the front, where she could best feel movement and body heat as the locals arrived. They came clutching iPads and laptops and sat facing Lana and the screen behind her. Morton Campininni brought his fat Chihuahua, Spot, and Mrs Goldsack requested that the animal be removed, please. Spot waited patiently outside with Larry Purfeat's greyhounds. Next to join the group were two farmers and their wives, then Denise and Kelli and Kelli's round, colourful mother. Cyril Horrick's wife Pam clomped in, wearing a red cowboy shirt with black piping and pearl snaps, then Paul arrived with the regulars – the much-loved barflies and pub philosophers. The regulars brought no electronic devices but they supported all community occasions . . . mostly for the free supper or the party after, but also to swell numbers. Mrs Goldsack read a list of those who had overdue library books, and Lana pressed something on her laptop. An image appeared on the screen. 'I'll email this presentation to you all, so you can look at it again later, but for now, find the button to switch on.'

'Where do I find the email and how do I get one and send one?'

'You've got to turn it on first.'

'Yes, but once it's turned on –'

'The button . . . just find it.'

'Mine hasn't got one.'

'Yes, it has.' She pointed to the screen, which showed clearly all buttons on a variety of devices. Most of the group turned their devices over, searching for the switch. Lana waited, then went around the room showing them how to open them and turn them on, and was then compelled to pause to explain why iPads didn't have a keyboard and why some laptops did nothing if you tapped the screen. She waited while they all wrote it down on notepads. ('Is keyboard one word or two?')

And then someone asked if you could find a library book on a computer and Mrs Goldsack said, 'Definitely not,' and then there was an argument because you could do that very thing on the computers at the Riverglen library.

Lana had hoped to have them all setting up mail accounts on that first night but all they managed to do was find the on button and the internet server on the screen. Then it was time for *Australian Story* so she went around and showed each of them how to switch their devices off again.

oOo

Not far away, as the gloom of evening descended, Mitch's unloving and unloved wife was marching around the swimming-hole exercise track in stretchy black attire. She finished her second lap and stopped, lifted her hand weights five times each arm, bent to touch her ankles five times, then continued back towards the newsagency, taking the route past the library. She noted the cars and utes parked outside and the dogs tied to the bench. The street was devoid of people, all windows were empty and the curtains static, so she selected a car that was far from the glow of the streetlamp and bent its radio aerial.

oOo

Outside the library, Mrs Horrick stopped to watch Kelli straighten her car aerial. 'Why would someone do that?'

Kelli's corpulent mother dragged on her cigarette and snarled, 'Someone doesn't like the computer classes.'

They got into the car and Kelli turned the radio on. It worked. She gave Pam the thumbs-up and drove home with her mother to their government house on Single Mothers Street.

oOo

Passing Jasey's, Lana slowed, thinking she might call in for a drink, but Kevin's car was parked outside. Inside, Jasey and Kevin froze as the car engine approached and slowed, but she relaxed into his arms again as Lana drove away and Kevin resumed his exploration of Jasey's pliant body.

Lana stayed in her car smoking, blowing the plume out into the dry, purple sunset. Her computer class was a long way from reading newspapers online and Mrs Goldsack would be there every week, willing the technology to fail.

Later, she curled up in bed with her copy of *The Woman in White*. Anne Catherick died and Lana said, 'Oh well, she caused a lot of trouble.'

6.

A CIRCULAR SUBJECT

Gottlob and Vorbach Bergen located the dust cloud and knew that Mitch was heading to the far north paddock to feed and water his rams. The two utes approached and slowed and braked. The tidy Bergens, in their clean truck with their bowling green–neat beards, looked at Mitch, in his dusty heap with his smiling dog. Mitch raised his thumb on the steering wheel in greeting.

Vorbach said, 'You get that letter last week?'

'I did.'

'What you going to do, Mitchell?'

'Whatever I can.'

They looked over to the new solar-powered meters on the banks of the Jeongs' raw irrigation ditches, just waiting to be installed.

'What are you two going to do?'

Gottlob said, 'It's our superannuation, that water, we'll sell it when the price is better. You want to lease our land?'

Mitch shook his head. It held little value without the water allocation. 'Thanks anyway. I hear you're opening a cafe?'

'We applied to the council. Maria will still do the hamburgers and pizzas and ice creams but we'll do delicatessen and snack food.'

'Looking forward to takeaway schnitzel and strudel.'

As they watched his ute disappear into the billowing dust, Vorbach said, '*Er gefickt,*' and Gottlob said, '*Er kann nach Bali oder Batemans Bay gehen,* get a surfboard.'

'*Callum muss zuerst sterben.*'

oOo

While water from the tank filled the troughs for the thirsty rams, Mitch climbed to the roof of the ute, waited for the internet to drop in. He paid his phone bill online, trashed the bill, emptied the trash and told himself to remember to delete it from his home email account. It was cold, so he pulled his beanie down over his ears and pushed his collar up. All around him was dull brown and blue, the farm a chilly dead place save for the wind battering the feeble saltbush. But over the horizon, above some distant continent, rain clouds were building and they would float to Bishops Corner and fall on his land at just the right time and grow a fat crop. One day he would press a button from his recliner rocker and the telemetry system would water itself from his vertical sprinkler system, but in the meantime the sound of a speeding vehicle, like a jet plane in the wide open, needed attention. It braked and parked at the fence. The Water Authority. He'd heard about Stacey Masterson. The young man in pale moleskins got out and came towards him, the collar on his blue wool shirt stiff against his neck in the cold wind.

'How are ya?'

'Fair to middling.'

'Stacey Masterson, I'm with the Water Authority renewal project. You'd be Mitch.'

'Spies, you lot, aren't you?'

'For a good reason.' Stacey rested his foot on Mitch's wheel rim and pointed some rolled-up brochures at the empty, weed-choked irrigation channel and static waterwheel beside him. 'Did you know that you forfeit about twenty-five percent of your water allocation annually because of those twelve kilometres of open channel you're still using?'

'I do know that.'

'It's all lost to leakage and evaporation.'

'Like I said . . . Why don't you just give me a couple of million bucks and I'll upgrade and grow more grain with the megalitres I save.'

Stacey smiled and shook his head. 'The government can't possibly be that generous.'

'Broke after the drought too, are they?'

'We can help you replace your waterwheels.'

'But I'll have to relinquish about three hundred gigalitres, I gather.'

'But' – Stacey spread his hands, god-like – 'you farmers will get that *all* back in saved water over time, and with the help of our new computer system and a solar-powered pump system. Your neighbours, the Jeongs, have a system just like it.'

'They also have good IT skills, an internet receiver booster and money to pay for it all.'

'We'll teach you all about the computer, it's part of the deal.'

'It's too expensive.'

Stacey beamed up at Mitch. 'But you need to upgrade. It's a dry continent, and we need to secure the future of water for all.' It was a quote directly from the front page of the brochures he was holding in his soft fist.

'I've heard all of this before, and I've crunched the numbers. Say I trade you four thousand megalitres of my water assets in exchange for an efficient irrigation system, those new pumps, meters and flume gates will have to work for many years to pay me back in water gains, which means I have to live even more frugally than I do now, but here's the crunch – I've also lost equity in my assets, yet I'm still paying the same for my mortgage at the same rate as I always have, so that means I'm paying more on my mortgage than the farm's worth, not to mention my loans, so there's a gap between what I actually have left and what I'm paying for. Sort of paying a hundred bucks, plus interest, for a farm that's worth fifty, and devaluing as the seconds pass and the cost of running it escalates. And given we can only produce according to the weather, which is traditionally shit of late, then overall it's not a good business plan for me.'

'Yes, but –'

'And I'll have to maintain all the new equipment, which means I'm paying for that too, as well as maintaining an expensive twelve-kilometre pipe.'

'Right.' Stacey nodded, trying to think quickly. 'But . . . our aim is to save water *for you*, for everyone.' The conversation wasn't going as well as Stacey had imagined. Farmers were meant to leap at the chance to become more efficient. 'Why don't you come on in to the office one day and I'll re-crunch those numbers for you. Or I could come to you in your own home?'

Mitch said, 'I've just explained it but I'll keep trying, for your sake. On top of paying too much to maintain a farm and business that's depreciated, I'll also lose access to water for my sheep. Fewer channels means fewer sheep, and I'll spend more time and energy moving flocks from dam to dam or trough to trough. Sheep won't be a viable product anymore, so the only thing I can rely on is crops and the expensive high-maintenance telemetry and machinery needed to grow them on my drought-ravaged farm. It's a circular subject, mate.'

Stacey looked at the farmer sitting cross-legged on the roof of his ute wearing a beanie and work shorts. 'It's a prick of a business for those who choose to do it, eh?'

'What the fuck else can I do? Sell the land from under my father's geriatric arse, hand all the money over to the bank and get a job at the hairdressers?' This clean-cut guy was giving Mitch the shits. 'Mate, it's been a long drought and I've got worn-out machinery and sick donkeys, an unhappy wife, a deaf father and there are dogs and foxes happy to eat my only profitable thing, my sheep, and I'm about up to pussy's bow with every fucking thing at the moment, alright?'

It seemed to Stacey that, above, clouds had just formed in the dry spring sky. He had neglected to anticipate this; he had not perfected his counterarguments.

'You could not have picked a worse time to try to get money out of us, truly you couldn't.'

Stacey pointed to the clouds. 'Things are about to turn.'

'You know these things too, do you? Know I can rely on the elements?'

The representative from the Water Authority renewal project tried a different tack. 'We just want to make things better for everyone. We're all here for the same purpose.'

Mitch looked at his phone.

'Can I leave the brochures with you?'

'You're going to need all the help you can get to tackle old Esther Shugg.'

Stacey smiled. 'Cyril's got her.' He saluted Mitch with the brochures – 'Talk soon' – and walked away, trying to appear more dignified than he felt.

In his car he opened his iPad to write notes on Bishops Corner and email them to Cyril, but there wasn't any reception so he just took notes and hoped no one stole the device.

Mitch watched him drive away then turned off the tank and hauled in the hose. 'I'm worn out,' he said, knowing it to be true. 'But at least I have you.'

Tink turned an ear to him, her eyes still fixed on the dirt-grey and solemn flock, drinking earnestly.

And then his phone pinged. It was Neralie. *I hear you got rain.*

Any time was a good time to text Neralie, but he'd rather talk to her, preferably in person, in the flesh, in 3D, standing there in front of him.

He texted back. *A sprinkle. Whatcha doin'?*

There was just the sound of the wind, then, *Not much. Pissing down here.*

You coming home for Christmas?

And then the reception failed. He deleted the text and pushed Neralie from his mind; it was time to go home. As he passed the thick bushy island cupped in the riverbend on Esther Shugg's eastern boundary, the place everyone called 'the spot' – the spot where he often met Neralie – he imagined hiding a pump in that impenetrable wall of weeds where snakes bred. It was a simple thing to bury a pipe and suck himself up a bit of free water. But the consequences . . .

oOo

Esther roared westwards in her old green Dodge, Peppy on the back, face into the wind. Something caught her eye over at the Jeongs' so she slowed and stopped. The paddocks were ploughed and ready to sow and new small black pipes jutted at regular intervals along the furrows. When they first settled, the Jeongs planted fancy lettuce, butternut pumpkins and broccoli and, as farmers in the district gave up, sold up and retired to the coast, the Jeongs bought their properties. Now they owned most of the land either side of Bishops Road – river frontage – and the access that came with them. They grew everything, even cotton. People parked on the roadside to see the cotton sown, returned to oversee its harvest, took photos of the great ragged cotton bales lined up, and collected the dregs, blown like tissues across the land to catch in trees and fences. Since the arrival of cotton, wealthy farmers with independent water had gained confidence and fields of the crop were spreading; a great gin was under construction at Riverglen.

Esther was wondering over the tiny periscopes protruding from the brown furrows when Sam Jeong rolled along the fence line. It was too late to flee. She watched him get out of his ute and climb through his newly restrung fence. He was too tidy to be a farmer.

'Hello, Miss Shugg, are you well?'

'I'm perfectly well, thank you, but your cotton makes this environment sick. It's alien.'

Sam looked beyond her truck to her paddocks, where weeds thrived and pests bred, then to the Bergens' property, where hard-hoofed goats pucked the ground. 'Everyone use chemical for the crops. Good for production. Many thing alien, some thing not good.'

'Cotton takes all our water, big farm takes big water.'

Sam explained that the small black sprinklers peeping from the dirt were his new underground drip system. 'We calculate that dollar per megalitre of water, cotton has better outcome, so we conserve water because our return much bigger.'

But Esther narrowed her eyes and asked if they'd sell the cotton to their relatives in China.

Sam smiled and shook his head. 'I not from China. I sell to Riverglen.'

Esther felt slightly ashamed, so she asked him how his family was, since she knew at least one of them was expecting a new baby.

Sam nodded. 'Good. Happy here, is better place to prosper. Good people.'

Then she didn't feel so ashamed because he'd reminded her that he was prospering more than most and she didn't think that was fair, so she roared off as Sam climbed back through the fence.

Esther turned her Dodge off the road, bounced across the dry irrigation channel and the stock grate, and headed to Bishops Corner homestead. She waved at the donkeys, fat and big-headed at the helm of the mob of ewes and lambs. Callum Bishop rose from the seat by the back door and limped to her, carrying his lunchbox. He closed the house gate behind him and climbed up into the cab. He gestured at the sky, now vacant of clouds. 'Gone.'

'All gone,' Esther said.

The two old friends rumbled back past the donkeys, who sniffed the dirt at their hoofs in case the passing vehicle had dropped sweet lucerne hay by accident. They roared east towards Esther's at sixty kilometres an hour and Callum said, 'She's an inconsistent housekeeper.'

As ever, he was complaining about his daughter-in-law, so Esther knew what to say next. 'Makes her expensive to run.'

Cal went on to expand – again – on why Mandy's brain would never save her feet, said that she wasted perfectly good water taking baths and hosing spiders from the window frames and failed to notice they rebuilt their webs by morning. On sunny days she put wet washing in the dryer and then she blew the thing up because she didn't clean the fluff filter. 'That was Margot's dryer.' Callum's wife was dead five long years.

Mandy also talked while they tried to watch footy and expected them to come to the table for dinner during the weather report. Her spaghetti bolognaise always sat in a pool of reddish water and her roasts were always dry. 'It's not tasty,' he said, and Esther said, 'No love in it.' She missed Margot's excellent cooking too.

'Elsie McIntosh tells me that daughter of hers is coming home,' she ventured.

Cal retrieved the image of the sprightly lass with the nut-coloured voice and a pleasing disposition. 'Neralie?'

'Top secret,' she said, taking her foot off the accelerator. 'Don't tell Mitch.'

'That'll set the cat among the pigeons.' Cal felt more hopeful than he had in years. Neralie was coming home, and somewhere in the blue void above more rain clouds were forming and wind was gathering to push them to Bishops Corner.

Esther pulled the stick out of gear and they coasted over the channel bridge onto her property, past her little corrugated-iron cottage towards the sheep yards. Dust rose and curled and was whipped away. Callum was amazed again at the luscious strength of thistles and morning glory, Bathurst burrs and paspalum and the wide fat carpets of bindi-eye, the thick scrub thrumming with vermin. A rough calculation told him he'd need about sixty litres of heavy-duty chemicals to get rid of it all. Vermin was vermin, it had to go. There was good soil under all that toxic scrub.

They drove towards a stand of old pines to a sick ewe

huddled against a fallen trunk, its lamb folded at its side. The ewe bleated, struggled, but was very weak. The two old farmers opened the doors and eased themselves down from the cab. Esther wound the winch on the back of her truck, lowering the sling. Callum picked up the lamb and dumped it gently on the cabin seat while Esther spread the sling on the ground and they rolled the ewe onto it. Esther wound the winch again and the ewe rose in her old jute cradle and was lowered softly onto the back of the truck.

They unloaded her at the yards and took the lamb into Esther's shack. She made up some milk feed and poked the teat into its mouth. It kissed the pale liquid, shook its head and turned away. Persistence paid off and it finally suckled, nudging violently at the teat, then it put its head on the floor to sleep and Cal and Esther ate their lunch with the ABC news blaring from the old wireless. They attended to the fly-struck ewe, clipping away the sodden, fetid wool, leaving her raw, pink skin exposed. Esther sprayed Tri-Solfen on her wounds and put her in the small yard by the house that boasted a patch of green grass. They washed and gathered up the lamb and headed back to the old green Dodge.

oOo

Cyril Horrick wore his fear on the inside as he drove towards Esther and Cal, one arm hanging from the open window and one wrist draped over the steering wheel. He was fearful from early morning, when the sky revealed its pure, rainless blue, until sleep finally came. He wasn't a God-believing man, but he prayed for grey skies every night. He passed the idle water-wheel on the crusty bank of Bishops Corner's condemned supply channel and continued on to Esther Shugg's property, snug against the river at the culmination of the road. He parked his late-model fleet car close to the bridge, making escape difficult for Esther's green Dodge.

Cyril applied his smile and walked towards the two old people, hand extended. He shook Callum's hand vigorously and ignored Esther. 'Not every day you get a visit from the regional manager for the State Water Authority, eh?'

'Thankfully,' Esther said, putting her hands deep in the pockets of her bib-and-brace overalls.

Cyril looked at the vast paddocks of exposed clay and the arcs of bleached sheep ribs dotting them. 'Nothing like it, is there? These plains – miles of beautiful barley grass curving over the wide earth . . .'

'It'd be better if it was wheat.'

'It will be when we get water again!'

Esther jerked her thumb towards the riverbank. 'That old pump I have on my river frontage will see me out and I'm not selling my water, so good day to you.'

The two old folk made for the truck.

'I understand, Mrs Shugg,' he said, overtaking them.

'*Miss* Shugg.'

He stood in front of them. 'It's complicated, so I just thought I'd make a few things clear.'

'You don't need to.'

'Your water entitlements were once tied to your quota of land.'

'I know.'

'But this has changed.'

'I *know*.' Some men couldn't help themselves.

'You can sell your water entitlements to us for just one season, if you like.'

103

'I'm keeping all my water,' Callum said, and Esther said, 'So am I.'

Cyril stepped towards them. 'Well, that's good, because I can get a qualified, certified contractor, government supplemented, to install a new pipe to replace that old channel of yours there. As neighbours, you'll share costs, and what you save on evaporation and seepage and leakage you can put towards a solar-powered meter, very efficient, a most impressive piece of technology. We'll also take away your old Dethridge wheel, free of charge, and you'll be all set to install new hi-tech flume gates to monitor and control water flow into your bays . . . you don't have to do a thing.'

'Neither do you,' Esther said. In the cab of the truck, the lamb bleated feebly.

Callum said, 'My waterwheel costs me about a hundred dollars a year. Your fancy solar-powered torch system will cost me ten times as much and I'll have to replace it every time someone in a city office has a new idea, and my water rates will go up to keep the whole thing spinning so you can get overpaid.'

'Anyway,' Esther said, 'we don't need any of it because there's a drought – there *is* no water.'

'But when the drought's over you won't lose six hundred megalitres per annum anymore.'

Callum narrowed his eyes. 'Spies, you lot, aren't you?'

'Sounds pretty good, wouldn't you say, Mr Bishop? Mrs Shugg?'

'*Miss* Shugg.'

He was standing in front of two bloody ancient trees and he was beginning to think they were not going to fall over. It was a bad way to start the day. 'Think about it! How much more attractive will your land be to prospective buyers with a new system in place?'

Anger at the thought of someone else owning her land sped the blood through Esther's veins. 'Why would I sell my home? Anyway, I might want to lease it when I'm old.'

'Well, then, you may as well increase its value!'

'There's a drought, Mr Horrick. Miss Shugg and I haven't got enough money to buy a new bucket.'

Inside the cab, the lamb bleated again.

Esther said, 'It's my land and water, I'll do what I want with it.'

Cyril looked at the old girl, who needed a shave, and the old bloke holding on to the back of the ute like a man standing knee-deep in a strong current. 'You can't. The water is actually ours, not yours. *But* you can trade, lease or sell your water entitlement to . . . let's say, Mr Bishop here . . . or to us!'

'Ha!' The two old people moved to the doors and held the handles.

'Think of the saving for the environment. And some will go to the bank of water, so to speak: more water for everyone, whenever you need it!'

'The bank of water, my arse. You'll just wait till we're desperate and sell it back to everyone at even more inflated prices.'

Esther and Callum opened their doors, heaved themselves up into the Dodge, tumbled onto the seat and sat where they landed, Esther clinging to the steering wheel and Callum clutching the seatbelt hanging beside him. The lamb bleated again.

Esther started up the truck but Cyril clung to the window-sill, thinking of Glenys Dingle and the dozens of bloody pumps and meters in the shed. His wife wanted her shed back.

Callum was winding up the window, the truck creeping forward.

'See you at the meeting,' Cyril called as Esther's Dodge moved away. It clipped Cyril's rear-vision mirror, bending it flat against the duco.

'I would never give the hard work of my ancestors to a man like Cyril Horrick,' Esther said.

'I wouldn't like to be him,' Callum said, and Esther thought of his poor wife.

As the sun slipped low in the west they turned into Bishops Corner's gate. Mitch and Tink and their tall sunset shadows were nudging a mass of garrulous rams towards their new paddock. There was no sign of Mandy's car over by the house.

Cal opened the door, got out, closed the door and thumped it lightly. Esther raised her finger on the steering wheel and drove away with her lamb, now sleeping.

The donkeys watched her drive past again then turned to Mitch and the sheep, getting smaller in the distance. Mark and Cleopatra sniffed the air in case it held a whiff of wheat.

7.

PREDATORY

The people along the main street began to stand in their windows and on their stoops to watch Stacey Masterson and the smart set check their wrist monitors and set off on their bikes, a flock of bright cyclists bobbing away on the black asphalt until they were consumed by the plains. On the first day Kelli let it be known that Stacey wore a helmet with little care for his carefully constructed hairstyle, Jasey took up checking her wristwatch each time they left and when they returned, and Denise re-dressed her op shop window with second-hand bicycle gear. Mandy checked daily with Paul for the cheap activity tracker she'd ordered online. This morning, she looked up from admiring her black-lace fingernails just in time to see Lana pass en route to Jasey's IGA. Three minutes later they walked out of the supermarket and across the road and vanished through the front door of the Bong.

oOo

The main bar was a gutted shell featuring naked furniture, so Jasey and Lana headed to the beer garden, ordered wine and scratchie tickets from Levon, and found a seat under an umbrella beside a gas heater with a clear view of the TV.

107

The current topic of bar conversation was the upcoming meeting with the Water Authority. Levon said, 'They're the Charon in the story, keep a dollar in your pocket for them or you'll be left wandering for a hundred years.' His companions in the bar told him that he read too many novels. The girls scratched their tickets, swapped, checked, then Jasey went for another round and asked Levon for a couple of steaks for the barbecue.

Levon said, 'It is *not* a barbecue. It is a new top-of-the-range outdoor grill, the very latest one.'

Jasey said she was pleased for him, but she didn't give a fat rat's clacker what it was as long as it cooked steak the way she instructed it to.

Lana was poised with the tongs over the potato salad when Stacey clicked through the playground and beer garden in cleated shoes and a cycling outfit. He was sweating, and Levon put a glass of water and a steak on the makeshift bar in front of him. He drank the water in one gulp, dropped the meat onto the top-of-the-range grill and continued through the renovations to the stairs leading to the accommodation rooms without looking at anyone in the bar.

Lana signalled to Levon for two more wines and said, 'I suspected he'd be the reason we're here.'

'Kelli says he uses product.'

'Kelli uses product.'

When he came down again he sat at the bar in the beer garden-cum-playground to watch the news and eat his steak. The girls were careful not to look at him because they knew he could see their reflections in the TV screen. Everything stopped when the weather report came on. All catchments remained dangerously depleted but possible light rain was forecast because of a threatening low.

Then the local carpenter suggested to Stacey that the meeting was pointless. 'You won't listen to us . . . our fate has been decided.'

The regulars focused their gaze on Stacey, who said, 'Not necessarily. Depends how much sense your task force makes.'

Levon asked, 'Exactly who is the task force?'

The people in the beer garden all looked at each other. No one knew anyone in a task force.

'We've got one – it said so in the newspaper,' the farmer said, and Levon said it was a myth. Then the carpenter said, 'But it's no myth that the Water Authority will eventually take all our water,' and someone else said that the Asians would take all the land, and the farmer said, 'Don't pick on the Asians. They've discovered wool – *my* wool. The Chinese are importing a hundred and fifty thousand tonnes of the stuff!' But the drinkers on the other side of the state-of-the-art grill argued foreigners imported their own machinery and workers – 'Foreigners employ foreigners' – and someone else said, 'Thank God for the backpackers,' looking at the perennially unemployed locals, sitting benignly at the bar. The regulars always sat in the same spot and referred to their area as Neutral Bay. Then someone pointed out that foreign investment had always existed, foreigners had always come and gone or stayed, and some of them even paid taxes. Levon asked Stacey what he thought, and Stacey said, 'It is what it is,' and left.

The girls leaned over to watch him climb the stairs two at a time and Jasey said, 'Few changes coming, Lana?' and Lana said, 'A few changes.'

o0o

As he drove to Mark and Cleo they hawed, and he knew they were feeling better. Green shoots had sprung over the mounds of manure they expelled, like green profiteroles crisscrossing the dirt. Mitch was happy that the ewes had soft, sweet fronds to nibble on. 'Good work,' he called. 'But you've missed Animal Therapy with the oldies. Morton's fat dog will get the scones this month.' His barrel-bellied donkeys showed no remorse, so he nudged them until they scrambled up on their thin, aching knees then tied them to the ute. He dragged them to walk in circles, some ewes and lambs straggling along behind, Tink watching the sad, fat procession from the back of the ute. When Mark's furry knees gave way again, exercise came to a halt. The sheep stopped. Cleopatra stood protectively beside her brother and readied her hind leg to disable Mitch should he further mistreat them. 'Very well,' he said. 'I'll let you win . . . just for today.'

Mitch fed his farm dogs and let them off for a run, then headed home. He took the long way to the laundry to wash and found his wife searching for racing bikes on the computer and eating crispy things in loud packaging. She would have already checked the trash file. He plugged his phone in to recharge it and noted the frozen pizzas bases thawing on the sink. He turned the oven on, showered and dressed. When he returned to the kitchen, Callum had turned the oven off. 'Wasting electricity,' he said, but Mitch told him (again) that pizzas were better if you put them into a really hot oven. He chopped bacon, sprinkled cheese and some pitted tinned olives on the pizzas, scattered some pineapple pieces on and shoved them into the warm oven. His housemates were both mesmerised by screens and he considered adding rat shit to their pizzas but set the timer instead and rang Bennett

Mockett. He ordered drench for his lambs and a truck to take away his Sunday sheep then fell into his chair in front of the TV to endure the daily talk from Callum. Today's was on raven traps and how to cull lambs for market, which Mitch had spent the day doing, and had been doing for twenty years or so. Then Cal retold the story of Cyril and his desire to trade water. He rubbed his stiff hip with his palm and said, 'Just knives into the wound.'

The stove called and Mitch served the pizza. He placed a plate at his wife's elbow near the keyboard and settled in front of the TV again with his father and their stable tables. The news told them that crops were failing in Russia and Mitch's heart sprang and kicked its heels together. His miserable crop might sell if there was no wheat anywhere else. Then the weather map showed a low in the bight pushing a half-moon of white clouds over the Riverina. They seemed to him to be rain clouds. The BOM site showed 'possible scattered showers'.

oOo

In the night they woke and left their beds and lairs, backyards and kennels, scraping between palings and slipping under mesh. They moved through streets and joined the group at the river. They mingled silently, tails wagging, ears up, big dogs, small dogs and dogs in between, fat Labradors and half-breed terriers and cattle dogs and a Corgi, a conspiratorial pack with wild blood come to the surface, instincts rousing. Then one moved off, running low, and the others followed, a stream of panting dogs moving with intent, killing in their eyes. Again they followed the river, east this time, running in a pack, tongues lolling, away from the town and far from the road, upstream to the far-flung farms and sheep on the riverbanks.

Mitch woke, unsettled by a cloudburst travelling through his sleep, and listened for the donkeys, but all he heard was the rain rumbling across the iron roof then pattering off to the east. He sank again into nothing, but not before he felt the warm mass of his wife beside him. He moved a little further from the middle of the bed. There was a time when he could have reached for her but the protocols had altered. If there was to be any intimacy it was Mandy who reached, squirmed and straddled, but that was something he no longer anticipated, though in their early days he'd looked for her.

A few weeks into their relationship he'd decided to end what he considered a fling. His happiness at finding her waiting at the pub after a long lonely day had waned. 'It's been good, but I don't want to be in a relationship,' he told her, and she said, 'But you promised to take me to Melbourne for my birthday.' So he did. He took her to Melbourne and they went to the footy and shopping at Queen Vic Market and ate lovely meals in nice restaurants and went to the cinema and the air dried up and crops failed and the drought was made official and life got lean and miserable and the Mandy affair seemed to be a good thing in the mess of it all, but then it became a marriage.

'I should have stopped it,' he said to the damp black night.

8.

DIVIDE AND CONQUER

The following week, there was a morning that arrived muted, the air smelling of rain on dust, and Mitch was both buoyant and fearful for his miserly crop, possibly damp and ruined. Mitch's wife was up early, again. She'd taken to wearing knee-length tight black things and a T-shirt whose purpose was to disguise the body beneath it. Mitch accommodated her shrill presence as he organised Cal's breakfast, though he hankered for the peace that her past, sullen presence had offered. He took breakfast to his father and she followed him, yakking on about things being quiet in town though there was plenty going on at the pub and how it was all very well that Maria at the cafe was making a fortune from the tradies but she wasn't really up to making six hamburgers at a time, 'but if it was me, I'd just make more pizzas and if that's all there is to eat, then that's all there is'. Joe Islip had told her that so-and-so was about to go bust and oh my God the price of pushbikes online, and then she asked what he would have to say for himself at the water meeting and, if you asked her, the meeting wouldn't get anyone anywhere, and Glenys Dingle was 'only in it for herself', because 'Glenys only married that Dingle guy so she could get divorced and take half his farm and money', and all the while Mitch wondered how it had got this far and why hadn't he seen what she was like? And then she said she was going to take up cycling again, *seriously*.

'You should ride your bike to town,' Cal said. 'Keep fit, save on fuel.'

'I'd need a much better bike. Want to buy me one?'

Callum said he didn't have long enough to see his money's worth.

'I used to be a triathlete!' She turned to Mitch. 'How about a bit of support, back me up for a change?'

He considered starting an argument, pissing her off so she'd go to work, but Mandy was the stand-and-fight type. It would be better for Callum if she left before the weather came on, so he told her she was more than capable of standing up for herself and pecked her cheek, and off she went. The men watched through the window as she vanished into the gloom of the shed then rolled her old bike out into the sunshine. She slapped the red-backs and cobwebs from under the seat with a rag, leaned it on the air compressor and drove away. The donkeys, tall and alert amid the ewes and lambs, watched her little white wagon pass. Mitch turned to Cal. 'Want some bacon and eggs?'

'My legs are alright, it's my hip that's the problem.'

oOo

His happy dog patiently watched him fill the wood box and check the rain gauge then followed him across the yard, the tiny craters the raindrops had left in the dirt tickling her soft paws. She watched him turn Mandy's bike upside down and blow the bird shit from the spokes and pump up the tyres, run a bit of oil along the chain, adjust the gears and lean the contraption against the tree. Then they spent some time with the disgruntled donkeys, keeping some distance from their rear hoofs, and left some hay for them. Tinka leaped up onto the tray again and barked once at the glorious day because the ute would take them to more places where they would do things together, and she smelled a storm coming. Overhead, clouds gathered in fluffy grey bunches.

oOo

The showers in the night washed the dust from the eucalypt leaves, perfuming the air with clean trees and wetted dirt. Mild morning sunshine steeped the air, illuminating the landscape. The bush and clouds were tinted gold and the brittle grasses fringed white. On their low perch the ducks ruffled their feathers and stared down, their dark eyes wary in their little matchbox heads. Jasey followed their gaze and found the white breast and dull red coat of Mr Fox. She raised the rifle, put her eye to the scope and steadied the crosshairs. She held her breath, felt the steel curve of the trigger holding back the rush of bloody victory and squeezed when a snap, loud as a gun blast, split the morning, sending the birds flapping. It was a branch cracking. An impatient gum had chosen that moment to shed one of its thirsty limbs. The mighty branch thudded onto the hard ground, twigs and leaves crashing across the bare slope of the river's edge, the loud echo of screaming, fleeing ducks and birds travelling up and down the water. Jasey walked down to the tree, the gun in the crook of her arm, and studied the fleshy cavity where the limb had ripped from the trunk. It smelled sweet, and was cool and moist to the touch, though not as moist as it should have been. She patted the tree and looked again to the promising clouds.

Lana's royal blue Commodore came up Jasey's gravel drive, sun shafts spotlighting the vivid plains behind it and music rumbling through its doors. The girls drove away singing but midway through the first lap around the barbecue area their singing ceased. Lana braked suddenly. Jasey reached over to the CD player and shut the chorus down. An army of colourful marchers circled the swimming hole. Everyone was there, even the 35-year-old grandmothers from Single Mothers Street were rushing along. The briskly fit Rural Women's Club, headed by Megan Mockett, in her white tracksuit, overtook the single mums on the outside, their hand weights lending extra push, and all the town girls – Keira and Madison, Amelia and Bree-Anna and Loren and Trixie and Nicole and Debbie and Coral and Kelli – were racing against the flow and jabbering as if they did it every day. Even Mandy was there, so early!

'Jesus Christ,' Lana said, 'Mandy's jogging,' and Jasey said, 'Struggling's more the word.'

And then they saw the swimmer. A figure in a partial wetsuit was splashing along in the chilly spring water from the jetty to the pontoon. He wore goggles and had the fluid action of a competitive swimmer – the new boy in town.

Stacey located the round black forms in the dull freezing water and knew they were the forty-four-gallon drums holding up the pontoon. He executed an Ian Thorpe turn and pushed through the churning murk. At the jetty, he climbed the small ladder and stood on the planks, water dripping from him, while the women turned to stare. The new man in town had a swimmer's broad torso, a cyclist's calves and curated biceps. Breathing hard, he pressed the activity tracker on his wrist, removed his goggles and earplugs and checked his time. Slow, but that was okay – new pool, muddy water and all that.

Lana looked at Jasey and shook her head. 'I'm not scared of the competition, but exercising . . . I don't even do stairs.'

Jasey studied the waddling walkers in their thrusting lycra. 'No way. Your strategy will be allure, Lana. Be alluring.'

'If he waterskis I could watch.'

'We'll get Megan to take us out. You can sit in the corner with the wind through your hair and call out when someone falls off.'

oOo

Mandy peeled away from the exercising scrum as soon as Stacey turned on the tap at the rainwater shower, so that by the time he got to the newsagency, she was leaning on the counter with her cleavage on show and her lipstick fresh. He stood in the middle of her shop stabbing at his phone, wearing a wool jumper and towel. Water flowed from his hairless legs and rolled off his feet. 'Reception's patchy.'

Paul said, 'The government's fault.'

'How am I s'posed to get the daily prices?'

Paul looked at the puddle growing in front of his counter. 'Like to keep fit, do you?'

'Comes in handy,' Stacey replied.

'And you've started a trend,' Mandy said, tossing her hair. 'I've never seen that exercise track so crowded.'

The newsagent was smiling at him. Again, he took this as an indication that she wanted him, which was all very well, but after a while you needed someone you could talk to.

'How do you find the swimming facility?'

He took his newspapers from her. 'It'll have to do, eh?'

'There's a filter on the inlet from the river, but you never quite know what you're swimming in.'

He walked towards the door, searching through the pages for the market prices.

'You staying at the pub?'

'Yep.'

'It's got new owners.'

'Bonza!'

'I can get the key to the footy club gym,' she called, but Stacey called back, 'So can I,' and Paul said, 'He could get just about anything he wanted, I bet.'

She rolled the newspapers, put elastic bands around them and dumped them on Paul's counter for the mail run, and spent the rest of the morning leaning in the doorway. No one looked in her direction. Tradies came and went from the pub, yet each time she checked, its back gate was padlocked.

At lunchtime Mandy went for a stroll that took her to the library. She borrowed a novel, which Mrs Goldsack said was due back in three weeks, but Mandy's main interest was in the computer room. Only one person was using the computers. She wandered back to the IGA, where she found Jasey standing proudly in front of her vast and brilliant display of notepads, stickers, satin-covered horseshoes, confetti, sequins and streamers and the box of Christmas decorations. She paid for her tins of creamed corn, and neither woman spoke to the other.

When she got back to the shop, Paul announced that he'd be putting in more postboxes, and it dawned on her that the postie was providing a service that meant no one ever had to cross the stoop. 'That'll bring the customers into the shop, won't it, Paul?' she said, wanting to plunge a knife into his soft body. Paul knew then that she'd probably never let him root her again.

oOo

The rain followed Levon's ute all the way from Sydney. It burst from the sky as they left the lovely beaches of Clovelly and pooled in the tarp protecting Neralie's possessions. It rained

118

while they ate toasted sandwiches at the Gundagai cafe and it rained while Levon drove and Neralie talked like she hadn't talked to anyone in five years, the wipers a rhythmic nuisance on the windscreen. Then she drove while he read *An Obolus for the Styx*, and when he finally closed his thick book he said he'd better drive the last leg into town.

It stopped raining when they pulled up at Esther's front gate. Neralie stood on the wet asphalt in the silence and inhaled the rain-washed, pre-dawn air. Faint birdcall came from the spot where the land formed an oxbow and leeches as fat as thumbs bred in the cumbungi. Everything she would encounter from this point held her life to date, and Mitch.

Levon said, 'On we go, Nelly,' and they drove on towards Bishops Corner. There were no lights shining from the house, no headlights sweeping across sleeping lambs or irrigation bays, just the woolshed and the yards silhouetted against a sky faintly illuminated by stars.

'Those donkeys alright?'

'They fronted up Anzac Day and they still do Animal Therapy even though they ate the vegetable garden at the nursing home. Don't know about the nativity scene.'

They laughed, remembering that day at primary school, the end-of-year concert and the nativity, and Mitch with his donkeys, just foals at the time, and one of them shitting on baby Jesus in his manger.

Levon said, 'They must be about twenty-five or thirty years old by now.'

'Old,' she said, and felt the pang for the last five years wasted. Impulse wanted her to run up the gravel driveway, skip through the house and jump on Mitch in his boyhood bed, but he didn't sleep there anymore because he was married.

'Why didn't anyone stop him?' she asked, and Levon shrugged. 'We just didn't think it'd actually happen.'

She glared at him.

'I'll tell you right now, no one wants to be told that they failed to stop Mandy from trapping Mitch, alright? We know already. We don't see him anymore . . .' She'd used the old divide-and-conquer tactic. First her sullen presence was like an infection in the corner, then she accused Mitch's friends of being mean to her, slighting her; Mitch was compelled to support her, defend her; friends retreated then became estranged, and Mandy had Mitch all to herself. It was easier for him, for everyone, that way.

'And anyway,' Levon continued, 'you left! And how were we supposed to know she'd sneak him off to Melbourne? Not even Isobel knew. Apparently she said she was pregnant.'

'That old trick. Almost serves him right for believing it.' She wanted to cry. How stupid of Mitch, how stupid!

The town came into view and her palms started to itch and her heart raced because soon she'd be standing in the kitchen with her mum and dad, and Lana and Jasey and Kev, and she wanted to cry more.

'Just focus on the pub, Nelly.' Her brother glanced across at her. 'It'll all work out, nothing surer.'

'It has to.'

They turned and drove over the bridge and pump station and there was the asphalt track that led to home, and there was Elsie's struggling orchard and the corrugated-iron roof of her parents' house. The biggest decision she'd ever made was to leave home. She found out that coming back was the best decision she'd ever made.

9.

I KNEW ALL ALONG

He wasn't sure if he'd harvest or plough in his crop. There was no point spraying. Was it worth the effort, or the fuel, to plough it? He gave the old header harvester a bit of a service and was grinding a few tines, just in case, when his wife wheeled her bicycle into the tool shed. 'I'm taking up swimming again,' she declared, as if she'd been a swimmer in the recent past.

'It's a bit cold.'

'It's spring. The water'll be warm.'

'Swimming and cycling?'

'Yes.'

Mitch shrugged. 'Whatever floats your boat.'

He watched her ride back over to the house and manipulate her bike into the back of her little wagon and drive away to work.

In town she sold a few papers to customers who speculated about the meeting the following day. 'I bet they say they're taking five hundred gigs, not three hundred . . . I bet they put the rates up again.' When she could, Mandy ducked out the back to monitor a truck she heard driving up the lane towards the pub. A group of men unloaded a new stove, and when she got back to her shop, Paul was there reading the paper, so she stuck her *Back in 5* note to her cash register and rode her reconstructed bicycle to the swimming hole.

Stacey was not splashing up and down between the jetty and the pontoon, but the 35-year-old grandmothers from Single Mothers Street were huddled with the briskly fit Rural Women's Club. She slid quietly up to them – 'Morning' – and they squirted off in all directions. When she was young and sad and searching, before she'd found Mitch, Mandy found companionship in food, as the unloved sometimes do, and occasionally she got pissed at the Bong and lurched off into the night with some boy she'd been to school with, and so she'd become accustomed to these huddles, seen them disintegrate the second she rounded a corner. It got worse when she married Mitch, so she rode along behind the walking women, pushing them, so that their arms pumped enough to ache and they peeled from the frantic pack, one by one, to bend over gasping at the grass between their expensive exercise shoes.

When they were all lying exhausted either side of the exercise track, she rode over to the outdoor fitness equipment, where the carpenter lay on his back on the soft rubber cover, his right toe placed on the ground next to his left knee and his face reflecting his pain. She got off her bike and put her foot up on the stretch station. 'How are you?'

'How do I look?' He straightened his leg and put it back where it belonged, raised his left foot and tried to make it go to the other side of his right leg, but it hurt too much.

'What is it?' Mandy asked.

'Slipped disc, sciatica.' He rolled carefully onto his stomach and raised and lowered his feet. Mandy held the stretch station and lifted her foot against her disappointed buttock. 'What's happening at the pub?'

'No idea.'

'How come you didn't get the job?'

'You might have noticed, Mandy, I'm not fit to demolish anything, build walls or carry plaster.' He rose to all fours.

'They could have given you something to do – paint stools or something – just to support local business.'

He cut his stretching session short and went back to his ute, a hand on his lower back. Mandy got back on her bike and rode around and around the swimming hole, her direction anticlockwise so she had a clear view of the main street as she pedalled. Someone in this town knew who bought the pub. The townies knew everything. Denise usually told her things, or Kelli. Someone always let something slip because that's what they liked doing. It made them feel powerful, no matter how small the news. But they were not telling her anything and she couldn't think why.

She called in to see Denise. 'What's happening?'

Denise shrugged. 'Looks like rain.'

'It won't rain.' Mandy picked a cardigan from the box Denise was sorting. 'How much?'

'Ten bucks.'

'I'll give you five.'

'It's for the church, you're not broke or homeless.'

'Yet.'

'Make it eight bucks?'

'Seven.'

'Done.'

Then Levon McIntosh's ute cruised past and Mandy took a step towards the window, so Denise asked if she was going to the water meeting.

'Of course.' She looked at Denise. 'I bet *someone* knows who bought that pub.'

'We'll all know soon enough.'

Mandy went next door to Kelli, who was studying the *Women's Weekly*. 'See this bald girl on the cover?'

'Cancer,' Mandy snapped.

'She died. She had the most beautiful long dark hair.' Kelli sighed then looked at her iPhone. 'Gawd, is that the time? I'm too busy to chat.'

'I can't see any customers in here.'

Kelli looked at her from beneath her cherry pink eyelids and her blue-striped fringe and said, 'You always have to argue. I've got to go out, alright?'

As Mandy left, she slid the door so hard that it bounced out of its tracks.

Back in her newsagency she found a nail file and ground her fingernail art to a rounded shovel shape, eradicating the lacework.

It was another quiet day in Mandy's shop. It was those computer lessons of Lana's. People were reading the paper online. Or were they?

oOo

'Cirrostratus,' he said to the grey skies, but the clouds were hanging. 'Thick cirrostratus? Or maybe nimbostratus?' Mitch lowered the plough and was about to drive off, ripping the crop to shreds behind him, but couldn't. Would it rain, and if it did would the crop be shot and sprung or would it dry out? What if he spent all that time and effort ploughing it in and the cloudburst drifted away? But if he left it to harvest, would it be worth the cost of fuel, the wear and tear on his ancient header, to strip this piss-weak crop before him? And what if the ominous clouds did spill their guts and he bogged the combine

124

harvester? Could he bear the sight of Kev's laughing face? And what would he say to the bank manager? And what of the stubble, the acres of weed-riddled, rodent-infested straw? Was there any kind of future in trying to farm like this? He sat in the tractor cab under the churning sky with his hands on the steering wheel.

'It's a circular subject, Mitchell,' he said, and wished he had someone to tell him what to do. And then it was too late. He ignored the first crack on the cabin roof but the drops started coming in twos and threes, big fat splats on the tin, and then drops came steadily, heavy racking the air and stirring a cold breeze.

'Well, holy frigging shitballs.' He let go of the steering wheel and then could scarcely hear himself think for the sound of rain on the metal cab. A wide wisp of steam shifted across the bonnet and dust slid down the windows in beige trickles. The sweet smell of rain on dirt came to him and he opened the little window vent at the side and inhaled, the sound of rain swelling and loud drops pelting his crop and a thunderclap rumbling past. Lightning split the boiling, grey sky and water hammered down, a great roar of it, and his eyes filled with tears and he hoped Tinka had thought to shelter under the ute.

Then he thought he heard something, a call, but when he listened all he heard was rain on metal, so it must have been a bird. The birds bathing on branches! A crow. Spiders would be scurrying to their funnels, snakes racing across roads, the lambs confused, never having experienced water falling through the air. Then something moved beyond the streaky windscreen – a figure of blue and pink shimmering behind the rainy glass. And then the figure was climbing up the ladder at the side of his tractor and the door opened and there was a woman, familiar, sudden and very real, crouching in the dreamy solitude of his cold grey cabin in the middle of a miserable crop. It was Neralie, smiling at him, rain dripping from her hair.

'Thought I'd better meet you here rather than . . . you know . . . giving you a fright in the pub or something,' she said.

Neralie McIntosh was sitting beside him with her teeth and her face and her eyes. A real thing. A person.

'Say, "Hello, Neralie, nice to see you."'

'I can't speak.' He couldn't take his eyes off her. There she was, in his cabin, sitting right next to him on the little plastic cover that protected something in the engine. It was for guests, kids who wanted a ride on a tractor, and she was sitting on it and then he felt her arms around his waist. She squeezed against him. She was just the same, only smoother or something.

'You've lost weight.'

'No,' she said, 'it's my hair.' She wiped the top of her hair with her hand. 'I'm brunette . . . for a while, anyway. I just came to tell you I'm back. What are you up to?'

'I'm ironing shirts.'

'Still a funny bugger, eh?'

'I was thinking about either ploughing in my so-called crop or maybe spraying, but now it's raining.'

She nodded. 'I know.'

Neither could think of anything to say so she looked out the window. 'My car's over there. Your wife will see it if she comes home.'

'She's at work . . . in the main street, where everyone knows everything.'

'There are some secrets the good people of the town keep.'

He could see the little white lines in her blue irises. 'Who knows?'

126

'Everyone. Except you . . . until now.' She sniffed, the damp air and dust making her nose run, and they just sat there looking at each other because it seemed the natural thing to do. Normal, yet extraordinary. Mitch looked the same – he was tanned, the creases at his eyes were still white when he wasn't smiling, his shiny black hair was still sitting up at the crown, his mouth open, perfect teeth, neat biceps that moved up and down under his firm skin and the kind of thighs men used to have, and she remembered what it was like to be enveloped in that lovely torso.

And there she was, in the flesh. Neralie, with her lovely skin and lovely mouth and all he wanted to do was take her home with him. Forever. And then the enormity of their situation was filling the cab.

Mitch was married to Mandy.

But Mitch loved Neralie and Neralie loved Mitch.

'Meet you at the pub's opening night?'

At the pub. In front of everyone.

'Everyone will finally get to see the new owner.'

'Most people have seen me before.' She put her hand on his knee, because she just wanted to feel him. 'But not as much of me as you have.' And though she'd promised herself she wouldn't, she kissed him on the lips. It was the best kiss she'd ever fallen into.

She pushed the door open and said, 'By the way, you've got a flat.'

He didn't understand what she meant.

'Your tyre is flat, the big one.' And then she was gone, her blue jeans and striped top flitting over the wet clods behind the rain-splattered windscreen while the meaning of what Neralie had just said fell like Smarties into a pretty cup. He looked up at the ceiling of the cab, at the dust and the yellowed plastic over the light globe, and he said, 'Friggin' PERFECT! I can't *not* see her. She's bought the pub.' He slammed his palm onto the steering wheel and stamped his feet. He'd often lamented that there was only one pub, meaning there was no escaping the usual crowd when you wanted a quiet drink or a meal with Isobel or Cal without some half-pissed local plonking down and hijacking the occasion. But now he knew why there was only one pub. 'Thank you, God, or town planners, whoever . . .'

Neralie was back, everything would be alright, and they knew now that in going away it was proved – things were only right when they were near each other. Nothing had been alright for a long time. And there was still the matter of Mandy, and the farm. But the universe would align, sooner or later, and things would be right again. They could wait a little longer to live in the manner where all things were correct. Good. He stood, banged his head, fumbled at the door, opened it and called out through the driving rain, 'Come back!' But she'd run too far from him through the useless crop. He looked at his tyres. One was indeed flat. He wondered if Neralie still ate her Weet-Bix with a fork and drank the milk from the bowl, if she still preferred her toast cold, if she would be at the meeting tomorrow night.

Neralie watched her sneakers chopping through the low sparse wheat, felt the dull stalks slap against her jeans and the raindrops tap her shoulders. She put her tongue out to catch a drop and tasted salt because she had started to cry. She was surprised to feel a huge tension drain away, and then so much happiness it made her ache.

oOo

It was going to rain any minute, so Lana stopped at her beautiful blue Holden, parked outside the empty butcher's shop. She knew Mandy was lurking in her gloomy shop, taking in everything from Lana's boots to her earrings. She hoped there was no toilet paper hanging from the back of her skirt, no line across her bum from elastic in her undies, but then she summoned the power of the secret she held and waved. 'Hi, Mandy!'

She saw a faint movement of Mandy's hand.

When Debbie dropped in with her kids they found the newsagency deserted and Mandy out in the back lane staring at the pub gate.

'I see new bar stools have arrived.'

'And a new pool table. You got my knitting magazine?'

Mandy handed it to her. 'It's like the whole town knows everything about that pub and no one's telling me.'

Debbie flicked through her magazine. 'There's dogs about.'

'I know. You gunna pay for that magazine or leave without paying again?'

'I did that once, by accident, five years ago.' Debbie paid and waited with her hand out for her change, which she checked carefully.

'You suspicious about your change?'

Debbie put the coins into the appropriate compartment in her purse and left, just as thunder rumbled from the east and travelled off to the west. A moment later, lightning cracked the sky and rain began to pour.

'Shit,' Mandy said. She could hardly go out walking now. From her stoop she saw a figure leave the pub and get into Levon's ute – a dark smudge of a figure wearing overalls and a baseball cap pulled low, like a celebrity buying toilet paper.

And there was a man on a ladder leaning over the door of the pub, painting something. She stuck her *Back in 5* note on the door, grabbed her plastic bike poncho and hurried up the back lane to the pub. She peeped through the gap between the tall corrugated-iron gates, the rain drenching her hair, more alive than she'd ever been, yet slightly nauseous, and her bladder was suddenly full and pressing. She hurried around to the front of the pub.

The man and his ladder were gone, but there, painted in bold black on gold, was a sign: BILLABONG HOTEL, LICENSEES L. AND N. MCINTOSH.

Goosebumps puckered her flesh and she flushed hot, but forced herself to walk, not run, the rain hard and loud against her poncho. She squelched around the track circling the swimming hole and followed it along the river past Mrs Maloney's house on the opposite side, her cow grazing on the meander, then the Jovetics' neat vegetable garden, Jasey's very tidy yard and finally she was opposite the sprawl of the McIntoshes' house, rain pelting down on its small orchard. She leaned on a tree to dig into her shoe for a stone that wasn't there and surveyed the scene. The McIntosh house was deserted . . . but then the screen door opened and a slight figure wearing denim overalls stepped onto the back verandah and stood at the top of the steps. It was Neralie McIntosh. And emerging from the gloom were Jasey and Lana, who came to stand either side of her. Between Mandy and her nemesis, the river flowed sluggishly, raindrops hitting it like thousands of falling marbles, carp leaped and splashed, the ducks swam in happy circles.

They had not told her. The entire town had kept a secret. This was far worse than her rejection from the Rural Women's Club. Mandy realised her mouth was hanging open, so she closed it. How could she possibly go to the new pub and have fun and be happy with Mitch again when that woman ran the place, when the entire family plus frigging Jasey and fucking Lana would be there twenty-four hours a day? How could Mitch do this to her? He must have known.

Mandy stepped away from the tree and faced them across the swollen, littered waterway, the rain bellowing in her ears and water sliding from the tip of her nose down her shirtfront. Jasey smiled and Lana waved for the second time that day.

Mandy turned and walked away.

oOo

Jasey and Lana followed Neralie into the house, where they picked up their glasses of wine and sat on the couch side by side, looking at the wall and the array of snack foods in front of them. Lana lit a cigarette and Neralie said, 'Give me one of those, will ya?'

And Jasey said she might as well have one too. They went back out onto the verandah to smoke and look at the spot where Mandy had stood dripping in a clear plastic poncho.

'We'll fix it,' Jasey said.

'We will,' Lana said.

Neralie nodded but she still couldn't quite trust them because, after all, they'd let Mitch be captured by that woman.

oOo

It continued to pour down on the drive to Bishops Corner, the windscreen wipers flapping and the dull wintry landscape rolling past, and Mandy replayed the scene in which the new publican had stepped onto the verandah with her two bitch friends. But they hadn't *really* won, the people of the town.

131

She'd known all along something was up. They hadn't told her, but they didn't have to. She knew. Neralie McIntosh might hold prime position at the pub, but Mandy had Mitch. Really, it was Neralie who would fail, *had* failed. She hadn't married that guy in Sydney. She hadn't snared a rich property developer or a smart city businessman, she didn't have a fabulous career on telly or a baby or nice shoes. She didn't even look any different. She had come back, *sneaked* back, and now she would work as a barmaid in a small town until she died.

But Mitch probably still liked her – possibly loved her.

Mandy would hang on to him. He'd married her, after all. She was Mrs Mitchell Bishop. Then hate and disappointment rose up, so bitter that she could taste it inside; something felt bad, wrong. She'd thought she'd be *somebody* when she married Mitch. She'd been swindled. Again. Nothing had changed in her life except she'd moved twelve kilometres from nowhere to an old house on a failing farm with two farmers in the dried-up countryside where gunshots thwacked through the thin air as farmers assassinated starving stock then, one by one, sold up and went to better lives, leaving houses emptied of living souls and a void of paddocks of grass and no hope. Not one single thing held any inclination to thrive except for weeds and rodents and predators. And now, it was raining, pissing down, and rural life would wake, smiling. Things were about to get better and Neralie bloody McIntosh swans back into town and sucks out the centre of her future. Everywhere Mandy went from now on she'd have to anticipate her, *them*. It wasn't fair. Her entire life would be shadowed, ruined, by Neralie and Jasey and Lana and that pub just down from where she, Mandy, worked, and there was only one pub for a hundred kilometres: one place to eat, meet, celebrate, dance, sing, live. It was all ruined forever.

Perhaps she could ruin *their* lives?

An oncoming car flashed its lights and she gripped the steering wheel, preparing to scare the car into the sodden irrigation ditch; they'd never know for sure in the fading light with headlights blinding . . . But that's what it was: a friendly reminder – dusk, rain, time to turn your headlights on. In the rear-vision mirror she could just make out the shape of the car. Stacey Masterson. She watched his glowing tail-lights and smiled. Lana and Jasey had their sights set on him, nothing surer. The water meeting was tomorrow. And he lived at the pub, the one place to eat, meet, celebrate, dance and sing.

She swung through the gates and over the bridge and rumbled across the stock grid. 'Fuck you,' Mandy cried to the dull house through the rain. 'I will not be dumped for a barmaid.' And she felt happy – started to laugh, in fact.

oOo

It was the way she drove into the yard, the way she splashed through the puddles at speed and braked, sat there with the rain falling down all over her little white wagon, and then the look on her face as she strolled across the wet yard that confirmed it.

'Shit,' Mitch said, and Cal took possession of the remote and reached for his hearing aids.

He felt her eyes on him while the frozen patties spat and sizzled under the grill. While water dripped from her wet hair and ran down her face, he opened and rinsed a packet of salad leaves and arranged them on buttered bread rolls with some sliced beetroot. He knew she liked chicken-flavoured onion rings, but Mitch didn't bother with them. And while the eggs burned, he put some tomato sauce, salt, pepper and cutlery on the table, and as he put the plate in front of her, she said quietly, 'I'm not hungry,' and left. The bathroom door slammed and the house winced, then was sucked by the violent surge of hot water through resting pipes.

Cal said, 'Crikey,' and bit into his hamburger. Mitch put his aside.

oOo

She would hurt them, she would pour salt into the barrel of Mitch's precious guns hiding there on top of the laundry cupboard, see how he felt about that. Then she would leave and take her half of the farm, finally have what she'd been denied by her grandmother and parents. But then she'd be alone again in a town with her failed relationship with the most popular bloke in town or she'd be forced out, made to leave, to start again. But where to? She rubbed the towel over the foggy mirror in the warm, steamy bathroom and saw her pink face. Her future was a void, and she felt the comfort of coming home to those two men, irritating as they could be. They were harmless, well-mannered, old-fashioned men who deferred to her on womanly matters and opened doors for her and serviced her bicycle and said thank you when she cooked dinner. And there was no one else for her. The void widened and all she registered was rejection and loneliness. Mitch wouldn't want her now.

But if he didn't have her . . . he would get everything he wanted. And she wouldn't get anything she wanted. 'Fuck that,' she said.

10.

THE MEETING

Mandy was not surprised to wake to a quiet house, her father-in-law in bed and her husband away with his sheep – or donkeys or machines, whatever it was he did out there in the wilderness. She would not squib. She dressed carefully and was behind her counter early. Stacey was her first customer and he set the tone for the day, hurrying in and out, the meeting on his mind. Her customers followed suit, rushing in (bearing correct change) and leaving quickly, saying nothing apart from, 'See you at the meeting tonight,' or similar. But they found that outwardly, the newspaper proprietor appeared her usual self. Mandy noted that Debbie sent the kids in for the Saturday papers.

At noon, and not before, Mandy shut up shop and drove home. A new banner at the pub replaced the SOLD sign. This one announced, in bold red letters, a GRAND OPENING. Mandy smiled, knowing she had a couple of weeks to prepare, but first, the meeting.

She spent most of the afternoon in the bathroom. Cal remained in his study and her husband enjoyed the company of his dog, somewhere.

Though her face was still hot-water pink, the mirror reflected an attractive woman with lovely hair, curled, but not too much. Her make-up was pleasing, unlike the overdone paint jobs Lana and Jasey made of their faces. And though Lana would be up the front at the meeting with Stacey, Mandy had plenty to say. She had opinions, and not many of the other girls who came to stare at Stacey would offer opinions on irrigation, that's for sure. Again, she dressed carefully. Her jeans were tight, but not as tight as Lana Jovetic's. She chose a cowl-necked blouse and rope wedges, then added pearl drop earrings and red lipstick. Rural, but not Isobel Prestwich rural. She raised her chin and squared her shoulders, flicking her tresses.

In the kitchen she stood next to Mitch as he washed dishes. 'You look nice,' he said, but it was not sincere.

'I knew all along something was going on.'

Cal leaned in his recliner to listen.

'Well, I only found out yesterday.'

'And of course you didn't ring to warn me.'

'I didn't want to upset you.'

'Oh? There's a reason I should be upset, then? Well, I'm not upset. I'm inspired. But I'm not prepared to have a threesome, like Kevin, Jasey and Lana.'

'What people do is their own business.' He just wanted to keep things as calm as possible, take it slow, establish what, if anything, might unfold.

'I'm quite content here,' she said, admiring her new fingernails. 'But you can go if you're not.' She would not be left homeless again.

And now Mitch was faced with the future, and the one worry that was always circling in the background – for reasons to do with debt, banks, breakdowns, fire, flood, the weather in general or any sort of setback – was staring back at him. The farm might be at stake, the legacy, a hundred years of hard work; but, above all, at risk was his father.

oOo

Cyril Horrick had one finger poised above a green button on a control panel. All around him, water was falling in tumbling cascades. Jasey said, 'Don't,' but he pressed the button with his extraordinarily long finger and a huge wall of water burst from the dam, rolling down the river along with homes and livestock, and then it was a giant flow of thick, muddy slush laced with European carp, rotted boats and drowned fishermen, eskies and rusted drum nets brimming with dead turtles and lost children. The wave, high as a building, rolled towards the town, consuming the bridge and the refurbished water pump station, and then it crashed into Bennett and Megan Mockett's boxy concrete castle, spoiling the white carpet, and Jasey was swimming, struggling against the flow, and somewhere, way off, an alarm was ringing. She reached out and shut it off. Kevin was looking at her and the sound of water tapping on tin filled the room. 'Oh my God,' she said. 'You'll never believe what I just saw.'

'I heard. Sounded bad.'

They flung back the covers, still dopey from their post-root afternoon snooze, and tottered on swollen, sleepy feet to the window. The sky was wet and the driveway shiny with water. They went to stand on the back verandah, put their hands out to let the steady rain splash onto their palms and smiled at each other. At the river's edge the ducks preened. Mr Fox was nowhere to be seen. 'He knows I'm watching him,' Jasey said.

'He doesn't want to get wet, but he'll get hungry again.'

It was still raining an hour later when Jasey and Lana faced each other over the rumpled bed in the master bedroom of Jasey's ancestral riverbank cottage.

'You'll look stupid prancing about in high heels with your tits hanging out at a meeting full of farmers. Let Glenys Dingle be the one who looks stupid. Alluring, remember. Alluring.'

Lana buttoned her shirt, then they dashed through the rain and climbed into Kev's van. Kevin was whistling.

'This might be an obvious question,' Lana said to him, 'but I'll ask anyway: why are you so friggin' happy?'

'Because tonight is a perfect opportunity to air grievances, and that fills me with rare . . . um, bonhomie.'

'False bonhomie,' Jasey said. 'No one can pay you, Kevvy, no one's got any money.'

Kevin pointed at the sky. 'It's raining.'

They drove the short distance to the hall and Jasey and Kevin helped Lana set up. They lined up chairs and tested the PA and checked the restrooms had toilet paper. Cyril strode into the hall with Stacey, whom Lana acknowledged with a professional nod. Close up, he was not as handsome as she'd thought; his hair was receding at the temples and he had the kind of build that would thicken after forty, but he was a young man in full command of himself and he was standing in front of her wearing a nice shirt, and a yearning swelled inside her. Then Cyril was in her face. He waved at the PA microphone and whiteboard. 'You want some help to work all those hurdy-gurdies?'

Lana looked at the man in charge of the Water Authority and said, 'Want me to tell you how to move papers around on a desk, Cyril?'

Cyril shrugged. He was only trying to help the girl.

oOo

At the pub, Neralie farewelled her mother and said, 'You can't say anything, they'll say you're taking sides.'

'Your father's staying home,' Elsie said. 'I'm about to be the cook at the one and only pub. No one'll say anything to upset me.'

Neralie went to the balcony to watch the passing utes. They were mostly the same utes, though sun-bleached and rattly. She imagined all those people in the hall, the *yadda-yadda* and *blah-blah*, and thought she might sneak into the old projection room to hear the arguments unfold, see her old mates. But then Mandy's little white wagon rolled past and she leaned back into the shadows behind the falling rain.

oOo

A chair scraped, and the five people in the hall turned to see Elsie McIntosh rearranging her chair so that she could view the entire audience as well as the presenters.

'Good to see you, Mrs McIntosh,' Cyril said, and wondered why she never bothered to put a ribbon in her hair or something.

Elsie replied, 'Get to the point tonight, Cyril, and speak up so the people up the back can hear.'

The population of the town and surrounds began to filter into the hundred-year-old hall. The farmers came early, slapping the drips from their hats against their jeans. They sat together at the back with their arms crossed, the women chatting like happy cousins. The townies – residents, businesspeople and shopkeepers – came in next, their shoulders rain-streaked, and walked past the farmers, pretending they hadn't noticed them. Then Mrs Maloney led the other riparians, Mati and Papa Jovetic. They claimed the middle seats around Elsie and assumed a determined air.

The ferals, grubby, rope-haired ring-ins, Centrelink avoiders all, leaned along the walls around the exit, wary and ready to flee. The regulars swelled at the door and retreated, but dribbled back in and relocated chairs into the shadows cast by the old projection box. Then the women from Single Mothers Street arrived and the single girls, always in pairs, left their umbrellas dripping at the door and made their entrance, conspicuously rather than grandly. They sat in the front row, positioned their hair and smiled directly at Stacey. Lana appraised them and felt confident Stacey Masterson would be hers before the end of the week.

The air was damp, condensation already dripping down the windows, and the sound of rain swelled, filling the hall with a tinny din. Mandy Bishop appeared and boldly led her husband and father-in-law up the centre aisle, Callum leaning on his stick, his tam-o'-shanter beaded with rain. Callum and Mitch peeled off to sit with the farmers, but Mandy continued on and took a vacant seat next to Denise, who immediately turned to speak to a townie across the aisle. Mandy pretended there was something to see on her phone.

A glance around the hall told Mitch that all eyes were on him. His wife was sitting with the townies . . . and they knew, they all knew Neralie was back, had probably known for weeks, perhaps months, that the McIntosh family and their Sydney partners had bought the pub.

Dread settled in his heart and he shivered, conscious of the clammy atmosphere. Someone turned the ceiling fans on.

At the back of the hall, Glenys Dingle extended her hand and Stacey placed her hat in it. She positioned the pristine Akubra on her carefully constructed golden curls and walked importantly up the centre aisle with the new boy in town following.

Glenys looked out at the 'task force' around her – just petals floating above a bed of colourful grasses really, since Glenys always wore reading glasses to blur the hostile faces. Lana stood at the lectern and blew into the PA and the din ceased. She introduced Mr Cyril Horrick and Mr Stacey Masterson, and said that the first address of the evening would come from the head of the State Water Authority, Ms Glenys Dingle.

No one clapped.

Glenys ran her manicured fingers over her plaited stockman's kangaroo-skin belt and the women in the audience decided she was too old to wear jeans that tight. She smiled and thanked the audience for attending, and said that it was 'greatly amusing that they could hear rain on the roof at a meeting about water!' Then she told them how bright the future looked and that she was proud of her long association with the area and that she *adored* the landscape and the aroma of irrigated crops at sunset and the sound of frogs and crickets that irrigation produced and that she had fond memories of the town when it was a thriving place and she was 'just a girl'. Some smart-arse called out, 'It's good you can remember back to 1898.'

Glenys pressed on, reading from a government brochure titled 'Our Farmers. Our Future'.

'This year is your year,' she declared sweetly. 'The farmers *are* appreciated and *all water authorities* aim to celebrate and support the farmers and the vital role they play in feeding, clothing and sheltering us all.'

Esther said, 'Well, why don't you allow us to get on with it, then?'

And Elsie added, 'We need you to get to the point, Glenys.'

At the sound of Elsie's voice Mitch's heart quickened.

141

Glenys dropped the fake smile. 'A key benefit of our Water Authority renewal project will be that *all* of you who use the river – the irrigators who use the water for rural business, the town folk, and those of you who choose to live along the river and to be part of its natural fluctuations – will achieve long-term sustainability via the procedures we are forced to put in place to rectify the accumulated problems. Going forward there will be water and economic security.'

She paused so that the subtext – *We're in this mess because of you* – filled the room.

'Our campaign publicity is clear about the new efficient infrastructure we are in the process of installing throughout the region.'

And it was true, the brochures showed acres and acres of irrigation ditches and thick green crops with metal constructions dotting their peripheries, and horizontal sprinklers spraying clean water, and smiling happy models dressed as farmers holding iPads.

'We need your help to put more water into the river system and this in turn means you can get more water whenever you want, even if there's a drought, because we'll have some put aside for you, *your* water, which *you* will have accumulated through efficient savings. And there'll be more water for recreation and the environment as well, and so with more water running your rivers will be healthier . . .' She flung her arm out in an embracing way, gathering in her flock, but inadvertently toppled her pristine hat from her perfect curls. She continued, as though she was used to wearing an Akubra with a wide brim and that it often fell from her head. 'Everyone will benefit.' Cyril picked up the hat and put it on her head, giving it a bit of a tap, then gave a thumbs-up to the audience.

'You'll need to get to a point quite soon,' Esther said, 'or I'll either wet my pants or die of old age.'

Glenys identified those with urban clothing and less seared complexions and addressed that group, knowing they'd be townies. 'We'll be able to regulate flow and get rid of weirs and some remaining levee banks upstream so your water quality will improve through less silting, and fewer silt nutrients means fewer weeds.'

One of the ferals called, 'At last! Liberation for the fish!' and the audience shifted impatiently in their chairs.

'There'll be job creation, so all communities along the river system will benefit. I know Cyril Horrick, and your local stock agent, Bernard Mockett –'

'It's Bennett. *Bennett* Mockett, not Bernard,' Esther said.

'– agree that the wetlands and river communities, both natural and manmade, through increased water flow will see a boost in wetland plant and animal species.'

A farmer cried, 'Like mosquitoes and Ross River fever!' Mrs Maloney muttered something about her cow and Elsie and Papa Jovetic murmured about their orchard and vegetable garden respectively.

Glenys Dingle folded the piece of paper on the lectern, looked defiantly at the crowd and used her hard, flat voice. 'It is a well-known fact that clearing land for farming means soil gets swept away and builds up in the channels, and that means fertiliser, pesticides and herbicides build up in the waterways. And there is also more salinity because there are no more trees left and the water table rises, bringing salt, and then there's stock eating everything, more erosion, and tonnes of stock effluent washed into the waterways.'

The farmer yelled, 'You gunna blame us for the melting

ice caps as well?' And a feral yelled out that it was in fact true that too many animals was a contributing factor to climate change.

Glenys called, 'The water saved for improved reliability will benefit the towns, their productivity and profit.'

There was a crack of lightning and the rain dumped its load on the roof so that Jasey had to raise her voice. 'But I'll lose my profit because I'll have to pay more for my water because of the irrigators and their bloody upgrades.'

Mitch spoke up above the dark noise. 'Just put your prices up again. We've got no choice, we have to go on being the primary producers making more and more cuts to meet everyone else's demands. We sell wholesale but *pay retail.*'

'Well, Mitchell, *someone's* gotta be a retailer, isn't that right, Vorbach?' That's when everyone knew for sure that Vorbach and Gottlob Bergen had sold their water to the Jeongs and had council approval for their cafe. They had defected to the townies to survive.

That same voice from the ferals' camp screamed, 'If you all sacrificed a bit of water there'd be more in the river for long-term health!'

'Yes.' Glenys tapped the lectern with the microphone.

Mitch pointed to the ferals. 'If youse relinquish one percent of your water, you lose one dope bush, but if I relinquish one percent I've lost the income that pays my fuel costs.'

Stacey, surprised by the division in the community, realised again that he hadn't thought through the other sides of the story. Beside him, Cyril was actually perspiring.

Sam Jeong called out, 'We lose water allocation, it hard on us how to plan for the future as demand for our produce get bigger but we have less water.'

The feral responded, 'You're growing cotton, man, lots of water and poison.'

'I growing what market want and what water allocation will let me.'

A farmer called, 'What's the water delivery plan and how much are the townies sacrificing for *your* objectives?'

A townie bellowed, 'Every megalitre that leaves the area takes jobs and people. And we're still broke from the bloody drought.'

A backpacker with matted hair and a nose ring said, 'Consider the waterbirds and wildlife. It's their water you're taking too.'

Sam Jeong called again, 'If no water regulation for irrigation the river dry up.'

The crowd swayed, like long grass buffeted in a breeze. An angler bellowed that weirs prevented spawning and chemical runoffs contaminated waterways. The farmers retaliated by telling him to take his shit and his discarded fishing lines with him so they wouldn't kill birds and then the townies copped it for their polluting industries and what about the fluoride they put in the water? Lana lifted the whistle to her mouth but Stacey, thinking of the Ford 290 HP 3.5-litre V6 and Giant Defy Advanced bicycle, motioned for her not to intervene. 'It's good to hear what they're saying – ammunition.'

She felt the close mingling presence of aftershave and warm male and fought a need to pull his tie back into place given he was the general enemy.

Then Mandy stood up and looked directly at Stacey. 'It's obvious we all have to sacrifice for the benefit of the *whole* system otherwise it won't work.' She saw that people were looking at her. Since when did Mandy know anything about anything?

'The one we've got was built a hundred years ago, we need a new one.' She looked at Lana. *Bet you didn't know that!*

'Hear, hear,' said Glenys.

Mitch turned to Glenys. 'But thing is, you lot are making me pay for it. You're taking my water and making me pay for it. You're asking me to work for nothing to feed everyone.'

Glenys stamped her foot. 'You're not listening to me.'

'No, you're not listening to me. I'm just telling you my side of the story, *our* side of the story. We're your customers, the *source*, you were elected to hear us, so you need to help us, not just take our water and let us die. We are the reason you are standing there.'

Mitch had seen the expression Glenys wore. It was the look of someone being affronted, of someone being found out, exposed. 'I did not come here to be treated like this.'

The room fell silent, but gradually a disgruntled rumble rose and amplified, moving along the rows of dissatisfied constituents. For Glenys it was time to take off her silly hat and sit down with a bottle of chardonnay and a slab of double brie and seedless crackers and watch the sun set over her empty lake. She handed the microphone to Cyril, who suddenly found he had to step up with just the lectern between him and the fierce crowd. Everyone knew where he lived; he had to see these people every day.

Nurse Leonie Bergen, sitting with Gottlob and her brother-in-law, decided Cyril's actions would see him rewarded, but as she watched Glenys duck into the wings she thought it would have been better all those years ago to ignore baby Glenys's chest infection, dismiss it as a cold and put her aside to fight it out, or not. Before the stage door had clicked shut behind her, Glenys was in her big black Ford Territory speeding towards her new Riverglen apartment. Beside her, back in its box, the Akubra waited for the next meeting with rural types.

Elsie stood up and cried, 'She snuck out. I knew all along that would happen.'

Cyril held the microphone too close and boomed, 'A bit of shush, please,' but the argument resumed. Mitchell kept raising points and could hear himself getting louder to be heard above the sparring factions, so he stopped. It was an argument he had been waging for years, a situation he'd been living with forever, and it felt pointless to persist. On top of that his marriage was shit, his wife took the side of the water traders in a publicly defiant act and his girlfriend was just down the road, totally out of reach. He stood amid the yabbering crowd and understood his insignificance. Not only was it all his own fault, but whatever happened next would be played out in the full glare of town scrutiny, and opinion.

Just then, Mandy made her way to the front of the hall and stood next to Stacey. 'As you know, Stacey, I don't belong to any club or faction here.'

It was a statement no one disagreed with.

'I think that because everyone uses water, everyone's rates should go up. I run a business in town and I don't actually see why my taxes should fund the irrigators, but I live with it. Everyone should proportionally pay their fair share. So, my point is, the farmers use the most water so they should pay the most, and it should be strictly monitored because my husband once told me it'd be easy to put a pump in the reeds and suck up a bit of free water.'

The crowd roared. The ladies from the Rural Women's Club were affirmed in their decision to reject this woman's membership application. The rest of the town knew Mandy to be always objectionable, but this was treason. And Mitch could not believe what he was witnessing. His wife was standing in the middle of a meeting about water accusing him of theft, or intention to thieve, and exposing herself as a supporter of the Water Authority – *everyone's* enemy. He was almost happy about it. How could anyone possibly imagine he could maintain a relationship with her?

'But it's *not* fair,' he shouted. 'That's my point!'

Isobel Prestwich's distinctive voice, a voice that advanced the cause for good elocution, came from the back of the hall. 'And water shouldn't be used to fill a recreational lake – not now, anyway.' She was leaning on the doorjamb, arms crossed, still windswept and damp from the dash from her ute.

Mandy didn't miss a beat. 'You can't prove they're using water to fill the lake.'

'That's the point.'

'You'll still sail your boat on it, I bet.'

'You'd love to go on my boat; you're just jealous because you never get invited.'

'Instead of taking the money for a boat, you should have let Mitch keep it, you've got enough.'

Jasey came out of the crowd, Kevin lunging to restrain her, 'You'd be happy to shoot through with Mitch's money at the first opportunity.'

'I'm not going anywhere, I like where I am.'

'Well, you're the only one who does!' Lana said and Mitch rushed to put himself in the middle of the women.

Kevin appeared at the lectern, his pale skin glowing in the overlit hall. 'I'm going to change the subject but not the method. I'm subsidising every one of you through the water rates I pay *and* the income I let you all keep instead of paying me for the work I've done to keep you viable. These bloody ferals are the only ones who actually pay me – cash! I can see about three thousand dollars at the very least that's owed to me in just the back row and I have to sit in the pub with all youse freeloaders while you splurge on counter meals and seventeen bloody rum and Cokes and I won't get paid until you've paid off your maxed-out credit cards.'

A farmer condemned to bachelorhood said loudly, 'And I guess you need to pay your credit cards since you've got two wives to support, more than your fair share.' The crowd booed and before Kev could move Mitch grabbed his arm and said, 'Steady . . .'

Someone said they'd pay him if they could and a ropey-haired scruff yelled, 'Man, I thought we were all here for the water. If there's no river there's no water, there's no nature, no farms, no food, no one to sell food, no town, no animals . . . nothing.'

Elsie grabbed the microphone from Cyril. 'Next time you venture out of your air-conditioned office, come for a drive to where the water is, why don't you, see what it is that you're actually monopolising! Take a look at what remains of our mighty river before you decide to take more water and sell it cheap to your mates who contribute to your political party.'

Mandy Bishop grabbed the microphone from her and turned to Stacey, who was now filming it all on his iPad. 'It seems I'm the only one here who's *happy* to pay my share and willing to stand up for a better water system that'll help us all.'

Her husband, red now with frustration, said, 'Your point would be reasonable except that farmers are expected to pay to maintain a new system that makes life *even better* for the people who control the water while the pressure on us is impossible!

We grow all the bloody food!' He was shouting at his wife in front of the entire town but it didn't matter; he would not lie down, he would fight his point because it was the truth. His wife was loving it, partly because he was showing Stacey and everyone else that her marriage wasn't happy. Let Mitch fight for his water because when it all finally fell over, she would get half of it. She deserved at least that.

It was one of the ferals who broke the awkward silence. 'We thought we could negotiate something here tonight but it's got angry and out of hand and Glenys is gone, which means now no one's voice is being heard.'

Mitch said firmly, 'She wasn't here to listen to you, pal.'

Some feral's wife started clapping and chanting and the silence was drowned out by '*The riv-er, the riv-er, save the riv-er . . .*'

Paper aeroplanes made from meeting agendas flew across the top of the disintegrating tribes to the sound of scraping chairs and chanting, clapping ferals. Jasey texted a thumbs-up emoji and a smiley face to Neralie, and Mitch watched the crowd file to the exit. No one looked at him. His wife was standing beside him, smiling.

Lana, Cyril and Stacey watched the last backs disappear through the dark doorway, leaving their carefully arranged chairs in disarray.

Stacey said, 'That went well.'

'Got them all on side now,' said Lana, and Cyril said he needed a drink. Lana wished she could tag along with Stacey and Cyril for a drink, but that would mean betraying the riparians, townies and farmers. And the ferals.

oOo

The bedroom door was wide open and he wondered if he could actually lie down next to Mandy, that solid form nestled a little too close to the low ridge dividing the mattress. He felt silly standing there in his pyjamas, his underpants underneath in case she touched him. Why did he even sleep in the same bed? He failed to find the courage to sleep in Isobel's old room so kept his back to her and stayed on the edge of the bed. Beyond his window the world was still damp and his pitiful crop was soft, wet and ruined, but in light of his fiscal dilemma and his water issues and the state of his life, it was probably irrelevant.

On her side of the bed Mandy plotted. She deserved what she was owed and the longer she stayed the more it would hurt everyone and the more she could take from them. But they had not won yet. She had not yet lost. Her husband was still there, on the other side of the bed.

11.

CONSEQUENCES

The caravan park proprietor wasn't surprised when he saw the Water Authority car turn down the track to the ferals' camp – he'd seen all types go down there at all hours – but he figured this visit was about the dogs. They barked half the night and the other half they roamed, and no amount of warning would make his new, smelly tenants tie them up. The skinny one with the ropey hair just said, 'We don't like to tie creatures up. The greater one's humanity, the greater one's free will.' Then he started talking about Queequeg, and Captain Ahab's great ship *Pequod*: 'We look like the devil but we're angels, saviours. We settled in this peaceful place to embrace the symbol of nature and freedom . . . Ahab's great white whale.'

The caravan park proprietor said, 'Two things, mate: there are no whales in the river and there's no such thing as free will. It's all about instinct, so that's why you have to tie up your dogs, and their instinct.' These days, he turned away those who tried to book in with a dog.

Stacey hummed along to the radio, his fingers tapping on the steering wheel as the car lolloped through the muddy potholes and wound between the grey gums and the tents and vans. He wanted to catch them before they dispersed to the scrub and their crops, wanted to settle the deal and get back to thinking about the lovely Lana. He stopped his car and studied the river as he took a piss. A dozen dogs came barking up to him and vans rocked as sleeping people rolled over or snuggled back down. There was a slight increase to the flow in the river, a little noticeable, but not so much for this stoned lot. Anyway, they'd be pleased, as would the riparians. A young woman stuck her head out the end of a tie-dyed teepee and a miniature pig tottered out. 'Alice,' she called, but the pig scampered up to Stacey and sniffed his boots. Someone whistled, but the dogs and the pig paid no heed. Soon there were children crying and people emerging from burrows all over the site, clutching sarongs to their thin bodies.

A skinny bloke with a third eye tattooed on his face approached Stacey, flicking ropes of hair out of his eyes, and said, 'Wow, man?'

'I've got a proposition for you.'

Third Eye shook his head and held up his hands, *No*, but Stacey said, 'I'm offering cash, for work. It's outdoors, you work in threes or in pairs, up to you, you split the fee, and it involves installing solar-powered meters.'

'Solar power. Cool. Where's the rip?'

'Rip?'

'The invisible grasp that drags you down, man, the silent stranglehold that steals from the truth.'

'You'll be taking water from the river, but ethically, and it's to feed the masses.'

'Feed the masses.'

'Now that has to be good karma.'

Suddenly, the hippie dropped his spiritual preceptor impersonation and turned into a bloke. 'Cash, you said?'

'Cash.'

He sat down on a log and the dogs stopped barking.

'Cuppa tea?'

'Lovely, thanks.' Stacey sat and the dogs lay down around them.

The women retreated with their snag-haired kiddies and the men attended to matters around the fire while the billy boiled. A bloke with plugs in his earlobes as big as a tribesman's lip plate kicked away a few coals and found a camp oven. He took the lid off the oven and started tearing chunks of thick-crusted damper from the hard mound. He gave Stacey a chunk with jam on it, as a bald guy wearing a loincloth arrived and sat cross-legged on a nearby stump.

'Politicians know nothing about anything,' said the dread-locked bloke, pointing to his third eye.

'But *we're* trying,' Stacey said.

Third Eye said his name was Edward Hull-Jones. Edward introduced the guy with the lip-plug ears as Jonathan Rhys. They didn't mention the bald guy in the loincloth.

After a pannikin of gritty river-water tea, Stacey showed them the certifications they'd receive once the pumps were up and running. 'Certified! Last thing we ever thought we'd be, eh?'

The bloke in the loincloth said, 'I'm certified,' and Stacey talked through the instructions on the back of the certificates. 'I'll pay you a minimum fee, with cash bonuses for each func-tioning meter installed. Just sign the contract here . . . and we'd like as many as we can done in the next few weeks, before Christmas.'

oOo

Neralie woke in her room at the Bong to the sound of nothing. Sun was streaming through the window and the smell of rain on wet asphalt rose. She stretched, and thought of Mitch lying in his bed, brown skin against white sheets, and she walked in and lay right down on top of him, naked, head to toe. But she removed the image because Bicycle Mandy was lurking so she moved Mitch to the AGA, had him standing there, dressed in work shorts and stirring his dad's porridge. But Mandy was still in the living room or bathroom, so Neralie got out of bed and went to the balcony, where she found the perfect distraction in the glassy sunshine. The horizon was coloured by dark clouds; more rain was coming. Across the road, Jasey was standing in front of her shop. Its window featured a crudely painted sign: SAVE OUR RIVER. SAVE OUR LIVELIHOODS. Neralie went back through her room, down the stairs and out onto the street and stood on the white lines in the middle of the road. Kevin was reclining in a deckchair between the bowsers, studying a hydraulic hose. A sign above him read: NO CASH NO FUEL.

'Morning, Kev.'

'Nelly.'

Jasey joined Neralie in the middle of the road and they watched a farmer's wife drive past. She didn't wave to them. 'She's driving to Riverglen to do her shopping. I've only had one customer, and that was Elsie to buy milk, but they'll be back. It's expensive to drive to Riverglen.'

'I've got a grand opening in a couple of weeks. I need a pub full of happy, friendly people spending money.'

A local with a Commodore full of kids and balding tyres pulled up at Kev's bowsers. When Kevin said, 'Cash only, mate,' the driver placed the fuel pump back in its cradle.

Kev thought about phoning the new servo to warn them a bolter might be on the way, but they could afford a drive-off every now and then and, anyway, they'd swallowed up two family-run fuel outlets in the area when they set up shop.

Then Bennett Mockett nosed his late-model Ford into Kev's drive. 'Mate?'

'Nah, stuff it,' Kevin said, pointing the hydraulic hose at the injured harvesters, tractors and trucks waiting in his huge yard and workshop. 'I've spent months fixing all those vehicles so people can get on with harvest and no one – no one – wants to pay me for 'em.'

'We're all in the same sinking boat, mate. How can they pay you when they can't strip their crops?'

'I must be the only sucker on the planet who runs a credit book and sends monthly accounts.'

'Everyone here has to. You know that. I bet I'm owed more than you. I'm owed tens of thousands.' But Two-shits Mockett was a company man. He got a wage.

Next, Sam Jeong swung into the drive. He paid for a drum of oil with cash, and Kev told him he was a rare thing, 'rare as frog feathers'.

Bennett drove the very short distance to Mocketts' Stock Agency and parked outside. Someone had scrawled *Steal our liFeblood and see what happens to your liFe* on the window.

'There's only one person in this whole town who uses a capital "f" in the wrong place,' he yelled. Kev looked at the sign he'd written: NO CASH NO FUEL.

In his ute, Sam searched for 'Australian colloquialisms' and found 'rare as frog feathers', smiled and nodded at his phone.

oOo

When Mitch had gone for the day, she'd gleefully set about cleaning out cupboards, and now Mandy was driving to the tip with his precious childhood treasures piled on the passenger seat. There were his balsawood aeroplanes and plastic warships, his old footy and cricket trophies, his first riding boots and photos of every puppy he'd ever owned, every fish he'd ever caught, his pet turtle, pet lizard and galah. Also in the pile was the collar from his long-dead curly-haired retriever and, of course, pictures of Mark and Cleo as foals. She'd considered stealing something from Callum's office, but there was time yet.

Mandy Bishop changed up to fifth gear, cranked the music up and sang, all the while playing the film in her head of how Mitch would look when he opened the cupboard and found his treasures gone. Then she went to the new servo and sat at a window seat devouring her sticky bun and cappuccino, watching the sun find its way through the floating rain clouds.

oOo

Mitch worked at the head of the race, drafting ewes from their lambs, all loudly bleating in distress at their separation. A ewe slipped through and milled with the lambs. Tink ceased her yapping and watched Mitch. He stopped, looked beyond the wet sheep to the barren paddocks, greyed by rain, the topsoil puddling and sliding away down between the clay cracks. His hands were stiff and water puttered off his oilskin down the front of his shirt and soaked his jeans. His feet were cold and heavy with shitty mud. He felt very alone and a little bereft in the vast acres while the rest of the world was inside, warm and dry. And he was separating ewes from their lambs. And a few hundred metres away, the rain was ruining his mature seed heads, folding them, bending stalks. Oh, to be at the pub, near the fire, with Neralie. He grabbed the ewe from the pen and dropped it over the fence to its sisters and cousins and there was a swell from the crying lambs. 'Weaning is a fretful time,' he told them. 'But you'll still live with your brothers and sisters, for a while anyway.' Behind him, Tink fidgeted and yapped, so he worked the drafting gate and the dog was happy pushing the sodden and splattered flock through the mud and shit. Cal arrived in his Driza-Bone and tam-o'-shanter and they pushed on, separating ewes from lambs until everyone was orphaned.

Then Mitch went to the donkeys and the lambs and they dropped their heads to sniff their substandard dinner. Mitch tried to pat Cleo but she moved, so he said, 'Be like that,' and Tink – sodden, mud-caked – trotted along behind him to the ute, the farm dogs circling. The lambs called plaintively to their mothers through the fence. Isobel kept her sheep in family groups and she swore they were happier and easy to manage. He wondered about her happiness, the husband and children who loved her.

He texted Neralie: *The spot, when?*

He had loved Neralie McIntosh since they were both eight years old. Little Neralie had stood in front of Mitch in the school choir. One day Mitch pulled her pigtail and was perplexed when she didn't whine or tell on him but just kept singing 'Puff the Magic Dragon', so he didn't bother with her again. The following Friday, during sport, Mitch ambled across to the crease, picked up the bat, planted it in front of the wicket and faced the bowler, his face screwed up against the harsh summer sun. Neralie stood at the other end, flipping the hard red ball from hand to hand, calm and pale despite the heat. The teacher watched Neralie turn and walk back, almost as far as the boundary fence, the ball snug between her cupped hands and her brows furrowed by tactical planning. The teacher signalled the fielders and they turned and moved further afield and the wicketkeeper stepped back. Little Neralie ran, her thick curls bending back high in the wind and her thumb and fingers tight and light around the hard ball. She lifted her elbow and swung her arm forward and the missile shot from her fist, an apple-sized cannonball heading straight for Mitch, armed only with a thin oblong of willow. The red missile whistled through the thin air above the baked pitch and bounced a yard in front of him. He stepped towards it, the flat of the bat addressing the deadly thing, but it stayed low, bounced, spun, whipped behind his bat and slammed into the inside of his rear knee. It ricocheted and shattered the stumps, flipping the bails from their tiny nests into the dust beside Mitch, lying on his side in the dirt, holding his burning knee. The ball rolled on, bouncing over low tussocks and disappearing into the clumps of galvanised burr beyond the wire boundary fence. At the other end of the pitch Neralie raised her hand, ready to catch the ball when the fielder found it.

The following day, Mitch pedalled the twelve kilometres to town to the swimming hole. The steadily flowing creek was tea-coloured and tasted like fresh water. You could see your feet when you were standing up to your knees, and in the shallows you could watch turtles going about their business. Later, you wouldn't see anything in the churning, clay-coloured mire, stygian and sad, because of the carp. He swam out to the pontoon where Neralie was lying on her tummy in the sun. He lay down next to her. She opened her eyes and looked into his and closed them again. After a while they stood up and looked at the wet patches their bodies had left, side by side on the planks, then dived into the creek.

Treading water, Mitch said, 'I know where there's a barn owl's nest.'

She screwed up her nose in disgust. 'You collect eggs?'

'No,' he said, appalled. He would never murder owls.

'Where?'

'At Esther Shugg's. Got your bike?'

'Nah.' Her little brother, Levon, had the bike that day.

'I'll dink you.'

They remained firm allies and strong sporting opponents. Mitch remembered the kids at school saying that if you gave Mandy Roper a sherbet bomb you could meet her behind the weather shed and she would pull down her pants and 'show you'. But he never did. He didn't want to and he never bought sherbet bombs.

The first day Mitch came home from boarding school forever, he and Neralie eagerly consummated the adoring friendship that had been swelling for years. It was a loose, intermittent pairing, clan and tribe boundaries dictating, but they'd belonged to each other.

When her grandmother died, Mandy lost weight. Then she inserted herself as much as she could into the pub hierarchy. The whole town was at the pub the night Mandy Roper smiled at Mitch and told him she'd like to buy his dead mother's little white wagon. 'Can you come and take me for a ride in it?'

Lana said, 'Do something,' but Kevin said, 'You can't deny anyone a root,' and Jasey said, 'She'll be hard to get rid of.'

They had failed to rescue Mitch, and now Neralie was back they felt that failure.

The rain ceased so Mitch went to the silo and filled the

feeder bin for his suffering ewes, the cry of their lambs close. He felt a little better and gathered some nice lucerne hay and fed it to his chastened donkeys. They looked at him warily, so he assured them that everything was alright. Since he was still harvesting fecund mounds of sprouting manure, he had no doubt they still felt unwell – 'You're probably coeliac now.' Cleo let him put a lead on her halter and, after a gentle tug and a snap at her heels from Tink, she let herself be led, Mark following. Mitch drew them slowly to the yard and put them in with the weaners. There was a greeting of sorts, the lambs bunting and the donkeys sniffing their charges. 'God,' he said, 'that's lovely,' and Tink closed her panting mouth.

o0o

Because she was late, Callum assumed Esther was dead – she'd passed away in her sleep or slipped in the mud and died of exposure in the wet, windy night. There was nothing to be done. They would take the useless dog – one more mouth to feed – the Jeongs would buy the property and Mitch would lose the supply channel. He rubbed his sore hip and looked out to the rain falling on Mitch's crop. The wind rattled the drips from the trees, willie wagtails ruffled their feathers in the bare fruit trees and galahs trilled as they showered on the clothesline. The lambs were still bleating in the distance and once in a while rain rumbled across the verandah roof. Cal hauled himself up and crept inside to wash three analgesics down with sweet black tea. He reached for the telephone.

o0o

It was the letter from the Department of Primary Industries that had thrown Esther's routine. She read it while the wood stove gained purchase on the morning chill. 'Threats,' she said, but Peppy, curled on the hearth, was oblivious to all but the biting wind slicing through the gaps in the walls and around the doors. 'Fines, "involuntary action", "compulsory rabbit baiting" and "interventions". I'm besieged.'

She put on her coat and hat and went to her Dodge, Peppy following. They sat in the warm dry cab, Esther's eyes watering in the glare bouncing off puddles, like welding light. Unidentifiable birds dived and circled around the gums by the stock ramp and a peregrine hung in the cold air. Butterflies flapped prettily over some dock weed and a pair of kooka-burras watched them from the sheep yard fence. She studied her little corrugated-iron and timber house, the water dripping from the roof and into the rooms through the cracks. This year, spring had brought rain and wind; summer was coming and the house would thrum with heat and hot dust would pierce the gaps like soldering flames. It would bring snakes to curl around the eaves and eat the owl chicks and then autumn would herald another winter to cut to her old bones. 'I am in my eighty-fifth year,' she said. 'This is where I have always lived and it might just kill me.'

She drove to the haystack and lowered the sling, readied it to receive a fresh bale. She leaned the ladder carefully against the haystack and climbed. At the top, she reached over to a sweet bale and everything shifted. She couldn't recall the view on the way down, exactly, but was relieved when she landed and found herself alive, though covered in mouse shit and dust, fetid hay and straw. She also found she couldn't move, that she was wedged with her feet above her shoulders and her chin pressed to her chest in a collapsed chasm in the middle of the stack. 'Oops,' she said.

After a short while she understood that struggle was pointless so she reconciled herself to missing the grand opening at the pub due to her slow death wedged in a nation of tunnelling mice and their small wet nests. Millions of the filthy little shitters and their pink wormy babies pattering all over her. There would be a snake, possibly several, fat and full and torpid in a smooth crevice. Esther Shugg prepared to meet her Maker, but was called back when she suddenly understood that her death meant Cyril Horrick would get her water and the Jeongs would pay money to take the land her ancestors had bequeathed her. She knew then that she wasn't honouring the land – she was honouring an obligation to people who were dead. Gone. There was no point honouring them. They didn't know. They'd never know what she did with the land, and once she was dead, like them – gone – the people she was keeping the land from would simply take it. She looked into the longing face of death and said, 'To you I might look like a fool, and I see now that all my yesterdays have lit the way to this dusty trench, but I am not a wisp of candle smoke yet, no sir.' She closed her eyes and waited because Callum possibly hadn't died in his sleep and he would realise soon that she hadn't arrived to collect him for their regular drive around their ancestral lands.

Mitchell's phone rang and Callum said that Esther hadn't showed up.

'Righto,' Mitch said, knowing his father thought Esther was dead of a stroke in her bed, but if she was dead Mitch could just continue to herd his ewes to the low paddock, away from the lambs he had just stolen from them. Or perhaps Esther was not quite dead. He could leave her to proceed alone towards her end, thus avoiding the slow rotting death of an invalid at the nursing home. But if he rushed to save her he would have to go on enduring her weeds and vermin. 'Probably just got a flat tyre,' he said, and finished droving his ewes to their new paddock.

oOo

The sound of Mitch's approaching ute woke her. She gathered her breath when the tyres rumbled on the familiar dirt and stones of her very own yard, then a puddle splashed and brakes squealed. The pumping of her heart made it difficult but she used what she had in her lungs to cooee.

He stood in her yard and beneath the sound of wind against corrugated iron, he heard a faint sound and moved towards it. The ladder was discarded alongside the haystack. 'That you, Esther?'

'No, it's Hillary Clinton.'

He rested the ladder against the haystack and was about to climb when she said, 'Don't climb, you'll drown me. Get help.'

She stifled a small sob when she heard the message go out to the entire district on Mitch's CB radio. 'The haystack has given way under Esther Shugg, she's trapped and injured.' She heard the waves of voices from all over the Riverina planning her rescue, and then many utes and trucks slowed and rumbled over her small bridge and stopped alongside her dry irrigation channel and people walked up the drive and she said through the hay, 'I think I've wet my pants,' and Mitch said, 'People piss themselves at the Bong every Saturday night, Esther.' Then a blanket fell from above and, a little while later, the Bergens arrived with their cherry picker, and a medic was lowered, and Esther Shugg was delivered to the ambulance and driven to the hospital and given over to the capable care of Nurse Leonie Bergen.

Mitch lifted Esther's warm, dehydrated dog from the cab, saying, 'You'll have to come and stay with us, Peppy,' and she sneezed.

oOo

In his ute, Sam Jeong followed the events of Esther Shugg's rescue blow by blow via the CB radio and imagined sneaking a kilometre-wide, self-propelled boom spray filled with herbicide defoliant onto her land while she was away and annihilating every atom of chlorophyll on the place. In his mind's eye he saw poisoned vermin fleeing in every direction and a future without the need to spray chemicals around so often. But it was a pointless fantasy and he let it go when he saw the ambulance drive past his gate, two utes and three cars following. Instead, he phoned Bennett Mockett, who told him he wasn't the first to mention Esther's vermin problem. He rang off, saying, 'Mum's the word.' Sam googled the expression, and was pleased.

oOo

The small neutral areas between factions had thickened with bitter offence. The riparians were cool to the townies and farmers when they arrived to purchase cow's milk or fresh-grown vegetables, and the townies were cool to the farmers when they put goods on credit, and the farmers gathered a little more tightly in the corner of the beer garden at the Bong of an evening. But when the ambulance drove past bearing Esther to the hospital, all the people in the main street – Lana and Jasey, Kevin, Debbie, Paul, Elsie, Levon and Darryl, Denise and Kelli, Cyril and Stacey, Joe Islip and even Mrs Goldsack – stood together on the footpath to watch. In the beer garden at the Bong, to the sound of nail guns and bench saws, the customers speculated on Esther's recovery and placed a few bets. No money changed hands – that would have been shoddy – but predictions were made. Cyril was waiting on the edge of the footpath when Stacey swung into the kerb. He hurried him into the office, saying, 'You'll never guess what God's just granted us.'

'Probably not, so you'd better tell me.'

'Give it an hour or so, then get up to that hospital and get old Esther to sign over her water.'

'Oh, that – I heard on the CB. We should wait a bit; she might cark it.'

'I'll send Bennett,' Cyril said. 'She likes him.'

Then the phone rang. It was Glenys Dingle. 'I hear there's been an accident.'

'On to it. Her allocation's fairly insubstantial, but we can certainly –'

'Just let me know what the outcome is.' She hung up.

oOo

The smell of warm bathwater and skin moisturiser told Mitch his wife was close. She looked over his shoulder at the Water Authority website. 'What are you looking for?'

'The next round of buybacks,' he lied.

'You going to sell your water?'

'Some of it – have to.'

'Well, what's the deal with the supply channel now Esther's gone?' Mandy chewed her thumbnail. 'Esther's had a fall, that always changes things for old people; she'll be rethinking everything. Ask her for it. The worst she can do is say no. She uses you all the time.'

'We help each other.' He didn't want to ask an old lady to hand over the family farm while she was in a vulnerable state. Yet it was the perfect time.

'She might even be relieved. Just bloody ask her. *Try.* Put your money where your mouth is.' She left and Mitch's tension eased, but then she was there again in her snakeskin dressing-gown. 'If you don't ask, I will.'

12.

NO HARM ASKING

To get to the spot, you could drive along the eastern road, past Bishops Corner, and take a shortcut across Esther's messy paddocks to the riverfront – and most did. But those who wanted to avoid a drive through town followed the track the Water Authority and Fisheries and Wildlife used to check pumps and meters, or fishermen, drum nets and campers – 'campers' being a euphemism for shooters who drove up from the city to hide in the elbows of the creeks and annihilate every rabbit, fox, pelican, eagle, duck and grasshopper they sighted. The spot was a U-shape of land, a fat tick hanging off the river's meander, the neck of which would eventually erode completely if too much water was released from the catchments. The meander would then become a noose-shaped island with a billabong moat. Esther would lose land, be it only about half a square mile of inaccessible and useless, weed-infested, willow-choked clay. But it was a slow, safe place to swim and fish, and the neck was easily blocked off with a vehicle or a log, a signal that it was occupied, because it was the spot for couples to absent themselves from intrusion on moonless nights. The spot was also an Aboriginal midden site, black soil and ash that threw up bits of bone and shell, axe heads and waddies, reminding everyone that once the mussels had been edible and the First Nation people were gone.

Esther's river pump was located far enough away not to disturb the silence, and the forest of willow trees, thick cumbungi and reeds on the river fold provided a camouflage. If he could only have Esther's water, if he could take water directly from the river instead of paying through the nose to have it pumped from town . . . but the water traders would not see the sense of it.

He parked his motorbike on the narrow neck, made his way to the far side of the meander and sat on the log. It had dawned warm and dry, the air was sweet with morning dew and damp dust on eucalyptus, the sun warmed his back, and the birds, high and free around him, sang as they set off for the day. There was a breeze to dry out his bedraggled crop and the sun to make it shot and sprung, but there was also Neralie, waving to him from the opposite shore. She made her way cautiously across the top of the old weir on her lovely legs. On safe ground, she fussed over the friendly dog, Tink's body wagging in three sections, and came and sat next to Mitch.

It was such a normal thing to see her sitting there, every freckle familiar. There was no tension attached to Neralie, no need to be anything other than how he was, and again he wanted to take her home and keep her.

'How are ya?' she asked, meaning it.

'Much, much better now,' he said. 'How's the renovation coming along?'

'Good,' she said. 'Grand opening soon.'

'It'll be good, no worries.'

'Someone drinks or eats a counter meal every day in this town; I can't see myself getting many days off for a while.'

'You will – they'll just help themselves.'

She picked up a stick and started flicking leaves away with it. Water trickled through the broken weir, a raven carked and a carp jumped along the edge of the low creek. They both looked up. Was someone watching? They glanced at each other, acknowledged their nervousness.

Tink came and sat at their legs, nudged Mitch's calf, and Neralie turned and straddled the log, a leg either side. 'What are we going to do, Mitchy?'

'Job'll be right.'

They watched a thin line of bull ants detour around Tink, her ears back, alert to the falling leaves, rabbits' traces and far-off farm engines. Then Neralie slid along the log and scrambled onto his lap, her legs around him, and they held each other and kissed for a long time, until she said, 'We'd better not,' and Mitch knew it didn't feel right. For the first time ever, it felt like they were doing something wrong, but it wasn't because Mitch was married. It was because the dark, eroding power of Mandy Roper's presence was moving towards them like spilled paint over tiles.

Mitch gave Neralie a final hug then watched her make her way across the top of the old weir. As her car rolled away along the back track he felt desolate. Tink nudged his fingers, pressed her wet nose up into his palm, and he rubbed her bony occipital.

'Do not worry, Tinka,' he said, his tone earnest. 'I will always love you more than anyone else . . . more than the donkeys.'

oOo

It was possible that the light rain was the reason Stacey wasn't at the swimming hole again. But every girl in town was still walking hopefully around the small lake as if they'd been doing it forever. Lana was not there, of course, nor Jasey. No doubt they were huddled with the barmaid – the barmaid who still had not appeared in public. Afraid, possibly; definitely not confident. If she wanted to, Mandy could have the new water taker. And boy, would that upset everyone. She might even dine out with Gravedigger Dingle at the Riverglen Lake Restaurant, or join Cyril Horrick and his bootscooting wife for a meal at the Bong.

Then Stacey's car turned into the car park and Mandy let her bike fall to the grass, tore off her plastic poncho and dived in. It was freezing and her ears were filling up with microscopic creatures and she wished she'd remembered earplugs. Stacey soon churned past her, stirring the mud and rousing the weeds to brush her legs. Too puffed to continue, her lungs hot from the effort, she heaved herself up onto the jetty and rinsed off under the rainwater shower, then sat heaving until her lungs and heart stabilised. The waddlers circling the swimming hole in the drizzle giggled at her, but she called, 'Got a question,' and Stacey stopped to talk to her, rubbing his towel over his goose-fleshed body.

'Do you get commission every time you persuade someone to sell water back to you?' she asked him.

'No.' He patted his thinning hair with the towel. It was getting thinner each time it encountered water, but there were hair transplants these days.

'My husband wants to upgrade his irrigation system.'

'Great. Tell him to give me a call.'

She glanced at the waddlers on the other side of the swimming hole and stepped closer to him. 'He's got a rich aunt, almost dead from eating too much European chocolate, so he'll get her money, and there's Esther Shugg's water – he'll get that, most likely.'

He wrapped his towel around his waist. She had his full attention now. 'He still has to pay us for the water he takes even if it is from Esther Shugg's pump.' And it meant more water back in the system, more revenue generated. And the Water Authority still received money for the water Mitch currently owned.

'You'll lose the channel,' she said.

'That's what we want – water efficiency. Pipes and efficient meters. Channel maintenance costs a lot.' Around them, light rain fell. He pulled his jumper over his head but had to stop to gently ease his goggles from his hair.

'It costs Mitch a lot, and it also goes all the way to Riverglen.'

'So?' His head appeared through the woolly neck of his jumper.

'Think about it,' she said, and decided this would be the last time she'd swim. The water was slimy in her hair and mouth and she felt faintly nauseous.

Stacey watched her walk through the spitting rain to her car. She was affecting a slow, sexy walk, but she didn't possess the physical attributes required to create the appropriate impact, even draped in a towel and dripping wet. She was obviously still hot for him, but what was the deal with the threat about Esther's water? He dried himself too quickly; his wet foot caught in his tracksuit pants and he stumbled and fell into the puddle under the rainwater shower. Thankfully, the damp stalkers were marching towards Maria's for their skinny cappuccinos.

By mid-morning, Stacey still wasn't sure what Mandy was implying. Maintaining twelve kilometres of channel for one farmer was pointless, extravagant. But he had missed things before, failed to see beyond the obvious, and he wanted a new car and hair treatments, and a bicycle that suited flat terrain better. A builder from the pub strolled in just then and asked Bennett Mockett about the apartments at Riverglen Lake Resort. When would the lake be full? he asked. A light bulb switched on in Stacey's mind and glowed, faintly.

oOo

Bennett told Esther that she was lucky and she told him that depended on what he was about to say to her, really. Her lower leg was heavily bandaged, her chin resting on a neck brace and her arms blotchy, like the tattooist's ink gun had burst. In front of her, a dinner plate was wiped clean and the contents of the dessert bowl erased. The old dear's over-bed table and bedside locker were piled high with biscuit tins, plates of cakes and slices, bowls of fruit and bottles of sherry. Vases of flowers, mostly garden-fresh, decorated the remaining flat surfaces. She held the remote control in her good hand and looked at the TV the whole time he was there, the sound on mute and subtitles telling her everything.

'The Department of Primary Industries is preparing to bait your land,' Bennett said. 'Carrots. They'll start with the bunnies then drop a bit of Foxoff later in the week once we get things organised.'

Her eyes left the TV and she pointed the remote at him. 'You'll kill my barn owls!'

'They won't eat Foxoff and they won't eat fox. Better tie your dog up, though.'

'She's with Mitch. What about the eagles?'

Bennett shrugged. 'Collateral damage? Vermin? We'll let your neighbours know so they can protect as much as they can . . .'

'It was the Jeongs, wasn't it? They complained.'

'It was the department.'

Her eyes had drifted back to the television. What of her lizards, skinks and monitors, the boree tree saplings taking hold and the bulokes and cypress pines regenerating over on the sandy rise? 'You'll kill everything else with the slasher too, I bet.'

Bennett said they would save the native vegetation, and asked again if she'd consider selling her water back to the authorities so that other people could use it.

'No,' she said. 'I might just use that Dethridge wheel again one day.'

'They'll decommission the channel, even Mitch knows that.'

'If there are two of us using it they won't.'

He shook his head. It wasn't true. Why didn't these people think about these things? Why couldn't they see the need for change, believe in the experts? And Esther used her allocation to water her weeds, which was why the department had to spray her land, why her neighbours were annoyed by the hellhag. He left when she started banging on about 'corrupt' water traders.

Esther snuggled low in her crisp white bed. There were no draughts and no insects in hospital, no wind coursing up between the floorboards or sun baking the corrugated roof, no damp crumbling wattle-and-daub walls. The noises were different. Her clock wasn't beside her. She missed its tick-tock. She pressed the buzzer. No one came. She pressed again and still no one came, so she held her thumb on the remote volume button until it was at fifty-eight and when Nurse Leonie Bergen appeared, a soft white cloud dimming the room, Esther asked for the portable telephone.

'Who do you want to ring?'

'Mitchell. He's got my dog and I need my clock.'

'Very well.'

'The stew was delicious.'

'Delicious?' Nurse Leonie knew that if it wasn't for roast lamb and tinned peaches, Esther Shugg would have starved after her mother died. The stew she'd just consumed had been cooked in bulk weeks ago, frozen, transported, thawed and reheated. Esther was the first person ever to appreciate the grey slush and soggy vegetables.

'My word, very tasty. Tell the cook it was splendid.'

Leonie loosened the bedclothes over Esther's toes and said she'd bring the phone.

Esther tried to sleep, but it was frightening without the ticking clock reminding her that she was still in the realm of earthly time.

That afternoon, they brought old Mr Gammon in. Eavesdropping told Esther that he'd tripped on his cat in the kitchen and broken his hip. In the quiet, as the soft shoes of the nurses quickened along the corridors, a voice said, 'This one'll be a short stay, poor old bugger.'

Esther thought about her river, the way it curved around the spot, and its busy population of fish, snakes, frogs, lizards and birds. She used the hospital phone to ring Mitch and remind him she needed her clock, then she spoke to Lana about moving into the retirement flats opposite the swimming hole. Lana brought up the forms to sign and Esther said she needed a view to the river.

'How about the swimming hole?'

'It'll do. I'm ready to move in now, if you don't mind.'

'You're on the waiting list.'

'Yes, but I'm the only one on it.'

'Right now there's nothing available.'

'Fred Gammon was brought in today; his flat's vacant.'

'Fred's still here. On this earth with us.'

Esther stuck her nose in the air. 'Thank you for bringing the forms.'

'Until you can wipe your own bum you're not going anywhere.'

Esther smiled. 'You have a point.'

oOo

The ping told Kevin he had a message. It was a text reminding him he hadn't paid his telephone bill. He leaned back in his office chair, crossed his grease-stained hands in his lap and looked to the ceiling for an answer to his precarious financial future, and the women in his life. Summer was around the corner, farmers would want their vehicles. How was he to manage that situation? And what was he to do if he wanted to marry Jasey? Did Lana really want or *need* him? And would she corner the flash-smelling, taut-bodied water trader in his white jeans and new boots? 'Sort it out,' he told himself. It couldn't just go on, could it? No one gets everything. It would come to a head; why not find a solution before it did? He turned his thoughts to the diesel engine injector – it was either the worn components inside, or the casing was cracked. He'd give it a few kilometres, see if the crank time was slow or if the oil levels changed. Then, of course, it was a matter of determining which injector was faulty, and that took time. And money, which he knew the customer didn't have, but neither did Kevin, and if he didn't fix the truck, he'd never get any. 'What's a man to do?' He chucked it in for the day and headed off to weigh up his life with the wise men at the Bong and devise a plan of action.

Neralie put a beer in front of him and said, 'Kevin, you were pondering the very same problem five years ago. Maybe it's a situation rather than a problem.'

'You've got a point, there, oh, wise barmaid.'

o0o

Tink jumped up onto the back of the ute where Peppy waited, wagging her tail, and they drove away. The sun was shining and Mitch looked at his limp, sparse crop and decided he should have stripped some of it earlier, put a bit of seed aside, or just ploughed the whole lot in. As he put the ute into gear his phone rang. It was his sister.

'You going in to see Esther?'

'Yes.'

'I've just been. Ask her for her water.'

'Are women psychic, or something worse?'

'Just ask – she might even say yes!'

He drove towards town, into the sunset. The main street was pretty quiet: dead, in fact – not a soul around. It was the rain. As he passed the pub he looked up at the balcony but saw no one. He backed the ute into the kerb outside the hospital so Esther could see Peppy and arrived at her room just as the doctor from Riverglen left.

Mitch placed her alarm clock on the bedside table. 'It sounds like a time bomb.'

Esther said, 'It is, if you think about it. Put it on its side. The three to the top.'

'Why?'

'It's fast. How is my dog?'

Mitch pointed to the window and Peppy, shiny and black with a white blaze on her chest, smiled at Esther from the ute. 'She sleeps beside the ute – waiting for a lift home, I guess.'

'My sick ewe and lamb?'

'Fed, watered and safe.'

Esther was shiningly clean, her hair parted neatly and brushed to the side.

'You look like a month-old cygnet.'

Esther moved her arms in her fluffy crocheted bedjacket. 'Isobel brought it. It's the nicest thing I've ever had.' She looked up into the eyes of her handsome young neighbour, her saviour, a man who was content where he was and would be happy given time – and the McIntosh girl. Mitch would journey but not abandon home, kith and kin, or his land.

'You can have my land and water.'

He straightened, shifted his feet, folded and unfolded his arms and cleared his throat. 'Jeez. Well. Thanks. You can keep your sheep there and I'll fix the fences for you. We can do a temporary transfer or a permanent transfer. If you want to.'

She looked down at her arms in their fluffy sleeves. 'I don't want a lot of money in my account. I'm entitled to my part-pension. Let's say a hundred dollars a year for the land. The water takers will have something to say about leasing you my water, but let them say it.'

He smiled, enjoying the second-best week in his entire life, the first one being last week, when Neralie came home.

'We'll negotiate the lease again in twenty-five years.'

'You're pushing eighty-five.'

She smiled at him. 'True. We'll make the lease watertight until I'm a hundred and ten.'

'Done.'

He shook her hand, made firm and grateful eye contact, and a couple of tears welled and almost fell down his burnished cheek. This was going to be Mitch's year.

'You'd better go and see Joe Islip,' she said, and Mitch left. As he passed Nurse Leonie Bergen he said, 'Keep her alive until I come back, will ya?'

'Won't let a thing happen until the ink's dry on the signature,' the nurse promised.

oOo

'See the water?' Jasey moved the rifle so that her eye scoped the reeds below the ducks along the branches. 'He won't expect us at sunset, old Mr Fox. I'll get him eventually, nothing surer.'

Lana was watching the centre current moving rapidly. It carried detritus, slimy leaves, twigs and branches, and the black stagnant water from the depths swelled across the surface. And there were dead fish rolling past. It was more than just rainwater. Something was wrong.

Cyril and Stacey Masterson must have known. In the drizzle, Lana drew her cardigan tighter and looked at the cloudy sky, a few golden seams pointing down between the clouds. 'Everyone is going to be upset by this, just everyone.'

oOo

With the rain came a lift, some hope, the idea that a future was possible. But still, Callum waited until Mitchell finished drinking a beer before he mentioned that there were dogs about.

'I heard.' He had a vision of dogs roaming in the cloudy night, teeth bared, coming out of the dark, scattering the sheep, snapping at their hindquarters, pushing them until they crashed to the ground or were cornered and killed.

Cal wiped his mouth with his napkin and threw it across the remains of his hamburger. 'It'll take another attack before that bloody useless Bennett Mockett does anything about them, you can bet your bottom dollar on that.'

His father was waiting for a discussion about the dogs, but Mitch was pondering the fact that Mandy wasn't about to leave. She continued to monopolise the computer; she ran deep, hot baths, keeping the bathroom to herself far too long; and slammed about the kitchen when they were trying to catch the weather on TV. Should *he* leave? Go and live at the pub?

'Next year, things will be better,' Cal said, and from the study, Mandy called, 'It'll be better for me, you can bet your last dollar on that.'

Mitch said there was a documentary on irrigation in North Africa on the telly and Cal said, 'Good-o, but that TV screen needs a clean.'

Mitch put his newspaper aside, took his father's glasses, polished them and put them back on Cal's face. While Mandy played online solitaire, father and son watched the documentary on qanat water distribution systems in North Africa. As he crept off to bed, Cal said, 'A community around water. Cohesion in the society. Marvellous.'

Mitch was still sitting there watching the screen long after the smiling villagers of North Africa had stopped hauling animal-skin buckets of water to the desert surface, his thoughts and his guts churning over Neralie, Mandy, Esther's water, the farm, Callum, his dead mother, and the consequences of his impulses.

13.

SKULLDUGGERY

When Paul's phone sang 'Blister in the Sun' to him, he pressed decline, but he couldn't really decline the presence of Morton Campininni, stepping from one foot to the other, waving a sign that said LOST DOG. The others – Larry and the greyhounds, old people with walking sticks and gopher carts – waited supportively with him, on the stoop . . . in the drizzle.

He unlocked the doors. 'Spot?'

'Gone,' Morton said, breaking down. A kindly mother patted his fleshy upper arm.

Paul pinned the photo of the obese Chihuahua on the noticeboard and while he retrieved the bundle of newspapers and cut the packaging the locals read the noticeboard and learned that the Department of Primary Industries had listed its interventions for weed infestation and compulsory rabbit-baiting. 'Our dogs will be safe,' the dog-loving customers said. 'They don't roam.'

They took their papers and left their coins on Mandy's counter. Larry needed change so Paul had to open Mandy's cash register, but there was no money. He found change in his own pocket and then a lady wanted a lotto ticket so he told her to come back. She said she'd get her son to buy one on the computer.

oOo

Cyril answered the door at his mock plantation homestead in pale pants and leather slippers, one of two twin Cavalier King Charles Spaniels in his arms. Stacey said proudly, 'I've got rid of the supply channel, secured us maybe . . . a coupla hundred thousand megs, so we'll write it off as evaporation and claim it, eh? No one'll ever know.' He smiled.

Behind him, Cyril's wife held the other puppy. Pam was a woman who reminded herself each morning that smiling was a normal thing to do and that people liked it when you did, but when she stepped in front of her husband and snarled, 'I suppose you'll want breakfast; Cyril's workers always show up at mealtimes,' Stacey felt like he'd been burned by steam.

Cyril moved the big-eared, doe-eyed dog from one arm to the other. 'You've met the wife?'

'Good morning, Mrs Horrick.'

Cyril said to the puppy, 'Mum's done bacon-and-egg muffins, hasn't she?' He kissed its ear. 'And there's cellulose and sugar with condensed cow juice, too.'

'Thank you, Mrs Horrick, you're very kind. Will I take my shoes off?'

'If you want to. But nobody else does.' Happily, Pam Horrick's presence was stolen from them by the duties imposed upon her by the unexpected guest. While Stacey scraped his boots on the doormat, Cyril waved at Mandy Bishop, who happened to drive by.

Stacey explained that he'd been thinking a lot, and had talked Mandy into decommissioning the channel. 'The

182

Masterson masterstroke. I haven't done the exact calculation but, mate, we'll save a shitload of water.'

'Good, mate, very good.' Cyril patted the dog's head.

'But I've been considering outcomes, moving forward, and maybe we should reassess the worth of that channel.'

Cyril's dull eyebrows moved towards his receding sideways fringe.

'Think about it,' Stacey urged.

'I'm thinking,' Cyril said.

'The existing supply channel goes all the way to Riverglen, right? A kind of back door, if you get my drift.'

Cyril's eyebrows came down. 'It's obvious. We don't want too much scrutiny; I've got a shed full of pumps to sell.'

'Glenys will be happy.'

'Shoosh!' Cyril glanced into the kitchen where his wife was setting another place at the table. He stepped closer to Stacey. 'As I say, a little knowledge is a good leader.'

Mrs Horrick called the men. In one of the many pauses over breakfast, she said she wouldn't attend the pub grand opening because since the water meeting, she'd been informed that her bridge club had been cancelled. 'But I know they still meet to play . . . without me. I sit at home, alone. I've lost all my friends.' The ladies weren't friendly when she met them at the IGA, either, she continued. 'Jasey doesn't speak to me. No one likes us.'

'It's a temporary thing,' Stacey said. 'People don't like change, even if it's to preserve the planet and the best interests of the primary production industry.'

'They also don't like lack of consultation, secrecy, coercion and the fact that they'll struggle to live while feeling dispossessed and bullied.' Mrs Horrick rose and cleared the dishes.

Cyril picked up one of the spaniels. 'She reads too much, just gets upset.'

oOo

Cyril and Stacey pulled up outside their office then ducked down to the newsagency. Cyril looked at Paul's empty counter and raised his eyebrows.

'Delivering mail,' the newsagent said without taking her eyes from her phone. She wrote 'shark' and gained four points on her word game.

Cyril leaned on her counter. 'Your husband thinks he's going to lose his channel.'

'So,' Stacey added, 'he'll be really happy when we tell him he's not – and that he doesn't have to replace it with an expensive pipe.'

Mandy shook her head. 'He won't be happy at all.'

Cyril straightened. 'You don't understand, all he's got to do is replace one old pump, that black Dethridge wheel.'

'I understand perfectly, Cyril. Mitch is going to pump water from the river. He's done a deal with Esther Shugg and that means he can afford to lose his channel, which is what you want, isn't it?'

'Yes, but –'

'But you'll also lose about forty thousand a year, probably more.'

'That can't happen.' Cyril searched his pockets for a cigarette then remembered he'd given up smoking.

Stacey frowned. 'We'll still get some of that money, though. We'll get paid for pipe maintenance, pumps and stuff.'

'Not as much. I looked it all up.' She tapped the computer screen with a blunt, black fingernail. 'If Mitch pumps from the river you lose the forty grand the Bishops pay for channel upkeep and you don't get to replace the Dethridge with one of your new kits.'

It was all starting to dawn on Cyril. 'We lose the water entitlements the new meter and pump would have controlled too, and the water that your husband would have traded for the new meter and pump in the first place.'

'You lose, big time.'

'And,' Cyril added, 'on top of that, he's taking Esther Shugg's water *from us*.'

Stacey clarified matters. 'All he has to do is trade enough water for one lousy upgraded river pump, a meter and a few flume gates.'

'Mitch wins.'

Mandy was enjoying the angst she was causing, so pointed out that Mitch owned his own grader and would probably even dig and maintain his own channels.

Stacy folded his arms and said, 'And once he's got his very, very efficient above-ground sprinklers, he'll pay us even less, and what about the meter reader? He's doing us out of our livelihoods.'

'You'll have to put the water rates up,' Mandy said, but they didn't see the irony. In fact, Cyril didn't seem able to respond at all. Then the penny dropped, and he turned white. 'So we're actually looking at losing a hundred grand or so all up just from that one channel?'

'Plus you get less water to play with, but the irrigators get more efficient. That's the point, isn't it?' Mandy was really enjoying herself now. The men just stood there while, outside, sun shafts turned the rain on the asphalt to low wisps of warm, curling steam.

Mandy smiled. 'But I can help you even more.'

Stacey's phone rang. He looked at it and turned away. 'Gottlob, what's up, mate?'

When he got off the phone he looked at Cyril and said, 'The Bergens will drop in later to finalise the sale of their water to the Jeongs.'

'Friggin' hell,' Cyril said. 'Next we'll have every bloody farmer racing around, opening up cafes and organising schemes and task forces.' He looked at Mandy. 'I hear you loud and clear. We appreciate that you understand that we're only trying to help. You get your husband and the old man to do the right thing by us and we'll do the right thing by you.' He winked.

'I can get him to do anything I want. It's either please me or I take everything.'

oOo

Cyril hid behind the potted palm until big old Nurse Leonie Bergen was at the end of the passage with her drug trolley, then he darted down to Mrs Shugg's room. She was sitting up in bed, looking very neat, and he suspected she'd even had a shave. He tapped on the open door with his most mischievous grin in place. 'Well, hello! Look who's as smart as the new peg on the Hills hoist.'

Esther glanced at Cyril. 'No one's expecting visitors in this room. You'll have a better welcome down the hall in the morgue.'

He stayed close to the door. 'Sense of humour – gotta have one, eh?'

Esther reached for the newspaper.

'I was just passing so I thought I'd drop in and update you on the wonderful water deal I'm offering.'

She held a *Weekly Times*. The headline read: WATER BROKERS BLAMED FOR IRRIGATION PRICE RISE.

'It says here, Mr Horrick, that "Texts and emails were sent to irrigators informing them that prices for temporary water allocations had fallen from $280 to about $100 a megalitre".'

'Not us,' Cyril said.

Esther said, 'If you tell farmers that the price has fallen, you get more water sales, which in turn pushes prices up. You're manipulating water for profit, aren't you?'

'That's just a beat-up to sell newspapers.'

'There's no point you being here,' she snapped.

'Fair enough.' He glanced down the hallway in case Nurse Leonie Bergen was loitering. 'You can't trade any water without letting us know; you're aware of that, aren't you?'

'When it's necessary to involve you in my affairs, Mr Horrick, you'll be informed.'

'You can trade through a *temporary* transfer and you can transfer just part of your water, if you like, to more than one person.'

'I know.'

'You can even lease it out over a set period of years, subject to our approval, so does your *transaction comply with trading rules that are designed to accommodate environmental objectives*? Or do you need some *assistance* with that?'

'You don't need to bribe me, we comply with all rules.' Esther picked up the remote control and turned the TV volume up to ninety-six, and Cyril shot past Nurse Leonie Bergen as she came through the door.

14.

ONE BEER AT THE PUB

It took a week, but Mr Gammon died. The Rural Women's Club ladies quickly started dismantling his flat and the solitary life he'd lived, and Lana arrived to complete the transformation.

'Okay, you can move into your new flat now.'

'I've never left home before,' Esther said.

It was Thursday, so Kelli was part of Activities. She trimmed, washed and set hair, and did manicures as well. She swept into Esther's room, pushing a portable beauty and cosmetic trolley and mobile adjustable hairdressing sink, and offered her the works. 'And I'll throw in a top lip wax and a bit of chin wax for free!'

Esther looked at her, puzzled. 'Why?'

'Well, okay, but your sun-damaged hair desperately needs a treatment.'

'It's already dead,' Esther said. 'Hair is dead cells.'

'How about a manicure?'

'I'll have a pedicure if you've got one.'

They settled on the pedicure and a good old-fashioned short back and sides. Esther looked at her reflection in the mirror and saw old Tom Joad looking back. She told Kelli she preferred Gary Cooper but Henry Fonda was acceptable. Kelli said she didn't know them and asked where they lived.

Nurse Leonie Bergen handed Esther the keys to Mr Gammon's electric gopher buggy, tightened the velcro on her moon boot, and off Esther went to her flat in the main street, which also boasted electricity, hot and cold running water and a front garden with a view to the swimming hole.

Callum arrived, went for a walk through her humourless new home, came back and poured them a cup of tea from his thermos. He handed her a jam roll from the supermarket. 'I see you've got good light and a spare bedroom?'

'It's not spare,' Esther snapped. It wasn't her problem that he wasn't happy in his own home.

'The qanats,' he said, 'are a very efficient irrigation system. The Persians started digging it in the early part of the first millennium BC. They raise water in animal hide from deep beneath the desert through man-sized shafts burrowed into the sand and rock. Plenty of water down there.'

'I know.'

'Rivers of the stuff. Clean too. And they still use it to this day. They gather and swap information and it builds a cohesive –'

'I saw it! They have television in the hospital.'

Callum wondered if the girlie in the barber's shop would be interested. He stood up, put his tam-o'-shanter on and left to go and make an appointment for a trim.

The Rural Women's Club ladies arrived with baskets and filled Esther's fridge with casseroles and asked her to sign a petition to have a pedestrian crossing constructed outside the school. Jasey dropped off Esther's weekly order of a leg of lamb and three tins of peaches, some rolled oats and sugar and a packet of dried milk, gave herself a tour of the flat and left, saying, 'Be a change for you, having air con, glass in your windows and doors that close. Need anything, just give us a call.'

Then Lana came with an iPad and ticked things off on it and asked how she liked living in town.

'My social life has increased five hundred percent.'

'You'll have your own stool at the Bong soon.'

'Hopefully.'

Lana put a shire magnet on the fridge door and explained the phone numbers on it: fire, ambulance, cops . . . 'and me'.

'Thanks.'

'You want to join my computer class of a Monday night at the library?'

'No.'

Nurse Leonie Bergen arrived and unpacked Esther's suitcase, putting the clock on her bedside table.

'Put it on its side,' Esther said. 'The three to the top.'

Mitch was her last visitor for the day. Peppy walked in, sniffed the air and hopped up into the chair next to her, circling and settling with her chin on the armrest to watch her new life through the front window. Mitch put the paperwork on the table and drank a mug of tea while gazing out at the swimming hole. 'I've got a tractor inner tube you can have. Summer's almost here, you can float across the swimming hole, feed a few leeches.'

Esther said she'd rush out and buy a bikini the next morning.

Mitch smiled at the thought. 'Joe Islip says the Water Authority can't stop us. He went straight to State Water, just phoned them up there and then.'

'He's a lawyer.'

She signed her land and water entitlements over to Mitch and he told her about the paperwork to decommission the supply channel, pages and pages of it designed to deter anyone. Printing it out had drained his ink cartridge.

'I know,' the old lady said. 'I signed it.'

He thanked her and headed off to the pub, and she hopped into bed with the blind up so she could watch the evening joggers and strollers working off dinner under the lamplight. Out at her farm the huntsman would creep out from behind the calendar, her barn owls would fly silently away from the bustle and clatter in the trees as birds roosted and possums roused. The poorly ewe and its thriving lamb would snuggle down in the corner of the yard. Esther was seized with home-sickness and guilt at abandoning her home and family. As soon as she could, she would drive out to collect her father's butcher's knife, the one plate that remained from her mother's dinner set and her grandfather's gun, which she'd forgotten to hand over in the 1996 gun buyback.

oOo

The regulars sat on their stools like three treble clefs in the nook in Neutral Bay. Each had a beer on the temporary bar in front of them. They were captivated by the barmaid, who came through the door for the early shift preoccupied, her brow creased, and swung to look at the gate every time someone stepped into the beer garden. Her brother arrived for the second shift and the barmaid went upstairs and the regulars turned to the TV.

Mitch walked swiftly and sheepishly past the swing and slippery dip and through the renovated bar towards the accommodation rooms, taking the stairs three at a time. He did not notice Levon under the telly with his face in *An Obolus for the Styx*.

Levon was one and a half pages from The End. When he finally closed the book, he looked at the back page, then turned the tome over and looked at the front cover, then he flicked through the pages, held it to his breast and gazed at the slippery dip for a while. Finally, he put the book down, stretched, checked that the regulars had beer in their glasses and headed towards the stairs. One of the regulars picked up the remote and turned the telly down.

Levon rapped on Neralie's door and her voice came thinly: 'Hang on.'

She was fully clothed but a little flushed when she opened the door. Mitch was nowhere in sight. Levon pointed his finger at his big sister and said, 'People will still come to this pub because no one actually gives a shit who puts their bits where, but Mitch is still married . . . to Mandy Roper, of all people. Isn't that right, Mitch?'

Mitch stepped out from behind the door. He and Neralie were just standing there like two kids who'd been caught smoking.

'I think this story will end with a union and the enemy vanquished, but the innocent should not be killed. Make no cause for recrimination or angst so that those who deserve a happy ending will get one and the baddies will be suitably punished, alright?'

They nodded.

Levon went back down the stairs and as he did the volume of the TV rose.

'We can't upset anybody because that'll just upset everybody and they're already upset, and I'm a townie and you're a farmer and I've got a grand opening and business to make a success of and there's that bloody wife of yours. We have to try to make it all work.'

'If I knew how to, I would.'

She shoved him out the door and he went back down the stairs to where the regulars and a beer waited.

oOo

When he got home, Mitch's wife trapped him in the corner where the iPad and phones were charging beside the microwave, though he was not afraid of Mandy anymore and no longer bothered to delete texts from Neralie.

'I saw your ute today. Don't ever think I won't know things.'

'I had one beer at the pub.'

'Anyway, I've got some news for you.'

Mitch said nothing.

'Stacey Masterson came into my shop today.'

'And?'

'Well, here's the thing. You'll save money by leasing Esther's riverfront pump and water, won't you?'

'Yes, and by bulldozing the channel flat.'

'Stacey says he'll make up the difference and increase your water allocation to forty percent if you agree to keep the channel.'

'He said that? Forty percent?'

'Forty percent.'

'I'm not keeping the channel.' He didn't want to discuss what she'd said or why she'd conjured that story, so he walked away from her.

'I'd keep that channel if I were you.'

'Why? What's in it for you?'

'Everything.'

In the night, he dreamed of Neralie and of being in her messy bedroom, holding her, the small dresses she wore, with their zippers and buttons and ribbons looped on doorhandles, and her underthings rolling from the tallboy. He got up and went to sleep in Isobel's room.

15.

FOR THE GREATER GOOD

As the first fingers of dawn melted the dewy morning, Mitch stretched in his sister's bed, but his feet hit the end. He half hoped it was still wet and that the crew wouldn't come to crutch his rams so he could park his ute behind the pub again and go and see Neralie while his wife pedalled around the swimming hole, but it was a clear day, no rain. As he passed Cal's room he heard him fart and turn over. It was a glorious day, the future looked good, and Tink sat at the gate, watching the house. He went outside and stood with her on the wet dirt, breathing the freshness. He climbed into the back of his ute, holding his phone high until he could see the internet wave to life in the corner of the screen. The BOM website said to expect a top temperature of twenty-three degrees and a slight breeze. 'A bit cooler, please,' he said, then the signal cut out. 'Please, goddess Demeter, or whoever's in charge of weather, please don't let the sun shine warmly on my wet crop, don't let my seed heads shoot. I just want a return, one that'll cover the cost of sowing. Please.'

He went back inside and made his father porridge, toast and tea and took it to him with his analgesics. Cal said, 'Summer's on its way. A top of twenty-three degrees, twenty-six tomorrow. Just enough to shoot every single grain in every head of wheat.'

'At least we can cut hay.'

'Why don't you listen? I said, it's going to be a warm *day*.'

Mitch picked up the tin of hearing aid batteries and handed it to Cal, who put it aside in disgust. 'If you articulated, spoke clearly . . .'

Their attention was seized by Tink, barking into the empty sky, and over at the wool shed the farm dogs started yapping. Something was wrong.

Mitch went to the yard and stood on the cab of his ute but saw no smoke from grassfires or bushrangers approaching, just his wethers nonchalantly chewing their way through his one and only crop. He swore, whistled Tink over, and went to the bike, the dog jumping up to her seat before he got there. Just then, the crew bounced over the stock grate, and while they set about sharpening blades and oiling handsets and hanging their slings, Mitch collected the farm dogs and spent an hour riding all over the damp soil, getting bogged, leaving gouges and swathes of flattened, small, weak stalks, gathering the happy diners and pushing them through the crop to the gates. The crew rested and smoked and thought about the money they were making lying on the greasy shed floor, then Mitch came and announced the yards were full of rams and set about herding them into pens while the crew roused, stretched and prepared to work.

Mitch's sheep came in woolly and went out trimmed and tidy; the morning passed like any crutching day, except that Neralie was a mere twelve kilometres away and it had been over a week since they'd enjoyed five or so urgent minutes alone. But the grand opening was in just twenty-four hours. He swept the small scraps of fleece aside with the vigour of a man with prospects and whistled as he pitched the woolly missiles into bins with uncanny accuracy and sang along to eighties rock songs, because they were what made shearers happy. He sent the wary, dignified rams into the holding yards, Tink and Peppy bouncing around him like dogs on elastic.

oOo

Isobel put a cake and a casserole in the fridge, which contained nothing appetising, then kissed her father's bald pate and wiped his stable table and checked his medications and changed the sheets on his bed and put a load of washing on. While he gathered himself for a morning at the shed, she walked through the cold and grubby house. She sighed at Mitch's boyhood room, now her father's, but she was pleased. Mitch was not sleeping with his wife. Then she took a breath, smoothed her palms on her jeans and walked through the study and the living room to the main bedroom. She stood in front of Mandy, sitting up in Isobel's parents' bed, her thick hair in coils about her shoulders.

'This is my house now, Isobel,' Mandy said.

Isobel ran her fingers over the dust and scars on her mother's mahogany dressing table. 'It is not your house and it never will be.'

'You're in my room. This is where I sleep with your brother, my husband.'

Isobel shuddered. 'Looks to me like he sleeps elsewhere.'

Mandy looked around the room at the curtains she'd bought and the bedspread. 'I'm perfectly happy here. This is my home now and forever.'

'No, it isn't.'

'We'll see.'

'We will.' Then Isobel felt silly standing there, fighting the urge to scream at Mandy like a child, so she went calmly to her father, walked him to her ute and drove carefully away, knowing that for as long as Mandy lived at Bishops Corner, she would spend her everyday life with curiosity, jealousy and rage chewing at her. But so would Isobel.

Callum looked out at the track ahead, saying nothing.

'So, Dad? What do you think of it all?'

'It's a mess, and I'd like it to be set right before I go.'

She patted his knee. 'You've got years left.' But they both knew it might not be so.

While Isobel herded sheep and sorted wool, Callum worked the broom along the board to the extent his worn hip permitted, all the while trying to keep his gout toe away from the ceiling of his boot.

Esther arrived and sat in a corner with her neck in a brace and her leg in a moon boot.

oOo

Digby Prestwich came in from the yards and paused on the front verandah, clutching Isobel's treadmill for support. He took his hat off and fanned himself. The first warm day of summer was always hard, and the recent rain made this one humid. He washed his hands and face in the laundry and found his meal served and waiting under a gauze dome on the dining table. Isobel had thoughtfully left a quarter of a carafe of wine and a thermos of coffee next to a jug of water and a tumbler. A pert bread roll waited with a wedge of heart-safe yellow stuff on the butter plate. The grandfather clock *tick-tocked* and chimed twelve. He sighed, settled at the head of the graceful twenty-seat dining table with a linen napkin on his lap, and looked down to the peaceful riverbank, the noise of his own mastication loud in his ears. Rainwater, or something, from the catchments further west had swelled the river. Good for the river gums. He focused again on his sans-pastry quiche and salad. She would come home sooner or later, his wife. She always did, his thorough and dutiful partner, the superb hostess and fabulous cook. Jolly handy about the property too. And she could be fun, but he never got to *talk* to her anymore. It was like being married to a homing pigeon. The last thing he wanted was a marriage in name only . . . like those marriages where no one was happy but there was a farm at stake so they stayed for that. And the children. And because there was nowhere else to go.

He placed his plate and cutlery on the sink, checked the fridge and the cake tin – muesli slice again – drained the last of the red into his wineglass and found *The Land* and the *Stock and Land*. He turned to the back page and worked his way to the front of both papers then started searching for the *Weekly Times*. He found it shoved down the side of the couch, read WATER BROKERS BLAMED FOR IRRIGATION PRICE RISE, and when he got to the centre pages, there was his wife. She was standing outside Verity's shop in Collins Street and he read that her fine merino pashminas were 'walking out the door'. Another photo showed her standing beside a fleece draped with a blue sash. Most of the ribbons she won were yellow, but they weren't in the photo. And that's when he realised where she was. 'Crutching,' he said out loud.

o0o

At Bishops Corner, Isobel parted the wool on stud rams and ewes, checking micron and strength and colour. She chose the best fleeces and sprayed the letter 'I' in orange paint down the back of the sheep with good fleeces. 'Jesus,' Mitch said, 'they're my best ones.'

'You didn't expect I'd choose your worst? And I'm taking one of your rams for my girls.'

They went on classing wool and talking wool prices and what to do about Cal's worn-out hip, his gout and his sluggish old heart, and also about Esther's bung leg and her land and water allocation and Aunt Opal and what to do for Christmas and other family stuff, and then Isobel said, 'And so, little brother, what about Neralie?'

'Christ.'

'This mess has to be resolved.'

He took his hat off and fanned his red face. It was a windless, warm day and he knew that every seed in what remained of his measly crop was swelling and splitting husks, and sprouts were reaching for the sun and air. He put his hat on. 'It's so bloody complicated.'

If it were a story, Isobel would have put her arms around his broad back and said she loved him and would support him, but it wasn't a story and she was buggered if she wanted the tragic ending where her brother had to find vast sums to pay Mandy out or possibly lose the farm because of that gold-digging opportunist, and she didn't want the house ruined and Callum forced out. 'Sell some water,' she advised. 'Pay her out now.'

'She wants me to keep the channel.'

'It suits her and *them*. Water is money, Mitchell.'

'If I sell water I lose, if Mandy leaves I lose, and if I do nothing I still lose. Just wait until I sort out the channel and harvest and see what I've got left . . . minimise the losses, or something.' There was so much debt, she had no idea . . .

'But you could do *something*, surely? Go and see Joe Islip, do a deal, pay her a wage or something. If you don't, I will.'

'Jesus, Bel, don't do anything drastic.'

'If I do anything, it'll be for the greater good.'

They picked a ram and ran it up the ramp onto her ute and then she helped Mitch move his groomed and handsome prize stud rams across two bare paddocks to a paradise with rare green shoots and bins of molasses and cages of lucerne and troughs of wheat to set them up to endure the summer, a paradise where the prize stud ewes waited. 'Men,' he said, as the rams strolled through the gate, 'I want you to enjoy yourselves, be good to the ewes and make good strong lambs.'

They would be relatively safe in this paddock – not far from the shed and the donkeys nearby. But, most importantly, they were far from the river and the ferals' camp . . . where the dogs lived. 'They look handsome, don't they, for their wives?'

Isobel looked at them and saw wide royal blue sashes across the fluffy creamy fleeces at the Royal Melbourne Show, and the craft ladies holding glasses of bubbles, and Pipparoy fleeces in Chinese factories, and pashminas and hats and shawls and socks in the window at Verity's shop in Collins Street. Bishops Corner was her farm, not Mandy Roper's, and she would not let her take it. She'd rather shoot the little guttersnipe.

oOo

Cal and Esther finished their morning of helping in the shed and came home for lunch. Mandy's car remained parked in the middle of the yard, exposed to the elements, as it had been all day. The old friends settled in front of the television in the recliner rockers with a wedge of Isobel's cake. Soon they heard a noise in the kitchen; Esther tucked the remote control under her stable table just as Mandy flopped down on the couch with a slab of cake. She looked around for the remote control, then finished her cake in silence, licked her fingertips, wiped them on the floral couch upholstery and went back to the kitchen, where she switched on the radio. It blared, and then the vacuum cleaner roared to life. Esther pressed her thumb to the volume control while Cal closed the door, and the images of life and death and war and weather and stock market prices and advertisements for things they didn't need played across the TV screen. Mandy vacuumed her way into the living room. She shoved the nozzle under the TV – knocking the plug from the socket – then vacuumed her way to a far corner. Cal looked at Esther's moon boot then struggled out of his chair and, with great difficulty, bent over, but he could not plug in the TV. Mandy vacuumed her way past them to the kitchen, the cord trailing, catching on chairs and rattling the standard lamps.

When all was quiet Cal limped to the kitchen to boil the kettle. He poured water into two cups with tea bags while Mandy grabbed the remote control. 'I wouldn't mind a cup of tea myself after all that work I've just done,' she said, and Cal said, 'Water's boiled,' and moved to the lounge room with the cups, spilling tea on Mandy's clean floor. He didn't mean to spill it, but when she unnerved him his limp was worse and his hands shook more.

When the old lady finally left, Mandy came and plugged the TV back in, then pointed the remote control at the telly – 'Just want to check something' – and switched channels. She watched all the ads on a commercial channel then went to the kitchen, leaving the remote control on the mantelpiece. Callum had just got out of his chair again when she came back, took the remote control and stretched out on the couch. He limped towards the study, defeated.

oOo

Mitch saw Esther's ute turn east at the gate and head to her farm. As soon as he could he went home. He found Mandy at the computer, the TV blaring on a game show and his father lying on his bed clutching his walking stick, eyes shut and mouth open. He couldn't, in all good conscience, leave the old man trapped and vulnerable in his own home with Mandy while he stood at the pub looking at Neralie.

'Pop? Callum?' His father started swinging his walking stick before his eyes were open. Mitch ducked, said, 'Want to go to the pub?'

'No fear. That woman'll burn the house down while we're gone.'

He went to face the letters waiting on the kitchen table. The one from the Water Authority was headed: 'Re: Renewal project. The case for Jeong–Bishop road'. In four dot points, it scuttled his water dreams and business plan. They ignored the demands he'd already met for their '*long-term outcome goals for the health of the river, the town and its irrigators*', and made new demands. Since there were fewer irrigators in the area, water rates would rise. Recent re-evaluation meant Mitch would also have to forfeit more water to install the upgrade he needed, and Esther's river pump 'compromised the health of the river so required a much more comprehensive upgrade system, and therefore it was more viable to maintain the supply channel on the Jeong–Bishop road. It was no longer efficient to decommission that same supply channel.' The letter ended by stating, 'You have failed to provide us with all the information we require and therefore we are unable to process your request to acquire the water allocation of Miss Esther Shugg at this time . . .'

'Bullshit,' he said.

A second envelope also bore the Water Authority logo. It was a bill for $45,000 for supply channel costs, maintenance and retaining infrastructure. Mitch turned his mind to Shane Warne's slow run-up, the roll of his right arm, the ball travelling straight down the cricket pitch, spinning, the drift to leg, Gatting moving forward, the bouncing ball, the bat to the fore, but it was hard to do when he was sitting at his sister's pink fluffy dressing-table seat with Tina Arena and Natalie Imbruglia gazing at him from the wall. The reel went straight to Gatting staring at the ground where the ball had bounced.

'Try to make it work,' he told himself, and went to the computer to compose a passionate email to Glenys Dingle, but in Cal's cold study, with the tall shelves of books, the farm's history and statistics observing, the voice of the feral at the water meeting echoed: 'Man, we are all here for the water.' Well, they all were, but there was no way Mitch was going to keep that supply channel now he had Esther's riverfront access. There was no way he was going to give anymore. Enough was enough. He would fight for his land and his livelihood, and so he might as well fight for everyone. If he didn't fight, no one would.

'Dear Ms Dingle . . .'

oOo

Esther's farm was peaceful, as ever, but desolate as well, for the department had been and the vegetation, burned by chemicals, was rigid against the wind. The same wind thrummed through the cracks of Esther's old home and swirled between the eaves.

A nest of kittens had settled happily in her wardrobe. Mother cat wasn't there – probably out chewing on the long nose and large brown eyes of a potoroo, or perhaps playing with a palm-sized pygmy possum? Esther's thoughts turned to the owl chicks and she headed for the barn. There was no sign of life up in the nesting box, but the splatters of fresh shit and the casts on the ground told her life was continuing for that family. She retrieved the 1943 Remington .22 from its hidey-hole and was careful to close the barn doors behind her against mother cat. In the house, she gathered her father's butcher's knife and the one plate that remained from her mother's dinner set and told the kittens that they were responsible for millions of deaths every hour and that seven fewer cats equalled seven million live animals less than eighteen inches tall. Then she blithely ended their killing future.

She went to her ewe and lamb, stronger now, standing and eating oats and hay in the shed yard, the lamb gambolling, and on the way home, she took her moon boot from the accelerator as she passed the ferals' camp. Their pointless, flea-bitten mongrel dogs barked. Behind her, Peppy lowered her ears and growled, showing her teeth.

o0o

Stacey had followed the road alongside the empty supply channel in search of friendly gateways leading to malleable farmers in their lunchtime kitchens. If he could just get a few new pumps installed, a few more solar-powered meters ticking over on channel banks and riverbanks, then others would follow.

'I'm a nice guy,' he said to the passing paddocks. 'I'll do the right thing by you if you do the right thing by me.'

But at the end of the day, Stacey had consumed many cups of tea at many kitchen tables and had just one handshake agreement to sell a quantity of water for a bargain price of $150 a megalitre.

The farmer looked at him. 'One fifty a meg? Cheap!'

Stacey winked at the man. 'You do right by me, I'll do right by you. I'll phone with my bank account details. Let me know how you feel about the new pumps and meters, and we'll see what we can do with your buyback limit. You might not have to forfeit as much as you imagine.'

The second time he stopped for a piss he heard the breeze through a small stand of boree trees and the thistles squeaking together along the crumbling ditches. Summer weed seedlings – burrs, rolling hogweed, goosefoot and wild rye – stretched all the way across to the liquid horizon and birds searched the thick puddles in the bed of the irrigation ditch. A kestrel hung in the clear sky. Surely those small-acre farmers knew that the banks were just allowing them to tread water before swimming up to effortlessly eat their legs? He checked his list of irrigators and found he didn't have the stamina, or the front, to drink more tea and connive. He stashed the folder in his boot and went to the pub.

He took up his usual spot at the corner of the bar where the internet signal was strong and free, and Levon plonked a raw steak in front of him.

'Think I'll go for the schnitzel and mashed potato.'

'None left,' Levon said, and turned his back.

Everyone in the beer garden was looking at him. He cooked his steak and went to the far corner near the playpen to eat it, then retired to his room and pondered his chances of ever getting anything in this town. He'd dearly love a root, and it was beginning to look like it would have to be the newsagent, though he'd prefer Lana from the shire office.

16.
GRAND OPENING

At breakfast the next morning the snazzy little barmaid travelled about the kitchen in her thongs, shorts and large jumper. She was, as ever, efficient but not particularly friendly – curt, in fact. Stacey had to actually ask for breakfast.

'We've only got cereal,' she said, and dumped a plastic jar of what looked like half-digested cow shit in front of him. He wondered if it was poisoned.

'You can't blame me for what my bosses dictate,' he said.

Her brother said, 'You denied an irrigator his right to thrive.' He poured his whisked eggs into a hot pan in which the Bergens' bacon sizzled. 'You might as well have cut Mitch's nuts off.'

Stacey poured milk on his cow shit.

Neralie poured herself a cup of tea and sat at the other end of the kitchen table to eat a stack of toast with spoonfuls of the Bergens' honey.

Stacey ate his surprisingly tasty seedy slosh, suspecting he'd never, ever get a warm reception from anyone around here, and that's when the conversation turned to preparations for the grand opening that night.

'Should be good,' he said.

'Yes, about time something good happened for the locals,' Neralie said.

Stacey gave up. He got in his car and drove the twenty metres to his office. There Cyril and Stacey greeted each other loudly and shook hands firmly and Cyril rubbed his hands together and said, 'How'd we go yesterday?'

'Pretty good – got a couple of handshake deals.'

Cyril nodded knowingly. 'I had a shit day too, but I have a plan. We'll write a letter.'

'They don't like letters.'

'They'll like this one.'

o0o

'I don't think those earrings are right, Lana. Try the pearl studs.'

Lana changed them.

'Good,' Jasey said, crossing her arms. 'I just need to say this, alright?'

Lana stood to attention.

'With regards to our plan . . .'

'Right.'

'Lana, I love you but it's time you had a boyfriend of your own.'

'I know.'

'Do not drink too much too early or you'll start dancing on your own –'

'I won't, Kev hates it.'

'And don't smoke, do not leave the table to pop out for a ciggie.'

Kevin's van slid into place at the front verandah. He tooted, and they picked up their handbags and went out. Their boyfriend's hands were scrubbed clean of grease, and

207

his bright red hair was wet and flattened. 'Don't we all look lovely?'

'We do,' they chorused, and Lana put her earrings back in while Jasey turned the radio up very loud and they sang on their way to the pub.

oOo

Levon climbed the stairs to Neralie's room and found his sister sitting on the edge of her bed, wrapped in a damp towel, with a shoe in each hand.

'You right?'

'Yep.' But at some point tonight, Mitch was going to step through the door with his wife.

'Well, why are you staring at a wall?'

'I'm not,' she said, putting on a shoe.

Her brother leaned down and looked into his sister's worried eyes. 'You just keep your mind on your job, Nelly. There's more than one customer in town and we want Steve and Wanda, our investors and partners, to be happy with their opening night, even if we're not.'

When Neralie finally walked down the stairs, she felt hot yet cold, and like she'd swallowed a cup of marbles. But after a few minutes in her funky new bar, with its edgy though under-stated decor, she started to feel proud. And the menu was perfect – the same but better, with something for everyone. She would smile at her true love and his wife when they came through the door. She smoothed her new skirt, pushed her hair into place and smiled. Steve and Wanda unlocked the front door and looked ruefully at the regulars spilling in, combed and smiling. Levon offered them a complimentary beer of their choice but they told him they'd have a single malt whisky and took possession of their new stools in Neutral Bay. Their view across the bar to the door was clear and the TV was brand-new with a bigger screen. The 'frosted' windows, which were always just plain filthy, had been replaced but still prevented passing wives from spotting their husbands. Larry Purfeat came in and put the exact money for three beers on the bar. Neralie pointed to the bar taps and the bottle fridge and said, 'Take your pick.'

'Just the usual.' Larry allocated himself three beers each pub visit, four nights a week, a ritual constrained by his meagre pension.

'First one's on the house.'

'Well, I might try one from another country, if I may?'

She turned to the fridge, searching for a beer that had no adverse religious, military, cultural or political reverberations. She reached for a Tsingtao, but remembered the rumour about Chinese investors inspecting local properties with Joe Islip. 'Belgium?'

Larry looked doubtful, so she whipped the top off a Westmalle and put it on the bar with a chilled glass. 'Suck it and see.'

Then the locals came dribbling through the door, took their complimentary drink and stood about like they always had in the same places they always had and got on with having a nice time. It was like Neralie McIntosh had always been there. She positioned Steve and Wanda in Neutral Bay, knowing the regulars would point out the factions – townies, farmers and riparians. 'It comes down to where your spiritual home is,' they explained.

'Where's your spiritual home?' asked Wanda.

'You're sitting on it.'

209

Neralie's world became a steady circle of filling beers and pouring wine and mixing drinks and keeping an eye on the kitchen, from which meals came at a regular pace. It was like her whole life had been a road to here, and she was loving it, but fifteen minutes later she wanted to cry. 'They just won't stop coming,' she hissed to Levon, and he told her that people were meant to come and buy beer and food, 'the more the better'.

Finally, Callum's fingers appeared around the door and a gust of cold air swept through the bar and there were Callum, Mitch and Mandy, smiling. Tonight they had Happy Mandy. In the ensuing lull, the kiddies in the beer garden squealed and all eyes went to Neralie, but the barmaid just smiled and waved. Behind Neralie, the regulars threw kisses to Mitch, who was dressed like a boy in his Sunday best for a family photo.

To Mandy, it was as if someone had tugged an invisible cord and the people turned like vertical blinds, presenting their shoulders to her. It was only the dickhead drunks who acknowledged her, waving like mad men and blowing kisses. And there was Lana, on her skinny legs, and beside her Jasey with her fake blonde hair and flowery dress, looking like an upholstered chair. Mandy clung to her husband. She was still Mrs Mitchell Bishop and she would be so until she decided otherwise. Her husband asked the barmaid for two beers and a glass of wine, and she put her arm around his waist and rubbed his back, because she wanted the barmaid to suffer.

'Red,' she said, 'a double,' so Neralie filled her glass to the top with one of Bergen's best shiraz. 'On the house,' she said, and Mitch wanted to reach over, grab her and drag her to the storeroom or somewhere.

Levon turned the music up a decibel and the bar resumed its hum, then Stacey and Cyril stepped in and for two heartbeats it went quiet again. Cyril asked for four beers – 'Always have one on hand to give to a potential client' – and Stacey became conscious that his swimming hole stalkers were there, the neat and tidy ones with swinging ponytails and the older ones with their dogs or frail spouses and the fat-bummed cast from Single Mothers Street, wearing snug outfits that afforded no speculation, but should have. A display of twenty-somethings occupied the table near the door so that the eligible bachelors had to pass them to go outside for a smoke, and one sad bloke wore a T-shirt with a picture of what looked like an inflated pufferfish and the caption MISSING: SPOT, and in the middle of it all was the bottle-blonde check-out chick, the red-headed mechanic stuck to her like wet tar to a thong. And there was *Lana*, the lithe and raven-haired meeting moderator, and she was pretending to ignore him so it was only a matter of time before her big, longing eyes would be looking back at him from between the backs of her knees, her toes touching the bedhead. And there was his and Cyril's new friend, the loosely upholstered newsagent, walking away from her tall husband and ancient father-in-law, towards him, smiling.

'My husband will maintain the channel if you double his water allocation for next season, making it forty percent of the total.'

'Funny.'

'You can take the Dethridge, too, install all his new pumps along the river.'

'I can't do forty percent.'

'You can agree to it, at least.'

The hairdresser, whose dyed hair made her look like a rainbow lorikeet, cried, 'Oh my God, Mandy! The torlets! Awesome.'

'Someone'll spew all over them before the night's out,' Mandy said, and turned back to Stacey. 'Just *tell* him you will, that's all. I don't want him to lose water just now. He knows it's either the channel or lose everything.'

The plump hairdresser was beside them now and she handed Stacey her card. Each of her fingernails featured a landscape: a pastoral scene, a mountain range, an island with a palm tree, waves on a beach. 'Did I tell you that when anyone moves to this town they get a complimentary haircut, shampoo and trim included? I can do a style that means you won't have to use product.' She sucked a yellow drink through a clear straw.

'You use product, why can't I?'

'You can if you want to, but I could just cut it so you can't see your bald patch.' She lifted his fringe. 'You're receding at the temples too.'

'Thanks,' he said, and looked at Lana sitting on a stool, being demure and poised. He imagined her breasts standing up, smiling at him.

In the dining room, Isobel, a green drink in her hand, kissed her father and settled next to him at the table she'd reserved for dinner; she decided there were too many seats. Then Mandy plonked down next to her. 'I got Levon to sit us all together. Seen the prices? Hope the food's worth it.'

Isobel turned her attention to the menu.

Mitch arrived. 'What's the green drink?'

'Darryl's giving them out. He told me it would put hairs on my chest.'

Mandy said, 'I didn't get one,' and Digby said, 'You've probably already got hairs on your chest,' and was surprised when no one laughed.

Isobel handed her father the menu then took his glasses from his pocket and gave them to him; he told her to stop interfering, and Digby said good job no one had a crop because the rain meant they'd be harvesting Christmas Day, and Mandy pointed to the notice on the fine old restored mantelpiece – DINING ROOM OPEN FOR CHRISTMAS LUNCH – and said, 'It's our turn to host, so since we're all here I'll make it official: we'll have Christmas at Bishops Corner this year. Mitchy and I are really looking forward to having you all back at your old home. For a change.' She was beaming at them, really overdoing the Happy Mandy act, Isobel thought, so she told her that they couldn't possibly, there were seven of them, including Digby's parents and Aunt Opal. 'But thanks anyway.'

Mandy's cheery voice cut right to the end of the table. 'We won't take no for an answer. We're doing Christmas lunch and everyone's coming. I'll even fire up the AGA.'

Isobel said, 'There's no air conditioning, so it's impossible for the oldies.' Then she turned to Mitch. 'Did you get my email about harvest?'

'No.'

She looked at Mandy. 'It was probably deleted.'

Mandy folded her napkin across her lap. 'No need to bring anything,' she said. 'I'll cook. It'll be traditional – turkey and ham with the lot.'

'We'd have to take two cars,' Digby said, suddenly realising he'd have to minimise his wine consumption.

Mandy said, 'That's okay, plenty of parking. That's settled then.'

Callum, who'd missed the whole conversation because he didn't have his hearing aids in, started to give a talk on forward-selling as a ploy for international corporations to hold the world to ransom and those present knew this speech would segue into the loss of the single desk system; thankfully their meals arrived.

Mandy sent hers back, telling Elsie, 'I asked for a well-done steak.' By the time the steak came out again, everyone else had finished eating.

Callum put his knife and fork down. 'That was a jolly good steak.'

Isobel said, 'It was rabbit, Dad.'

Everyone agreed the food was excellent and drifted to the bar.

Mandy was left chewing her hard, brown T-bone with Callum, who was explaining the crippling effect the loss of the single desk policy had on the wheat export industry but she could see what was going on in the bar, and she could see Stacey.

Cyril was digging the remnants of his steak from between his teeth and telling Stacey that he had old Glenys right where he wanted her, and that his company, C. & P. Water, was in a prime position to unload all the pumps and meters he had in the wife's shed. He put his toothpick carefully in his blazer pocket and gazed across the bar to Mandy, eating with the old man in the dining room. 'They're all the same with a paper bag over their head, but happy wife, happy life.'

Stacey followed his gaze to Mandy and thought about his new red Ford 290 HP 3.5-litre V6, his new bike, his hair transplant, the money they'd make selling pumps and water, and the promotion he'd get from Glenys. He decided it would be best to shag the newsagent with her clothes on. But Stacey needed to get to Lana first. She had maintained her tactic of sitting with her back to him. He'd make a move before closing time. Then she turned and smiled at him and Stacey's sense of manhood swelled with hot hope; he told himself that since he was a mover and shaker, a modern man in a cutting-edge industry that would change the world for good, he could have both women, as long as they didn't find out about each other too soon. And when they did they could just fight it out. The music was good, the barmaid was working the crowd like a professional and his future looked set. And then, the blonde shopkeeper went to the bar to buy another Fluffy Duck, so he stood up and took two big steps and sat in her spot between Lana and Kevin. He said hello to Lana but addressed Kevin. 'Our fuel account's with the top servo, eh?'

'Apparently.'

'I'll change that.' He gave Kevin his card, but Kevin gave it back. 'I know where to send the bill.' They shook hands and Kevin looked over to Jasey and she beckoned him to join her.

Stacey smiled at the lovely Lana but at that moment the newsagent settled herself on Kev's chair. 'Drought nearly ruined this town,' she said loudly. 'The best thing for the whole district were the restrictions your company put into place.'

'Bullshit – my grandmother's roses died,' Jasey called.

Mandy replied, 'So did your grandmother; old things die.'

Lana said, 'I'm surprised you weren't killed years ago.'

'What about you? You can't tell me you're not dreaming of sitting on top of him later tonight.'

'In my role with the shire, I maintain a neutral position.'

'You live on the river and you think you own it and so do the farmers. You're the reason everyone in town's sniping at each other. The Water Authority *employs* people.'

Neralie came out from behind the bar and everyone turned to watch as she walked over to stand in front of Mandy, hands on hips. 'You want to start a fight, don't you?'

Mandy leaned in. 'It's the perfect time: everyone's here.'

Neralie pointed to Stacey. 'The argument is with Don Juan here.'

Mandy stood up. Mitch put his beer on the bar and took a step towards his wife. Levon called, 'Last drinks,' and the crowd took the warning and the general hubbub recommenced and the sniping women were forgotten, though Mandy was reasonably pleased with the disruption she'd instigated.

When Mandy returned from checking out the new torlets, she joined her husband at the bar. Kevin was boasting to Mitch that his future was set now that he'd scored the Water Authority's petrol account. 'That's the water-meter men, the maintenance workers, Cyril and his wife, Bennett Mockett. I'll shout you a beer, Mitch.' Kevin held up his empty glass to Darryl and gestured for two more, then Mandy said she'd have another one too, so Kev yelled, 'And a wine for Bicycle Mandy . . . I mean, Mandy Roper . . . Bishop . . .'

Neralie threw her hands in the air. Mandy calmly walked out the door. Mitch drank the rest of his beer in one gulp and put his hand on the shoulder of his best mate, who was white with terror. 'Thanks, Kev.'

'I'm sorry, mate, it just came out.'

Mitch turned to Neralie. 'Thank you, I've had a mostly lovely evening, but my fate awaits and I must go and drive it home, so to speak.'

The regulars explained to Wanda and Steve that Kevin had unintentionally insulted Mandy and made his best mate's life either better or worse, which meant that Neralie's life was either better or worse.

oOo

In the car Mitch said, 'I do not want to live like this. Surely you can't be happy either?'

'I'm not,' said Cal from the back seat.

'I was fine until a few days ago,' Mandy snarled.

They drove the rest of the way in loud silence, then Mitch went to lie on his sister's narrow bed and search his mind for a solution to the current mess.

His wife entered the room. 'People in this town think you're nice but you're just a prick, you're weak as piss. I have done everything to fit into this family – your father sits around all day sulking and watching everything I do, I can't move anything, I can't even have my own stuff in this house. You could have stuck up for me tonight. There's not one single person in that entire town who hasn't got something in their past to regret. Like I said, weak as piss.'

She had a point, he knew, but as she stood there he understood that she was never going to fit. *Pick a suitable wife*, his mother had said. 'You're right, I could have stuck up for you.' He would have defended anyone else but he didn't defend her, so why was she still standing there? Why didn't she pack her bags and leave?

'You can fuck off,' she said. 'Just fuck off.'

'Fine,' he said. *I am free.*

'*Fine*,' she mimicked, and the plump, sneering girl who'd hogged the swing at school left to go to her end of the house, far away from the dispossessed men's end. Could he really be free to go to Neralie? How could he leave Cal there? What about the donkeys? The sheep? Well, fuck it. He would sell his half-starved bloody sheep. Then a memory of Neralie walking through a flock of scattering ewes and lambs came to him. She was carrying a picnic basket, her smile as wide as the sky, and all around her sheep bleated and fled back to the plains, Tink scrambling to retrieve them. He'd spent all morning herding the ewes and their unsteady lambs towards the stubble, good stubble in those pre-drought days, and then his kind and lovely girlfriend brought lunch, scattering all his work for miles. They ate lunch sitting on a log beneath the eyrie, then they rode away to gather the sheep again, Neralie clinging to him, Tink leaning on Neralie. During that week, their final week together before she went to Sydney, he discovered many more things about his childhood sweetheart. Her life on the banks of the river had taught her about birds and trees, water and fish, yabbies, leeches and turtles, spiders and snakes, flood plains and wetlands, and he learned she could also open any configuration of gate. He had always known that she was excellent company and that she liked to win, especially at Strip Scrabble, but the thing he liked best about her was that she was happy to drop anything she was doing for a shag, almost anywhere, almost anytime.

Across the hall Callum's thoughts were of his ancestors. They'd be disappointed about the failing farm. He should have bought more land and built up a profitable business . . . but there was the 1963–64 drought, and another in '82–83 . . . and the years of Margot's illness, the medical bills. A business needs capital to work, especially a small business, otherwise it starves to death. He had gifted his son a perilous future that was now doomed.

He would find a way to set things right.

oOo

Elsie reported that they'd done forty plates and fifteen bar meals and taken bookings for Christmas lunch. They agreed

218

they needed better internet access and Steve said he'd see about an antenna. Wanda wanted to know about the divisions, how the locals would cope with conflict over their 'spiritual homes', and Darryl said it'd take more than a war to stop the locals coming to their own damned pub. Steve suggested the regulars should be moved outside with the hippies, who'd been smoking wacky-baccy. Elsie said you couldn't put smokers in with the kiddies and Levon said the ferals paid cash and they'd harvest soon and be too stoned to go anywhere.

Then Neralie finally spoke: 'It was a disaster. It was all over by ten-thirty and it was all because of that woman.'

'Nah,' Darryl said. 'It wasn't the worst night we've had here, and they'll all be back for episode two.'

But it was a disaster for Neralie. She'd wanted it to be perfect, wanted it to fix everything, get it back to how it was. But it was impossible, she could see that now. She'd left for Sydney and discovered that she wanted to be home and she wanted Mitch. But if she took him, well, there was Cal's farm . . . And now her calves burned, her feet told her she would have to buy her first pair of cushioned orthopaedic shoes and she stank of beer . . . but you couldn't erase the past and you couldn't deny something that was.

She climbed the stairs to her room with thoughts of crawling under her sheets to weep, but when she opened her door, something was wrong. In the pink glow of her bedside lamp her room usually looked soft and fleshy, but tonight her bed was stripped and her messy room was very tidy – rudely bare, in fact. The cupboard doors were open and the drawers emptied. In the middle of the room was a big fat bundle. It appeared someone had taken the linen from her bed, spread it on the floor and dropped the entire contents of her room onto the sheets. That person had handled her bras, panties, frocks, hairclips, socks, shoes, notebooks, postcards, photos, pyjamas, face cream, lipstick, tweezers, mirror, mascara, earrings and purse. Everything had been dumped onto the sheet, and her entire life now sat like a large, alien pudding, the sheet ends tying it all up with a bow. The skin up her spine crawled and she felt nauseous.

17.

UNACCEPTABLE

The grain report told them nothing they wanted to hear. More local rain was forecast and the strong US dollar was pressuring commodity prices down, but the forward-selling market was looking positive because the American crops looked grim – no rain – and rain was expected in Europe, which the grain producers there didn't want. On top of that, Canada, too, was wet and the Black Sea region was too hot. So if Mitch had even a reasonable crop he'd be able to sell it for a top price. But his crop was poor. Then the reporter told them that fuel costs were rising because of some war somewhere.

Mitch's phone rang and Mandy brought it to him. 'We're not going to Girri Girri for Christmas,' she said, and the rest of the rural report was lost.

'There have been more dog attacks,' Isobel said. 'Out your way this time. And we're not going there for Christmas, we're having it here. Come if you want.'

He watched his wife through the window. As she stomped past Tink, the dog leaped up onto the back of the ute and flattened her ears, keeping her eyes on the little white wagon. As it sped away, Mandy's fist came out the window, her rude finger pointed to the sky. Tink hopped down and sat at the yard gate again. 'I can't come for Christmas,' he said, feeling wretched, because he wanted a peaceful Christmas; he wanted Mandy to be approachable; he wanted to talk to her about Christmas, and the future.

o0o

He parked his motorbike near an outlet on his neglected irrigation bank and glanced around for sunbaking snakes. Finding none, he took his shovel from its holder and dropped the blade onto the bank of the ditch, compacted by hard hoofs and blasting sunshine. The blade bounced like metal off cement, and then, of course, the flume gates wouldn't budge in their concrete runners. But the infrastructure was nothing he couldn't rebuild with the tractor and the grader blade. So he replaced the shovel, Tink jumped up and they headed for his stud rams and their ewes, content in their new marriages, grazing together in the crop stubble, making pure-bred stud Merino lambs. As he drove towards their rounded grey forms, he dismissed his fear of wild dogs and dreamed of a hundred-percent pregnancy rate, even some twins. This year he'd cull the barren ewes again so that in a few years' time every sheep on the property would be paying for its own upkeep.

At the sound of the motorbike, the sheep raised their heads. There was something about some of the pale faces and legs and the fluffy torsos among his thick-set, dusty Merinos. He stopped the bike. It was the ears. They were at the top of the head, almost upright, not the leisurely downwards incline of the Merino ear. His guts turned and his saliva thinned. Among the rounded, fluffy polls were bald polls and bald faces, pale and narrow . . . and bald legs . . . and, finally, the profiles: those distinctive snouts. Border Leicesters. Esther

Shugg's Border Leicester rams were in with his stud ewes and Christ knew what the fuck they'd produce now. He got off his bike and turned in circles with his fists clenched. 'Faaarrrrrkkkkkkk!' he roared. 'I do *not* want Border Leicester cross sheep!'

Tinka jumped down. Mitch reached for the .22, emptied a few bullets into his palm, loaded up and took aim at the imposters, but they gazed calmly back at him through their innocent green eyes and he lowered the gun, swore, and put it back in its holder. His hands went to his knees and he dry-retched into the sharp stubble, hating everything and everyone.

oOo

Nurse Leonie Bergen, on her way from a maternity visit to Mary-Lou Jeong, an expecting mum with a one-year-old and a dose of hyperemesis gravidarum, saw Mitch dancing exuberantly with his gun and slowed a little. 'Border Leicesters,' she said, knowing full well that the gate had been closed when she'd driven past earlier and now it was open. Nurse Leonie had passed only one car that morning. Her mind went back to the day Gloria Roper forced her baby into the world and Nurse Leonie momentarily regretted the battle she had waged to get baby Mandy to breathe.

Nurse Leonie Bergen saw her patients and then, at the end of the day, lumbered across the road from the hospital to see her husband in his thriving new shop, the German Shepherd. Gottlob turned to her as she came in, relieved she wasn't another bloody customer. He placed a cucumber salad in front of her with his large farmer's hands and wiped them on his German Shepherd—emblazoned linen apron. They talked about the

223

day's trade – brisk and constant – and the day's news. Behind him, Vorbach washed dishes and placed them gently onto a drying rack.

Then Leonie went to the IGA and the pub, so by five o'clock that evening, every person in town knew Mitch's breeding stock had been sabotaged.

oOo

Lana had an inkling the presence dimming the light around her desk wasn't a local – the smell and the substance of the air lit her senses – so she looked up from her screen, her pleasant expression in place, and met the eyes of Stacey Masterson, leaning on her counter like a cowboy at a saloon bar. 'Lovely morning.'

'How are ya?'

'Same as I look.' He smiled, then straightened, businesslike. 'I'm after a map.'

'Topographical or road?'

'Both.'

'The shire?'

'Please.'

He watched her stand and walk into the back offices, the door behind her clicking shut, and while he waited he circled the spacious vestibule, looking at aerial shots of the town, black-and-white photos of the opening of the Water Authority Plant, and photos of the local Aborigines, long gone, in the early 1880s. When Lana returned she carried two fat, neatly folded maps and asked if he'd like to look at them before he took them.

'Nah, you'll find out I can't refold maps.'

'Other stuff you're good at, I bet.'

'Yep,' he said. 'Thanks.'

She nodded, sat back down again, smiling stupidly, though a little deflated that it was just maps he wanted. At the door, he turned. 'Got a question. If I wanted to take someone out Friday night, impress them, eat nice food somewhere different . . . where would I go?'

'Well,' she said, 'twenty minutes away there's Riverglen, and they have the Riverglen Lake Resort restaurant. Excellent food, I hear, but a bit pricey.'

'The Riverglen Lake Resort restaurant, you reckon?'

'I reckon.'

She watched him type in his password and do a search on his iPad. He told her reception was good in her foyer and that he might drop in more often, and then he looked her dead in the eye and said, 'All booked. Pick you up about seven, okay?'

At the door, he turned and smiled at her, and she wished she could think of something witty to say, but she couldn't, so she just smiled and waved until the door had closed behind him. Then she walked across the reception area to the table under the photo of the vanquished Aborigines and tidied the magazines. When she saw his car reverse out of its spot, she skipped back to her desk and dialled Jasey's number.

oOo

The lunchtime pub topic was how to get a truck back from Kev before harvest. Neralie, who appeared to be out of sorts, suggested the farmer just pay him if he wanted his truck, but he shook his head, finished his beer and left. The topic moved to dogs, which had torn apart a few thousand dollars' worth of that farmer's sheep in the night.

'Bennett Mockett is responsible for culls, isn't he?'

Everyone agreed.

Neralie turned to the regulars. 'Which one of you lot's responsible for your bar tab?'

'We'll pay after harvest.' Then one looked at the other and said, 'It's your turn this year,' and the other said it wasn't and the third said he'd worked the last harvest but the other two disagreed.

Two minutes into the argument, Neralie interrupted. 'It's been five years! Does it make any bloody difference whose turn it is?'

'Absolutely,' they said in unison.

She was anxious, fretting and impatient. Steve and Wanda had left for Sydney, not entirely happy, so her bar had to thrive, and there was a better life to get on with after five years of only half living. Neralie was tired of seeing with only one eye, missing the middle of everything, catching the edges and not feeling the relevance. And then the door opened . . . but it was just her friends, Lana looking as if she'd been elected shire president and Jasey looking like she'd just won lotto. They stood beaming at her.

Neralie called, 'Dad?'

He didn't reply.

'DARRYL!'

Her father rushed in from the kitchen, a tea towel and saucepan in his hand. 'What's happened?'

'Hold the fort.' As the three girls left the bar and ascended the stairs, Darryl looked at the regulars and said, 'Secret women's business.'

They nodded. 'Won't be secret for long.'

oOo

When Isobel mentioned Mandy's plans for Christmas, Aunt Opal said, 'It's unacceptable. She doesn't cook well. I'm not going.'

'It would be easier just to go to Bishops Corner. There's always next year.'

'At my age, "next year" is a wish rather than a promise.' She hung up and slumped in her Victorian spoon-backed bedroom chair and let her bottom lip drop. 'Blast.' She folded her lace handkerchief and popped it back in her large bra, recalling the happy Christmas images of 1940 onwards from her aged but remarkably reliable memory. She didn't want these memories sullied, nor did she want to drive all over the countryside in the searing heat in that high square machine Isobel drove. And why endure bad food, second-rate wine and paper serviettes on Christmas Day? Or *any* day, for that matter? Plus, she'd be a guest in her own home.

At Girri Girri, Isobel put the phone in her pocket and said to her husband, 'Mandy Roper is the arse through which the devil herself shits.' She rode to her flock and prodded them homewards on the quad bike. Closer to the yards, she parked and walked ahead so that they followed her, mothers and their lambs, some yearling siblings, and even a few old muttons. She closed the gates and they turned their triangular faces to the ram in the next yard and huddled closer together, a group of boulders wearing woolly coats. Isobel decided they no longer felt safe in their fold. 'I'm going to shed them,' she said.

Digby reminded her that the dogs were over at the other side of town.

'Dogs travel,' she said. 'And my sheep aren't happy.'

He looked at the ram, a beautiful specimen, pale curled horns, straight-backed, deep-shouldered and square-hipped, with a large, firm, woolly scrotum. She had a good eye, his wife. 'I don't think it's necessary but we could put the ram in.'

'Fuck off, Digby,' she said in her cultivated accent. '*All* the sheep should be up close to the house.'

But Digby had too many sheep; it was too impractical and far too much work.

They drove over the plains to check on the dust-coloured Dorper ewes and their new lambs gathered in small, bewildered mobs across the paddock. Small patches of green phalaris and ryegrass, temperate grasses, reminded Digby that his property, Girri Girri, was ideal pastoralists' land. He felt successful and proud, but when they came to the river he saw that the tide had risen. 'Released water. Too much there just to be rainwater.'

Isobel said, 'I didn't see anything from the Water Authority about it, did you?'

'No one sent warnings to me.'

So they drove to the old barrages and stood on the bank, watching the tide carry steady islands of branches and debris westwards into the pink-tinged sky. A swamp harrier skimmed past, on the lookout for dinner, and a gull-billed tern stood up to its knees in the reeds watching for fish. The evidence of returned wildlife and the majesty of the river flowing strongly after all these years made Digby nostalgic, so he told Isobel – as he had many times before – that Prestwich ancestors had built the barrages, now frail and elderly, back in the days of steam-boats and Aborigines. 'And in the 1870s, there was a pier to transport wool to the railway station, but this water will revive the river gums, give a bit of stability to the dry banks. I'll start the reticulation, have a green lawn by Christmas.'

And that was when Isobel pointed to the great log. 'You might not have a lawn if that log takes out the ancestral barrages.'

The log was drifting towards the fast lee side of the river-bend. It swung wide, revealing the detritus propelling it – an ammunition island – and it *was* aiming straight for the ancient barrages beneath them. They stepped back, Digby glancing to the vehicle. At the last second the log missed the barrages but its wandering tail caught a massive red gum root reaching down to water from the high, bald bank and the whole mess turned like a great wreath and finally rammed the giant tree trunk and its dunnage into the bank, brittle from the drought and soft with water, and Isobel and Digby watched as the bank dissolved, dragging the old barrage planks, about one hundred and fifty years of history, with it, yowling and splintering. Then another few metres of rich alluvial bluff sank and all that was left was a great chunk of exposed riverbank, like the centre of a warm cake.

Isobel swore and Digby said, 'That was a few hundred thousand dollars of my prime grazing land that just washed away.' He'd have a glass of thick red wine then sit down and write a stern letter to the ombudsman. No, damn it – he'd ring the chair of the Australian Competition and Consumer Commission. They'd rowed together at school. Isobel would phone Cyril, and Bennett. 'We should have been warned, and Bennett has to organise a dog cull. It's all very unacceptable.'

oOo

He didn't hear the back door slam, just her quick, hard foot-steps. 'You phoned your old aunt yet?'

He got up and went to shut the door. Family skirmishes were new to Mitch and he didn't quite know how to please his recalcitrant aunt, his stormy sister, his garrulous father or his furious wife.

'I said, have you phoned –'

'No!'

'Okay, I will.' She snatched up the phone and dialled, so Mitch grabbed it from her and held it high.

'No one wants to come.' He enjoyed the words coming out of his mouth, but hoped that if Mandy did anything terrible, it would be to him, the damage contained.

'Do something for me, just once! It might make me happy.' She stomped out.

He sat at his sister's dressing table feeling Mandy's presence eking through the house like carbon monoxide. From the wall, pop princesses – talented people who'd seized the day – looked down at him. Shane Warne and his Ball of the Century would not come, just a stark pitch in a green oval with a few seagulls and someone sweeping the seats in the grandstand. He was a grown man sitting in a small frilly bedroom and he was forced to move furtively through his own home, hiding from his wife. And so was his father.

oOo

Over the next few nights, the erosion continued. The main stream coursed down, carrying the weak and untethered, and it gradually consumed the manmade levee that separated the swimming hole from the river. One night, the last chunk of levee gave in to the flow and was carried away in a brown gritty cloud, leaving the flume gate and filter standing alone in its concrete housing. The swimming hole and creek were finally one again and around its banks, the remaining snakes slid away from their hollows and holes, lizards scurried further afield and spiders scrambled up trees. Out at the camp, the sleeping ferals turned and their swags squelched beneath them. Cooking utensils, buckets, branches lifted and circled away, and plastic chairs slowly rose with the creeping water and followed as the wheels of campervans were hidden by the river. People cried out and babies started to bawl.

There had been no warning, no dogs barking at the slippery, quiet chaos, for the dogs just slid from their beds and kennels and verandahs and set off low in a hunting pack, following the river eastwards again. The alpha dog turned away from the river and headed south, the pack following through the Bergens' orchards and the Jeongs' ploughed rows, up and down irrigation ditches and dry channels, past Esther's old house and barn, beyond the haystack to the yards, tongues hanging and dripping.

18.

TWELVE KILOMETRES OF CHANNEL

Mitch put the idea to his father, but his father shook his head and turned to look at the paddocks and the ivory hue in the morning sky, at the sheep grazing and the donkeys looking glumly towards the house, and the trees dotting the landscape all the way to the wall of dark gums lining the river beyond the property line. He did not want a new landscape. 'You can go to live at the pub, but I'll stay . . . though she'll probably smother me in the night then set fire to the pub.'

oOo

Mandy joined the fit and thin Rural Women's Club members to take in the changed circumstances. The swimming hole was gone. All that remained was a vast expanse of water and the concrete frame where the pump had once been. The filter was also gone, leaving lonely flume gates. The pontoon strained to free itself from its mooring wires and the jetty leaned with the new current.

Mandy rode back to her newsagency and waited for Stacey. When the customers found her there instead of Paul, they went home to read their papers online, and Mandy spent a great deal of time on her stoop watching the awful people of the town come and go from the Bergens' new delicatessen. She was eating two-minute noodles when Kelli walked past. 'What did you buy?'

'Lentils,' she said, shoving a spoonful between her painted lips.

'Fart material.' Mandy stared hatefully at the German Shepherd. 'Hippies eat lentils. That's why those flea-bitten ferals smell.'

'I'd love to cut their hair, or at least brush it.'

'They've probably got lice.'

Kelli decided she'd had just about enough of Mandy Roper. Everybody said, 'Give her enough rope,' but Kelli wasn't in the mood. 'You were a nit farm at primary school yourself.'

Mandy straightened. 'You pooed your pants.'

'I was sick!' Kelli's tolerance for Mandy evaporated completely and she envisioned pushing her and her bicycle into the swimming hole one foggy morning, her fancy riding shoes jammed fast to the pedals. 'Stacey Masterson and Lana are having dinner Friday night at the Riverglen Lake Resort restaurant. What are you doing, Mandy?'

Mandy stepped back into the gloom of her newsagency and its lotto tickets and gossip magazines and wanted to cry. They always had the last fucking word, this town. Well, not for much longer . . .

At lunchtime Kev's van left the garage and headed east. Mandy swung her attention to the shire offices and, sure enough, a few minutes later Lana went to her car and also drove east, as if she was heading somewhere for shire business. When Paul wandered down to the German Shepherd for potato soup, Mandy stuck her *Back in 5* sticker to the door and followed.

oOo

Kev arrived at Bishops Corner in his all-purpose service and maintenance van, and in the sunshine, flies buzzing and small things rustling in the ticking crop around them, he and Mitch gave the combine harvester the once-over. They greased nipples and checked fanbelts, oil and air filters, then listened for squeals, grumbles or thuds coming from the huge rattling engine. Kevin declared the leviathan fit for the thin sea of ruined wheat, then reminded Mitch that 'eighty percent of crop loss occurs at the platform or cutter bar or gatherer, so maintenance is imperative'. Then he wished his friend a good harvest and drove away.

Mitch emptied the last bit of feed from the storage silo into the trailer and thought that if he did lose the farm to the banks and his so-called wife, then at least he'd never have to feed sheep again. He opened the manholes and walked around his silos, banging the sides until the remnants of grain peppered the dirt beneath the outlet hatch; then he climbed to the top and reached in with his long broom and brushed the sides as far as he could reach and stood up to peruse the sad patchy crop he'd soon be harvesting. The donkeys watched him from their paddocks. A pair of brolgas he had known for many years, which had returned with the rain, rested at the water trough in the house paddock. Beyond them, a white vehicle waited at the house – State Water Authority. He cleaned a couple more silos but the white sedan remained parked at the house and he felt the angst his father was suffering so he gave in and went home, leaving the hatches and manholes open to the cleansing power of the elements. The donkeys watched him drive past then moved to press their furry breasts against the fence and inhaled the trail of sweet grain.

Stacey was sitting at the kitchen table with Cal, drinking tea. When Mitch came in he stood just a little too eagerly and shook hands a little too sincerely. He started the discussion by mentioning that he cycled, or rather exercised, in the morning with Mitch's wife, hoping Mitch wouldn't think he was back-dooring him.

Mitch said, 'Comes in handy, being fit.'

'Now, the supply channel –'

'I don't want it anymore.'

'But the deal, as far as I understand it, is that if we match the water saving you'd have made on Miss Shugg's deal, you'll retain and maintain the channel.'

'I haven't heard that version. I was told you'd up my water allocation to forty percent, but I think that's just a tactic for an alternative motivation.'

'I'll match you on the water savings you'd get from Miss Shugg's proposal.'

'Not interested.'

'If you keep the channel I'll make sure you get a good deal on a sprinkler system.'

'What about Esther's water?'

'You won't need it.'

'It's mine already.'

'Your proposal for a new riverfront system at Esther Shugg's does not meet our environmental outcomes.'

'Jesus, mate, this is another circular subject. It does. Joe Islip's checked. You just want me to buy pipes and pumps and meters and the rest of the gear. I don't need it, I can't afford it, especially when my wife gets going; I'm ruined if she asks for money.'

'Then there's no need to do a thing if you keep the channel.'

Mitch straightened, his voice rising. 'You're talking to a man who's not winning anything at the moment, but I know I can win this one because I know what you're up to.'

'What if we pay to upgrade the supply channel?'

Stacey could see his new car slipping away; he was sitting at the table facing the truth, completely stumped.

Then the old man said, '*You* need the channel, and you are a fox in a trap with a dead lamb in your mouth, son.'

Mitch pulled out a chair and sat down to face the man. 'The relevant officials at the Water Authority tell me Esther's water is mine, and so is her pump. You and Cyril tell me Esther's water can't be mine. You are lying, and they know you are, and my question is, why aren't your superiors doing anything about that?'

Stacey blinked. Mitch had gone around them. Joe Islip had gone straight to State Water; he had gone straight over Glenys's head. A tumour-like presence pressed on his bladder. Was it his prostate or just tea? He noticed his white-knuckled hands and stood up, banging his chair on the antique sideboard. 'Thanks for your time.'

Stacey wound his window down as he drove towards the gate and inhaled the warm air. Two donkeys stood forlornly beside an empty silo and he felt their hunger and disappointment, so he turned the car radio up, put his hand on the roof of the car and tapped along as the brown and green paddocks slipped past. If he was in the shit, he was in the same shit as Glenys. It would be their heads that would roll. Stacey was just a young man doing as he was told.

oOo

He talked to Bennett about wild dogs and Bennett said the cull was planned for Boxing Day. 'I sent an email to everyone.'

'Mine get deleted,' Mitch said, though he could have checked the website.

Bennett dropped a box of Foxoff on the back of Mitch's ute. 'The ferals say their dogs are vegetarian – "peaceful and domesticated", they reckon. Leave a bit of bait about and then we'll cull, just need the authorisation. Remind your neighbours.'

Mitch's ute found its way around the corner and down the back lane into the yard behind the pub. He came through the kitchen and said hi to Elsie, who was holding a pen and frowning at a newspaper. '*Still lacking subject for debate*, ten letters starting with M?'

'Motionless.'

'Thanks.'

When Neralie saw him alongside the regulars, her face lit up.

The regulars gushed and gasped. 'Oh my . . . and when he stepped into the room . . . everything else fell away . . . and we were alone together.'

Neralie pulled a beer for Mitch and watched him drink it. 'How's things?' she asked.

'Same. How's yours?'

And the regulars shrugged and said, 'Same.'

They stood on either side of the bar and a sweet urge swelled between them. One day they would settle into whatever it was they'd end up as and make their lives excellent, and she'd feel alive and amazed again. He asked for another beer and she put one in front of him, smiling all the while, and the regulars said, 'My heart is heaving under my bodice.'

Mitch looked at the regulars. 'You blokes right for harvest?'

'We are,' they said.

Mitch turned at the door to throw Neralie a kiss and the regulars threw kisses back. 'It was only a moment . . .'

'. . . but it will last for eternity.'

237

Mitch and Tink took a drive to the spot. The sky remained blue and dotted with fluffy white clouds, and puddles shone like silver plates all the way to the horizon. The air was soft, but when they swung through the gate, it became thick with the stink of rotting rabbits and the gut-churning stench of a dead fox emanating from the acres of brittle foliage. They passed Esther's dear old house and her dear old tractor heading towards Esther's old pump. There was more water in the river and it brought rubbish and black water, but the birds were back. He planted the pellets by the weir where the dogs and foxes crossed, hoping they'd get them before anything else ate them, and his thoughts turned to the wedge-tailed eagles. He had not seen them for days, possibly longer, but in the thin, crisp canopies of the stressed gums, sulphur-crested cockatoos cackled and screeched, and on a partially submerged trunk the pelicans lined up, and a cormorant sat close by on the old weir. A few herons and a handful of ibis lingered, watching the increased flow on its way to the sea. 'Where do you think most of that water's going, Tink?' He put the ute in gear.

As they drove back towards the road, they spied the blue roof of Lana's Commodore and the rusted roof of Kev's ancient repair van hiding together behind a tall stand of thick cumbungi, so Mitch turned and headed the long way to Esther's. The ewe was huddled under the water trough, her legs folded beneath her, exhausted, head drooping, and Mitch felt a brick of cold fear in his guts. There was no sign of the lamb but the prints were everywhere, the frantic splayed hoof and paw prints.

'Dogs.'

The ewe didn't try to move or draw away from Mitch, so he carried her bleeding, torn body to his ute. He looked at

Esther's old house, the barn where the owls were, and he hated the townies and their pet puppies and the ferals and their shitty, smelly, dusty, flea-bitten camp and their dogs.

Later, when he told Esther he'd shot her ewe, she looked at the sun glittering off the swimming hole opposite and said, 'I should never have left.'

oOo

When he stepped into the office after his disappointing day trying to unload solar-powered meters, Stacey said, 'Mitchell Bishop has already contacted the State Water Authority. He told them we won't let him bulldoze his channel. Next they'll be wanting to know why. I don't want to be part of it anymore.'

'Son,' Cyril said, and slapped his shoulder, 'you're already part of it.' He patted his pockets, looking for cigarettes, but found only his phone. There were three missed calls from Glenys Dingle.

Stacey rubbed his temples and remembered the hair there was receding. 'The Water Authority knows –'

'They just want to be able to report the required water savings to the government so they can put it in a media release.' He winked at Stacey. 'Enjoy your night.'

Cyril went home to his wife's shed and counted his unsold meters and pumps and calculated how much he still owed on them. Then he checked his super balance online. He wondered how much the Water Authority actually did know about the supply channel, his pumps and meters, and Riverglen Lake. His phone rang again so he turned it to silent and went to the new servo and bought a packet of cigarettes.

oOo

At the appointed time Neralie turned up at Jasey's. When Lana tugged off her rhinestone skirt and turned to pick up a dress, Neralie hissed, 'Jesus, Lana! You've got sump oil on your arse!' and went to guard the bedroom door.

Lana turned her bottom to the mirror. Greasy handprints darkened the pale skin of her buttocks and bruised the elastic of her G-string. 'Oops,' she said, and the crack of the .22 made them freeze. They heard Jasey say, 'I missed.'

Neralie said quietly, 'Many lovely, single farmers come into my bar every night, Lana.'

'So why don't you get yourself one?'

'Touché.'

Then Jasey was there. 'You stuff this date up, Lana, and I'll shoot you.'

'Don't have sexual intercourse with him,' Neralie said. 'Definitely do not do any sexing.'

'And don't tell him *everything*. Remember – be alluring,' Jasey added.

'Stay sober.'

'Get drunk when you get home instead.'

'We'll be waiting.'

Stacey pulled up outside Jasey's house, approached the door, knocked and checked his hair in the window they were standing behind. When Lana opened the door – 'How are ya?' – he told her she looked nice. Neralie and Jasey watched him watch her arse all the way to the company car. He let her open her own door because women in the country thought you thought they were helpless if you opened a door for them. Lana didn't look back to the house, just drove off with the new boy in town and his pale jeans and brand-new boots.

Kev sauntered in from the back verandah, a gasping redfin

in his hands, and said, 'What stinks?'

'Cologne,' Jasey said.

'I've got to get back to work,' Neralie said, and left.

Jasey took a step towards her boyfriend, her one and only ever boyfriend, and she took the fish from his hand and drew his arms around her waist. 'It's time for the next phase, Kevvy,' she said affectionately, pressing against him.

He looked afraid.

'You should marry me.'

'Sounds good to me.' And he wondered what Lana and Stacey were talking about.

oOo

For the first five miles or so, the atmosphere in the car was stiff, the pauses thick and the commonplace dialogue a little too loud and eager as they drove past flat land and dry trees. Then Stacey asked Lana what she wanted in life.

'I want us to all go back to how we used to be five years ago.'

'How was that?'

'I want the farmers to hang at the pub, joking and laughing, and I want lots of mums at school fetes, and I want fundraising film nights and cocktail parties again, and kids screaming on the footy oval and in cricket teams and at the swimming hole, and I want the town to show up for gymkhanas and sheep shows and race meetings, and I want Christmas parties that go for three days.'

'Really? That all?'

'I reckon that's all there is. The rest is just killing time.'

They were shown to a seat by the window at the restaurant. Orange streetlights glowed from tall poles around the dark chasm that was the new lake, but only two lights twinkled

241

from the new resort apartments on the manmade hill above it. Stacey asked the waiter for their best champagne and studied the wine list. Lana decided on the yabby cocktail and the smoked cod salad and hoped they'd sourced their produce from the river now that it was flowing rather than stagnant. Her date would have steak, she knew. Or the roast.

'It's dark so I can't see,' Lana said. 'But is there any water in that lake yet?'

'A bit. Not much spare water about.'

'No.'

'So, whose side are you on?'

'I went to school with all of them, so everyone. But officially I'm a riparian. It's hard.'

Then they changed the subject and had a lovely meal and when he pulled up outside her house, Stacey put his arm on the seat behind her and leaned in close. 'I really, really want to get to know you better. *All* of you.'

She kissed him, longingly and deeply, but when he reached for her breast she pulled away and said, 'On the first date I don't sleep with boys.'

'What about the second date?'

'Possibly the third date, but depending.'

'Want to go out for dinner tomorrow?'

She opened the car door. 'That was a great night.'

'See you tomorrow?'

'Phone me.'

He watched her vanish into the gloom behind her parents' house and drove to the pub and fell onto his bed, congratulating himself for not persisting. His reputation had to remain intact for a little longer. But he kept an ear out anyway, just in case the door swung open and Lana with the pert breasts was there, her nightie sliding down her long, long legs to pool about her thin ankles.

Lana texted to report she was home – her two best friends replied immediately, awarding her ten out of ten for poise and decorum – then she undressed, hopped into bed and closed her eyes. A few minutes later she got up, dressed in a tracksuit and sneaked past her parents' bedroom to the back door . . . where she found Jasey and Kevin, who sent her straight back to bed.

At the pub, Neralie stood at the door of her room, listening. Then her phone buzzed in her hands. The message from Jasey read: *Intercepted*. But Neralie understood Lana's need. During holidays when Mitch was home from boarding school, she'd say goodnight to her parents and brother, close her bedroom door and climb straight out her window. They'd cycle towards each other under the dome of stars, each appearing out of the tinkling gloom, and spend a pleasing time together in Esther Shugg's haystack. And then, one Christmas morning, Santa left Neralie a packet of contraceptive pills and a reflector bike vest.

19.

SHOT AND SPRUNG

Mitch flicked on the computer, waited, and waited some more, and finally the grain market website loaded. Nothing had changed, with the strong US dollar and downward commodity prices. The drought was breaking all over the eastern states so exports were up and the dollar falling, making export industries competitive. But he'd probably only get less than $100 per tonne. He could possibly still break even if he kept harvest costs low, if his machinery held out, if storage costs were consistent . . . Next year would be better. He would go to the bank, sit in the air-conditioned office opposite the fragrant young man with the hairdo of many textures and tell him the good news. Then he would swan in to see Bennett Mockett with the proof of sales, and ask for brochures on a new tractor, a new ute and, most especially, a new harvester. He would pay off Mandy and wave her goodbye from the back door and take Neralie to the Riverglen Lake Resort restaurant and formally ask for her hand in lifetime companionship and permanent, exclusive rooting. 'You're full of shit, Mitchell Bishop,' he said aloud. 'You'll be lucky if you've got a farm next year.'

He grabbed a Weet-Bix, spread some butter on it and went to his dog, waiting on the ute. It was the smell of water on dry mud that made him stop, and then sunshine glinting off the surface. Water was flowing in his supply channel. He stood with Tink on the hard, dry bank looking down at it, remembering what it was like to see a flowering crop on a warm spring day, and it made him thirsty, and he wanted to strip off and jump in and get thoroughly wet, hide under the smooth, murky stuff, leaving his troubles in the other world. But it wasn't his. It was theirs. All the water belonged to Cyril and Glenys Gravedigger and the polished chap with the gender-neutral name and $450 boots who fought with an iPad full of lies.

'That is a ploy,' he said to Tink. 'A trap.'

He waved to his donkeys and drove to check his crop. The soil was soft under his feet and he was pleased there was subsoil moisture, but that also meant that heavy machinery – a tractor or a harvester – could bog. He inspected a few seed heads and found them definitely shot and sprung. 'There you have it, Tink. We're pretty much sunk.'

He put her in the cab with him and just sat for a while behind the wheel, Tinka panting, the spider repairing its web in his cracked rear-vision mirror, but he finally headed through Esther's to the river. He travelled slowly, his arm resting on the open window. At the Jeongs' westernmost boundary, Tink's ears whipped forwards and her mouth closed; he followed her unwavering gaze. He reached to the glove box and found the binoculars. The men were on the riverbank near an old pump. Next to it, the bald guy with the big earlobes was working away at a very big hole with a crowbar and another was mixing cement with a shovel on a sheet of plywood, while the skinny bloke with ropey hair studied a sheet of paper. They wore brand-new workboots and their high-vis vests were discarded on the ground. 'There you go, Tink. Gravedigger said she'd create employment. You could get a job installing meters. They'll pay you more than me, but you'll do a better job than these chaps.'

The meter installers stopped to watch Mitch's ute approach, holding their implements like Romans on guard.

'You should tie your dogs up at night.'

'You should stop exporting live animals, genetically fucking the food we eat, using all the water and polluting the air and the earth with chemicals.'

'You certified and trained to install those meters?'

'You certified to give dog-management instructions?'

'Dogs eat sheep and lizards and Christ knows what, including fox bait.'

'My dog doesn't go anywhere. I know that for a fact, because she sleeps with me.'

'Right,' Mitch said, and put his ute in gear. 'That's no way to speak about your missus.' He drove away and in his rear-vision mirror he saw the feral throw his shovel down and walk in a circle.

'Well,' he said, reflecting, 'I've just about had a gutful.'

20.

A HARVEST, OF SORTS

In the cab of his harvester, Mitch prodded the screen with his grimy thumb to adjust the satellite configurations. The B-double pulled up and his big sister descended from the cab into the new morning, wearing clean work clothes and lipstick. For a couple of years she'd arrived with Rory and Philippa in booster seats beside her, and the first time she'd backed the B-double up to a loading ramp, she'd squared it.

Though he'd long been made redundant, Cal also fronted for harvest. He gave the advice he gave every year, then limped away with Tink – also redundant – to watch events from afar. The regular chaser-bin driver arrived and went to the tractor, and Mitch turned the ignition on, pressing the starter button, and the old harvester engine lurched and failed and lurched again and then turned over and kicked into life. He lowered the head. Every adjustment he made and every button he pressed lit a rattle somewhere way back in the contraption but, like a cruise ship, the harvester moved forward, the reel spun and the great combs brushed the crop into the cutters and the weak heads of the sad, shot crop vanished into the churning, thrumming machinations beneath him. He stripped through the first thin tonne in record time and as the seed spewed from the auger into the chaser bin, he acknowledged it was dull, weed-contaminated rubbish.

It was when Isobel's truck was three-quarters full and waiting for a final load from the chaser bin that the header slowed and came to a halt. Something always went wrong, and it was always because of wear and tear. The reels stopped and rose and the CB radio clicked and Mitch said, 'The keys.'

The cabin door opened and he climbed down from the cab to reach through the wall of wheat at the head into the keyway.

He had sharpened the tines, but cut stalks and weeds had gathered in one of the reels and bunched against the drapers and cutters, clogging the feeder and leaving the thresher to thrash away at nothing. Friction and metal fatigue.

They started again and soon the light flashed on the harvester and the chaser bin was unloaded into Isobel's truck and Isobel drove to the silos at Riverglen. Once there, she eased the truck up to the small cabin, where the lass on the testing deck worked the probe through the load, spilled the sample onto a dish and went inside to test it. The girls, in shorts and Blundstones, *Southern Grain* stitched to their shirts, worked away at the samples, testing and weighing and logging readings. Isobel handed over Mitch's grower registration card and the tester handed back a small square ticket, which showed the impurity content of the grain was high, as was moisture, but protein was low. They offered her a very low cash price, which Isobel accepted. There was no point paying storage fees; grain like that would not sell for much no matter how long it sat there waiting for a price rise.

Eventually the truck in front of Isobel rolled away and she drove onto the weighbridge, where another girl in a booth

248

took her ticket, studied the screen in front of her, wrote the weight and handed it back to Isobel, who took her place in the next queue to unload.

Mitch had just read her text – *2 hr wait* – when the affirming thrum and grind coming from the drive component behind him groaned and the harvester stalled, as if the system was threshing a horse. There was a judder, everything seized, and the stink of burnt oil filled the cab. Something watery shifted in Mitch's belly and acrid saliva filled his mouth. He sat there in the ruined header, eighty percent of his miserly income remaining in the paddock, wheat grit under his sweaty shirt and prickles in his socks, the air dusty and dry and filled with the alarming smell of hot metal and the sound of nothing.

The CB clicked and the chaser-bin driver said, 'May as well go home, then?'

'Just give us a hand first, will ya? Please?'

The old man saw it all through high-powered binoculars. He rubbed his sore hip with his palm and said, 'We're buggered now,' and then his son disconnected the chaser bin from the old tractor, drove the tractor away and came back with the grain head trailer. They raised the reel and grain head, manoeuvred the trailer under it and dragged it away, leaving the castrated monster in the middle of the paddock, acres of unharvested wheat before it, a couple of rows of stubble behind.

Later, in the subdued comfort of the pub, the discussion was about what might have caused Mitch's header harvester to pack it in.

oOo

Sam Jeong parked his shiny ute, with its logo and multiple lights and aerials, next to the river. He stood in front of one of his new pumps, in the small square of shade from the solar panel. The concrete was still wet but the metal post held firm. He used the key to open the small metal box. Nothing registered on the screen. Water was flowing through the flume gates, but no flow was registering here. He opened the power control box, but the motor didn't seem to be working. Cyril Horrick's solar-powered pumps didn't work, his new meter was useless, and an unknown quantity of water was flowing, flooding his crop. He reached into his back pocket for his phone, but there was no reception, so he drove to town.

oOo

The class had made great progress over the weeks, and so it was that the riparians, townies and farmers arrived at Lana's computer class, sat with their respective clans and turned their devices on. The atmosphere was aloof, but not hostile. Some took advantage of the library's free wifi, some discussed new tasks they'd discovered the machines could do. Mrs Goldsack sent the moneybox around for tea and biscuits and scolded those with overdue library books.

Lana took her position before the class, the screen behind her. 'Everyone turn on their computer or iPad,' she said, her tone unusually cheerful.

They adjusted their glasses and squinted at the screen and put their fat fingers over buttons or thumped too hard with their fingernails, but Lana waited, her screen projected onto the big whiteboard.

'On my screen behind me, you can watch what I'm doing with my fingers, if you're confused, okay? So, there's an email

I've sent you all. Remember what an email is?'

Some nodded, others looked to their neighbour's screen instead.

'Look for an email with lana@srgv when you've opened your email account. You can search for a keyword, remember, or just scroll down.'

The students, dutifully mimicking Lana's actions as displayed on the screen, searched for and found an email in their inbox from her and opened it. Some read the message, *Congratulations! You've just received your first email!*, while others had a photo attached. It was a blurry photo, the lines ill-defined and the colours block-like, but it was of two people having sexual intercourse against the front of a white van. The pale-skinned man had bright red hair and the girl's head was thrown back in ecstasy, her dark hair vivid against the white bonnet of the van, and it was projected on the screen behind Lana.

The members of the technology class closed their devices. Those who knew how pressed delete. Someone went and closed Lana's screen and sat her down. 'It's never been an issue for any of us, Lana. It's none of our business.'

Then someone leaned over to Mrs Goldsack and whispered why the room was deathly silent and Lana's glowing presence had suddenly radiated such heat at Mrs Goldsack's side. Eventually, they helped Lana to her feet and took her across to the pub. When they stepped into the bar, all talk ceased. Neralie put a bottle of top-shelf Scotch whisky in front of her friend, saying, 'You'll smile about it in five years' time,' and the regulars patted the vacant stool and told her, 'It's safe harbour here.'

Levon phoned Kev and asked him if he'd checked his emails, then suggested he go see Jasey. And then the topic of conversation turned to Foxoff, the dog cull and the benefits to the community of exterminating vermin.

oOo

The letters were fanned across the kitchen table like brochures in a real estate office. Mitch had anticipated the abysmal bank balance, knew the end-of-year rate rise notice from the council was due, and expected Cyril's formal rejection of his application for the riverfront pump. It was the invoice from Bennett Mockett that hurt the most. Everything from spray chemicals and inoculation products to fencing wire – even the cost of ear tags – had gone up. So he loaded a lucerne bale onto the back of the ute and drove away towards his friends, Mark and Cleopatra. As they crossed the supply channel, still full and flowing with other people's water, a flock of starlings rose and folded and fell in a whorl over the grass. He looked to the fat messy eyrie in the old pine but Mr and Mrs Eagle were not there. The donkeys were in the far back corner of the paddock so he dumped the food and filled their trough, but only the weaners came towards Mitch. Cleo just raised her head and Mark swung his low head to see. He called, 'I have put the feed over there, and over there is a trough of water. You can remain undecided, do nothing, but you'll die . . .'

The sky turned brilliant pink and he turned again to look up at the eyrie, but it remained lifeless, and he knew that his eagles had eaten something that had died from bait at Esther's. Everything had a price. There were always consequences, good and bad. He set off for home and in the rear-vision mirror he saw the donkeys still standing there between the hay and the trough, and the weaners nibbling at the feed and drinking the water.

He found the washing he'd done days before stuck against the spinner and hung it on the clothesline, matching trousers seam to seam so he only had to iron the cuffs and pockets, and then he stood back and admired his handiwork, enjoyed a moment of what life was like when it was just him and Cal, when he could drink beer in the shower and read the paper on the toilet with a cup of tea. He remembered the week he'd had with Neralie before she went away; she used all the dishwashing liquid to shampoo the donkeys, and when he came in for lunch he found her lying on the couch in her pyjamas, her nose in a book, the house around her a complete mess. Mitch tidied their bedroom, hung her dresses and blouses according to colour and picked up her soiled garments. As he shoved them in the washing machine he called, 'Don't you know how to use a washing machine?' and she reached for her mobile phone saying, 'I'll ask Mum.'

Then his phone rang. It was Neralie. 'What are you doing?'

'Fretting.'

'I've got a bar full of fretters here. Why don't you join us?'

oOo

When he arrived at the pub, tanned and handsome in a sleeveless torn cotton shirt, Neralie was at once pleased, afraid and triumphant. He said hello, kissed her across the bar, and she gave him a beer. He joined the united front of Kev, Jasey and Lana in the corner where Stacey usually sat. He stood by the stool with a beer in his hand and spewed forth his latest tragedy. 'Production squeeze,' he said, and the people in the bar rumbled and shifted on their stools and shook their heads. 'Bennett Mockett has just put all his prices up.'

Levon, Darryl, Elsie, Neralie, Kev, Jasey, Lana and a couple of farmers just looked at him sympathetically. In Neutral Bay, the regulars stared.

He drank his beer and put the glass behind the bar. 'What?'

Kev cleared his throat. 'You've got metal filings in your harvester oil and petrol tank.'

'Filings?'

'Filings.'

Mitch couldn't speak. Neralie put another beer in front of him. Kev explained, finishing with 'and that's not all'. They told him about Kelli's bent aerial, the poaching of Paul from the IGA, Neralie's possessions molested and tied in a bundle in her room, and Morton Campininni said she'd once short-changed him five cents. 'She didn't return a book to Mrs Goldsack,' Larry added. There were things she had done in primary school, too, and finally, Kev explained that they'd found his balsawood planes and treasures at the town tip, '. . . but we saved them, or as many as we could.'

'Small person, big grudges,' Levon said.

He could have cried but the love of his life, his soul mate and friend, was smiling at him from behind the bar, because soon they would be together. 'Enough is enough,' she said, and he saw now that everyone was smiling.

oOo

The Friday evening view was spectacular from Bennett Mockett's rooftop terrace. The sinking sun turned the new, strong flow of release water orange, the shining flow pushing past the refurbished pump station and its extraction pipes, enormous drinking straws reaching down to the water. Cyril, Stacey, Glenys and Bennett and his wife Megan, cocktails in hand, toasted themselves. They talked of their successes – the reinvigorated river, its flood plains, ecosystems and wildlife, as well as the encouraging responses from the federal government and, most especially, the business investments, jobs and tourism that the Riverglen Lake Resort was bound to attract once the lake was filled. No one mentioned the loss of the swimming hole. Pam Horrick sat with the doggies at her feet discussing Megan's new boatshed on the riverbank at Riverglen. When Glenys threw her head back to laugh loudly at something the others had shared, she stepped back, treading on one of the spaniels. The dog yelped and held its paw aloft. Glenys looked down at the dog and said, 'Oops.' Pam clutched the whimpering animal to her breast.

With his back to the orange orb in the golden sky, Stacey watched Jasey, Kevin and Lana come out of their little flood-plain house and drive away. When pissed Cyril, dull Pam, ripe and bossy Glenys and Two-shits Mockett were at the height of their boasting, Stacey looked again at his phone. The image was grainy, just blurry shapes really, but it was clearly two people shagging, and Lana looked just how he'd imagined. He could have her now. If he claimed Lana, surely Jasey, Kevin, and everyone, really, would be grateful?

oOo

The pub was full now, though Mitch had gone home to his father long ago. Darryl was behind the bar and Levon adjudicated proceedings for the newly formed task force. Paul was handing out photocopied Certified Accreditation certificates, pink-trimmed, while the topic moved through water released from catchments with no warning, the loss of the swimming hole and Digby's barrages, black water, and Sam's new you-beaut solar-powered water flow pumps and meters, which had not been earthed and therefore didn't work. Then there was the lack of water, the fact that a twenty-percent allocation wasn't enough to grow anything or save anyone, so the factions joined to discuss corruption and set in place a plan. Then the topic arrived at the dog cull, and the reasons to kill: food, suffering and vermin. They had no choice, they reasoned, since it was all for the community . . . for the greater good. Levon asked for eradication volunteers. Esther was first to nominate. She would work with Callum.

oOo

Mrs Maloney set off to fetch her cow, which had been grazing near a great toe of riverbank on the lee side of the main river meander, just upstream from the swimming hole. She wobbled along the north side of the river, alarmed at how much the river was up, how much dead water and detritus had swelled to the surface, and the mighty push of it, like one long container ship. She found her brown and white Guernsey cow standing in the river, straining to keep her chin above the water, the whites of her eyes showing, the water lapping all the way up to her thurl. When she saw Mrs Maloney, the cow bellowed.

It took the bleary people at the cocktail party on the roof terrace some time to identify the sound of metal on metal and breaking glass, and by the time they negotiated the stairs, drinks in hand, Mrs Maloney had smashed the windscreen of Cyril Horrick's Water Authority car and was slamming the star picket fence post across the bonnet of Glenys Dingle's Ford Territory. Cyril threw himself at Glenys's car, but Mrs Maloney was undeterred, and he suffered a split philtrum and several broken yellowed crowns.

Mrs Maloney yelled, 'The bank under my cow has washed away – get her out!' She swung the star picket into the headlights of Stacey's car as Glenys put her drink down and searched for her phone to take pictures – evidence in the court case.

'They won't put me in jail,' Mrs Maloney called. 'I'm too old. But you're not.' She raised the metal fence post again.

From the deck, Pam watched Bennett and Cyril run towards the river, Megan following with their shoes. Mrs Maloney finished off the cars and turned on Bennett's double-glazed front windows.

21.
COLLATERAL DAMAGE

By the time Glenys could face the sun, it was high, yellow-white and blazing. She stood behind her mirrored glass windows, her one-hundred-percent Egyptian cotton dressing-gown tied tight to contain her struggling waist, and her serum-enhanced eyelashes bending against the binocular lenses trained on the water flowing into her lake. Beside her on the glass-topped dining table, two soluble Panadeine and a Berocca gently fizzed in a glass of soda water. She noted the water level in the lake and looked at her wrist to check the time and date then remembered she used her phone for such things these days, so set off to see where she'd left her bag after the joint SWS/SWA meeting at the Mocketts' fabulously intelligent, sustainably green, low-impact, high-performance, carbon-neutral, climate- and eco-friendly home with efficient air flow and light access. Then she remembered Mrs Maloney's cow, and closed her eyes for a moment. SWA would give her a new car. She would tell the board it was the fault of the drunken task force.

Glenys upended her bag onto the kitchen table but found no phone. The stove clock wasn't yet working and she didn't have a television, so she searched for her watch, strapped it to her wrist and prepared to drive all the way back to that wretched town with those barbaric, provincial people. A memory of Mrs Maloney slamming the star picket fence post across her Ford Territory thumped against the inside of her head, and she knew she couldn't possibly be seen driving a car like that in broad daylight. She reached for her phone, but she didn't have her phone. A tear escaped from her blood-shot eye and she suspected it might ruin her eyelashes so she went back to bed to lie on her back until she felt better.

o0o

Isobel was at a furious six kilometres on her treadmill, four hundred calories burned and her head filled with acid thoughts of celebrating Christmas without her ancient aunt or dear father, and Border Leicesters contaminating her breeding line, and bloody Mandy. A conspiracy of ravens swooped down and settled on the fence at the yards to stare boldly at her prize Merinos. She hopped off the treadmill, letting it run, imagining the murderers wouldn't notice she'd left the apparatus, and went to the office. She unlocked the gun safe, loaded the rifle and sneaked to the side verandah. From behind the purple bougainvillea, she raised the rifle butt to snuggle into her shoulder. Isobel closed one eye, trained the crosshairs onto the fattest of the sleek, black vermin. It turned and looked at the bougainvillea, crouched as if to fly away, and she pulled the trigger. Digby sat up in bed.

It was when he was squeezing his morning orange that he saw, beyond his lovely wife on the treadmill, a dead bird nailed to the fence at the yards. The rifle rested on the verandah.

'Bel, you shot a raven?' They were the hardest things in Australia to shoot.

'They're corpse-eating scavengers and murderers of the inno-cent. They're cruel, selfish and entirely unnecessary to anyone.

Vermin. I will get rid of every one of them.' She stopped the treadmill and started crying.

Digby went to her. 'This is no good, Bel, old thing. I can't have you upset.'

'Mitchell will lose the farm.'

He handed her his breakfast napkin. 'But Philippa will still get the sheep.'

'Oh, bugger the fucking sheep. Why can't she have a whole farm? Rory will get one.' She blew her nose. 'And I don't know what to do about Christmas. It's a mess, Opal hates me.'

'Let's take Christmas off this year. We always host and everyone always eats and drinks everything in the house.'

'Mitch brings beer. And peanuts.'

'And Cal gives speeches and cleans his spectacles with a crusty hanky.'

'Careful, that's my old dad.'

'Let's all go to the pub. I'll book it for everyone.'

'Neralie will be there.'

'Good. I hope she spills the burning bombe Alaska all over Mandy.'

'We can't,' she said. 'We're trying to appease, not incite murder.'

'Depends who gets murdered.'

Later, when her nose was very red and she'd filled a bin with damp tissues, Isobel stood forlornly at the kitchen window watching her lovely Merinos grazing contentedly in the paddock as a family. They would live to their full potential before a humane end saw them consumed for the greater good. It was their right. 'You want a fight, Bicycle Mandy, you've got one.'

She phoned her aunt, who picked up the phone and said, 'I know it's you, Isobel, and the answer is no, definitely not. I will not attend Christmas lunch. I won't travel to Girri Girri this year and there's nothing you can say or do that will make me change my mind.'

'We've decided we'll all go to the pub for Christmas lunch.'

'Oh, excellent, I'll catch the bus.'

oOo

Stacey parked his bike, removed his aerodynamic sunglasses and unzipped his riding suit. He checked his activity tracker as he moved towards the swimming hole, then remembered the swimming hole was gone, consumed by the river. He set off on his bike again.

When he got to the shop, the newsagent was reading the paper. She smiled at him. 'I see you've got a tender in to reinstall the solar-powered meters that don't work?'

Stacey went pale. 'A tender in to reinstall the solar-powered meters that don't work?'

She handed him his newspaper. 'Page fifteen. I wonder who'll get that job?'

'We didn't put that in, we didn't advertise . . .'

He found his office crowded with a slightly odorous groups of irrigators, riparians, townies and ferals. They each had a Certified Accreditation certificate and were busy filling out application forms to reinstall the faulty solar-powered meters out along the creek at the Jeongs'. Cyril opened his mouth to say something. There was a gap where his front teeth once were, and the crusted blood in his nostrils cracked, oozing fresh blood over his swollen top lip.

Stacey said, 'Well, at least the golf course and the tennis courts are green.'

They asked when the levee across the swimming hole – or the place where the swimming hole used to be – would be rebuilt.

'It was due for renovation anyway,' Stacey said.

Mitch handed him two pieces of paper. 'This piece of paper says you are qualified to certify meters, the instructions are on the back, just fill in your name . . . and the second certificate says that all your meters are certified. Again, you have to fill in your own name. The Water Authority will pay you for the installation, and Cyril will supply the meters and pumps from his back shed. Oh, and the tender application is on page fifteen of the newspaper you've got there. Give it to me when you finish and I'll post them off to the Water Authority . . . unless the tender's been won?'

Stacey was in strife, for sure, and he might just need a new job.

Cyril managed to say, 'The tender's been awarded.'

'Oh, really? Who to?'

'Experienced workers,' Stacey said.

'You mean the ferals? They work for C. & P. Water, don't they, Cyril? You've given the tender to *yourself*?'

'Gosh,' Kev said. 'Weren't they the ones who stuffed them up in the first place?'

The office filled with 'Oh my goodness' and 'That's not very smart' and 'I wonder if they'll get a raise' and Sam started asking Cyril really curly questions about the new pumps and meters and their maintenance needs, the high-end weather parts and durability in pH or salinity ranges, if the meter could read muddy water accurately, if the coils in the sensor were resin-lined to stop rust (or had he messed that up too?), but most importantly, would the meters be properly installed this time? Cyril nodded, dabbing his raw, shredded face with a bloody hanky.

When the mob finally dribbled out of the office, Bennett

came out of hiding. 'They sound scarier than they are,' he said, and fled.

oOo

Pam Horrick was bootscooting in her shed, so Cyril left her with her music and used the calculator on his phone to confirm his figures again. If he could just sell another dozen pumps he'd break even and his wife could stomp, slide and clap all the way from one end of the shed to the other without boxes to obstruct her. He'd get a pretty bloody good boost to the little retirement nest egg and a nice website spruiking him as a 'consultant'. Bennett Mockett would hire him. He looked to the sky – 'Please, God?' – and was disappointed to see foliage regeneration in the sparse canopy of the kurrajongs. If bloody flowers were bursting across the land the irrigators would get all hopeful and hold off selling water to see how the recent rain would affect quotas. His phone rang. It was Glenys Dingle.

'Top of the morning to you, Glenys,' he tried to say, using his best Irish accent. Blood oozed again from his lips and into his mouth.

'You're not at the top of anything. You're deep at the bottom of a shit pit. Be in my office this afternoon with a full explanation for everything, alright?'

Blood dribbled onto his tie.

oOo

Jasey was scanning Mandy's cake mix and dried fruits when she decided to chuck iron filings into the enemy engine that was Mandy. 'So, off to the pub for Christmas?'

'No, it's at my place this year.'

Jasey leaned over the counter and looked at the floor beside

263

Mandy's feet. 'Didn't bring your own bag? Have one of ours for twenty cents.'

'I'm cooking a traditional Christmas lunch for my husband and extended family, and I have my own bag.' Mandy handed Jasey a used plastic bag from the Riverglen supermarket.

Jasey ignored the bag. 'Isobel told me she'd booked a table at the pub. It's going to be a good day. I'm looking forward to it.'

'We won't bother – it'll be too hot for Callum.'

'I see,' Jasey said, making it clear that she understood exactly. 'If you bring your own bag you have to pack your own groceries. That'll be twenty-six dollars fifty.'

It was humiliating. They had not told her about Neralie (even though she knew) and now everyone knew she'd been excluded from the Bishop–Prestwich Christmas celebration. For five years she'd wanted people to see that she was part of that family, *in* it, attending nice gatherings with her *husband*. She'd have loved to post photos on social media, everyone in paper hats over a feast, champagne and smiles. All she ever got to do was ride out to the cemetery and stand by the heap of gravel that was her grandmother's grave and shout, 'Guess who I married?'

Her phone beeped. She didn't recognise the number. The text message read: *Have booked table at pub for all for Christmas lunch. Expect to see you about 12.30. Digby Prestwich. Ho ho ho.*

'Well,' she said triumphantly, 'seems we're having Christmas together after all, the whole family.'

'Me and you and everybody and the McIntosh family,' said Jasey.

Mandy fought an urge to punch Jasey's round, lipless face.

22.

DATE NUMBER TWO

The next day, the regulars watched Neralie, Jasey and Lana rub away at scratchie tickets, the small table rocking and the sound of scratching filling the pub silence. They let their coins drop, one by one, and looked sullenly at the small mound of discarded tickets in front of them.

'Nothing?'

'Nothing.'

'Nothing.'

The regulars moved their focus back to the silent TV.

'Wait – three two thousands, I got!'

The regulars drained their beers in anticipation as Jasey grabbed Lana's tickets and studied the numbers. 'No, you didn't, you got two two thousands and one twenty thousand.'

'Oh.'

The girls swapped piles and checked each other's tickets again anyway.

oOo

Upstairs, Stacey watched his reflection in the wardrobe mirror as he completed another fifty bent-over rows with cumulative eight-kilogram weights on his barbell. Then he attached his ankle weights and did some pull-ups using a bar fitted across his doorway. He finished off his session with some flexing in front of the mirror before taking a quick shower and getting himself spruced up for the afternoon. He found he was ready far too early so sat down and tried not to think of the meters or the water mess he was hoping would evaporate.

Lana was a Holden girl, he was a Ford man, specifically a 290 HP 3.5-litre V6, red or possibly midnight blue, though dark colours showed the dirt . . . What he really wanted was a Mustang, and Lana sitting next to him with her big blue eyes and her fine legs. But if he showed up with an imported car when people were already suspicious, and if Lana found out . . . He took one last look at himself, checked the condom was in his back pocket and that his hair was brushed over his temples so as to conceal the fact that it was receding, then bounded down the stairs into the quiet bar. At the bottom, he met Neralie. She looked trim and compact in short slacks, a light sweater and strappy sandals. He found her appealing, though she didn't really wear make-up or do girly things with her hair or anything.

She handed him the picnic basket. 'On a day like this you gotta love a picnic, eh?'

'Sure do,' he said, and continued on his happy way.

He collected Lana from the bar, waited while goodbyes were said to Jasey, then took her hand. 'You look pretty. You should wear a dress more often.'

Neralie trailed after them, but he only became concerned when the barmaid opened the back door of the car, settled into the back seat, buckled up and said, 'I think the east side of the lake will be best. We'll get the setting sun.'

'Best for what?'

'Our picnic. We're off to Riverglen, aren't we? Just chuck a U-ey, there's no cars coming.'

'You're coming too?'

'Is there a reason you haven't paid your rent this month, Mr Masterson, or is it because you forgot? You can pay Elsie when you give her ninety dollars for the hamper.'

'Ninety bucks?'

'Bergens' sauerkraut and German tube steak, prosciutto, quinoa salad, crusty bread, cheese and olives and apple strudel with fresh cream – everything we need for a quality day out. I'm looking forward to a day off, actually.'

'Me too,' said Lana. She reached over to pat Stacey's thigh like a mother reassuring a kid about to have a flu shot.

'You a brut man when it comes to champagne or will you be sticking to the beer?' Then Neralie slapped her forehead with her palm. 'What am I saying? You're *driving*, you can't have anything.'

In Stacey's mind, the images of naked Lana on the new carpet in the vacant resort apartments at Lake Riverglen pixelated and vanished, and he wondered if the newsagent was an easier prospect after all. Then Lana smiled at him. 'He can have a glass or two.'

As they drove away from the town, the locals dribbled into the bar and gathered together – as one – to plan events and procedures for the night of the cull.

oOo

They ate sitting on a rug on the brand-new bank and looked at the low tide along the dried clay sides of the reservoir. The bottom of the lake was barely covered, but it was alive with creatures, and even the gum seedlings waiting hopefully on the nude shoreline looked perky.

Stacey pointed to the galahs, cockatoos, corellas, white ibis, magpies, crested pigeons and even a seagull, all circling, paddling and squawking. 'Wildlife,' he said.

'Invasive wildlife.'

'It's a start.'

'Jasey would say it's only successful once the ducks arrive.'

'And herons, water hens . . . other animals.'

'Toucans and shoebills?'

'And turtles, platypuses,' he said earnestly.

The barmaid stood and walked away, shaking her head, but he didn't care what she thought; he was pissed off. What was the point of trying to do the right thing, show women a good time, spend money on them, if they undermined the purpose? He twisted the lid off the ice-cold Crownie and lay back on the rug next to Lana while Neralie squatted on the shore with her glass of champers. Lana leaned down and kissed him. 'Next date, just us.' His heart lifted, his faith in humanity flickered, and then his phone rang. Lana thought the noise on the phone sounded like a far-off panicked cockatoo. As he listened, his smile dropped, and then he hung up and stared at the bare concrete apartments for a while. 'Gotta go, girls. Sorry.'

He drove as slowly as he could to the Riverglen Water Authority offices.

oOo

Glenys Dingle stood at the marble handbasin in the sparkling, private, corporate bathroom re-reading another letter from Mitchell Bishop. This letter boasted a couple of dozen signatures in support of his arguments. She dabbed at her teary eyes and applied a new layer of creamy powder to her cheeks and walked through the deserted office building calmly, her bottom unmoving in the control panties beneath her casual weekend slacks. As she passed the men waiting in the foyer, she beckoned them to follow. In her bright office she sat at her desk and narrowed her eyes at the two men settling into their chairs. A pile of printed emails and letters from locals sat between them, about solar meters that didn't work and water that flowed through decommissioned channels at night and black market water for $150 a megalitre.

Cyril thought she might enquire as to his recovery, his facial fractures, but she just said, 'Well?'

He felt in his pockets for something and Stacey turned in his chair to watch.

'Let me be specific,' Glenys said. 'There is a situation with the supply channel, which I understand is the responsibility of Miss Esther Shugg and Messrs Callum and Mitchell Bishop, so why am I getting garrulous emails and phone calls from people I've never heard of but who appear to be quite closely associated with you two and that particular channel? Why can't you appease these people, find solutions, keep them thinking they're happy? Make them *fit the plan*.'

'You see, Glenys –'

'I have spoken to you about this vicious task force, have I not?'

'We've retained the channel so we can divert water to the lake at Riverglen – *your* lake. We can make a lot of money by maintaining that one channel. We can use it to store water, use it as an overflow, and we can show any "inquisitive people"' – he pointed at the ceiling – 'where water is if they question the figures.'

She pointed to the ceiling. 'The "inquisitive people" you refer to, Mr Horrick, otherwise known as directors, chief executive officers, and the minister, have all received the same communication I have, and those letters assert quite clearly that you want to charge Mr Bishop to maintain a decommissioned channel for *your* water management arrangements.'

'As you say, it's just a matter of a failed negotiation – for *our* purposes, I stress. We'll sort it out.'

'Why were the solar meters along the river not earthed, Mr Horrick?'

'Faulty earth rings. A technical glitch, all quite fixable. The tender to reinstall them's already filled.'

'A private company,' Stacey said, and Cyril added hastily that they'd used them before. 'So there's no need for you to worry.'

Her fingers drummed on the glass-topped desk, the aquamarines glittering. 'I don't respond well when people patronise me, Mr Horrick. Nor do I respond well to disgruntled irrigators when they're disgruntled because someone I'm responsible for has failed, when you put us all at risk of *undue scrutiny*. You will make sure we are not the subject of harassment again, as I imagine you two don't want to find yourselves jobless at this point of your careers.'

But Stacey had thought this through; he was prepared for Glenys Gravedigger Dingle. He was not going to sit there and lose his future – he'd made a choice: he would stand and fight. 'Neither do you.'

Glenys Dingle turned her heavily made-up face to Stacey and blinked. 'I beg your pardon?'

'You don't want to find yourself jobless either.'

Cyril spoke a little too loudly. 'What young Stacey means is he doesn't want you to find yourself jobless because of *us*.'

'No,' Stacey said. 'She's criticising us for doing what she wants us to do and she's meant to be representing the people. She's meant to be looking after *their* interests, not her own.'

Glenys remained speechless no longer. 'How dare you!'

'If we lose our jobs then we're free agents – I can say what I bloody like.' How proud Lana would be when he described how he'd called the corruptor's bluff. Then his guts churned with Bergens' sauerkraut and German tube steak and he desperately needed to fart.

Glenys's fury broke free. 'I am the person here with the power,' she said, her voice high and thin. 'I have summoned you here on a Saturday for obvious reasons, but I can, at any time, choose to *expose* mismanagement or corruption simply by ordering an audit of you two.' She stood up. 'You men are so full of shit.'

Stacey felt the pressure of his large intestine and shifted in his chair. Cyril was paralysed. His face ached and his nose was clogged with dried blood and shredded cartilage.

Glenys screeched, 'I've had a phone call from the chair of the Australian Competition and Consumer Commission. He accused me of sending half of the riverfront properties and their thirsty livestock out to sea, so I now look incompetent, callous and careless, and next I'll have the fucking greenies and PETA outside, chucking drowned fish at me. I've had to stop releasing water! Now go and meet your targets! Release water but do it using less water. And appease that bloody task force or I'll see you all charged with theft, corruption, embezzlement and environmental vandalism and anything else I can find in your shed, Mr Horrick.'

They felt her eyes on them, like needles in their necks, as they stood and went to the door.

Cyril turned and said, 'But we did manage to put some water in the lake.'

'It's almost Christmas, Mr Horrick, and I don't see enough water for paying customers to float a matchbox yacht let alone paddle, swim or waterski.'

oOo

It was Nurse Leonie Bergen, returning from a visit to Mary-Lou Jeong and her brand-new baby, who alerted Mitch to the donkeys. 'I see you've got them closer to the road, all ready for their Christmas visit.'

He'd entirely forgotten the nativity scene for the oldies.

Then Nurse Leonie said carefully, 'They've been in the same spot since yesterday, possibly the day before.'

'I'll get them ready,' he said. 'Give them a bit of a brush-up and polish their hoofs.' He went straight to them, taking lucerne hay and oats. The hay and water he'd left for them days ago had been nibbled, but the donkeys were still under the same stand of shade trees. Unease entered his unhappy heart; something was wrong. Cleopatra turned to watch him drive up and her guts pumped out a violent heehaw, her head tossing and her teeth biting at the air. The dog barked and, as the ute slowed, she jumped, landed badly and recovered, stood and barked again, but by then Mitch knew something worse than anything else was about to unfold. Mark stood by the dilapidated fence with strands of rusted wire puddling around his fetlocks. Cleo watched, her nose near her brother's nose. Mitch heard the drone of swarming flies and caught a whiff of rotting flesh. In front of Mark the dry grass was nibbled to the ground in a wide arc as far as his mouth would reach and behind him was a compact pile of manure. He tried to step away but the wires hanging from the rotted fence post jangled and caught and his head jerked up in pain. Mitch spoke calmly to Cleo, gave her hay and stroked her neck. He wished he had an apple. The dog sat respectfully at a distance, her ears down and her two grey-flecked eyebrows close. Mitch extended lucerne to Mark, but the gelding was passive, defeated. He ran his hand down the donkey's flanks and over his rump and gently down his back leg to the hock. Mark stamped and squealed and Cleo honked, and Mitch said, 'I'm sorry.' The wire was pulled tight and cut deep into Mark's flesh, biting to the fetlock bone and exposing the cannon bone. Busy fat green flies worked in bunches along the lacerations. Mark swished his tail once, feebly, but the flies remained.

'I'm sorry,' Mitch said. 'So sorry.' Tears came and he saw himself as Mandy saw him: stupid, careless and weak. He had been distracted and now it was too late. 'You'll have a limp after this,' he said. 'And you can live in the house yard, alright? Eat all the apples and peaches.'

He went back to the ute and found the wire cutters, emptied his water flask into his hat and walked back slowly, Cleo watching his every move. He held the water under Mark's nose but the donkey just sniffed and turned his big head away. Mitch put the hat in front of Cleo then got down on his knees and cut the wire. But when he said, 'Walk on,' Mark stayed. Mitch turned to Cleopatra – 'Walk on' – and she looked at her brother then took two steps, so Mark took a step, limping, his head shooting up in pain. He lowered his head to fresh new lucerne sprouts, ripped a few sprigs from the bale and let them spill from his big floppy mouth. He looked at Cleo and took another step, then he swayed, righted himself, but buckled sideways and crumpled like a dropped sack, the wind leaving his lungs like air from a blacksmith's bellows and the light in his eyes dull.

Mitch called and called, patted him roughly, and finally sat with the great furry mound, weeping, apologising to Cleo. Then he phoned Isobel and told her that her donkey was dead.

'He was old,' Isobel said. 'Thank you for telling me,' and the phone went silent against his ear and he knew he had failed his sister, failed in his responsibilities to everyone: the donkeys, Neralie, Callum, even Mandy.

oOo

At Girri Girri, Digby found his wife in bed in the middle of the afternoon, crying again. 'What now?'

'Mark.'

'She's hurt the donkey?'

'No. He just died.' She wailed, 'I loved him,' and Digby said, 'I know,' and thought about Ralph, his long-dead lorikeet.

But Isobel hated herself. She'd made Mitch take money from the farm to pay her out when their mother died. 'You're entitled to it,' Mitch had said. But she didn't earn it, and she could have had his fences fixed. There were plenty of fine Merino sheep in the world, why did anyone need more sheep? Good farmers have good fences, but fences cost money, and there was no money in a drought, just dilapidated properties with aged, costly infrastructure, and how could Mitch reap anything when everything was broken? Of course he was going to lose the farm!

Digby patted his dear and lovely sobbing wife.

oOo

At Bishops Corner, Mitch put some baked beans in the microwave, and as he leaned and waited for the ping, he felt a warm

274

glow coming from the AGA stove. He opened the grate door and saw that someone had been burning documents.

Mandy said, 'Told you I'd fire up the AGA for Christmas.'

He didn't want to think about what she'd burned; he just served Callum baked beans and toast and said nothing. Neither he nor Callum was hungry, so they stared desolately at the TV. Mandy ate her dinner and left the kitchen without turning off the light, so small black insects arrived and got stuck in the beans in the saucepan.

23.

THE CAPITALIST SYSTEM DESTROYS

Tinka sniffed her breakfast and looked at Mitch. *Beans?* She ate, then joined her forlorn friend in the machinery shed, watching quietly, perusing the landscape and catching the odd passing fly while Mitch attached the grader blade to the tractor. As the loud tractor approached, Cleo did not move. She remained standing with her dead brother, Tink next to her as Mitch graded a great hole. When he placed the grader at Mark's back. Cleo sniffed him, then, ears pricked forward, watched as he gently pushed the poor lovely beast into the hole. Then Mark gradually vanished beneath waves of moist brown dirt.

Tink and Mitch left Cleo standing vigil at her brother's grave, and Mitch spent a terrible day mending fences in the loud sunshine with only the sound of tears running down his nose and dripping into the dirt.

Mid-afternoon, Cleo started crying. At first she was just squeaking, like a rusted axle, but she worked up to terrible squawks, long, loud and angry, sounds that scraped over the green shoots and dry grass, her heehaws stricken and grief-laced, her ribs blowing in and out, and her guts jumping inside her hide. Mitch gave her carrots and apples, wheat, oats and water, but she cried through lunch.

Cal said, 'You'll have to phone the vet.'

'He can't do anything.' It would just be a waste of money.

Cal went to the laundry and looked up at the gun safe, then limped back to his rocker and blew his nose, wiped his tears away and said, 'Three reasons to kill: food, vermin and suffering.'

oOo

Stacey eased out his door and crept down the back stairs, but Elsie was waiting. She handed him an invoice and he looked at it briefly, said, 'You can't charge me that much for a picnic basket, Elsie.'

'You ordered it, I made it.' She put her hand out. 'And your boss never paid his quite substantial tab on opening night.'

Stacey put the company credit card in her palm then went to collect Cyril, but his wife said he was still at the vet with one of the spaniels. 'He has an injured paw,' Mrs Horrick said. 'Glenys Dingle stood on it.'

Stacey stepped back, opening his mouth to say he'd better get cracking, but Mrs Horrick said, 'Come in, Cyril won't be long.' She almost smiled.

Stacey looked at his watch, at his car, but Mrs Horrick yanked him inside, waving to the woman across the road watching from behind her rosebush.

'That business you two are running, those meters taking up all the room in my studio?' She was standing very close. 'The business is in my name, but I've never been told anything about it, have I?'

The hairy folds on Stacey's body started to get damp. 'You haven't?'

Mrs Horrick waved a letter at him. 'This is from the State Water Authority. Paul put it in my mailbox "by mistake". It says C. & P. Water Pty Ltd has won the tender to reinstall all the solar-powered water pumps and meters along the river.'

Cyril's car pulled into the drive.

'Oh, that . . . They stuffed up the meter installation, Mrs Horrick, really stuffed it up, it was a big problem, but we sorted it out.'

'I knew nothing about being a company director, because if I had known, I'd have told you it's illegal to win your own tender.'

Cyril arrived with the spaniel in his arms, waving the dog's shaved, recovered paw, *Hello*. Behind him on the street, a van pulled up, and then another: brightly coloured vehicles that needed a run through the car wash. The woman over the road moved to her nature strip.

'How much did the vet charge you?'

'More than I'd anticipated.' He kissed the dog's ear. 'All better, though.'

'Did he give her pain medication and physio?'

'Yes, dear.'

Pam snatched the dog and pointed over his shoulder. 'Who are they?'

Thin dusty men came across the lawn. The least washed of them, a creature with earlobes you could see through to the landscape behind, stood in Pam's petunias. 'We didn't get our pay.'

'Well, the meters weren't installed properly,' Cyril explained.

'Because you didn't give us adequate or correct instructions.' The dusty man waved his long, grubby finger at Cyril. 'We are not surprised, man, nor are we disappointed. You use water for the accumulation of wealth, and that generates corruption for power. You use the *most important* thing that supports life to exploit people. Like Queequeg, we *cast the runes* and the *runes*, man, they've come back in the shape of the destructive capitalist system.'

The bloke behind, who had a third eye, said, 'Your system unfairly concentrates power, wealth and profit among that small segment of society that controls capital and it also gets its wealth through exploitation and maintains it through corruption. And politics.'

Earlobe man poked Cyril in the chest. 'And no one's going to leave a casket for you to float on when the destructive capitalist system comes back for you, and that's as sure as whales are big, man,' and, like krill from a whale, they scattered to their wheeled hovels.

He didn't fully understand what the hippies had said about 'ruins', but Stacey was more unsettled than he'd ever been and he knew for sure he was part of something with far more reach than he'd realised. He had not dedicated enough thought to this topic, it was clear, but instinct told him he no longer wanted to trade water.

Cyril said, 'Jesus, what a scruffy-looking lot. They'd better stay home the night of the cull,' and Pam sprayed antiseptic air freshener all around the porch and vestibule.

Then Cyril put his hand on his crestfallen accomplice's shoulder. 'Not a problem, young Stacey, not a problem at all.'

Stacey felt grubby. He needed to change his shirt and brush his teeth. Suddenly he longed for his corner at the Bong and Lana with the lovely smile.

Pam picked up the puppies and told Cyril he'd have to get his own dinner.

o0o

Mitch went to the laundry and retrieved the gun from the safe. He grabbed his swag and half-a-dozen beers and headed back to Cleopatra. She was folded on her legs with her nose in the dust, singing a low and guttural song of grief. Her furry body was juddering with anguish, so Mitch sat with her, and she was quiet. He opened a beer and sighed, but then her long, cruel heehaws recommenced, flooding the air with anguish, barbed wire in his soul, and the farm dogs started yelping and bouncing about on their chains. Nearby, sheep huddled together behind logs in the furthest corner. At times the noise died to a long, eerie keening and the air over the paddocks was quiet, but then Cleo regathered herself and resumed her loud squealing and honking. By nightfall Mitch was irritable and exhausted and could only imagine how the Jeongs were coping, but he rolled out his swag and stretched out next to his grieving donkey and closed his eyes.

24.

CHRISTMAS EVE

Christmas Eve arrived bright, and sunrise told Mitch it would be hot. Tink was sitting on top of the hill, alert to the world, fire-edged by the rising sun, and beside him Cleo slumped against the hill where her dead brother rested, whimpering. 'Cleo,' Mitch said, 'sleeping with you is like sleeping with a church organ on Sunday.' He patted her white belly, rude to the world, rubbed her furry cheek and tickled her nostrils, blowing small bare patches into the dirt. She closed her eyes.

He tried to get his jenny to stand. She would not move. She just cried for her brother like she was being sliced in half. The farm dogs responded with long bandsaw howls that made the hairs on Mitch's arms stand up.

'You are an exceptional donkey, you were good at your job, loyal and idiosyncratic, and I have always loved you and I always, always will.' He loaded the gun, nestled the butt against his clavicle, closed one eye and steadied the crosshairs on the whorl, like the crown on a baby's downy head, just above the beloved eyes of his jenny. Mitch's donkey ceased whimpering, sat up on her haunches and her ears rose to right angles. She looked directly at her human friend and he imagined she saw from the long, convex pupil of her round, wet eye a gun barrel, huge, hollow and black, and at the far end of it a small person, all elbows, shaking and bawling, like herself, with grief. He decided she might just come good. He lowered the gun and reached for a can of beer.

oOo

The text from Mitch said: *I need to see you.*

As she left the bar, Neralie yelled, 'LEVON!'

Upstairs, she applied lipstick and pulled the brush through her hair, then rubbed most of the lipstick off. She grabbed a handful of tissues as she stepped into her sandals. At the door she caught a glimpse of her reflection and decided to change, then remembered it was all about Mitch and his donkeys, and left.

oOo

Mandy's attention was captured by the sound of a throaty engine travelling too quickly, then suddenly braking. A black 2010 Audi RS Coupe did a quick U-turn and swung into the kerb at the Bong. A well-groomed chap in a pair of dark skinny-legged pants and a long-sleeved black shirt got out and stretched. He pointed his keys at the car and a loud *boink* slapped up and down the street. Definitely a city person. He vanished into the pub.

Over the road, Jasey was watching the smooth black-clad visitor too, her phone at her ear, and opposite, Kevin was standing between his bowsers, scrutinising the Audi.

Three barflies sat benignly at the counter looking at the blow-in. One smiled at the stranger, his teeth tiny and low in his gums. 'Get you a beer?'

While the stranger sized up the beer taps, the smart decor

282

and the pool table, a derelict bloke went behind the bar, poured a cold glass of amber liquid and put it in front of Beau. 'How was your trip?'

He sipped his beer. 'Long.'

'You wouldn't be here if you only took a short trip.'

Another barfly asked how things were in Sydney.

Beau looked around to see if there was someone normal. Then a short square woman in activewear entered the bar. She didn't seem to think it odd that no one was there to serve; she just sat on a stool and smiled at him. 'You from Sydney?'

He frowned, put his beer on the counter and looked to the nearest exit. The barfly poured the woman a very big glass of red wine.

'You won't get anyone to service that car of yours around here.'

'Right.'

'She'll be down soon,' the barfly said, and pointed to a door that led to a stairwell and the kitchen.

'Has to be,' the other one said. 'What goes up . . .'

And the other one said, '. . . must come down,' and then she was standing there in the doorway by the stairs, holding a basket spilling over with lettuce, carrots and apples. She was the only girlfriend he'd ever had who wore shorts, and her lips were painted red. 'Babe,' he said. 'Happy Christmas!'

The barflies cried, 'Sur-prise!'

Neralie said, 'I'm on my way out, actually.'

Beau sculled his beer and looked up. 'Let's go.'

But Neralie said, 'It's not something you'd enjoy. You see . . . there's been a death.'

Beau looked at the basket of produce, put his keys back down on the bar. 'I'll wait here.'

The short square woman said, 'She's off to see her boyfriend, who is actually my husband.'

Neralie walked towards the woman in activewear and pointed a finger in her face. 'I am off to support an old friend who is upset!'

The squat woman said, 'I wouldn't bother with apples for Cleopatra, I'd just shoot her if I was you.'

Beau put his beer down. 'Steady . . .'

'If anyone deserves shooting it's you.' Neralie turned to Beau. 'We've got water restrictions here. You can't take long showers.'

Beau watched her run to the ute and the woman said, 'I'm Mandy Bishop, and you are?'

Jasey and Lana burst through the pub door and began talking loudly and cheerfully to Beau, and then Levon arrived to pour drinks and they laughed about that time at the Spanish restaurant in Sydney when Jasey had complained that her soup was cold, but the wine was hot! And Mandy was left sitting at the bar, looking at the back of Beau's creased shirt.

oOo

The twelve-kilometre drive along the supply channel road through the dull flat landscape to Mitch took longer than it ever had. Neralie felt the pity of everything and wondered why it was so hard, so sad, when it should have been a straightforward thing to settle down and lead an uncomplicated life with Mitch and familiar people who cared about her pub.

He was sitting on the ground with Cleopatra, and neither of them looked up at her as she approached. Beside them a drum was full to the brim with fresh water; the hay, lucerne and oats were fresh too, but the carrots were limp and soft.

Ants devoured the apples. Neralie held out a fresh apple but Cleo kept her big brown eyes on the dirt at the end of her furry nose.

Mitch stroked her ears. 'I just don't know what to do.'

'Yes, you do, you just don't want to do it.'

'But what if she comes good? Do you think I should get another donkey to keep her company?'

'What would you do if they gave you someone to replace Isobel?' Neralie sat down on the ground in front of Cleopatra and stroked the donkey's thick fringe, and ran her fingers across the warm, moist muzzle. She offered Cleo the apple again. 'Please, it'll make you feel better.' Cleo moved her nose away and her long eyelashes closed over her eyes.

'I can't do it,' he said. 'It'd be like shooting Cal.'

'Mitch, she's pining, she's not eating or drinking, it'll kill her, you know that.'

He did know; there was only a slim chance she'd forget her brother, her twin.

'She's suffering.' Neralie picked up the gun, checked the chamber, wiping away tears.

Mitch got to his feet, 'You don't have to . . .' But she aimed, called, 'I'm sorry!' The shot whacked over the soft green paddock and Cleopatra settled sideways with a moan and was still. Neralie put the gun down, dropped to her knees and stroked Cleo's perfect chamois eyelids and long, straight lashes, and the blades of grass around them shifted and flickered as insects scurried away.

o0o

In his room, Callum, octogenarian, was roused from his doze by the sound of a gunshot. Then the dogs yowling and then dead silence. 'Now boast thee, death, in thy possession lies a lass unparallel'd,' he said, and as the air and the house eased in the calm, Callum felt the nosy hand of old age take hold of his left arm and squeeze. The blood vessels winced and the dull ache thickened and travelled to sit on his chest like an anvil. He arranged himself in case he didn't wake again and tried to think of what he hadn't said that he should have. Then his thoughts went to his wife, the lass he married and had lived with for all those years in partnership and love, working away at mutual happiness and succeeding, largely. He thought of his little girl, now a strong, capable and lovely person despite, or perhaps because of, her dill of a husband, and he wished his son had found what he'd had, wished his son was happy, wished that he'd bought more land when given the chance, but he'd been preoccupied with his wife's illness. 'Nonetheless,' he said, 'you failed in that regard . . . and now see what's happened.'

oOo

Mandy Bishop left the bar and headed to her newsagency. Neralie McIntosh had no right to come back here when she had a perfectly good boyfriend in Sydney. That was two-timing. How dare she? They all did it – Kev and Jasey and Lana – yet they called *her* Bicycle Mandy! And he – the beau – was unfriendly. All she did was tell the truth. And then those bitches turned up, as usual, to ruin everything. Mandy turned and walked back to the pub, marched through the bar and straight up the stairs.

In room nine, Stacey was resting on his Bodybuild Olympic Utility Bench, sweating, trying to catch his breath, pondering Christmas with his parents, his siblings and all their screaming shit machines, and regretting the fact that he never got to root Lana. Why hadn't she shown up at his room by now, just marched in, dropping her dress as she came towards him and flinging her G-string aside . . . Then the door opened and Mandy was standing there, her running shoes dangling from her hand. 'Not going home for Chrissy?'

'Heading home shortly, just got a few things to fix up.'

She dropped her shoes. 'I could do with a bit of fixing up.'

'No, look, I've got one more date with Lana –'

'Lana's not going to root you, you're a thieving water trader, everyone knows that. If she slept with you she'd be betraying five hundred people. Besides, there's a new bloke in town. A Sydney bloke.'

'Really?'

'You're attractive, but you're not so attractive that she wants to lose her family *and* her friends.' She leaned down and lifted the elastic waistband of his exercise shorts, and he sighed . . .

Afterwards, Mandy and Stacey stayed glued together, Mandy straddling him on the utility bench and clutching a barbell on the upright rack system, and Stacey facing the truth. He was a water trader and thief and Lana definitely wouldn't sleep with him now. 'Happy Christmas,' Mandy gasped.

Stacey said, 'Christ, I needed that.'

'Me too . . . let's do it again.'

'I thought you had your husband under control?'

'I do.'

'Tell him to back off, tell him to stop sending letters and emails to Glenys and the directors and the minister, tell him I'll sort the upgrade for him, I'll get him funds to subsidise a sprinkler irrigator, just stop the harassment. I'll do it sooner than you think, but no one needs to know my part in it, alright? No one.'

She smiled, shifted a little on top of him.

'Tell him, won't you?'

'I might,' she said, grinding a little more.

Stacey thought about Glenys. *I'll see you all charged with theft, corruption, embezzlement and environmental vandalism and anything else I can find in your shed.* Bennett Mockett's career would be ruined as well. 'Just tell him he can have a new horizontal sprinkler system, fifty spans if he wants, as long as he keeps the channel. Otherwise a lot of people are going to get hurt.'

'His debts could ruin him any second, his crop failed and his best friends are dead or dying and he wants the barmaid . . . and her old boyfriend has just arrived in town. I'll let Mitch have the barmaid if he keeps the channel, and I'll be happy because you'll let him have Esther's water and he'll still have his own water so the farm'll be worth lots and lots more money and I'll take as much of it as I can get.' Then she smiled, and leaned down to him. 'I might even try to take some of his water if I can, sell it to you . . . and Glenys Dingle.'

'Jesus,' he said. 'You sure are something, aren't you?'

'Yeah.' She smiled. 'I'm sick of being nothing.' She moved on top of him again.

Much later, Mandy left Stacey snoring gently and stepped out of his room to find the pub a ghostly hollow of stairwells and rooms. Pockets of old air – pub food and stale beer – hovered. The bedroom doors were shut and the place was silent. She crept down the stairs and was drawn to the glow from the main bar. The fridges lit the room, making the bottles shine prettily. It was entirely without activity and its stark emptiness surprised her. She was walking quietly towards the back door when a burst from the cool-room fan startled her. She stepped into the dark and humming kitchen and the smell of garlic, the deep fryer and disinfectant. Small switches illuminated the edges and surfaces. The stove still radiated heat and large pots waited on the hob. Puddings hung in the corner. Christmas.

25

PEACE, HARMONY AND GOODWILL TO ALL

On the drive from her riverfront house to the Bong early on Christmas morning, Elsie noted the storm clouds swelling on the eastern horizon. Sharp sunrays pierced the dark clouds and faint flashes of lightning glittered. It was hot and oppressive. 'Cabalistic,' she said, remembering the clue for the crossword. 'Relating to or associated with mystical interpretation; occult; having secret or hidden meaning.' Only rain would break the muggy tension.

In her sparkling kitchen she turned the air conditioner on, then the radio, and tied a fresh apron around her waist. She fired up the gas ovens, filled the pots with water and put them on to simmer for the puddings. She washed her hands and gazed at her list as she dried them and went to the cool room to get the pork for salting. She found the spring-loaded catch resting on its latch, holding the door ajar. In the cool room the air was humid and thick with the odour of tepid meat and fermenting trifles. Small drops of condensation pooled in the plastic covering food and the walls and the doors were slimy. The oysters and prawns stank, the yabbies and the redfin were off, the pork was sweaty and the turkey sticky. The milk, stacked in sturdy crates, was still cool to her touch but the cream on the trifles smelled of ripe butter. Three obese drunken flies tilted at the dead light globe.

The screaming woke Neralie, and Neralie's screams in turn drew Elsie from her rank and contaminated kitchen. She found Neralie standing at the top of the staircase, watching a trickle of water spilling down the steps into the bar. The dining area was flooded. Levon emerged from his room clutching a sheet, took in the situation and stepped into the bathroom. A moment later he emerged with the bath plug in his dripping hand. Beau appeared, neat in his monogrammed kimono. He looked down at his wet feet and rubbed his eyes. Neralie was glaring at him, so Levon said, 'It wasn't him, Nelly.'

The water had escaped under the front door and trickled down into the cellar, which explained why there was no electricity. The whole pub was shorted out. Elsie phoned Darryl and within twenty minutes he and the electrician had the power reconnected and the fan in the cool room spinning and the bar fridges cooling the boutique beer and Christmas wines. The electrician, dressed as Santa, leaned on the counter drinking tea while around him Neralie, Levon and Darryl waited, stunned. Elsie peeled potatoes, tears dripping.

'This is going to stop, right?' Neralie said, and the men replied, 'It is.'

Santa put his cup on the sink and said, 'You'll get a full house today even if you serve fried fox,' then said he'd better get back to the kids before Mrs Santa got her claws out. Beau joined them and asked what time breakfast was served.

'Whenever you feel like serving yourself,' Elsie said, and pointed to a packet of muesli on the counter.

The lawn roller was fetched from the bowling club to squeeze out the dining room carpet, the cool room was emptied onto the ute and water pumped out of the cellar.

oOo

Jasey had the fox in the crosshairs of her scope when Lana's scream shattered the morning quiet, waking the owls and possums in their cosy hollows. Jasey ran the short distance to her friend's house, gun in hand, to find Lana standing next to her precious blue Commodore. Someone had used a key or nail to etch a giant penis and testicles on the bonnet. Jasey reached into her bra and brought out a tissue for Lana's tears and put her arms around her. Kevin ambled over from Jasey's, his red hair screaming in the bright morning, and said, 'Nothing that can't be fixed,' and bit into his Vegemite toast. Then Jasey's phone started ringing in her pocket and she answered with: 'What now?'

oOo

He calculated that the donkeys were twenty-three years old, given they stumbled backwards out of the float the Christmas he got a cowboy suit. He remembered unwrapping it. Isobel got a portable record player but she sulked because she had no records. Then the truck came with the float and two Shetland-sized foals with long fat ears appeared and shuffled about side by side, as if they were glued together.

He got out of bed and found his way to the kitchen and took his phone from the charger, flicked on the torch and made his way as quietly as he could to the sleep-out. The box was not there so he made his way into his old room, got onto his hands and knees to the hollow sound of Cal's snores.

The box was not there, so he went back to the sleep-out cupboard. It was gone. The only photos he had of the foals, the balsawood war planes and ships, his footy and cricket trophies, and photos of all his pets and Goldie's collar, his adored long-dead retriever. Mitch did his crying for it all on a wool bale in the shearing shed, Tink watching from the greasy floor.

The first grey rays took an age to taint the black horizon then showed a thick grey sky. The air felt humid. Tink was asleep. 'Happy Christmas, Tink.' She didn't move. He placed his hand on the soft curve of her furry ribs and she opened her small black eyes and lifted her head, her tongue protruding slightly. 'You're getting old, Tink. And deaf.' But she sat up, turned her ear to nothing Mitch could hear, and then thunder rumbled a long way off, like a pumpkin rolling across the kitchen floor.

Because he could not stay at home they drove to the ruined fence. Straining wire in a storm was stupid, Mitch knew, but he felt only desolation, and there were lambs to keep safe, and they were his only remaining pure breeding stock; they were his future. The eyrie atop the dry old pine remained abandoned and he wished he knew where the eagles were – if they really were dead or if they had just moved house. He finished the strand, tied a knot with the key and straightened, uncurling slowly to accommodate his stiff farmer's back. Above, the fat clouds curled westwards. He made loops on the end of the broken strand, folding the wire back on itself, and tidied the tag ends as best he could. Another round of thunder rumbled, swelled and thumped in the distance, and then a bolt of lightning struck the sparse dark scrub far away, like an image from a horror movie. He worked at a quicker pace now, threading wire through one loop and putting the two ends of broken wire in the strainer jaws. He worked the strainer lever, inching the ends closer together, then joined and tied another wire knot with fencing pliers and twisted the tag end, winding the sharp snipped wire around itself. Thunder cracked like a cannon shot, louder than anything earthly. The ground at his feet erupted and he jumped, catching his finger in the sharp tag end of the rusty knot. Dust swirled all around him and, somewhere, wood was burning and grass singeing, and a sound like a tall building collapsing tore through the electric air.

He was on the ground, his head buried in his arms, his thoughts a jumble of Tink, his sheep, Callum and Neralie, and he looked up just in time to see the mighty pine lean, crack and smash to the earth. The steaming branches bounced and shuddered, smoke and dust ballooned, and almost immediately rain started falling, as if from a hose. His hand ached. The fence wire had ripped the soft flesh at the side of his index finger, catching the nail and ripping through it. He held up his wounded hand and swore, scowling at the giant old pine smouldering in a thousand steaming pieces on the ground around him. Rain ran from his back into his shorts and down his legs. He dropped his tools and went to the pine.

The eagles' nest was strewn across the wet mud near the head of the tree: sticks and branches, feathers and chick fluff, and bones of all shapes and sizes, stripped of lamb, possum, fish, snake, bird and rabbit flesh. He glimpsed a couple of cat collars, which was fair enough, and then his eye lit on a collar with a name tag that said 'Spot'. Poor Morton. But Mitch saw nothing in the debris to suggest a recent kill. Mr and Mrs Eagle must have died shortly after devouring Morton Campinnini's obese Chihuahua, or maybe they'd eaten a rabbit that had ingested the 1080 poison the department had dropped at Esther's.

He walked slowly to the ute, eyes to the teeming sky where the majestic raptors he'd known so long had once reigned. And his finger was hurting like nothing else. He scooped up his trembling, terrified dog and put her in the cab out of the storm. She snuggled beside him, her nose forced into the small gap between the seat and his back.

oOo

'I thought you were a goner,' Cal said.

Mitch sat beside the first-aid cupboard in the machinery shed amid the greasy tools, oil drums, files, anvils, clamps, welders, grinders and old filings while Callum washed his wound with a cotton ball dipped in Dettol and rainwater. He poked the jagged flesh back into place, distracting Mitch by telling the story of the lightning strike that shattered the old windmill and set the hay barn alight. Rain kept falling and they could almost hear the smouldering tree hiss and drown. Mitch patted Tinka, wedged under his seat, and tried not to wince. His father put a plastic finger guard on his wound and bound it with a wide roll of bandage, then made them each a cup of sweet black tea.

oOo

As the phone calls spread, the women of the town and surrounds – so recently divided – united, and many fridges were raided.

While the clouds above rumbled, Papa and Mati Jovetic stood in their precise, fecund vegetable garden, arguing, and Lana loaded her boot with salad and vegetables and strawberries. At the IGA, Jasey and Elsie loaded a frozen turkey, a leg of ham and some frozen seafood into a shopping trolley and pushed it across the road just as the rainclouds burst and water came tumbling down.

Meanwhile, Mandy Bishop lay in her bed in her lovely big room and thought about Stacey and his wonderfully convenient Bodybuild Olympic Utility Bench. Finally she flung the covers back, got up, bathed and dressed carefully and sat at the triptych mirrors to do her face and hair. Great claps of thunder smacked across the sky and lightning dimmed the lights; then rain fell, and that was annoying because her hair never sat well in damp air. She rested the curling wand on the dressing table so that it scorched the polish and bruised the mahogany. She checked her phone, but there was still no message from Stacey. 'Too soon yet,' she said, but in her heart she knew it wasn't.

She went for a walk through the big old house. Callum was in the shower, and the cover on Isobel's bed was tugged roughly into place, so she stood next to the tiny Christmas tree, a dry pine branch in a bucket of sand, its brittle needles falling on the carpet, and looked to the vista outside. There was no sign of human life, just a bleak sky purpled with thick clouds and blue rain above a vast yellow blanket, then lines of grey weeds along the channel bank, scrubby thistles and wild ryegrass, wet skeleton grass clinging to a shoddy fence along a puddled track that led to a small town where nothing happened . . . except for today. Christmas Day. Neralie McIntosh's big day. Startlingly, a feeling of utter isolation filled her, even though she'd been loved – *adored* – been possessed, body and soul, three times (!), and her eyes were bright with the afterglow. She turned sharply away from the window and went to the kitchen, where she filled the kettle – hearing a faint 'ouch' from the bathroom as the water falling onto Cal's old head suddenly thinned and scalded.

oOo

When Isobel arrived at the pub with her in-laws, husband, children and Aunt Opal, they found a loud pump sucking water from the cellar.

Inside, Neralie took their dripping umbrellas and gave them disposable plastic shower caps to cover their shoes. 'There's been a flood . . . but not from the rain.' She set them up with a bottle of local organic sparkling wine, chilled champagne flutes and a platter of seafood and explained that they'd had to change the menu a little. She hoped they didn't mind. Opal said archly, 'Well, we can hardly go home and cook a meal now, can we?' but Isobel looked hard into Neralie's blue eyes and asked, 'What happened?'

'Sabotage.'

'That's not very community-minded.'

'We can't prove anything.'

'But you've got a plan?'

Neralie gave the cricket signal for 'wide', indicating gathered locals eating, drinking, sitting at set tables, a fully functioning bar and restaurant filled with friendly, mingling customers – riparians, townies and farmers. Just then, the pump cut out. The cellar was empty of water.

'Marvellous,' Isobel said. She went back to the dining room and rearranged the seating so that she would be sitting opposite Mandy.

oOo

Much later than she'd hoped, they pulled up in the yard and got out of the ute. The old man shepherded Mitch, whose hand was bandaged. He walked as if he'd severed his arm at the shoulder. When he came into the kitchen, he smelled of burnt sheep shit. Then he took far too long to shower and Callum had to help him with his buttons. Finally, they climbed into her small wagon and headed for the Bong, and Christmas lunch.

There was a din, she was surprised to hear, when she cut the engine, so followed her decrepit father-in-law and injured husband inside, cautiously.

The entire town, it seemed, was at the pub, sloshing around in gumboots or standing on the damp floor of the bar in bare feet. There were frail elderly people, robust men and women with strong digestive tracts, thin weak women, men with high cholesterol, barflies with liver problems, lots of small children, toddlers and babies – all tucking into ham and turkey, roast spuds with cream and slow-cooked, crackling-crisp pork. And there was Neralie, with a Christmas tree hat on her head and small gift boxes dangling from her earlobes, smiling like she'd finally won three million dollars on pub scratchies.

'Merry Christmas! Get yourself a drink. Heaps to eat.' She shoved a seafood platter at Mandy. 'Warm day, isn't it?'

The attractive ex-boyfriend, Beau, was sitting at the bar forlornly reading the label on a bottle of red wine. Kelli was talking to him about a free hair consultation.

'Have an oyster,' Isobel said. She steered Mandy to their table in the dining room and put two oysters on her plate.

'Not a fan,' Mandy said, moving them to Mitch's plate.

Isobel shelled a prawn and ate it with sounds of appreciation. Beside her, Mitch tilted his head back and poured an oyster into his open mouth.

'I shouldn't eat so much . . .' Opal said, taking an oyster. 'But if I keel over I want you to know I've had an adequate life.' And she sucked another oyster.

Isobel pushed the plate of warm chicken salad towards Mandy. 'Dig in.'

Mandy shook her head. 'Not a fan of seafood *or* chicken.'

Neralie plonked a bowl of yabbies in front of her. 'You and your fitness friend, Stacey the water taker, have been swimming with them,' and Opal, who'd had two glasses of sparkling wine, said she hoped Mandy hadn't weed in there, then fell about in her chair laughing.

They gave Mandy eggnog and a plate piled with rich food – a slab of ham and a turkey leg snuggled closely to a cream-covered roast potato, some coleslaw and a mound of egg and sweet potato salad – and she spent a long time moving the food about her plate while everyone else stuffed themselves.

'Eat up,' Isobel said. 'It won't kill you . . . I don't think.'

Isobel cut Mitchell's food and Rory and Philippa peeled his yabby tails and his pub mates ferried drinks to him and he described his brush with heavenly death that morning. Lana joined the party, and with her came Jasey. Mandy was wedged into a corner with no way out. Lana said, 'What did you get from Santa, Mandy, or have you been naughty?' Jasey offered Mandy a creamy Brandy Alexander, and when Mandy declined she smiled. 'Don't want to live dangerously today, eh?' And Lana added, 'Something you afraid of?'

The noise in the bar faded and Mandy saw that the entire town was looking at her. The plate of food in front of her must be pure poison, and they wanted her to eat it.

At the other end of the table, some sort of gruesome truth was dawning on Mitch. He caught a movement out of the corner of his eye. Neralie was waving at him, so he went to her, like a man hypnotised, and she took him by the hand and led him towards the storeroom. Levon wheeled a flaming

Christmas pudding past on a trolley, and in the bar Darryl popped another bottle of champagne. There was some sort of commotion from the dining area and Kevin yelled, 'No, Lana – no!'

Mitch vaguely heard the ruckus from the storeroom, but he was kissing Neralie, at last, a long, deep and urgent kiss, and Neralie was running her hands under his nice blue shirt and Mitch's hand made its way up under Neralie's blouse . . . but his bandaged finger caught and he had to swap hands. He tried again, reaching for her breast, and from somewhere there was the sound of crockery being smashed. He ground against her and she reached for his fly but at that moment the door opened and there was Beau, looking at Neralie, her foot up on the shelf behind Mitch and Mitch's groin against hers. 'There's a fight, Neralie! Women fighting – grown women!' Then she was gone and Mitch was left in the storeroom with engorged genitals, a throbbing finger and Neralie's ex-boyfriend.

Beau said, 'You people are barbarians.'

Mitch replied, 'You should come out and give me a hand with the next killer, find out where your chops come from.'

When he finally got to the dining room, Mitch found a circle of shouting customers and Jasey and Mandy on their knees in a sea of smashed crockery and broken glass, each with a handful of the other's hair. Levon was trying to separate them, Kevin held Lana by her skirt to stop her diving into the fray, Larry Purfeat was taking bets in the corner, Isobel was standing on a chair with her glass of champagne while her kids filmed the whole thing on their phones. The Christmas lunchers clutched their drinks and held their food plates high to keep them out of harm's way. Then Elsie came running in with an ice bucket and threw the contents on the wrestling girls. Startled, they were momentarily motionless. Then Lana lunged, leaving her skirt in Kev's hands, and flipped Mandy onto her back. Jasey sat on her, pinning her arms to the floor.

'That'll do it, then,' Levon said, and Darryl helped them up and held their arms in the air, declaring a tie. Lana put her skirt back on.

Mandy wobbled over to Neutral Bay, sat next to Beau and asked for a whisky, which Levon gave her. 'They're upset because I ruined their Christmas Day,' she said to Beau. 'But I am going to ruin the Bishops, you just wait and see.'

'I can hardly wait for what happens next,' Beau said, and poured himself another glass of red wine.

Music played and people sat and talked, but the mood was flatter than it should have been. The first Bong Christmas was a slow, pissed day with very little laughter, made worse by Morton Campininni harping on about Spot and showing everyone the collar Mitch had found.

o0o

Later, at Esther's, Callum stared out the window to the street and the place where the swimming hole had been, with a cup of tea resting on the arm of his chair. Esther reached down between the wall and her chair and lifted her father's 1943 Remington .22 calibre rifle and checked the chamber. Then she applied her polishing rag to it.

'You got ammunition?'

'Plenty.'

Much later still, Cal struggled out of Esther's comfortable lounge chair and limped to the pub. He pushed the bar door open and found his drunk son sitting on a stool, looking at the floor between his knees, and his daughter-in-law stretched out along the bar, holding an empty bottle of crème de menthe, fast asleep.

oOo

Before climbing into the small bed in Isobel's old room, Mitch phoned Neralie. When she didn't answer he sent her a text message: *I love you like air but I've ruined everything for you and life's a clusterfuck-up of inestimable proportions but I know what to do to end it all.*

26.

BOXING DAY

Mandy's scun fist was tight and the noise was loud when she moved against the sheets. She needed to get to the bathroom, but it would hurt. Everything in her intestines would move. Sloppy, slimy food would shift and churn, and fetid wind would swell against her poor tender liver and her aching kidneys. Slowly, she raised her head from the pillow. She sat on the edge of the bed for a long time looking at the wall, then reached for the bedside table and levered herself up. With the help of friendly infrastructure she made it to the toilet, fighting dizziness and waves of feverish nausea. In the bathroom, her reflection didn't look as bad as she felt, but when she turned on the taps the thunderous cascading water made her weak. She sank to the floor, her mouth near the spill drain in the centre of the old green tiles. Footsteps, punctuated by the clack of Callum's stick, shuffled across the timber floor to the bathroom door then retreated. When the bath was full and hot, she crawled into it and sank so that her ears were submerged and the muffled thuds through the house softened. She let her tears drip straight from her eyes into the foamy beige water.

Then the door swung open and Mitch was standing over her, the .22 in his hand. He said, 'Morning, Mandy,' leaned the gun by the sink and brushed his teeth. He wet a comb and dragged it carefully through his hair – missing the bit at his crown – then picked up the .22 and left, slamming the door shut. It was like an explosion in her head, and as the water vibrated against the edge of the bath, Mandy whispered, 'I hate you.'

oOo

Neralie woke from a dead, exhausted sleep and rolled over in her bed. Then she remembered Christmas Day. 'Glad that's over,' she said to no one, but despite everything she felt quite cheerful. She reached for her phone.

The message from Mitch made her go cold.

oOo

Lana, Kevin and Jasey watched Boxing Day dawn from Jasey's back verandah. They were enjoying a Bundy and rum, Lana smoking a cigarette, while Beau snored gently in his chair, his mouth stained blue from red wine. Mist lingered over the water and pungent smoke wafted from the burning mosquito coils. The mozzies buzzed on anyway. Eddies curled over the river surface and the water moved steadily, forcefully. Jasey sat forward, her hands up, telling them, '*Shoosh.*' They looked to the rushes. Jasey quietly loaded a rifle.

Beau stirred, froze, then followed their gaze to the ducks. They were lined up, flat-footed, on the low branch, their neat beaks turning this way then that, unsettled. 'No, don't!' he said.

Lana put her hand over his mouth, Jasey raised the gun, aimed, squeezed, and there was a loud crack.

Beau jumped and the birds and mozzies stirred and the ducks flapped and scattered and the rushes shuddered then stilled. Beau looked at Jasey holding the smoking gun. 'It's like *Apocalypse Now*.'

'Stick around for the cull,' Jasey said. 'It'll be better than anything Marlon Brando ever did.'

He didn't follow his three new friends down to the river to retrieve the dead fox.

oOo

Neralie found Callum Bishop in his bed. His eyebrows rose and his wrinkled brow lifted. He just said, 'He went away in the ute.'

'Did he take a gun?'

He sat up. 'There's the cull tonight.' But she had gone, striding down the hall to the laundry. She pushed through the bathroom door and glanced down at Mandy in the warm brownish water, small islands of suds clinging to her knees like bubbling fungus. She was heavy-faced and greenish but had no visible bruises.

'Morning, Mandy,' she said loudly.

Mandy heard the linen cupboard in the laundry screech open, heard the bottom shelf creak as Neralie used it as a step-up to the top shelf.

The gun was not in its safe. Neralie raced back through the bathroom, letting the door slam. The contents of Mandy's Christmas Day rose up from her stomach and spilled out, turning the dull bathwater around her the colour of green algae. She was amazed at the amount of créme de menthe she'd consumed and grateful it was no longer hers.

oOo

Mitch fed his farm dogs, let them off for a run, then tied them up.

305

He cleaned the gun and blasted a few cans from fence posts. The scope crosshairs were accurate and he could shoot straight even with an injured finger.

Then he drove towards his pregnant ewes, but when he stopped to open a gate he was saddened by the absence of the guardian donkeys, his discerning, decisive, independent and fierce creatures. 'I'm going to be more like Cleopatra,' he told Tink.

In the thirty minutes or so that Mitch sat in the ute in the sunshine, birds flew past, sheep grazed, weeds grew and the eagles tended their new nest. He was on his knees finishing off the fence the day their shadow slid across the ground before him and he watched them glide towards the tall young pines a mile to the east. He needed to rebuild, but whatever he did, he'd have to pay, and it might result in the loss of the farm, but if he did nothing, he'd eventually lose it anyway. Then Tink woke from her doze and turned her ear to the sound of the approaching truck.

Neralie pulled up beside the ute, got out and climbed into the cab to sit on Mitch's lap, facing him.

'Good to see you,' he said.

'Really good to see you.' She kissed him. 'What are you doing?'

'Thinking.'

'What about?'

'Buridan's ass. It's a paradox; we studied it at school. Humans should choose for the greater good. But when faced with equally good choices, a rational choice can't be made – by donkeys or humans. It has to do with free will, some say instinct.'

'I'm about to employ my free will to satisfy my instinct,' she said, removing her shorts.

'I've decided to act for the greater good,' he said, as Neralie pulled his shirt over his head. 'Though it isn't rational.'

'I'm perfectly rational,' she said and helped him to remove his pants.

oOo

Mandy saw Mitch drive past with the grader blade on the front of the tractor. She abandoned the tub of ice cream she was eating and reached for the phone. Stacey had not phoned her; she would enjoy telling him his channel was lost.

In his library, Callum sat in his tweed coat with his tam-o'-shanter in place, dabbing at his cloudy old eyes with a hanky. In front of him, the cupboard doors were open and the shelves were bare. The logbooks were missing. A century's worth of data – the entire history of sheep-breeding records and statistics, as well as rainfall records and crop harvests – was gone. Three generations of work erased from the world. Callum pressed both palms to his wincing heart and gritted his teeth, waiting for the pressure to ease.

oOo

Over at the channel, Neralie held her phone up and said, 'Smile,' and Mitch smiled for the camera.

'I don't know why I didn't just do this in the first place.'

She took the photo. 'Because they control your water and therefore your life.'

oOo

At first Stacey ignored the ping, presuming it was Mandy again, but when he saw it wasn't he returned the call.

'Mate,' he said nervously, 'what's happening?'

'I'm about to bulldoze the channel flat and send a film of the event and a letter of complaint to every media outlet in the southern hemisphere and to every Opposition politician I can think of. I'll tell them about your scheme selling pumps and meters and installing them badly so you can get paid to reinstall them, and I'll tell them how you skimmed water off the top of allocations and sold it for a hundred and fifty dollars a megalitre while you frigged about reinstalling the pumps, and how you sent the water down my supply channel to fill Riverglen Lake and want me to pay for the upkeep of the channel. And I'll tell them that you want to give me a free sprinkler system to shut me up. Now I'm hanging up so I can phone old Gravedigger Dingle.'

In the past he'd done some impressive circle work, but the one-eighty the representative from the Southern Water Supply renewal project performed that day in the main street was perfectly executed and raised a cloud of rubber smoke that impressed Stacey himself as well as the patrons at the Bong.

oOo

Mitch lowered the blade to the bank at the point where the supply channel narrowed to travel under the small bridge at Bishops Corner's gate. The water underneath was invisible beneath the camouflage of newly multiplying weeds, lovingly germinated from Esther Shugg's stock. He revved so that the diesel smoke lifted the cap on the exhaust above his hat and he smiled and waved to his girlfriend. She gave him the thumbs-up and pressed record.

Then Stacey's car came tearing down the road and skidded to a halt in a dusty cloud and he burst from the driver's door, his hands held up in a gesture of surrender. 'Stop!'

'Facebook, YouTube, every newspaper and TV news program, mate,' Mitch yelled. 'The politicians are being paid by someone somewhere not to care, the water traders are in on it, no one'll do anything until it goes on *Four Corners*.'

'Please don't.'

'If you take my wife off my hands, I'll stop.'

'A lot of people will get hurt – innocent, defenceless scapegoats, people who were only doing what they were told.'

'This is *my year*. Take it or leave it.'

Stacey put his hands on his thinning hair and said, 'Oh fuck, I need to think this through.' He'd back-doored this determined man on his tractor and it was a shameful thing to do, but he could never submit to a meaningful relationship with someone who was prepared to ruin someone else for money, someone who'd deface a lovely 1990 Holden Commodore. Stealing water was an unacceptable practice, he knew, yet he was prepared to skim water off this channel and sell it on the sly for $150 a meg, and he'd agreed to suck water from the river and send it down this channel to fill Glenys's lake. And though he was reluctant to admit it, he really did like Lana, the riparian. It was all very confusing.

'Do what you have to,' he said to Mitch, and went and sat on the bonnet of his car and watched the grader blade shift the bank. Lovely water sloshed free and spilled, washing the dirt away, the brown fluid catching in the tyre imprints to run through the stubble, and Mitch just kept flattening the bank, shovelling it down into itself, mud spinning in the air from the rubber wheels and water spreading and seeping into the ground. When he'd erased a good couple of hundred metres of channel, Mitch got down and stood up to his ankles in the valuable water as it trickled to Esther's weeds and he poured his heart out to the phone Neralie held. He spoke of being an ass and how he was midway between the hay and the water, feeling paralysed by the choices he had to make, but he would not let himself be killed, and something had to change in order that he could go on living.

They emailed the video clip to Glenys Dingle, to various officials at the State Water Authority, to the federal minister for agriculture, to the Department of Primary Industries, and to newspapers and the ABC, and Mitch was pleased that his actions would produce consequences of some sort.

Stacey drove away and Mitch took a selfie in front of the grader blade of himself with an arm around Neralie, Tink by his knees, the sloppy heap of mud that was once a supply channel all around them.

oOo

Early evening, they started coming through Neralie's door. Esther drove past the kerb decorated with utes boasting spotlights and gun rests and boxes of ammunition, and parked her Dodge at the back of the pub. Everyone came. The Bishop arrived, Callum sat with Esther and Mitch joined Kev and Levon. Mandy followed in her little white wagon and joined Beau.

The local stock and station agent stood in the white light of the projector, a conductor with his baton, indicating shooting areas north of the riverbank and allocating drivers and shooters. 'As I predicted, it's a mild southerly tonight, so stay upwind. Keep the town behind you and the breeze in your face. I can tell you that a pack of wild dogs has travelled as far and wide as Girri Girri and Esther's property, so it's feasible that the culprits come out of the ferals' camp, or they're wild and live in the grassy box woodlands opposite the swimming hole. The night is all about apex predators.'

Bennett Mockett turned off the projector and the carpenter asked Two-shits why he had allocated the top shooting spot to himself and his Digital Night Vision Riflescope. Bennett replied that it was only right that he and Stacey and the officer from the Department of Primary Industries take responsibility, since they were the most qualified and had organised the authorisation.

Esther reminded them all that her Dodge was equipped with a sling and hoist should anyone need help to transport disposed vermin. Bennett eyed the hunters. 'I'm aware each group has reached their own arrangements with regard to appropriate transport and disposal.' Then suddenly, in groups of two and three, the councillors, irrigators, riparians and townies left the pub and went, united, into the black star-speckled night, the smooth barrels of their loaded guns frosted silver by the moonlight.

Mandy had a good view of the telly and the remaining patrons, including Callum, Esther . . . and Isobel Prestwich. She eyed Jasey sitting with her fighting partner, Lana, across the bar next to the single mothers. And there were the walkers too – Keira and Madison, Amelia and Bree-Anna and Loren and Trixie and Nicole and Debbie and Coral and Kelli – and the smart set, and Isobel's precious craft ladies, knitting. Mandy was not done with any of them yet. They deserved more. She moved her chair a little closer to the boy from Sydney and demanded wine from Neralie, who filled her glass, generously and graciously. Elsie turned the TV down; the patrons watched their phones for messages and photos. A song played through the sound system – '*I stopped loving you though I knew I could because you didn't love me as much as you should, so now it's your turn to die . . .'* – and faraway gun blasts spiked the tense atmosphere in the pub. Beau said, 'It's callous and primitive here, dangerous,' and Callum said, 'Not if you do the right thing.'

oOo

A round white glare caught the dogs coming out of the bush behind where the swimming hole used to be, heading west, a low puffing pack, the silver moon sliding across their fast backs. Bennett, Stacey and the officer from the Department of Primary Industries followed them in their crosshairs as they gathered pace, vanishing and emerging from lignum stands and tree trunks. When the pack hit a wide clearing shots cracked and dogs dropped, flipped and stumbled to the ground, dead. After two minutes of intense fire and a few more minutes of sporadic shooting, six dogs had been felled.

To the east of town, out towards Bishops Corner, Kevin manned the spotlight. Mitch and Levon sat beside him on the ute tray, waiting. Above, the black night sky held silver bursts of light and shone with washes of stardust and twinkling planets. Scraps of remaining cloud floated away quickly. Faint gunshots came to them but they saw no dogs, just many foxes chasing the call of the fox whistle, running to their deaths in the blinding spotlight.

oOo

When the gunfire surrounding the town thinned, patrons switched on their torches and drifted to their homes. 'May as well finish this,' Neralie said, emptying the bottle of wine they'd been drinking into Mandy's and Beau's glasses. Neralie locked the front door and soon Isobel, Callum and Esther left using the back door. The barmaid and her mother put up the stools, tidied the bar and counted the cash, then Elsie stood by the light switch and Neralie said, 'It's all over, Mandy, time to go.'

Beau said goodnight and Mandy scraped her change from the bar and followed him. Elsie shut all the lights down and the place went black. The odd shot rang out until dawn.

27.
TRY THE BILLABONG HOTEL

Cyril placed a cup of tea on his wife's bedside table. Pam was reading the newspaper on her iPad, so Cyril left and returned with his own cup of tea. 'Have you seen my watch?'

'Top drawer, bedside table,' she said, and Cyril strapped his watch onto his wrist. He pulled the covers back and sat on the bed. Pam looked at him over her glasses and said, 'I want you to go to the shed and get two large suitcases.'

'Of course.' He pulled the covers up.

'Now,' she said.

He pushed the covers back and went immediately to the shed, thinking, *It's a ruse, she's organised a surprise trip for my retirement.* He dusted the cases off, took them inside and put them down next to the wardrobe. 'Now what, my love?'

'Love is gone, Cyril, and so are you. Fill those suitcases with your possessions and leave this house.'

She flipped the iPad over and held it up. The headline of the online newspaper read: MINISTER FOR PRIMARY INDUSTRIES SACKS WATER AUTHORITY MANAGERS IN WATER FRAUD SCHEME. 'I didn't mind earning money from installing pumps and meters, Cyril, but stealing water from the locals and selling it back to them is unacceptable.'

On the kitchen bench his phone started to ring. At the same time the landline phone rang and someone knocked on the front door.

'You haven't started packing, Cyril.'

'Pam, darling – please . . .'

'"Investigations revealed that the Water Authority was using 60 percent of water buybacks and water-saving measures for the Riverglen Lake Resort project, funded and mostly owned by local and state government employees, and retaining a mere 35 percent for farming purposes, with 5 percent of the tally unaccounted for." You were selling that five percent, weren't you?'

'Where will I go?'

'You could try the Billabong Hotel. I hope they give you credit – I've emptied all our accounts.'

'I'll get time with the puppies, surely?'

'The Billabong Hotel is no place for puppies.'

Outside, the ferals rolled their vans up onto the lawn and parked next to the television trucks. Camera people focused lenses on the house and well-groomed TV anchors stood in Pam's petunias talking into microphones.

oOo

In the dining room at the Bong, a table of strangers – TV crews and reporters, men with very white teeth and women with fake tans wearing inappropriate shoes – were running up a huge tab. But Neralie had their company credit card, so she smiled while she pulled beers and served meals.

Levon looked at Cyril and his suitcases. 'First you have to pay for room nine – it was suddenly vacated by Stacey overnight. You can have his unpaid tab too.'

Cyril opened his mouth to object but thought about the puppies and handed over his credit card. On the TV above the bar, Glenys Dingle was elbowing her way to her office through a media pack wielding smartphones and microphones. 'Will you resign immediately, Ms Dingle?'

'Certainly not,' she said, and ran into the Water Authority offices.

Levon handed Cyril his card and said, 'We've got no room for you here, try the caravan park.'

oOo

Jasey had noticed Lana no longer bought lamingtons and chocolate milk for breakfast, opting for yoghurt and a banana instead. She had ceased buying cigarettes, too. But Jasey knew for sure what was going on when Lana declined a glass of wine and ordered mineral water. She watched her two friends work at their scratchies, the remains of lunch in front of them.

Neralie looked at her pile. 'Don't think I did much good.'

Lana said, 'Not a cent.'

They looked to Jasey, who dropped her five-cent piece. 'You're pregnant, aren't you, Lana?'

Neralie froze, Kevin put his beer on the table, a regular turned the TV down and Levon closed his book, anticipating intervention. The sound of the trucks at the silos in the quiet reminded them Kevin was back in business. Lana blinked and her big blue eyes filled with tears. Neralie looked from one to the other and was about to say, 'I'm sure we can work this out,' when Jasey said, 'Pretty radical step to take just to give up smoking.'

Lana said, 'Can I still be bridesmaid?'

316

'Mitch and Levon'd look pretty fucking stupid in the photos with only one bridesmaid between them.' Jasey held her hand out to Kevin. 'Come on, Kevvy, you've got work to do. I need to be pregnant by morning.'

oOo

Mitch finished typing his protest email and pressed send. Then he printed off a copy:

Dear Sirs,

Your letter tells me that I cannot clear the property I lease from Miss Esther Shugg to run a lateral above-ground sprinkler system because the trees are natives. I am writing to appeal for an exemption because I'm happy to clear around the stands and leave them undisturbed in order not to miss the coming sowing season. In the meantime, I will replant and establish another native forest . . .

On his drive to town, the rural news told him that if the predicted El Niño eventuated, it would have a devastating impact on cropping regions in the coming season, but if average rainfall was achieved then fifty-two percent of crops had a chance of making average yields.

'Mother Nature, please don't be a bitch,' he said, knowing the bank managers would swoop, like ravens to a dying lamb. But life looked promising. Mandy had vanished, shot through with Beau to a life she wanted – deserved – presumably in the vast mess of Sydney. There'd be a letter from a lawyer some day, some time, demanding something, but for the time being . . .

Mitch parked next to the ute that belonged to the hydraulic fracturing company. The new boy in town, known fondly as 'the frucker', was staying in room nine.

Tink watched the pub door open and saw Mitch vanish into the dark oblong, then she turned a circle, lay down and closed her eyes. When the sun came up he would appear again and they would go to the farm together.

When he stepped into the pub the regulars called, 'Welcome home, darling,' and Mitch studied the menu board. Neralie put a beer in front of him. 'Yabbies are off the menu, swimming hole's contaminated.'

'Right. The flood, I guess.'

Neralie smiled. 'Something like that. The council put a sign up.'

'I'll have the roast, please.'

She asked if he'd written to the Land Conservation Council.

'I did,' he said. 'And then I just walked out the door and came here without having to lie or make excuses to anyone. You heard from Beau?'

She shook her head, 'I bought you your own toothbrush.'

He leaned across and kissed her. 'I haven't heard from Mandy either.'

He sat with the farmers and they discussed the possibility of the El Niño event and their water allocations and what to do about the outbreak of Chilean needle grass left by drovers along the Jeong–Bishop road, and the action strategy to repel the frucker.

EPILOGUE

The following spring season brought weeks of unusually heavy rain. It fattened the crops, and the harvest was good, a bumper one, then plump green weeds contaminated the precise lines of stubble and sucked the life from the precious subsoil. Bennett Mockett put pesticides and weed killer on sale but rather than waste chemicals, useless against such thick infestations, the locals discussed the topic and decided to use the exacting efficiency of fire to eradicate the contaminated fallow and its nuisance tenants. So for days, the neat paddocks that contained the town burned low, spreading smoke and ash far.

Through the window of her joyless prefab across the street from the swimming hole, Esther watched. First, the Water Authority had rebuilt the levee and walking track, and now they were draining the swimming hole to clean it and repair the jetty and pontoon. As the pump sucked water from the small lake, a group of kids and the smart set paused by the 'Contaminated' sign to watch the tide fall and see what they had really been swimming with all these years, what fed the yabbies they'd caught and eaten with vinegar and salt.

No one took any notice of old Esther Shugg when she steered her electric buggy across the grass and pulled up next to the kids. 'It was 1940 – that was the last time they drained the swimming hole. Found a hundred-pound Murray cod.'

A tall boy glanced at her.

'They say they grow a pound a year,' Esther continued, 'and this one was as big as a small child. They put it in the rainwater tank at the pub until they filled the lake again.'

The boy had only ever seen the old lady in faded bib-and-brace overalls sitting at her front window, but up close she looked like a goanna. He nodded at the swimming hole. 'Is it still in there?'

'If it had any sense it would have swum off when the levee broke.'

The kids turned back to the water. The tide continued to subside, and something began to rise in the middle. An old gate? A drum net?

'Drum net,' a little girl said, pointing to the circular rusted thing. 'You're not allowed to have drum nets.'

'No, you're not,' Esther agreed.

Esther moved her buggy forward a few centimetres. The tide around the end of the suction pipe dropped abruptly, the engine on the truck screamed, and the worker cut the generator. In the abrupt quiet the willow trees around them relaxed and the stench of sour mud swelled.

'Smells like something dead,' said the tall boy, and the ladies in their exercise attire hurried off across the grass.

The small crowd scanned the slimy lakebed. Gathered against the end of the suction pipe was a pile of plastic bags iced in runny black clay. Beer bottles and cans rested in sheet-sized puddles and lying neatly in the weeds, a deflated tractor inner tube and a sheep skeleton. Most eyes settled on the rusty thing resting in the puddle in the middle of the small lake.

The worker called from his truck, 'Youse kids stay out of that swimming hole, y'hear?' and the kids nodded. He drove away with the pump.

Old Esther said, 'Mind what he says, alright?'

The kids nodded again.

Esther pushed the ignition button and her electric buggy sputtered to life. They watched her roll away, then turned back to the putrid lakebed and the brown rotting thing. They stepped into the slime, stopping to turn up old tin cans and piss into yabby holes. Shrimp flicked across the mud, brown bubbles rose and popped, and the fish, mostly carp, too heavy for the drag of the pump, writhed and gasped, but they saw no monster cod. On the horizon the sun sank to a molten half-circle, the burn-off appeared more sharply in glittering lines and the breeze dropped. The rank grey cloud of ash hovered above the kids.

They plodded on towards the thing, mud sucking their feet, and when they got there, they stared. In the grey sludgy bed, caught against what remained of a drum net, a human skeleton rested, its flesh long ago eaten.

The smallest boy asked, 'Did he drown?'

'Yep,' said the pale boy. 'Dived in and got caught. You can see where he broke his rib on impact.'

The little girl looked at the wormy ribbons of hair that clung to the head. 'It could be a lady. We'd better call the police.'

The tallest boy upended his yabby net, setting the freshwater crustacean free, and turned to look back at Esther Shugg's house with its two front windows. Inside, Esther Shugg picked up her phone and dialled. While she waited for the call to be answered, she closed her eyes and took a very deep breath.

'Hello, it's me . . . they just drained the swimming hole.'

o0o

He put the phone back in its cradle and sat in the kitchen chair, looking out through the window for a long time. Then he drove to the spot and parked in the afternoon sun. In the warm cab his cold hands eased and Callum turned his thoughts to his mother, then his father and sister. After a while he thought about his wife and daughter, and finally his wise and discreet friend and neighbour, Esther. He was tired, and his chest squeezed again. A year ago he'd ceased taking his medications, just left them in the sludge at the bottom of his porridge bowl, so he gave in to the malaise and enjoyed the rich sun on his skin.

Then the landscape of his life was below him and he could see the pattern of tracks fanning out from the water troughs, to and from, to and from, and it seemed to him that they should build more dams so the sheep didn't have to travel so far. The tracks he and Mitch made across the farm were deep and direct, also returning again and again to places of work, and to home. He'd led a useful life, though it had its share of disappointments. Then patches of landscape went missing from the picture, but it didn't matter because there was Mitch going around and around in the harvester, though harvest was over, and the grandkids driving the chaser bins and Isobel in the B-double, and there was the pine tree – tall and straight again, the last remaining tree of the whole forest that was there in his grandfather's time. And there was the woolshed, and the channel was back! Brand new! And he was standing with his father watching the first ever wave of tea-coloured water flow to them, cooling the air and bringing insects and birds. Sheep were grazing, and so were his cattle, though he'd taken them to market in 2002, and he smelled wet clay and animals, wheat and dust. Everything was wrong, yet nothing was wrong, and something was ceasing and draining away inside.

'These are my final minutes,' he said.

He had an inkling Margot was about, a thin, posh girl fresh from school, with city hair and high heels, not an entirely satisfactory person for a small community, as it turned out, with her ideas of class, but there was always the dirt, the soil, the life force . . . and he would be part of it soon. The sound of rushing water – or was it air? – brought the river to him, wide and flowing and clear enough to see snags at the bottom. But the very last thing Callum Bishop saw was a string of villages across North Africa, a few mud abodes sprinkled around a hole on a vast orange plain, and the smiling community were gathered, working at pulling an animal-skin bucket from a well that went deep in the earth. They spilled the fresh water into a trough, just enough for their needs, no more, and Callum rose high through blue sky and folding rain clouds, and a word came to him: *marvellous*.

ACKNOWLEDGEMENTS

I would like to extend thanks to The Bundanon trust, RMIT and McCraith House. Also to Janie and Rob Armitage, Antoni Jach and the masterclass writers, friends and family for the support and advice.